SHADES
OF
TRUTH

Charlie Hudson

Outskirts Press, Inc.
Denver, Colorado

Shades of Truth
All Rights Reserved
Copyright © 2005 Charlotte Kimball

Outskirts Press
http://www.outskirtspress.com

ISBN-10: 1-59800-093-4
ISBN-13: 978-1-59800-093-1

Outskirts Press and the "OP" logo are trademarks belonging to Outskirts Press, Inc.

Printed in the United States of America

ACKNOWLEDGEMENTS

Although I originally interviewed Sergeant Kevin Brinkley and Earl Murray of the Nags Head, NC Police Department when I wrote *Shades of Murder*, their technical advice about police procedures and operations was equally valuable for *Shades of Truth*.

My uncle, Judge John S. Pickett, Jr. and my cousin, Judge Elizabeth Pickett continue to be terrific sources for legal aspects of my books. I was fortunate this time to have made the acquaintance of Dr. Brad Harper (Colonel, US Army), an experienced pathologist who assisted me with some critical scenes.

My editor, Barbara Ledbetter, played the key role that good editors always do and Lewis Agrell of Outskirts Press created the cover.

In addition to being the love of my life and an unfailing supporter, my husband, Hugh, provided the underwater photographs that were used as part of the cover.

A word of appreciation also goes to Darla Bentley and the staff of Outskirts Press for their efforts. My thanks again to readers everywhere who make it possible for authors to have a voice beyond the confines of our offices.

Charlie Hudson

CHAPTER ONE

Warren stared at the pistol – a small one, all things considered. *Damn, why hadn't he seen it coming?* It was a stubby piece that hadn't made so much as a bulge in Jonah's briefcase. *Hell, he hadn't even blinked when he reached in and pulled it out.*

"Now, Jonah," he said in a surprisingly steady voice as he clutched the edge of the massive black walnut desk to keep his hands from trembling. "There's no call for this."

Jonah Shepard stood stiffly. He had risen from the upholstered chair that was placed at a slight angle, an angle chosen to make a visitor feel comfortable, yet aware of his suppliant posture as opposed to the power position of the man who sat behind the desk. Jonah held the pistol tightly in his right hand, his voice devoid of the pleasant tone he had used when Lila, Warren's secretary, greeted him, kept him waiting for ten minutes and then ushered him into the senator's office. Jonah was a man who didn't make an immediate impression – nice looking, neither particularly handsome nor ugly – nothing striking about him. The revolver was not as easy to overlook.

"You may be right, but I want to make sure I have your full attention," Jonah said and motioned for Warren to sit. "I'm not surprised you thought I would sell Lottie out, but I was curious to see what you thought my sister's life was worth," he continued as Warren eased into the brown leather, ergonomically designed executive chair.

"I meant no offense, Jonah," Warren replied, breathing as regularly as his palpitating heart allowed. "I merely meant I always understood Lottie's death was hard on you and your folks and there are ways I can help now." He slowly moved his foot beneath the desk searching for the alarm covered by an unobtrusive bump of carpet. *There, two quick presses! If Mike was doing his fucking job, he'd switch on the hidden camera. Three or four minutes to stall.*

"My parents are both dead, you son-of-a-bitch," Jonah said, his

1

voice choking on *dead*. "The only things I want from you are statements to the state attorney general and the press." He waved the gun to the clean legal pad resting inches from Warren's left elbow. "Pick up that fancy pen and start writing."

Warren lifted the gold Mont Blanc from the black marble holder. "A statement? What kind of statement?"

"We'll start with your relationship with the gentleman in Chicago, then go back to what you did to my sister," Jonah said coldly. "You don't have to put in too many details. The basic connections will generate plenty of questions that you won't be able to lie your way out of for once. People will finally know what you really are. You're going to pay for it all – for everything you've gotten away with your whole life."

Warren held the pen over the pad, his eyes fixed on Jonah's determined face. If he swung his gaze to the nearly invisible adjoining office door, Jonah would notice it too.

"Drop it and then freeze!" a voice commanded as Warren bailed from the chair to the floor. "Don't shoot!" he cried on his way down. A shot cracked almost as soon as the words left his mouth and he flinched at the explosion.

There was a gurgling sound, the heavy desk wobbled only a bit and then he heard his security chief. "You hurt?"

"Mike?" came simultaneously from the doorway and Warren lifted his head to see Rusty through the door, pistol ready. The ruddy-faced, barrel-chested young assistant stopped and looked at the points of the human triangle: Mike stepping to the body; the man slumped against the desk, eyes open in surprise, blood blossoming across his chest; the senator scrambling to his feet.

"Is he dead?" Warren asked in alarm.

Mike knelt, found the pulse in the neck and put his ear close as Jonah tried to speak and then stopped moving.

"Damn it, I said not to shoot," Warren said, raked his hand across his photogenic face and wondered if he was pale.

"He didn't drop the gun," the security chief replied calmly. "Standard procedure," – as if killing a man was equivalent to remembering to switch on the alarm system when you left the house.

"Yeah, well, in this case..." Warren started and pressed his lips together as he heard male voices in the outer office.

"The West Palm guys," Rusty said in response to Warren's

glare. "Standard procedure," he finished in a tepid mimic of Mike as he moved forward to open the double doors.

"Shit," Warren muttered and replaced his scowl with an appropriately grave demeanor. Lila led two city policemen into the office, her contact lens-enhanced green eyes wide in fear. She put a hand to her mouth when she took in the scene.

"Oh, my God," she started in a shaky voice, "Senator, I'm so sorry, I had no idea, oh, I…"

"Lila, honey, everything is under control," Warren said smoothly and crossed the sculpted taupe carpet to take her by the elbow. The older policemen knelt next to the body while Mike handed his pistol, butt first, to the other one.

Lila was still stammering an apology for what Warren assumed was her perceived failure in not having known that the Mr. Stanley Jones who made an appointment was in actuality Jonah Shepard, a man with a dangerous agenda. *A fucking numbers geek with a gun – go figure.* Hell, it had taken him nearly five minutes to realize the deception. The last person he'd ever expected to see in his office was Jonah.

"Lila, take a deep breath and listen to me," Warren said, his best baby-kissing, back-slapping, hand-shaking sincerity coming to the forefront. He maneuvered her into the outer office as the men behind him began an exchange of questions and answers. *Damn, he had to get back in there and buy some time!*

"It's going to get real crazy soon and the media will be on us like ticks on a hound dog, so I'm going to need you to get a pretty smile on and make sure no one except the police and Freddy Hartwell gets past your desk. Oh, and we'll probably need some fresh coffee and plenty of Cokes. Can you do that for me, Lila?"

Lila nodded her head so vigorously that a strand of sun-streaked blonde hair almost slipped out of its moussed, sprayed poof. Her teardrop gold earrings jiggled and she spoke with something close to her normal efficiency. "Yes, sir, if you're sure you're all right. I mean, when I heard the shot, I was just so afraid, well, I thought…" her voice caught again.

Warren squelched a sigh and smiled instead. "Certainly I understand, but everything is going to be all right and I need to get back inside," he said as all three telephone lines rang at once.

The action triggered the expected Pavlovian response. Lila

3

dropped into her chair and reached for the receiver with deep-red lips in an automatic curve, her charming drawl ready to shield her boss from unwanted queries.

Her concern was far more likely due to the fleeting idea of the loss of a prestigious and perk-filled job than for his physical being, but he could hardly begrudge her that.

He heard the elevator ping an arrival and swiftly went into his office. That was probably the medical team and homicide personnel would be next, soon followed by an assortment of other officials. He raised his voice just enough to remind the four men in the room of who the hell the big dog was.

"Gentlemen," he began solemnly, "I know there will be many questions and I'll answer you as quickly as possible, but I must take Mr. Noonan next door for a few minutes on another matter. Rusty, you carry on here."

Warren turned toward the conference room without the slightest thought his instructions would not be followed and side-stepped the two-person emergency medical team hurrying in from the hallway.

Mike Noonan was on his heels when they cleared the reception room. Warren swiveled abruptly. "Close the door, for Christ's sake, and why in the hell did you have to kill him?"

Noonan pushed his palm against the solid, soundproof door and raised one eyebrow with no discernible emotion. "To save your life?" he responded in the dry Midwestern tone made even more characterless when he was surrounded by Florida good-old-boys or displaced New Jersey and New York accents.

Warren backed up two steps to give Noonan more space and pressed his hands into the headrest of a leather conference room chair. "Mike, I know you did what you thought was right and believe me, under other circumstances, I would be thrilled, but there's a complication."

Noonan stood motionless, apparently not disturbed by having killed a man ten minutes earlier, nor by being told that perhaps he'd made a mistake. He merely lifted his gray eyes that reminded Warren of cold fog and waited.

Warren paced beside the polished mahogany table with its sixteen comfortable chairs. "Jonah Shepard, the man who presented himself as Stanley Jonah, is, I mean, was, no, is, a potential problem for me, that is, for us." Warren paused and looked directly at

4

Noonan. "I don't want to get into a lot of detail, but he claims to have, and quite probably does have, documents that would have serious consequences if put into the wrong hands."

Noonan still didn't move, except to arch the other eyebrow. "And you wanted him left alive?"

"Until we had the fucking documents," Warren snapped and resumed his pacing. "When I pressed the goddamn buzzer, I thought you would come in and disarm him, for Christ's sake, not put a hole in his chest."

"My mistake," Mike said flatly. "Now, tell me what you want done."

Warren stopped and fingered one of his brushed gold cuff links. "Jonah told me he didn't have the documents with him, so maybe he left them at home somewhere. If you can find out where that is, and if we can keep everyone focused here, then maybe you and Rusty can get to wherever *there* is and find the damn documents before anyone else does. Then we give the straight story of Jonah as a whacko who came gunning for me." Warren paused again. "Some shit from a long time ago will be coming up, but I can contain it."

"I won't be able to leave immediately," Noonan pointed out. "I've got to give my statement to the cops."

"I know that, for God's sake," Warren replied. "The last thing I want to do is get people to thinking there's more here than it looks like. I'll come up with some reason for his name not to be released, but I probably can't buy you more than twenty-four hours, maybe less. You cooperate fully about the shooting, get the information on Jonah and get your ass on the road. I want this kept totally fucking quiet. I wouldn't have you take Rusty, but I don't know what you're going to find and there wouldn't be time to send him if you need help. Can he keep his mouth shut, no matter what you run into?"

Noonan nodded curtly. "He's still learning, but he's close enough and he likes being on the inside. He'll do what he's told. What are we looking for?"

Warren twisted his other cuff link a full turn. "I'm pretty sure it's financial papers, maybe some kind of ledger or could be on a computer – accountant kind of shit. You'll recognize a few names if Jonah was on the level."

Noonan nodded again. "How about a wife, kids, home, office?"

"Hell if I know and he sure as hell can't tell us," Warren snarled and looked past Noonan's shoulder. The light blinked above the door indicating someone wanted in. He looked at his gold Piaget watch. Fifteen minutes had passed.

"I suspect we have visitors Lila can't stall," he said and stared at Noonan's calm face. His eyes, if you knew what to look for, held the expression of a brain kicked into full planning mode. He was plotting out the tactics of an operation and Warren relaxed a bit. "I may not have a chance to talk to you before you leave," he said and swept past to open the door. "Use my personal cell phone if you have to and if it's not safe to talk, I'll find a way to call you back."

He remolded his face into a now-don't-y'all-worry-about-me, everything-is-just-fine façade as he emerged from the room into a small crowd of men milling around engaged on telephones, with cameras and so forth.

Lila waved him toward Freddy Hartwell, his chief of staff, political advisor and spin master, not to mention ass-kisser of his father-in-law. Freddy did not have a don't-worry look on his square face. Warren clasped him on the shoulder in a comradely way and within seconds he was spouting the story that should stand up under police and media probing. Thank God the recorder was on the blink – the film would support his version of events.

Three hours later, Warren was finished with the police and the first quick press conference as he reiterated that, no, they couldn't provide the man's identity just yet and, yes, he was immensely grateful to, etc., etc. He'd spoken reassuringly to his wife during a brief call and promised his father-in-law that no harm was done, well, at least not to the grand personage of Senator Warren Blaine Randall. He'd been over the story with Freddy so many times it sounded true. Mike Noonan was released by the homicide detectives, gave him a silent thumbs-up signal from the doorway and melted out of the knot of men before Warren could get a verbal confirmation.

Warren sat safely behind his desk again with a well-deserved double Scotch with a splash of water and was only half-listening as Freddy bounced around the office with a cell phone clamped to his ear. He declined Lila's offer to call the Council for the Preservation of the Everglades to cancel his evening speaking engagement. A politician couldn't buy this kind of publicity – a dedicated public servant bravely making an appearance only hours after a brush with death.

Even better, Cecilia would no doubt be too distraught to accompany him. If he worked the timing properly, he could make a late night stop to see delectable little Amber. Lila made for damn fine eye candy in the office, but banging one's assistant was as stupid as a man could be. Amber was distanced enough from his circle and unlike Cecilia, she would physically and enthusiastically demonstrate her relief that he survived such a frightening ordeal. Maybe she would greet him in the black demi-bra and thong lingerie set he'd given her the week before. No, the red corset and stockings with those spiky heels.

Warren swished Scotch in his mouth as Freddy punched his phone off and started yammering about tomorrow's press conference. The only problem Warren could see at this point was it would be difficult for him to speak with Mike if he called. Fortunately, Mike was the kind of man who rarely needed guidance and the odds were he wouldn't call anyway.

Warren forced himself to pay attention to Freddy and hoped Mike would be back with the documents in hand before the nine a.m. press conference. If so, the pathetic Shepard family would be out of his life for good.

CHAPTER TWO

"Divers really don't have to worry about sharks," Chris had said confidently when one of the students mentioned the spate of attacks at Daytona. "When you're underwater, they can tell you're not a part of their food chain. Trying to corner one isn't something I recommend, but divers are rarely hurt if they use a little common sense."

Bev wasn't exactly concerned, but she involuntarily sucked a large amount of air through her regulator when Chris gave the *Shark* signal with her right hand and pointed her other arm to a coral-dotted rock ledge. Damn, the sudden breath caused Bev to lift and as she tried to correct her buoyancy, the air tank shifted enough to put her into a mild roll. She floundered and bumped against Kyle's leg. He was intent on the shark though and didn't seem to notice. Bev exhaled deliberately to descend the extra inches and kicked twice to join the second couple observing the nurse shark, a reportedly harmless variety. The fourish-foot long creature rewarded their presence by languidly swimming from underneath the outcropping and disappearing behind an adjoining section of reef.

Chris's experience as a dive instructor meant she could view the shark as a treat for her class, but Bev was just as glad to watch it depart. A school of tiny purple fish swirling across her vision was more her speed. She dutifully checked her air gauge and was surprised to see she was down to 1,000 pounds. She flashed her open hand twice to let Chris know and wondered if she was using air faster than everyone else. It wasn't a competition, but if she and Kyle continued to dive, it would be nice if they had similar consumption rates.

"Don't worry," Chris told them during the open water training dives, "air consumption, body alignment and buoyancy are tough for everyone in the beginning. It gets easier later."

The other female student, Nina, was also down on air and Chris turned the group back toward the waiting boat. All they had to do was make a proper ascent and she would issue their temporary Open

Water Certification cards when they returned to the dive shop. Bev and Kyle were the first on the rope. It was a mercifully calm day with virtually no current and they faced each other with one hand loosely holding the rope and the other on their inflator hoses. Bev had no air in the full-vest buoyancy compensator, but she could feel the upward lift as they slowly rose forty feet to the surface. The visibility had been excellent all afternoon and the orange float ball moved gently above them. A trio of some kind of silver fish zipped past them as Bev switched her attention to directly overhead. They had enough clearance not to worry about colliding with the twin propellers, but it was the correct ascent posture.

She put two pumps of air into her vest when they broke the surface and remembered not to spit out her regulator. Kyle indicated for her to move ahead of him, and Danny, who was their boat captain for the day, beckoned her forward. The ladder was the open-fin type so she clamored up it with some degree of grace and swung sideways onto the right-hand swim platform.

"Looking good, Bev," Danny said gleefully, as he held her tank steady while she unsnapped her fins, slipped them off and handed them back to him.

She pulled the regulator out and took the mask from her face. "Feels good, too," she replied and released the chest straps of her vest as Kyle came up the ladder.

"You were right, the nurse shark was still around," he said. "It was great! No eels, but a nice ray, too."

"Cool," Danny said with a grin and quickly had the thirty pounds of tank and attached gear off them and stowed. The second couple and Chris queued along the float ball line and Kyle and Bev moved to a seat on the back starboard bench in the full sun. They unzipped their wetsuits and Kyle helped Bev peel hers down to her waist before he shrugged out of his. Even with seventy-eight degree water temperature, an hour of check-out diving and touring around the reef could give a chill.

When Chris had asked if they could do their final class on Friday instead of Sunday to accommodate Nina and Louis, Bev called to check Kyle's schedule. Neither of them routinely had Fridays off, although crimes in Verde Key were pleasantly down. One of the advantages of dating an assistant district attorney was their workloads tended to match. She felt only a moment of guilt about taking a Friday since it wasn't as if she didn't pull her share of early morning and late night calls. With only two detectives in the department, a forty-hour work week was never guaranteed.

"Good job, everybody," Chris said after the quartet was comfortably on board and Danny cranked the powerful engines. "A great dive and all the requirements met. Congratulations and even though I usually only bring water and sodas, I do have some Sharkstooth ale to mark your graduation if anyone is interested."

Everyone nodded and Chris distributed iced long-neck bottles. She set hers aside, grabbed the nozzle of a hose secured to the side of the boat, sprayed her cropped, curly coppery hair and ran fresh water on her upper body. She'd pulled her faded blue, snag-marked wetsuit off completely and spread it across the port-side upper bench. The navy blue and red striped one-piece swimsuit looked new and fitted her lean body with no bulges of fat around waist or stomach. She twisted to spray her back and the high-quality seahorse tattoo on her left shoulder undulated with her movement. She stretched the sprayer and handed it around to her newly graduated students.

Bev barely squirted her hair – it was too long to benefit from anything other than a full dose of detangling solution. She would do that after they docked. After a quick rinse and hand-off to Kyle, she tilted the beer and welcomed the cold liquid. She lowered the bottle, savored the taste and watched water trickle down Kyle's muscled chest. Most of the droplets clung to light brown hair and glinted in the sunlight. He grinned at her and she wondered if he was feeling a wave of desire like she was. He passed the hose along and moved close to press his thigh against Bev's. Yep, they'd be celebrating their accomplishment with more than a cold brew.

"All right," Chris said happily and stood balanced in a wide-legged stance. "We'll get back to the shop, finish the paperwork, shoot the photos – always done after the dive to make sure everyone looks bad – and then give out the temporary C cards. We've got about a twenty-minute ride, so give me feedback about the classes."

The group spent the time chattering companionably and then pitched in to haul equipment from the boat. The Adventures Below Dive Shop was less than fifty yards from the dock and when Bev stepped inside the building, she paused to let her eyes adjust to the dimmer interior.

"Good dive?" George asked from behind the counter. He muted

the sound of the television mounted on the adjacent wall.

"Four down, four back – all certified," Chris announced and waved a digital camera around. "Anything exciting happen while we were out?" She waved Louis to stand in front of a poster with a sea turtle in turquoise water. It was a fitting backdrop for their photos.

"An uproar in West Palm," George said in general. "Not a lot of details yet, but some guy was in Senator Randall's office and went nuts or something. Pulled a gun and threatened him. The cops, or I guess it was one of the bodyguards, shot the guy. Killed him right out, I guess."

Bev and Kyle both turned automatically. "Anybody else hurt?"

"Don't think so," George replied and wrinkled his high forehead. "They had a quickie press conference a little while ago, but they're not identifying the guy yet. There wasn't any warning or anything. It looks like he made an appointment under some false pretense. Something happened and all hell broke loose. There's another conference set for tomorrow morning."

"Randall is pretty high on the totem pole for a state senator," Kyle said as he took his place for the photo. "The pucker factor will be up and all kinds of folks scrambling. Daddy-in-law DeLong will not take this lightly."

Bev snorted in a most unladylike fashion. "Yeah, but Randall will get great mileage out of it at no cost. His only regret will be it didn't happen closer to election time."

Everyone laughed. Verde Key was outside Randall's constituency and he wasn't held in high esteem by most of the town's residents. His ability to turn situations into frequent photo opportunities made it difficult to ignore him. There had been a great deal of recent press speculation that he was on the short list for a potential political appointment if the White House changed parties. There had been other rumors about him running for the U.S. Senate if either incumbent chose to retire. Few, if anyone, really cared except to feed empty conversation time.

"Okay, Bev, you're up next," Chris called. Bev stepped into the designated spot and involuntarily flashbacked to the shootout she'd been a part of thirteen months prior.

"Give me a smile," Chris instructed. Bev complied with no hesitation. She logically knew there were no visible signs of that night remaining. She pushed away unbidden recollections of a blood-

11

splattered floor and focused instead on how pleasant the day had been.

Bev had grown up around her father's love of deep sea fishing but knew little about the local diving community. She'd become interested while she was investigating the death of Greg Wiley, a partner in Adventures Below. It was the same case that brought her and Kyle together. They enjoyed cycling and kayaking and he broached the subject of taking dive classes carefully. She agreed that the grim outcome of the Wiley investigation shouldn't taint what looked to be an intriguing hobby.

They could have used any of several dive shops in Verde Key, but Bev had met Chris Green at her gym before she knew what Chris's job was. Chris had a quick sense of humor and the kind of extroverted personality that was inviting rather than in-your-face. They were chatting as they dressed after a charity ten-kilometer run and Bev was startled to find out she'd bought Adventures Below. The thought of a bungled robbery in which four men were killed had apparently dissuaded other potential buyers.

"Oh, yeah, you were the one, weren't you? You were there that night with the owner when those guys broke in? That was a hell of a thing the way I heard it."

Bev nodded. The story faded from the newspapers, although it was still occasionally discussed around town. "You knew everything when you made the decision?"

"Oh, hell, yeah," Chris replied undaunted. "The estate was muddled and the father of the one guy and ex-wife of the other were anxious to unload it. They dropped the price until it was going for a song and someone at the bank that held the mortgage told my sister about it. She called me and it was a great deal for someone without a lot of upfront capital. I don't believe in ghosts, haven't had anything weird happen yet. No matter what people say, I've had plenty of clients who come in just as an excuse to see the place. I admit it's not the kind of marketing I would normally do, but, hey, whatever works is okay by me."

"Hang on a few minutes and we'll be all done," Chris said, bringing Bev back to the present. She grinned at Chris's ebullience and shook off gritty memories. She'd done what needed to be done. As her father had often said when he was on the force, being willing to shoot wasn't the same as being trigger-happy.

Kyle slipped his arm around her waist. "Hey, new diver, you want to head over to the Scarlet Macaw for another drink? We can grab some appetizers and do steaks later at my place."

Bev smiled into his cornflower-blue eyes. "Sure. I am kind of hungry now that you mention it and it's a little early for steak. Why don't we go ahead and rinse off? Our cards should be ready by the time we're done."

Kyle leaned in and whispered with a grin. "Do we have to shower separately?"

"Behave, counselor," she laughingly chided and pushed him gently. "We can work off the appetizers before you grill the steaks."

"I like the way you think," he said as they found their gear bags and adjourned to respective bathrooms.

Detangling her long hair would take a few extra minutes, but she could braid it wet and use Kyle's dryer later. She showered quickly, rolled her wet swimsuit into a towel and changed into a pair of teal denim shorts, a matching sleeveless crochet top with tiny white anchors embroidered along the scooped neckline and slid her feet into saddle-tan leather sandals. She snapped a hammered-silver cuff bracelet on and did a rapid review in the narrow full-length mirror. The teal color worked well with her hazel eyes and the fit of the top was clingy without stretching too tightly. She'd have her full summer tan in another few weeks.

As she expected, Kyle was finished and looked delicious in khaki cargo shorts and a dusty-blue golf shirt. His short, straight ash-blonde hair was damp. He was talking to George and keeping an eye on the bathroom door so he smiled in her direction when she appeared. The other couple was gone and no new customers had come in.

Bev stepped beside Kyle, signed for her card and noticed Chris looked distracted.

"Is there something wrong?" Bev asked politely.

Chris jotted a note on the calendar spread before her and shook her head. "Not really. I called Cindy a few minutes ago to let her know about this client I recommended her to and she wasn't home. I thought she was supposed to be there all day, but I left a message that I would swing by. I've got to drop something off and Jonah is out of town. I figured we could do a girls' night with dinner or whatever."

"Well, unless you've got too much to do here, why don't you come to Steve's place with us and have a beer?" Kyle offered.

Chris looked at her chrome dive watch and around the room.

"Go ahead," George said. "Danny can take care of the tanks and I don't think we'll get a big rush during the last hour. Y'all will have a jump on the Friday evening crowd."

Chris snapped the elastic waistband of the quick-dry navy blue shorts she'd pulled over her swimsuit and rocked her head back and forth. "Why not? I'll shower up and meet you for a round. Cindy should be home by then," she said.

"Okay, see you in a bit," Bev said and retrieved her pistol from under the counter where George kept it for her. She slipped it into the specially designed holster of her purse and reached for her equipment bag. Kyle had beaten her to it and had a bag dangling from each hand.

They waved good-bye, dumped the bags into Kyle's Explorer and drove across two parking lots to the Scarlet Macaw. It wasn't in either Bev's or Kyle's neighborhood, but had become a favorite and they especially stopped by when it was combined with a trip to the dive shop. The owner, Steve Dillworth, had helped with technical information when she was investigating the death of Greg Wiley.

Steve was leaning across the bar signing off on something for the bartender when they entered. Desmonda, the bar's namesake, ruffled her brilliantly colored wings and squawked a greeting from the black wrought-iron cage that occupied a large space between the door and the end of the bar. Rattan-tipped ceiling fans revolved quietly without dislodging the stack of paper bar napkins.

Steve looked up, smiled and pointed them toward a round table in the middle of the room. George was right, only half the tables and a third of the rattan bar stools were occupied. Within an hour, the place would be crowded, although not elbow-to-elbow. It wasn't quite the kind of place where you threw peanut shells on the floor and the décor couldn't have been picked by anyone other than a diver. Old equipment from the pioneering days of Jacques Cousteau, photographs of dozens of divers that veterans would recognize and framed breathtaking underwater shots dominated rough wood walls.

Kyle and Bev stopped at the bar and ordered a pitcher of Shark-stooth ale. "Say hello to some of the newest divers in Verde Key," Kyle said when he and Steve shook hands. Bev nodded and told the bartender, Jack, to open a tab.

"Then that pitcher is on the house," Steve said. "Did you have any trouble?"

"Nothing to speak of," Kyle replied. "Chris is great and she's coming over as soon as she gets changed. Come join us," he invited and took the pitcher and both frosted mugs.

"Sure," Steve said and picked up his glass of what would be club soda. He liked to stay until closing time most nights and usually saved his drinking for later. He and Kyle moved to the table while Bev put in the order for the special crab and cheese dip, nachos, and potato skins. They'd skipped lunch and she was suddenly ravenous. A bowl of fresh popcorn was on the table and they could start with that. Steve took pride in the red and gold cart-style machine at the other end of the bar. It was meticulously maintained and emitted a buttery, taste-bud tempting fragrance throughout the day.

The Macaw was away from the franchise hotel clump and was a favored spot of divers as well as marina crewmembers and boat owners. Tourists, the economic lifeblood of the town, were welcome, although not courted through advertisements or fliers. Steve's reputation among the water-drawn crowd was enough to keep business afloat. He'd been an avid diver until an injury during Desert Storm left him with a collapsed lung and a series of scars on the side of his neck that extended below the collar of his shirt. He was forced to restrict his diving to occasional and shallow, but he stayed current with the industry and constantly encouraged non-divers like Bev and Kyle to give it a try.

Bev sat down and took the filled mug from Kyle. "Congratulations and here's to many happy dives to come," Steve said in a toast.

They drank and Kyle launched into a description of the afternoon. Bev watched for Chris and they were almost ready for the second pitcher when she arrived. Two hours passed with stories and other people clustering around as Steve moved about the place. The experienced divers seemed eager to assure the novices they'd made a wise choice for a hobby.

It was after six o'clock when Chris excused herself and shortly came back to the table, a puzzled look in her chocolate drop eyes.

"No luck with Cindy?" Bev asked. Cindy was a year or so older than Chris, but there was no mistaking that they were sisters. They had a best-friends kind of relationship as far as Bev could tell.

15

Chris shook her head and tapped deeply bronzed, blunt fingers along the back of the wooden chair before she sat down. "Well, maybe Jonah got back early and they went out to dinner or something, but I'm a little surprised she didn't call me. I didn't get a chance to see her yesterday and two days without a conversation is about as long as we ever go." Chris looked across the room when someone called her name.

"Well, I'll try again later and drop by in the morning on the way to work," she said and pushed back from the table. "I need to say hi to those folks. They've got a full boat booked on Sunday."

"We're getting ready to leave anyway," Bev said and Kyle nodded in agreement. "Thanks for everything and maybe we can book a dive next weekend. We don't get a lot of Fridays off."

"Give us a call – we'll be getting more tourists soon," Chris said in parting.

Kyle settled with Jack, the bartender, and they left Happy Hour in full swing. Kyle took Bev's hand as they walked out.

"I cheated and picked up prepared mashed potatoes, a loaf of fresh bread and salad mix at the store this morning. All I have to do is marinate the steaks and then we need to find some way to spend about half an hour before I light the grill."

"Hmmm," Bev said and briefly pressed her body against his back when he stopped to open the passenger side. "If I put my mind to it, I bet I can come up with an idea."

"If it's like the ideas you had last night, I'm all for them." He sneaked a quick pat on her butt before she plopped onto the seat.

Bev smiled without further comment. Finishing up their dive certification with no problem, a fun couple of hours at the Macaw, two juicy steaks waiting at Kyle's and time for hot sex before and after dinner. Now that was the way to spend a day off.

CHAPTER THREE

W arren Randall left the office immediately after his flaw-
less performance at the morning press conference and
smilingly refused to elaborate as he made his way through the building lobby with Freddy in attendance. He paused long enough to
shake hands with the patrolmen outside the automatic sliding glass
doors and threw a quick salute to lingering members of the press before he and Freddy disappeared into the idling black Cadillac.
Freddy stayed on the telephone for the less than twenty-minute drive
and Warren happily noted two squad cars at the entry of the wide
horseshoe driveway. The rest of the neighborhood was quiet, of
course. The occupants were accustomed to media attention and the
incident as it was probably being referred to *had* occurred outside the
landscaped lawns.

The driver pulled into the horseshoe to allow Warren to exit with
the car between him and the cluster of reporters and photographers.
Freddy stepped out to throw them miniscule morsels of information.
Warren assumed the camera crews had been instructed to at least get
footage of his impeccably restored, outrageously expensive, 1920s
creamy-yellow stucco house. A twenty-foot high arched cover over
an oval terrazzo entryway provided protection from the elements
while still letting in light to showcase twin, arched, copper-accented
wooden doors that had once belonged to a castle or cathedral or
some such horseshit. Cecilia had prattled on about it with the faggot
decorator who was *simply the man that everyone had to have.* Or,
hell, maybe he was a stallion in disguise and drilled the society ma-
tron crowd while the husbands avoided being in the same room with
him. Who knew?

Warren called out his presence and hurried into his study, or
gentleman's retreat, according to Cecilia, and pressed the remote to
the fifty-two inch television in the custom-built cherry cabinet. Hot
damn, they'd made CNN! He flicked to multiple screen mode and
heard Freddy come in.

"Cecilia's out and won't be back until after lunch," he said.

17

"Dora put coffee, juice and pastries on the bar unless you're ready for something stronger." He pointed to the set-up and grunted in satisfaction with his appearance on the ample screen. The navy-blue suit, ice-blue shirt and red tie with thin white stripes had been the right choice – set off his eyes and hard to go wrong with subtle patriotism.

"I almost hope she forgot the chocolate chip muffins," Freddy said and crossed the room. "You want a cup?"

Warren nodded and sat in one of four deep red chairs arranged around a chest-like thing instead of a normal coffee table. "Everything still under control?" he asked without looking at Freddy. He'd hustle Freddy out after one cup of coffee. Mike should be checking in soon. It would have been nice if he could have gotten an okay from him before the press conference, but there hadn't been a chance to talk discreetly anyway.

CNN switched to another story, but the local stations would use it as a trailer interspersed between Saturday programs. Images of him, the mayor and the chief of police would be shown together and separately as each news crew tried to come up with a slightly different angle. They'd interviewed the cops who had first responded, and pretty Lila, who knew how to stick to her scripted answers, had shown the ledger in the lobby where Jonah had signed himself in as Mr. Stanley Jones.

They were suckers for more information and he had to give Freddy partial credit for keeping the lid on Jonah's identity until the moment of revelation. Warren skirted the fact of the twenty-year old suicide during his discussion with the police and merely acknowledged an old grudge that had obviously become an obsession. The explosion of questions in the crowded room for details about Jonah Shepard competed with camera flashes and Warren had stepped back to let the chief of police field the queries. The early morning start meant that none of them could possibly make the connection with the death of Lottie Shepard. Even with a personal assault on a state senator, a press conference at nine o'clock on a Saturday morning guaranteed that junior members of the press had been dispatched rather than seasoned staff. It would be several hours or longer until some of the older reporters and researchers paused over the name *Shepard* and began to look into the archives. More importantly, the delay had given Noonan and Rusty plenty of time to get to Verde

Key. Not that it really mattered, but how the hell had Jonah ended up in the Keys?

"Today is okay, but you've got to fill me in about this Lottie Shepard thing," Freddy said and handed Warren a cup of coffee before he took the chair across the table.

Fuck, DeLong must have told him. You'd think the man's brain would be too busy with billion dollar deals to remember shit like that.

"Nothing really to tell," Warren said evenly. "It was a long damn time ago. She was a mixed-up kid who took some pills when she got knocked up. The whole family was weird. They had too much religion and it was hard on all of them to lose their daughter under those circumstances. Apparently Jonah never got over it." Warren muted the sound to the television, sipped his coffee and waited to see how much Freddy knew. Or how much he would admit to knowing.

"So why were you the one she called that night?"

Warren lifted his right shoulder in a semi-shrug. "She'd been tutoring me for a while, she got scared with what she'd done and I was the only one she could think of, I suppose. She was dead by the time I got there. No note or anything so there was no way to know. I called the ambulance and waited until they arrived."

Freddy set his cup down and lifted a chocolate muffin from the white china dessert plate. "But you went there first instead of calling the cops or the hospital or anything? Wasn't that a question during the inquest?"

Warren locked eyes with him and had no idea if Freddy could discern his lies. "Hell, I was seventeen and she was babbling on about being in trouble and needing help. How the fuck was I supposed to know she'd swallowed a batch of pills? It's not the kind of thing you think of. I only went over there because she sounded so upset and I figured maybe I could help."

"The inquest was routine, the family left town and nothing else came of it?" Freddy bit into the muffin.

"The brother tried to attack me during the inquest and accused me of knocking his sister up, but the cops grabbed him. His parents said they didn't blame me and understood I hadn't been involved. Jonah went back to college, they left town not long afterwards and, until yesterday, I had no idea what happened to them."

Freddy swallowed, broke eye contact and looked at the muffin as though he was trying to figure out the ingredients.

Warren sipped his coffee to appear calm. He'd wait Freddy out. DeLong could put his own man in and he had to admit Freddy had the right kind of contacts in more places than he'd thought, but there was no way he could know anything about what had happened. Nobody could after all this time. Not with Andy being dead too.

"Okay then," Freddy said and shrugged. "Seems like someone mentioned it was brought up in your first campaign, but didn't caused much of a ripple. I'll take a look at the old coverage to make sure we're ready. We ought to get nearly a week's worth of good press out of this one and might as well be prepared for the suicide stuff to get dragged around and second-guessed. Somebody will try to get mileage out of it."

He bit into the muffin again and Warren smiled.

"Always a step ahead of the crowd, Freddy," he said pleasantly and looked down at his watch. "Good to have someone like you on the team."

Freddy finished the muffin without a response, wiped his mouth, picked his cup up and put the napkin underneath it. He stood and inclined his head toward the door. "No problem. I'll give you a call later and we'll talk about Monday night. Senator Tynsdale has decided to come down too, and I'll find out if golf or the yacht would be better for Tuesday."

Warren stood and walked with Freddy to the door. Tynsdale himself, huh? That was unexpected.

"You looked good today, Warren," Freddy said as he stepped across the threshold. "My regards to Cecilia."

The driver jumped out to open the back door before Freddy had a chance to say anything else. Warren was ready for him to be gone. He slapped Freddy on the back in parting. It was something he knew Freddy disliked.

Christ, he missed Andy! Fucking aneurism at forty! Minding his own business

and his goddamn brain exploded. Well, not exploded exactly, but deader than a post anyway. And then DeLong makes his move practically before the body is cold and "strongly advises Freddy step in."

"Now, Warren, I know you and Andy were tight and he was a

good man, but after all, he was more locally oriented. He didn't have the kind of national scope Freddy brings to the table. And if we're going to look at the next rung up, there's a lot of work to be done."

Warren went inside, crossed the marbled foyer that housed the dramatic hand-crafted staircase and remembered the litany of pat phrases accompanying DeLong's pronouncement. Hell, yes, he understood what could be at stake and maybe Andy was a homeboy, but at least he could trust him with anything. Friends since grade school, jocks together later; Warren the best receiver on the team and Andy a hell of a blocker. They both knew where each other's skeletons were buried and Andy never gave a shit about not being the star. He might not have been a political or financial genius, but he knew his way around a smoky room or two. And he was the only other person who knew about Lottie – well, had known most of it.

Warren left the study door ajar and went straight to the bar. He pushed the carafe of coffee aside, poured icy orange juice into one of the tall crystal glasses and splashed enough gin in to make it interesting. The sound of the doorbell floated faintly to him. That was bound to be Noonan with his report. Good, they could have the whole thing wrapped up in less than twenty-four hours.

Warren heard Dora's voice as she led Noonan to the study. He smiled widely at the petite Hispanic woman and positioned his body to keep her from coming in to replenish drinks, clean up and otherwise get in the way. "Thanks, Dora, Mr. Noonan and I have a lot to discuss, so I won't be taking any calls for a while."

He closed the door almost in her face and looked hard at Noonan. The angular, ex-cop rarely registered emotion of any kind, but his face seemed stonier than usual and his frigid eyes could not possibly reflect news Warren wanted to hear.

"I hope you doctored that," Noonan said quietly before Warren could frame the question. "Because we ran into a problem I wasn't expecting."

CHAPTER FOUR

"All I'm saying is you're both old enough to know what you want and he's a perfectly nice young man." Emma Henderson huffed slightly, moved the colander filled with peeled potatoes to the sink and turned the cold water on low. "You've been keeping company with him for practically a year, and don't think everybody in town doesn't notice how often your cars are seen at each other's place. He may be a Yankee, but a proposal would be proper by now."

Bev gulped the last swallow of tea. She was perched on a cane-bottom wooden chair at the honey-pine table of the eat-in kitchen. This was a conversation to be headed off quickly. "Mom, we've talked about this before. Kyle and I want to take this slowly and really get to know one another. There's no hurry. Your potato salad is always a hit – what else are you taking to the dinner?"

Emma sniffed loudly, switched off the water and turned her head as she swung around to lower the potatoes into a pot of boiling water. "Changing the subject doesn't change my point," she said. "Why you young people try and make this complicated is beyond me. There's only so much you can learn about a person unless you're married. You're going to wind up like your Aunt Lorna if you're not careful, living all alone surrounded by a bunch of plants."

Bev laughed in spite of herself and pushed the chair back gently to the edge of the oval braided rug. She deposited her glass on the counter, opened the cabinet her mother had to stand on tiptoes to reach and took down the big green bowl decorated with miniature daisies that was always used for crowd-sized potato salad.

"Mom, I love you to death, but I wish you'd stop worrying about this."

Emma shook her head and extracted a long-handled wooden spoon from a blue and green striped ceramic kitchen utensil holder. She waved it in the direction of the sliding glass doors that overlooked the canal. "Oh, I know you'll do whatever it is you want anyway and just because your father doesn't nag you like I do, doesn't mean he isn't waiting to walk you down the aisle."

Bev's cell phone rang sharply as her mother *hmmpf'd* at the interruption.

Bev stepped back into the dining area and punched the button. "Henderson," she said thankfully.

"Hey, Bev, I know you're off this weekend, but we've got a bit of a situation you might want to know about," Les Martin said with no preamble. "The guy who got shot in Randall's office yesterday? Turns out he's from here and some shit is brewing."

"You're kidding," she said. "I don't think Randall's ever been in town – we're not much use to him. One of the gun-toting, swamp-dwelling boys go off the deep end and decide to kill whatever politician he saw on TV last?"

"Nope, looks like an accountant, if you can believe it. Jonah Shepard. They released the name during the news conference, but we got a call beforehand. The West Palm guys want us to do a search of his place and a couple of news crews are already poking around the neighborhood. I thought you might want to be in on it."

"Yeah, sure. It doesn't sound like it will take long. I'll be there in about fifteen minutes," Bev said and ended the call.

"You haven't had a bite of lunch and I bet you didn't have enough breakfast to count," Emma said and moved to open the refrigerator. "I'll make you a sandwich."

Bev crossed the few paces between them and put her hand on her mother's shoulder. "Thanks, Mom, but I'll get something later. I'll take one of those brownies instead."

"You eat like you're still in college," Emma said with only rote reproach as she popped open the container holding the rich chocolate and peanut butter squares she was known for. "You'll be here for dinner tomorrow? And it wouldn't hurt you to come to the church social tonight and bring Kyle along."

"Dinner tomorrow, yes, and maybe we'll catch next quarter's social. We've already made other plans," Bev said quickly and wrapped two brownies in a paper towel. She pecked a kiss on the top of her mother's head, her curls of light brown hair slightly crinkly from hair spray. Spending most of the day in the kitchen did not mean Emma Henderson would slouch around. Starting the day in a nice pair of loose-fitting, polyester brown slacks and shirt, with makeup in place and coiffure secured, was what respectable women did. One never knew when company might drop by. It wouldn't do to have anyone think she was a lay-about just because she no longer had teen-agers flowing in and out of the house.

"Got to go, my love to Dad and see you tomorrow."

Bev snagged her tan leather purse from the sofa in the den and whisked out the front door before her mother thought of any more last minute admonitions – sinfully cavorting with Kyle, neglecting nutrition and not going to church regularly were enough for one day.

Bev resisted the thought of leaping into her Spitfire and opened the door like a normal person. The sun-warmed black leather seat was tolerable since she was in khaki slacks rather than shorts and she backed out of the drive with barely a glance for on-coming cars. It wasn't a high-traffic neighborhood; there were mostly retired or semi-retired couples and the occasional requisite widow thrown in to keep the demographics balanced. She waved cheerily to Mrs. Fletcher who was spreading mulch in her curbside begonia beds at the entry of the cul-de-sac. Bev wasn't about to add bad manners to her list of social offenses.

She was at the police station in eleven minutes and couldn't discern a heightened state of activity. Les Martin was standing outside the maroon unmarked sedan with the door partially open and was speaking into the radio with the cord stretched across the space. He was in weekend attire: olive drab slacks and a short-sleeved, palm-leaf patterned cotton shirt in lieu of his usual out-of-date seersucker suit. His more-white-than-gray hair would have passed any military inspection although male pattern baldness was apparently not part of his genetic make-up.

Bev switched off her engine and looked up for clouds. Rain wasn't forecast and the scattered wisps weren't threatening. She'd risk leaving the top down.

Les lowered the radio and pointed to the passenger's side. "There's a patrol car keeping reporters off the property and I thought we'd go on unless you need to do something inside," he said and reached into his front shirt pocket for his sunglasses.

"Nope, I'm ready," Bev replied and climbed in. "What are we supposed to be looking for?"

"Covering all the bases," Les said. "Check around for notes or calendar entries; see if it looks like anybody else was involved. I've got a warrant, but there was no answer at the house when we called.

We don't know if there's a wife and no other relatives have shown up yet. I'm banking he does like most everybody and has a spare key under a mat or one of those fake frogs. Did you catch any of the details on this?"

Bev shook her head. "Can't say I was paying attention. All I heard was that the guy had made an appointment under false pretenses and I guess there was no way to ask questions later."

"No, and nothing to go on," Les said and tapped his long fingers against the steering wheel as he drove. His hands and feet were disproportionately large for his average height and frame and, according to Kyle, he had a hell of a drive matched with a respectable putt. "No evidence of him spending the night and it would have been easy to drive up yesterday morning. They found the car because he had one of those remote entry systems and the parking lot wasn't very big. Nothing important in it, but more than one set of fingerprints. They're running them and if there's somebody else involved, they might get lucky."

Les made another left and Bev could see the patrol car near the far end of the short connector street. Most of the cars were parked inside garages or carports. The neighborhood didn't have a fancy sign with an appealing name and the houses were predominantly brick rather than concrete block or frame. None looked to be larger than three-bedroom and it was the kind of area real estate agents would label as starter or empty-nest. Front lawns were deeper than in some of the new developments and there were either a number of gardening enthusiasts around or an efficient landscape service available. Some of the residents had opted for gravel, palms, flowering shrubs and ornamental grasses in lieu of higher maintenance sod.

Beau Wilson motioned Les to park in front of a trio of brick duplexes. They were of the same design, although the brick color varied. Kevin, the senior officer, stood at the sidewalk leading to the middle one that was light red with splotches of mossy green. One-car, window-less white garages attached on each side of the duplex were closed. Peach-colored mini-blinds blocked the front windows from what was probably the living room.

A white van with a news logo and a bright blue one with a competing sign sat empty on opposing sides of the street. A photographer and reporter were in a front yard two houses away talking to a woman with a child straddled on her hip. Bev recognized the profile of the interviewer, Sylvia Ruthven, a perpetually wired individual who could be a royal pain in the ass when she was tracking a story. On the other hand, she wrote well, tended to stick with facts and didn't exaggerate for the sake of dramatics. The other crew was filming from an angle out of speaking distance and swung the camera to catch Bev and Les. The detectives ignored them and stepped up to Kevin. He and Bev's brother played football together in high school, but Kevin had chosen the community college and signed onto the force instead of going to a university. With his boyish face he looked closer to Bev's age than the almost four years he had on her.

"Morning, Bev, Les," he said, as he held a key for them to see and inclined his head toward the vans. "Beau and I have kept folks out and checked around. Nobody here, both garages are locked and neighbors on either side are gone. The lady across the street, Mrs. Ridge, said the young couples on the right are off on vacation, and the sisters that share the other duplex went to Mississippi three days ago for a funeral. Mrs. Ridge also said a woman named Cynthia actually owns the duplex, but Mr. Shepard moved in more than a year ago as a renter. He's on the left, but apparently there's a lot of movement between the doors. Mrs. Ridge wasn't sure it was appropriate for a woman to allow a male tenant, although she decided they made a nice couple so it was probably okay given the way this generation behaves."

Kevin rolled his eyes. "Mrs. Ridge is a real talker, so Beau's making sure everyone else stays away until one of y'all says it's okay. She said she hadn't seen anyone for a couple of days, but told us a spare key was in the garden hose container."

"How convenient," Bev said as Kevin dropped the key into Les's open palm. The three filed onto the white porch that spanned the length of the duplex. A white wicker glider with a hunter-green cushion was on the right side. A healthy-looking spider plant, with small new sprouts draping halfway to the porch, hung from a ceiling hook between the door and the glider. Mr. Shepard's side was bare, uninspired rather than uninviting. There were no newspapers in sight and Bev opened the top of the standard, black wall-mounted mailbox. A colored sales flier and some envelopes were inside. She'd get them later.

The door unlocked with no resistance and Les called out their identification. The only noise was the sound of an air-conditioner. Les entered the dim interior and groped for a switch. The front porch light came on first, then the light to a short hardwood hallway. Bev pointed to a door cut into the hallway that evidently led to the other side of the duplex, like in adjoining hotel rooms. That seemed odd.

Bev and Kevin followed Les into the living room and they stood for a moment to get their bearings. The thermostat was either set high or the unit didn't work well. It wasn't uncomfortable, yet it had the stale smell of barely circulated air. The rectangular room had two windows to the front, one to the side, and an opening into a dining area with only enough room for a square table and four chairs. The beige, short-pile carpet looked fairly new, with no stains or worn patches. A single landscape painting that could have come from any of a thousand stores and a gold-framed oval mirror were all that broke up off-white walls with no marks of lived-in damage. Not sterile – more like unused. A wooden entertainment center held a television and some hardback books and a sofa with matching armchair were arranged in front. The furniture was covered in a dark blue patterned fabric Bev couldn't quite distinguish from across the room. A ficus tree sat in one corner. Despite realistic foliage, there wasn't enough light for it to be anything other than artificial. An extra three-shelf bookcase, a coffee table with scattered magazines and a brass floor lamp next to the armchair completed the scene.

A rapid, first tour provided no surprises: neater than one might expect, ghost odors of onion or garlic in the kitchen, one bedroom with a half-bath, one bedroom used as a study and a full bath between the two. The colors were neutral, the tile work and fixtures evidently updated in contrast to the 1960s construction of the buildings. Not a hint of avocado green, harvest gold or flamingo pink on the premises.

"Where do you want to start?" Bev asked Les. "The study?"

"Probably the best bet," he agreed and pulled three sets of disposable, hospital-type gloves from his pants pocket. "It's not very big, so I can take it and you and Kevin can split the rest."

They nodded, slipped the gloves on and Bev started toward the bookshelves in the living room.

The front door opened and Beau thrust his head and torso inside. "Detective Henderson? There's a lady out here who's pretty anxious. Name's Chris Green."

"Chris? Why is she here?"

"Something about her sister," Beau said. "The other half of the duplex?"

Bev waved for Les and Kevin to continue and she opened the door to see Chris standing behind Beau. He moved to the side and Chris pushed past him to grasp Bev's forearms.

The slender woman who dismissed sharks with a laugh, who was usually the image of self-confidence, was trembling, her eyes wide with fearful question.

"Oh, God, Bev, where is she?" Her hoarse voice broke on the *she*. "Could she have known about Jonah? Is she in trouble?"

Oh, shit, it suddenly clicked. Chris not able to reach her sister, Cindy, last night. The comment about Jonah being out of town. This Cindy, this Jonah.

"Chris," she said and drew the woman inside before the news crews could see. Beau pulled the door shut and stayed outside. "Chris, there's no one here, no one on either side. What do you know?"

She held Bev tightly, blinked her eyes and hoarseness melted into bleakness. "Nothing," she said. She dropped her hands and lifted one to rub her forehead. "I never got Cindy last night and I had a dive group early this morning. I was running a little late, so I didn't stop by like I planned. I didn't hear about Jonah until I got back to the shop maybe half an hour ago. I called Cindy again, got the machine, panicked and came right over. I was going to call you next."

Les and Kevin came to the edge of the living room and Chris jerked her head from one to the other. "Has anyone been next door? Have you seen my sister?"

"The woman the neighbor mentioned is Cynthia Green, Jonah Shepard's girlfriend," Bev explained.

Kevin cleared his throat. "Uh, no, ma'am, we looked around outside and knocked, but we didn't try to go inside."

Les looked at Bev and then Chris. "Is it possible that your sister had to go somewhere early this morning?" he asked logically.

"I suppose it could be," Chris said, a shade of hope sparking her eyes. "She's not really a morning person, but something could have come up. She never listens to the news on the weekend and doesn't get a newspaper. I mean, I was sure she said he was out of town for a day or two and if she didn't have the radio on in the car this morning, she wouldn't have heard." Her voice started to lift and she almost smiled. "If she did go out, maybe she left me a message at home to let me know when to come by. I'll go next door and see if there's a note on her calendar. She always writes down her appointments."

"I tell you what," Les said quickly. "Bev and I will go with you. If you can reach her, the news is going to be a shock and you can let her know that we're going to have to talk to her."

Chris was nodding and poking her hand into her pocket. "Yeah, yeah, you're right. It's going to be awfully tough. I mean, I still can't believe it – not Jonah. It doesn't make sense."

She tugged a key out, spun around and couldn't see the exchange between Les and Bev.

"Let's be ready," Bev mouthed. Jesus, she hoped it was a simple crisscross of schedules between sisters.

Les nodded once and followed Chris outside across the porch. She inserted the key, turned it and hit the front switch.

The fresher air and a hint of floral scent were immediately apparent even though the physical layout mirrored next door. Chris turned lights on as she moved down the hall and turned left into the kitchen.

"She keeps a calendar by the refrigerator," Chris said, "and one in her office."

Bev was watching carefully and stepped quickly to the side when Chris stopped abruptly after entering the kitchen.

"Oh, shit," Chris moaned and momentarily, instinctively slumped back against Bev. "Oh, shit."

CHAPTER FIVE

B ev steadied Chris and expertly scanned the room. On this side of the duplex, the wall between the kitchen and dining room had been removed to add a sense of space. A square, tile-topped wooden bistro table sat in front of a semi-circle of potted plants. A bentwood chair was shoved away from the table, a second chair lay on the floor. A yellow coffee mug was next to it, brown stains spread on the beige-flecked vinyl. A ceramic salt and pepper shaker set designed like light houses had been knocked over – black and white grains were spilled into tiny piles on the surface of the table. No blood was immediately visible.

"Please don't touch anything," Bev said when Chris righted herself and began to move forward.

She turned her head, looked at Bev blankly and registered comprehension.

Les moved in silently and touched Chris on the elbow. "Miss Green," he said calmly, officially. "We're going to need your help here if you can. Will you be okay?"

Chris drew in a deep, audible breath, exhaled slowly and answered in a firmer tone. "Yes. May I check the other rooms?"

Bev silently sighed relief although she wouldn't have expected Chris to fall apart. Now that it looked as if her foreboding had been justified, she would want to take action.

"Let me look first," Les replied and moved before he saw Chris nod her assent.

"We'll talk about time line in a minute," Bev said. "Let's see if her car is gone."

"The entrance is in the utility room," Chris said and angled toward a partially open door.

She stepped through and reached up for the light chain. The space was maybe ten by nine: water heater, stacked washer and dryer, pantry shelving and fuse box and the door into the garage.

They heard Les call from the bedroom area. "No one here."

"Let me open the door, please," Bev said and twisted the knob as lightly as possible with gloved hands.

"I don't understand," Chris said when they saw the empty space. "Where's her car?"

"There could be a couple of answers," Bev said. "Let's go sit down."

"Living room, Les," she said as they passed him in the kitchen.

He was on the cell phone; they would need photographs and the on-call forensics specialist.

Chris stood at the edge of the multi-colored striped sofa and stared as if she'd never seen the piece of furniture before. She gave herself a quick shake, sank sideways onto the sofa and faced Bev who took the sea-foam green upholstered chair.

The room seemed undisturbed by whatever happened in the kitchen. Unlike Jonah's place, there were more live plants and an Impressionist theme. A good quality Monet print – or maybe it was a Manet – dominated one wall and a pair of dried flower wreaths were displayed on another, but the floral effect wasn't overwhelming.

Bev slipped her notebook from her purse and focused on Chris's tightened face. "Is there any chance Cindy might have heard about Jonah on the news, been thrown into a state of confusion and left for some place, maybe to see you?"

Chris twisted her hands in her lap. "That's not Cindy's style and I'd think she would call first. She knows the number to the shop and I have voice mail on my cell phone." She hesitated and looked toward the kitchen. "This wouldn't be like anything she's ever handled though. It's possible she bolted instead."

"She doesn't have a cell phone?" Bev asked.

Chris moved her mouth in a half-smile. "No, that's one of those silly things about her – she doesn't like them." She reached out her hand. "Let me check my voice mail at home, just in case."

Bev gave the other woman her telephone and joined Les in the opening between the living room and dining area.

"The others will be here soon and I thought we'd wait to call the chief until after we finish the interview," he said. "You figuring this the same way I am?"

Bev spoke just above a whisper. "She finds out what he's planning, he strangles her, maybe, takes her in her car, dumps the body and car, gets back here somehow and takes off?"

"Gives us a lot to look for," Les said unemotionally. "Unless the sister can think of where she might be."

Chris was rubbing her forehead again and looked in their direction.

"My guess would be no," she said.

This time Bev sat next to Chris and let Les take the chair.

Chris took one more steadying breath and started in a controlled voice. "Cindy teaches English at the high school, but she's off for the summer. She does some freelance editing and newsletter work from here. We had a late lunch Wednesday and she told me Jonah was going out of town, but I don't think she mentioned where. I had an appointment at the bank Thursday afternoon and a night dive group Thursday evening. I ran by and borrowed one of Cindy's purses, but she wasn't home. I left a note and then I couldn't reach her Friday."

"You came by for a purse?" Les asked with a puzzled expression.

"Yeah, Cindy leaves her purses stacked on a trunk at the foot of her bed. The lady I was meeting with is one of those clothes-horse women. You know, the kind who looks like she belongs in some fashion magazine. The kind that thinks if you don't know how to dress, then you must not know anything else either. Anyway, I was wearing my blue suit with navy shoes and for whatever reason, I had my brown purse. This is on the way to the bank, so I dashed in and got Cindy's navy bag. The meeting took like forever and I barely made it back to the shop in time to get everything ready for the dive."

Bev tried not to smile at the baffled look on Les' face – she could give him a fashion lesson later. "Sure," she inserted smoothly. "I remember you were trying to call her Friday and you said you hadn't talked to her for a couple of days. Can you tell us about Jonah?"

"Jonah," Chris said and her voice quavered momentarily. "God, this makes no sense. I mean Jonah threatening anyone is hard enough to believe, but doing something to hurt Cindy is just, just..." she trailed off.

Kevin opened the front door. "Earl and Justin are outside and a county car is coming down the street. Should be forensics."

Les stood. "Bev, why don't you keep going with Miss Green

and I'll get everybody started. We'll take care of here and then go back next door."

"What do we do now?" Chris asked, her thoughts distracted from Jonah. "How do we find Cindy? Do you think he took her with him and she's locked away somewhere? That kind of thing happens, doesn't it?"

Interesting how people were willing to create alternate scenarios instead of recognizing the most likely one when it involved someone they cared for.

"We go over both sides of the duplex for clues," Bev said without answering the last question. "We interview everyone on the street, get word out to the public with a photo of Cindy and a description of her car and maybe we get lucky fast." It was, after all, a missing person case at this stage.

"If you can tell me everything you know about Jonah and their relationship, it will help. Give me as much detail as you can, even if it seems minor."

"Yeah sure," Chris replied and explained about her older sister and the quiet, sometimes melancholy – but who could have thought dangerous? – Jonah Shepard.

Chris regained most of her composure and concentrated on Bev's note-taking and intermittent questions. She faltered slightly when there appeared to be no more to tell.

"Uh, I guess that's it," she said and paused. "Is there anything I can do here? I mean, is there something I can get you, show you?"

Bev tapped her notebook with the tip of her pen. "Recent photographs and the details on her car would be helpful," she said. "And do you need us to contact your parents? The name recognition with the attempt on Senator Randall means the story will get picked up pretty quickly."

Chris rose and shook her head. "It will be better if I call them. I was waiting, hoping it was all some stupid conclusion I was jumping to. There are some extra copies of a studio portrait we had done for Christmas. She has a silver Taurus that's two, maybe three years old. She bought it new from Cotton's."

Les was giving Kevin instructions about next door when Bev and Chris entered Cindy's home office. The sparsely decorated, disgustingly tidy room showed no sign of invasion other than from the forensics expert.

Bev explained about the photo and Les cleared his throat. "I saw them in one of the desk drawers," he said to Chris. "We're finished, although we'll need to get your fingerprints for elimination purposes. Later this afternoon will be all right."

The room was done in oak with a corner computer armoire, the kind that could be shut to hide clutter if there was any clutter to hide. A large roll-top desk, also capable of closure for the sake of neatness, was open. Even the items tucked into the signature pigeonholes fit into the recesses without hanging over the edges. An ergonomically designed chair, a five-drawer wooden filing cabinet and a glass-fronted lawyer's bookcase were the remaining furnishings. It wasn't difficult to think of Cindy in terms of an English teacher.

"Will I be able to come and go from here?" Chris asked and offered two five-by-seven versions of what would have been a larger portrait. "I'll need to water the plants, get her mail, things like that." The mundane acts, the sort of things she would do if her sister had simply gone on vacation.

Would it give her a level of comfort or would an eerie emptiness take hold? Bev studied the picture while Les answered Chris. A bluish background and a fan-backed wicker chair. Cindy standing behind a seated Chris. Different coloring, but easy to identify as sisters. Cindy's hair was longer and lighter, the sort of dark blonde that would show sun streaks if she spent time outdoors. Green eyes instead of chocolate, the same oval face and wide mouth. Cindy's smile was pleasant, Chris's closer to a grin.

"This is fine," Les said and used his body to turn Chris toward the front door. She looked silently between them and nodded.

"Okay. Well, I've got to make a couple of phone calls and then I'll come to the station."

"I'll go with you to your car," Bev said. If the news crews were still around, she didn't want them catching Chris yet.

Chris started to say something, bit her lower lip instead and moved silently to the front door. She paused on the front porch and spoke so quietly that Bev almost missed the comment.

"Jonah's a gentle person – I can't understand any of this."

Bev put her hand lightly on Chris's shoulder. "It's hard to know people. We'll do everything we can to find her."

The two news vans were gone. They'd be pissed if they found

out they could have had a shot at a first interview. Bev moved down the short walk and around to the driver's side of Chris's silver PT Cruiser. She was the only person Bev knew that owned one and Chris had told her she'd bought it on a whim right after she'd left the Army.

"Is an hour okay? For the station, I mean?"

"Yeah, we'll be leaving here in a few minutes," Bev replied and gave Chris one of her cards. "Call if your folks have questions you don't want to get into, or you can call them again from my office."

"Sure, thanks." Chris climbed into the car and drove away.

Bev watched until she was out of sight and turned when she heard Les step up behind her.

"Will she hang in?"

"Yeah, she was thrown off balance, but she's tough. She's ex-Army as a matter of fact," Bev replied. "Where are we?"

Les jerked his thumb over his shoulder without looking. "The tech found some dried blood splatters on the seat of the chair, and some faint smearing on the edge of the table and floor. Not much spread. Probably a bloody nose, could have been a blow to the head with a minor cut. We'll get blood type info, but you can figure it'll be a match. We found an asthma inhaler partially underneath the refrigerator. Remind me to ask the sister if she needed it all the time. I called the chief a few minutes ago and he'll handle the press while we work. He'll meet us at the station and try and keep a lid on it for another couple of hours. Then we've got to go public and ask for help. Kevin said there's nothing from the neighbors so far."

"Anything useful in Shepard's place?"

"Not yet," Les said. "Several file folders with clippings about Randall – goes back to his college days if you can believe it. No other photos or scrapbooks, not some of the classic stalker indicators you hear about. If there was somebody else involved, there aren't any obvious clues. Unless maybe the sister was. It could be the other angle."

Bev squinted and remembered she'd left her sunglasses in her glove compartment. "Wouldn't that be a hell of a thing? I've never met Cindy, but hardly seems like something an English teacher would get mixed up in, although I guess we can't totally count it out yet."

"Shepard was an accountant," Les said and checked his watch.

35

"Be interesting to see if we get the, 'He was such a nice, quiet guy' bit from everybody we talk to, or the, 'There was always something really strange about him.' Unless you see it differently, we shift focus from the Randall piece and move out on the girl."

"Agree," Bev said. "What do we need from here?"

"The files and a few other things. Let's take stuff now, meet with the chief, then come back to do a second sweep with the neighbors. There are only ten houses total and Kevin's got a list on who all was home."

"Works for me," Bev said.

As unlikely as it was that Cindy was still alive, they would treat it as a missing person case until they had something definitive, if they ever did. It was a short distance to deep water where a body could be sunk and never found. But an accountant? What would someone like Shepard know about disposing of bodies?

CHAPTER SIX

Chief Taylor was leaning back in his chair, telephone to his ear, staring out the glass window of his office when Bev and Les entered the station. He flagged them with his free hand and stabbed the air toward the chairs in front of his desk. They silently entered, not certain of who Chief Taylor had on the other end.

He was dressed in jeans and a red polo shirt. If he'd been on his regular Saturday schedule, he would have been interrupted during the time he allotted for house maintenance and repairs. Bev saw a streak of dark across the back of one hand. It was probably grease that wouldn't come off in a quick wash-up.

"Give me the basics," he said as he dropped the telephone into the cradle and picked up the burning cigarette from the ashtray. Three squashed butts. At the rate he chain smoked, that meant he hadn't been in the office long. "Understand you had to shift gears when the sister showed up. I've already talked to more people than I particularly care to and we've got to give the news guys something. It's not like they get a chance at anything juicy very often."

Les inclined his head toward Bev. "Bev talked to the sister. There wasn't much in Shepard's place on the first run through. What physical evidence we have is from Miss Green's – Cynthia, Cindy. She's the owner of the duplex and girlfriend of Jonah Shepard, who rented the other half of the duplex. The sister, Chris, is the one who alerted us about Cindy and took us next door. Looks like there was a struggle. The tech found traces of blood on the scene, Miss Green's car is gone and there's been no contact with her sister since Wednesday."

He looked to Bev who nodded confirmation. He continued.

"It's not a densely populated neighborhood and this time of year, houses are mostly shut up with the air going and kids playing in fenced-in back yards. The two duplexes on either side were a bust – all the residents gone. A Mrs. Ridge across the street seems to know everybody's business, but she was nursing some kind of ailment and not out and about. Bottom line is that nobody saw anything unusual,

37

everybody is shocked about Jonah, nobody other than the sister is aware Miss Green is missing."

"Okay, what are you two figuring?" The chief blew a stream of smoke out the side of his mouth.

"Four possibilities," Les said, as he held up his fist and extended his thumb. "Most likely, Jonah did this independently, Cindy finds out what he's planning, he whacks her, disposes of the body late Thursday or early Friday and goes about his business."

His index finger went up. "Second is someone else is involved who took care of Cindy while Jonah had the West Palm end. Same outcome for Cindy as possibility one. Third, Cindy was in on it in some capacity and she either got cold feet or he didn't want loose ends. Same outcome as possibility one."

Fourth finger went up. "Less likely considering what we found at the house, but Cindy found out, bolted the premises and is lying low somewhere too scared to contact anyone."

Chief Taylor swung his glance to Bev when she lifted a hand. "The sister, Chris, can't imagine Cindy wouldn't come to her for help," she said. "She's holding on to the idea that Jonah took Cindy with him and she's stashed some place."

"A fifth idea," Les said and shrugged, an unspoken opinion of that possibility.

"Six if you count in something totally unrelated like a robbery gone bad," Chief Taylor said dryly. "That would be off-the-wall, but we wouldn't want to be accused of jumping to conclusions. What does the sister know?"

"They're close with lots of regular contact," Bev said. "Cindy's been here nearly four years; she's the one who got Chris hooked up with buying the Adventures Below Dive Shop last year."

"The Wiley/Farmer thing?" the chief asked in surprise.

Bev nodded. "Cindy is older, no other siblings, parents are in Kentucky. Jonah came into the picture right before Chris moved here. She stayed with Cindy for a few weeks and the romance hadn't started yet."

"Any history of violence?"

"No, just the opposite. *Sort of moody some times, but sweet and gentle, quiet, lost-soul kind of guy,*" Bev read from her notes. "They seemed to be a good couple. Cindy wasn't sure how permanent it was going to be, but Chris said it wasn't an issue with her. Technically Jonah lived on his side and Cindy on hers. The people who originally owned the duplex had an older parent living next door and installed a connecting door. Chris said it was dead-bolted from Cindy's side, although it was usually unlocked and they free-flowed back and forth. She's genuinely stunned and swears she didn't see or hear anything out of the ordinary leading up to this."

Bev paused and tapped her notebook with her pen. "One interesting thing.

Apparently Jonah had a sister who died when she was in high school and he was in college. Chris didn't know the whole story, but she has the impression it was a suicide and it tore up the family. I guess it was just Jonah and the sister and he never really got over it. The parents are no longer alive. That's the *lost-soul* part, I imagine. Chris's take is she doesn't think Jonah ever had a serious relationship before Cindy and she was helping him deal with his emotional baggage. I suspect that's a part of why she'd rather believe a kidnapping."

Chief Taylor scratched with two fingers at a spot on his head where Bev could recall thick, sandy brown hair. He'd been a sergeant in the department when her father signed on as a rookie. The remaining fringe encircling his skull was now mostly gray. His heavy brown eyebrows hadn't changed over the years though, nor had the intensity of his brown-eyed stare. "You voting with Les on Number One?"

"It makes the most sense. I mean, a quiet accountant going off the deep end and trying to shoot a state senator doesn't make sense to start with, but the idea of Cindy being in on it would seem really far-fetched. If he hauled her off alive, that means prior planning or off-the-cuff finding a place to leave her in addition to everything else he's got going. Same thing for her disappearing on her own. She might take off, but there would be no reason for her not to call her sister once she put some distance between her and Jonah. No, her discovering what he was up to and him getting rid of her is more reasonable. It's too bad we got nothing on the first round with the neighbors, although if he took her in her car, he had to get back some way. Most likely he hitched a ride."

"Photos of both and info on the car are in the system," Les said. "We let the television and papers have them and maybe we'll get somebody quick."

The chief stubbed out his cigarette. "Okay, missing person is the official call. We're not positive on the link with Shepard, but checking all possibilities and so forth. No speculation, we're looking for help on the missing woman. They'll pester the shit out of us for the lover/sex angle, but the neighbors can provide that grist. I'll handle the questions, you two get moving on all the pieces."

He had already picked up the receiver to the telephone. Les and Bev adjourned to their office to compare notes on actions left to be taken. The space they shared was about the same size as Chief Taylor's except it held both of them, a couple of extra chairs, black metal filing cabinets across one wall, a combination bulletin board and white board on one wall, an old refrigerator and table against the other painted wall with old thumbtack holes scattered like a teenager's acne scars. The table was devoted to coffee making and some of the lingering stains were impervious to known cleaning products.

"I didn't ask if you had plans for today," Les said. "I bet this is not what you had in mind for a Saturday." He pulled out the swivel, non-adjustable chair to his desk. The old chair with the annoying squeak had been discarded when Les came in to replace Jim Osborn when he retired. Les had come from Tallahassee, wanting a slower pace that allowed him to spend more time with his wife. She was a friendly woman who maintained a pleasant demeanor in spite of encroaching arthritis.

"Not a big deal," Bev said. "I'm good until later tonight. How's Blanche by the way?"

"Moving around a little better and doting on the new granddaughter. Hard to believe we've got six grandkids now. There are days when I have no idea where the years have gone." He snapped his fingers. "And speaking of not having any idea. What was the business with the sister and purses? That part about borrowing her sister's purse. Navy blue and brown?"

Bev laughed. "Oh, that. Chris said she was wearing a navy blue suit and I assume navy shoes to match. For those who care, that means she should have been carrying a navy purse to complete the ensemble."

"Why would you know this shit?"

Bev moved to the dented refrigerator in the corner, took out a diet Coke for herself and a Sprite for Les. "Too much exposure to my friend, Helen, a woman who never met a shoe store she didn't like. She rags me constantly about my lack of accessorizing. I'm willing to bet Cindy was the one who would have been into coordinated shoes and purses and warned Chris to spiffy up for her session at the bank."

Les took the cold can and shook his head. "Color coordination is another good reason I don't do my own shopping. Let's work through where we should start the search and if we get a decent lead, we can change tactics. I can't see it being the back yard. You're a native, where would you dump a body and car?"

"Water and that doesn't narrow the territory much," she said immediately. "But a body and car together means access to deep water and that helps a little. We don't have elevation with rocky cliffs and water below. You need a ramp or a bridge." Bev gave a wry semi-smile. "Unless you separate the body, dump it in one place and abandon the car somewhere else."

"So much for narrowing the search," Les said and took a swig.

The telephone on Bev's desk rang. She picked it up and spoke briefly to the desk sergeant. "Chris is here," she said. "I'll get her through fingerprinting and see if she's thought of anything new. Maybe she knows of a deep water place where Jonah liked to fish."

"I could handle a quick find," Les said. "In the meantime, I'll call your dad. He knows his way around as well as anyone."

"As long as you don't tell him I didn't think of him first," Bev said and let the laughter fade from her voice. She didn't want Chris to misinterpret banter for a lack of seriousness and Chris might be getting into earshot as she came down the hall.

Bev had instructed the desk sergeant to allow Chris into the open bay area and Bev raised her hand as Chris approached the administrative assistant's desk. Taliah wasn't in and Bev hoped they could keep the weekend staffing level down. They wouldn't need extra office personnel unless leads flooded in.

Chris had changed into a pair of black shorts and a green-print button-front shirt, no make-up or jewelry. Her eyes were calm and a casual observer might have missed the lingering red of dried tears.

"I told my parents I'd call them again after I leave here," she said by way of greeting. "And that I trusted you to do everything possible to find Cindy. I suggested they not come down yet. I didn't think there was anything for them to do and who knows, maybe

Cindy will try and reach them."

Bev stepped forward and put her hand on Chris's forearm. "That's a good idea; it's probably easier for them to be in familiar surroundings. Come on back and I'll tell you what we've done while they're getting the prints."

Chris followed Bev while she crafted the missing person version of the case, the version going to the media. Bev wondered how quickly the question of homicide would be asked. Or if it had been already.

Chief Taylor joined them after the fingerprinting and invited Chris to his office to talk about the conversations he'd had with which reporters. Bev quickly excused herself and found Les on the telephone at his desk.

Bev eased into her chair and reached for the telephone to call Kyle. She paused when Les held a finger up and pointed to the receiver he was holding. He said good-bye to whomever he was talking to and raised an eyebrow. "Well, shit's about to stir up for sure."

"What? You got something already?"

"No, not for our part, but do you remember what you said earlier about Chris telling you about Jonah's sister?" He didn't wait for her to respond.

"The deal with the sister was suicide. She took a bunch of pills when she was seventeen, which makes it more than twenty years ago. You get one guess as to the now well-known name of the male high school student who found her body and called the police."

Bev frowned and then opened her eyes wide. "Randall?"

"Damn, you *are* good," Les said. "Want to hear it and then I'll tell you what your dad and the search and rescue guys had to say?"

Bev nodded. A twenty-year-old connection would explain the multiple file folders they'd taken from Shepard's place.

"The Shepards and Randalls lived in Vero Beach at the time. The sister's name was Lottie and she and Jonah were the only children. The father was a blue-collar guy, the mother a housewife. Lottie was a high school junior, Jonah a college sophomore. The Randalls were up on the social scale, not in the top tier, but well-to-do. Young Randall was high school football star with all the trappings. What Lottie did have going for her was book smarts and the story gets a little fuzzy at this point, but for some reason, she starts tutoring Randall in a couple of classes. Several months pass and the parents are gone for a weekend. This next part is still up for grabs, but the bottom line is that Lottie takes a bunch of pills, calls Randall for help, he gets there too late and she's dead. He calls the cops and swears he didn't know what the problem was when he went to see her."

"And the brother blamed him for not getting there quick enough?"

"Added to the fact they discovered she was pregnant," Les said.

"Holy shit," Bev said. "It was Randall's?"

"Not according to him. His story was nothing beyond tutoring went on and he had no idea who the father could have been. The brother was pretty vocal with his opinion, went swinging for Randall during the inquest and had to be restrained. The parents put a stop to it, wouldn't pursue the question and the family packed up and moved not long after the funeral. The Randalls moved to West Palm, the elder Randall having had considerable success in his business. The Shepards disappeared, the Randalls moved up the social ladder and young Randall hit the jackpot when he became romantically involved with Cecilia DeLong, only daughter of William and Margaret DeLong. Doors magically fly open, he becomes a golden boy, they a golden couple and all the rest of the bullshit that goes with it."

"While a quiet, *lost-soul* accountant keeps tabs on him, plans some kind of revenge and picks a certain day, for reasons as yet unknown," Bev injected.

Les shrugged. "Oh, I imagine there'll be all kinds of speculation about why now. The only thing that will keep this from becoming a total circus is that Randall is a state politician instead of national. It's going to be a hell of a story when you add the Green girl into it."

Bev crossed her arms, stretched them over her head and arched her back slightly. "A hell of a story is right. It's too damn bad I don't see much chance for a happy ending."

"Probably not the way Senator Randall sees it," Les said.

"Guess you're right about that," Bev agreed, not the least concerned for the politician's perspective. "Okay, what are the suggestions about where we start looking for Cindy?"

CHAPTER SEVEN

Word about Cindy spread quickly for a Saturday afternoon. Non-fatal car wrecks, house fires and drug-related shootings were no competition and the press embraced the long-dead-sister-missing-girlfriend story with professional glee gloved in professionally somber tones. *"Breaking news in the recent attempt on Senator Warren Randall. In an unexpected twist..."*

The chief had been surprisingly patient with media queries and later with the mayor when he groused about tourist season and bad publicity. The chief reminded him of the value of notoriety.

Les made arrangements with the West Palm detectives for them to conduct a more thorough forensics check of Shepard's vehicle and a county technician was scheduled to retrieve the computers from the duplex. Bev told him she wasn't particularly concerned about the attack on the senator. If Jonah hadn't been solo, it would impact the search for Cindy. If there was a partner, West Palm could worry about protecting the senator. Jonah hadn't left incriminating notes tucked into his papers, but totally erasing data from a computer was more difficult than many people realized. And if Cindy had been using her computer, the technicians could see the date and time to the minute of when she was working on files, or sent and received electronic mail. If she was the kind of person who regularly surfed on-line, it could help narrow the time frame of when she was alive.

Bev linked a conference call with her dad and a representative from County Search and Rescue to map out potential body disposal areas in a widening circle. Teams would begin searching after forty-eight hours or sooner if a useful lead developed. Efforts until then would focus on the missing/kidnapped woman who might be hiding somewhere, hurt and/or frightened.

"Experts can't discount the possibility of psychosomatic amnesia, commonly referred to as hysterical amnesia, induced by the shock of discovering Mr. Shepard's actions..." had made it into the news anchors' copy. Bullshit for a movie script as far as Bev was concerned.

Chief Taylor left before the evening news; Bev sent Les home not long afterwards and she stayed to leave word about what kinds of calls should be forwarded to her in the middle of the night. She didn't expect any, but she wanted to make sure they used her cell number rather than her apartment phone. Kyle said the lobsters he'd picked up were two pounds if they were an ounce. She had no intention of spending the night in her own bed despite her mother's chiding.

Bev drove to Kyle's condominium, opened the door without bothering to ring and found him in the kitchen dicing tomatoes. The aroma of garlic bread baking reminded her that brownies and a bag of trail mix hadn't exactly constituted a meal.

His condo was a newer, more contemporary style than her apartment, although they shared an affinity for functional pieces with clean lines. The two bedrooms were upstairs and a clever architect had managed to fit a powder room and small storage space underneath the staircase in the entryway. The kitchen, den and dining area were all a part of a single room. Furniture and area rugs over the ceramic tile floor defined the spaces. It was obvious that Kyle's real thought had gone into the array of electronic equipment and accessories housed in the hefty maple entertainment center. One of the cubbyholes was home to multiple remote controls that between them had as many buttons as the console of a jet fighter. He never had to worry about Bev controlling the remote; she wouldn't know which one to pick up.

She deposited her purse and gym bag with overnight essentials on the leather recliner. "Great looking salad," she said and leaned across the kitchen peninsula to receive a light kiss.

"Love those bags," he said and raked the tomatoes into a mound of mixed greens. "Open, dump and toss – my kind of cooking. You want a beer or to open the wine? Or something stronger? I know this afternoon was hard. How's Chris doing?"

Bev took two beers and iced mugs from the refrigerator. "She's coping and hoping for the best. She's convinced herself Cindy is alive somewhere." She poured her beer, took a grateful swallow and replaced Kyle's empty mug with a fresh one.

"Stranger things have been known to happen. It's probably better for her for now," he said and pushed the bowl of salad aside. "Unless you're a purist about steaming, I thought I'd dismember the lobsters and throw them on the grill. And I found one of those chocolate mousse pies that you like."

"Lobster and chocolate mousse pie?" Bev almost moaned in pleasure. "You do realize we'll have to work all those calories off?"

He grinned and lifted his mug. "Well, I was sort of counting on that."

Bev smiled and wrinkled her nose. "Speaking of which, I got another lecture from my mother with hints of hellfire and damnation. It's a good thing she likes you because otherwise my wanton disregard for proper behavior would really be unforgivable."

"Your mom's a nice lady and I'll try to stay on her good side." Kyle reached into the freezer and removed a newspaper bundle covered with a sheen of ice crystals. "They should be numb by now," he said and rolled the large crustaceans into the sink. He took one, flopped it onto the cutting board and pierced it behind the head with the tip of his chef's knife. The body was separated from the tail within seconds. He whacked the claws loose at the joints, tossed the body into the sink and dispatched the other lobster just as efficiently.

"Wow, I'm impressed," Bev said. "Pretty good for a guy who claims not to be a cook."

Kyle shook his head and cut away the thin part of the shell on the underside of the tail. "During my economically challenged beginning-lawyer days, my roommate was an equally struggling chef. Mostly he cooked and I cleaned up, but he taught me the value of good knives and I picked up a few flashy dishes. I chop and grill and depend on packaged and frozen for the rest."

He loaded the lobster parts on the cutting board. "If you'll bring the beer, we'll throw these on. They don't take long and we can eat when they're ready or wait awhile. The bread is in one of those foil packs so just turn the oven off and it can sit."

"Sooner will be better. Eating didn't make the priority list today," Bev said and stepped across the den to open the sliding glass door for him.

She took the filled mugs in one hand, a pair of spare long necks in the other and sat on one of the short redwood benches that serviced the round table. The dark blue market umbrella was open even though the evening sun was a muted yellow. A breeze carried smells of grilled meats, clinking glasses and laughing, fractured conversations from other yards. The previous owner of Kyle's condo had replaced grass strips around the patio with raised beds defined by decorative concrete borders. Heat-tolerant greenery had been planted instead of flowers.

"You want to eat outside or in?" Kyle asked and turned the lobsters. Their brown shells were taking on the red hue that signaled Bev's hunger could soon be satisfied.

"I vote for out here," she said. "You watch those critters and I'll get everything else."

Bev unfolded from the bench and went inside. She moved around Kyle's kitchen as familiarly as in her own and piled almost everything on a tray decorated with a pair of parrots inlaid on red lacquered wood. She'd found it in a shop in Key West and given it to Kyle for his birthday.

"That's a handful you're carrying," Kyle said and transferred the steaming chunks to the plates Bev set down. "I'll get the wine and be right back."

Bev arranged the table, filled the plates and smiled when the voice of Nancy Griffith floated from the outdoor speakers. Kyle returned with the aquamarine acrylic wine bucket and Mexican goblets. They were heavy glass with the barest hint of blue and a band of darker blue around the rim. He poured pale sauvignon blanc and held her fingers for a moment when he handed her the wine glass.

"At least the day can have a better ending than the middle," he said. "Enjoy the sea bugs and tell me as much as you want to."

"Thanks," Bev said. She nearly always gained something listening to Kyle's perspective, even when he became lawyerish to her cop's preference for speedy results.

She cracked a lobster claw and began to relate the details of what they'd found and done and their expectations of how the case would play out. The sun sank lower behind another row of condos and solar-powered ground lights interspersed in the raised beds gained strength as natural light dwindled. Some of the neighbors lit candles or outdoor torches and Bev could hear the periodic *zzzt* of electronic bug killers. Kyle must have sprayed the yard before she arrived since the pleasure of the meal was not disturbed by blood-seeking insects probing exposed skin.

The temperature eased toward seventy and they decided to stay outside for coffee and dessert. Bev relaxed to near-drowsiness and pushed away the fleeting intrusion of thinking about what kind of evening Chris Green would be having.

CHAPTER EIGHT

W arren sat with his legs crossed and swirled Scotch in the finely crafted crystal glass – a glass designed for a man's hand, sturdy and expensive. Mike Noonan stood at the fireplace, no drink in hand. A fireplace in West Palm; more idiotic designer shit.

"Well, at least they're looking at Shepard," Warren acknowledged. His fury at Noonan's first report of the monumental fuck-up had passed through spasms of fear into pragmatism. He'd demanded that Mike return for a second meeting to try and re-kindle Warren's hope for a quick resolution to the mess that erupted without warning.

He ran his other hand down his tie. His schedule had been filled with an excruciating, unavoidable luncheon and another meeting with Freddy where he'd bluffed his way through more discussions about Jonah Shepard. Freddy, like everyone else, was assuming the missing girl had been a victim of the unbalanced assailant. Freddy's matter-of-fact acceptance of the link was what had calmed Warren. Except for the goddamn papers. Where were they? Had the girlfriend been in on it? Was anyone else?

"It's a round peg in a round hole. Cops like that," Noonan said in his irritatingly cool voice.

"You're certain you weren't seen? No one's going to come forward with a new story?"

Noonan lifted one shoulder and let it drop. "We were careful. I know how to do this shit and Rusty won't talk."

"And there's a dead girl and no fucking papers." Warren rested his glass on his knee and glared.

"It couldn't be helped," Noonan said with no concern for Warren's temper. "The girl showed up about the time we'd done the initial search. We thought he might have stashed whatever it is with her, but then her sister called and said she might come over. We had to get the girl out of there and we didn't get a chance to question her like I wanted to. I would have preferred more time for disposal, but we caught a tough break."

Noonan didn't alter his tone. It was moments like this when Warren reminded himself he could only push Noonan so far. He was not a man to be underestimated. "If they don't find her, great. If they do, there's nothing to change their minds about it being Jonah. As for the papers, we still need to go through the hard drives we snatched and if that's a bust, we head back down to the Keys. We can be in and out in a night and we should be able to gain access to his office without going through the cops. We claim potential conspiracy and the company will let us in to at least see the layout. They're small-time and will fall all over themselves to help."

Warren breathed in and out slowly. This was the best they could do. Jonah could have hidden the papers anywhere, but it wasn't likely he would have trusted many people. If not the girl, then maybe nobody else. A safe deposit box would be a danger if it was uncovered as a part of the estate, but wouldn't he have wanted to keep the documents close, somewhere with constant access? Maybe. But who had access to his belongings? There was no direct family left. If he could only count distant relatives and hadn't left a will, everything could languish for months or years while someone tried to straighten it out.

"No more screw-ups, Mike," Warren said evenly. "I either need those papers or to feel comfortable they can't be found by anyone else. I don't know what all he had, but I've already started moving assets around. I just need to do it slowly."

Noonan nodded and cocked his head at the sound of knocking.

Warren looked startled and then consulted the mahogany and brass mantle clock. The door swung open and Cecilia stopped a few paces into the room. This evening's look was lavender and purple. Silky, form fitting, and accessorized with amethysts and diamonds. Carefully chosen styles and colors. Wealth with a precise touch, never a seam too tight or a stone too large. Photogenic and instantaneously poised in front of television cameras. Admittedly not personally knowledgeable of working class woes, yet gracious and charitable. An ideal politician's wife.

"Mrs. Randall," Noonan said politely and stood straight.

"Mr. Noonan," she responded in kind, her right hand on the doorknob. "I am sorry to interrupt. I know it's been a busy day, but Mother's expecting us at seven."

Warren rose and smiled breezily. "Thank you for reminding me,

I did let the time get away from me. We're almost finished and I'll be up in a moment to change."

"All right," she said, "I thought perhaps the new Armani. It's on the foot of the bed unless you'd like something else."

"That will be fine. I'll walk Mike out and then be up." He lifted his glass in a gesture of dismissal. Cecilia turned and floated from the room.

Noonan was silent until they could no longer hear the tap of her heels on the marble. He crossed the room and stood closely to Warren as they traversed the foyer. "We'll have to wait a day or two in case the cops swing back through. They have no basis to be searching for documents though – they'll be looking for signs connected to the girl."

Warren clenched and unclenched his jaw. "Remember, no more screw-ups."

Noonan nodded curtly and walked away without responding.

Warren shut the door and mounted the unusually wide, hand-crafted staircase. It had supposedly been designed so the largest piece of furniture in the house could be carried up by two men abreast.

He sighed silently at the prospect of dinner at the DeLongs with a crowd of people. He hoped Cecilia had the limo service laid on. He needed at least one more drink before he faced his father-in-law. If the guest mix were weighted toward the corporate side, however, speculation about Jonah Shepard wouldn't make the conversation cut. DeLong would be giving or taking depending on the interests present and Warren could safely glide through those machinations. *Making life better for all by keeping Florida business-friendly – Randall, a leader for the 21st Century!*

Buoyed by the thought, he leisurely showered and dressed for his part. The dove-gray Armani draped elegantly across his shoulders and when Cecilia brought him a fresh drink she told him the limo was to arrive in ten minutes. The night might turn out to be pleasant after all. Too bad he couldn't find an excuse to break away for a quickie with Amber, but it was too risky. No, attentive husband would be a better role for tonight and Cecilia's unimaginative sexual tastes would have to do. Or maybe he wouldn't bother.

He continued to talk himself into a charming mood as he steered Cecilia into a recitation of the guest list and family or social relationships. The ride to the DeLong estate was buffered by a light Scotch and Cecilia cataloging the philanthropic deeds of various couples.

Warren compartmentalized the nagging worry about Jonah and spent four hours engaging in banal niceties and subtle business discussions. Thankfully, the chairman of a conglomerate DeLong recently closed a deal with monopolized the host's time for the entire evening. Warren took no chances though and circulated the rooms in constant motion, smiling, nodding, listening, advising. He wandered by his wife often enough to ensure she had a full glass and noted when her social smile softened with an amorous hint. It happened so seldom these days he took it as a signal for a graceful departure. Warren made another loop, watching for when Cecilia was standing alone with her mother. He saw them near the front hall, paused to call the driver to bring the car around and navigated across the parquet floor.

"Warren, I've hardly had a chance to speak with you this evening and now Cici tells me she's ready to leave," Margaret said and accepted a kiss on the cheek. Her superb bone structure augmented by exclusive salons blurred the age difference between mother and daughter.

"It's been a hectic week, but tonight was delightful," he said.

Margaret tucked her hand under his right arm as he offered his left to Cecilia. "Well, I think the whole business is simply horrid," she said. "I'm just glad you weren't hurt and you've been marvelously strong about it. I suppose this is the kind of story the media won't let go of until something else catches their fancy. I do hope they find that poor girl soon."

"Yes, it is tragic," Warren lied easily. "We can only wait and see what happens."

"All right, that's enough gloom," Cecilia interrupted with a flick of her hand. "I'll see you Monday, Mother. Tell Daddy good night for us. He's still trapped with that man who won't stop talking."

Margaret laughed her daughter's laugh. "Important business, darling, and I suppose I should tend to mine and see to the other guests. Call me tomorrow."

Warren ushered his slightly tipsy wife into the limo. She leaned against him on the way home and seemed receptive when he squeezed her hand with thoughts of Amber's acrobatic limberness in mind.

Cecilia's compliance carried through to the undressing stage and as she slid her toned body between the sheets he recalled the vision of a delicious little redhead he'd enjoyed on his last trip to New Orleans. He tuned out the sound of Cecilia's rapid breathing. She uttered no words of passion, of course. Would Amber be amenable to a threesome? What a pair she and the redhead would make! He thrust harder at the thought, but was careful not to collapse his weight onto Cecilia. Afterwards he rolled to his side of the king-size bed and exhaled in relief.

Cecilia fluttered her eyes drowsily. "Mother is right, you know, it really is horrid."

Where the hell did that come from? "Sssh," he said, startled fully awake. "There's nothing for you to worry about."

Cecilia turned and pulled the sheet over her shoulder. She mumbled something Warren couldn't understand and began to breathe shallowly.

He propped himself against the pillows. Damn, he needed another drink! He waited a few minutes so he wouldn't rouse Cecilia and slipped from bed into his master bath. He took his burgundy silk robe from the hook next to the door, wrapped it around himself and silently padded down the staircase. The exterior security lights provided a glow in the foyer and he waited until he was in the cavernous kitchen to switch on a light above the wet bar. He found the bottle of Scotch, a glass and scooped ice into a small silver bucket. No need to bother with water. He turned off the backyard security alarm, unlocked one set of French doors and stepped onto the stone terrace. He sat at the round mosaic-topped table closest to the water's edge and added Scotch and ice to the glass.

Warren sipped his drink and watched the reflection of perfectly placed outdoor lights shimmer on the perfectly replicated lagoon pool, complete with waterfall. It was a scaled-down version of a secluded resort on an island the name of which he couldn't recall.

Midnight was a bad time for memories, for speculation. Warren had no time for ghosts, no patience with men who let conscience stand in the way of practical decisions. God, he wished Andy was with him. Christ, he couldn't remember which one of them made the bet first about Lottie and what was the fuck was the other girl's name? Helen, Elaine, something, a frigid bitch who looked down on jocks. Christ, he'd damn near wet himself laughing when Andy did his falsetto rendition of her carrying on after he'd gotten into her pants. But he'd won the bet; he'd drilled Lottie first. And it wasn't like she'd been easy. Hell, no, he'd planned out the approach and figured it exactly right. Well, except for the part about dumping her. God, that nearly got out of control!

He took a long drink of the Scotch and forced the dead girl back to her grave. He'd come too far and too many years had passed. He inhaled the smell of tropical blossoms and listened to the night sounds of muffled sirens from a distance and frogs croaking in some kind of rhythm. These were the protected surroundings of a wealthy and powerful man, the surroundings he deserved. Maybe he'd married money, but goddamn it, he'd learned the ropes and kissed DeLong's rich ass enough to earn it. DeLong wanted power in politics as well as the boardrooms and Warren had delivered from the get-go. *Quid pro quo.*

Warren stirred the ice with his fingertip. Noonan would come through for him, but there were still unforeseen angles – hell, the week had been filled with them! If Noonan couldn't find the documents, it might be years before they surfaced, if they ever did. Thank God there were plenty of banks in the Caribbean he could deal with and he had a good system for diverting assets. He preferred the Turks and Caicos though; not as well known as some of the Bahamas and Cayman banks. Well, that was the way it went down sometimes. Aruba was a fine little island and once the old accounts were dissolved and new ones established, Warren was safe. If the documents did eventually appear, all he had to do was claim Jonah fabricated everything in a crazed plan for revenge. The theory would fit and who the fuck could challenge it?

Warren flexed his shoulders and stared toward the glimmering reflections on the dark water. Money and the willingness to make things happen the way you wanted was what mattered. Losers like Lottie and Jonah had no place in his world, not twenty years ago and not now. Warren tossed the rest of his drink down. He was ready to sleep, sleep without disturbance.

CHAPTER NINE

Bev tried not to growl at the computer technician. "Both of them? Ah, shit. No, I understand. Thanks, anyway."

Les turned from his monitor when she replaced the receiver with something similar to a slam. It wasn't quite as loud as a real slam, yet was not a gentle motion. "Bad news or more useless info?"

They'd met at the duplex before coming to the office and walked the yards, garages and rooms a second time. The deserted silence yielded no overlooked clues.

The few telephone calls they received were information they already knew or questions about the case. Well, there had been the man who insisted it was alien abduction, but they were holding that as a last resort.

Bev turned a thumb down and drew a line through a list on the pad in front of her. "The computer tech at the duplex is not a happy camper. We screwed up his Sunday and when he tried to boot up the computers, he discovered the hard drives had been taken out."

Les raised his eyebrows. "And we didn't find any disks labeled with anything that sounded promising?"

"No, we didn't," Bev said and massaged her temples. "I suppose we should have guessed an accountant would have been meticulous about removing files. I don't really give a shit about what he had unless it implicates an accomplice. I was more interested in checking Cindy's work to see if we could narrow down the time of disappearance. It might help if we knew whether it was Thursday night or early Friday morning. Damn."

Les scratched the back of his hand. "This almost makes me yearn for the days when everybody on your street knew what everybody else was doing. She didn't have a dog she walked, didn't make any calls, didn't go anywhere and use a credit card, no one can remember seeing her after late Wednesday afternoon. It's worse with Jonah. If we didn't know he existed, I'd have to wonder. The man left work Tuesday afternoon and there's no trace of him until he shows up in Randall's office as Mr. Stanley Jones. He seems to have been a blend-into-the-woodwork guy."

Bev picked up the photograph they had circulated. Moderately nice-looking – late thirties to early forties, short dark hair, wire-rimmed eyeglasses, pale eyes and no distinguishing facial features.

"I agree he's not a guy who would stick in your mind, but if someone picked him up hitchhiking late at night or early in the morning, it should have rung a bell."

"Unless it was an old coot who doesn't watch the news, a non-English-speaking person, of which we have no shortage, a trucker who by now is on the other coast, or someone who just doesn't want to get involved," Les said and hesitated. "Unless there *was* someone else, an accomplice. We don't have any real indication otherwise, but it's possible."

Bev did a slow neck roll left, then right. "If you look at case studies of this kind of attack, it's almost always a single individual. We could call that detective you talked to and see if they've turned up anything. Other than runaways and a couple of spouses that emp-tied checking accounts before disappearing, we don't get missing people or hidden bodies. It's straight domestic, drugs and barroom brawl fallout."

"Ah, don't forget the famous Wiley/Farmer case," Les teased.

The case that had been the last one Bev and Jim Osborn worked together. Tom Farmer and his partner, Greg Wiley, who had suf-fered shallow water blackout and drowned. A tricky case Bev solved despite being the only person who didn't believe it was an ac-cident. The case that ultimately resulted in Chris Green owning the dive shop.

Bev shrugged. "There has to be an exception," she admitted. "What was the name of the West Palm guy?"

"Hank Rodriguez. He's probably off for the weekend, but we could find him, I imagine."

Bev shook her head when the direct line rang on her desk. "Monday will do. Oh, hi, Kyle."

Les pushed his chair back and left the office to give her some privacy. Unlike her old partner, Jim Osborn, Les didn't joke around about her relationship with an assistant district attorney.

Kyle's voice was low, "Look, Bev, I hate to do this on short no-tice, but I'm going to have to cancel dinner with you and your folks tonight."

Bev sat straight up. "Oh, is something wrong? I mean, is there a problem?"

"Not exactly, I mean, it's nothing you can help with," Kyle said in an odd tone. "I mean, I'll take care of it. I know you were looking forward to tonight and I'm sorry."

Looking forward to tonight? Had she said that? "Uh, that's okay. It's not a big deal. Mom always cooks too much anyway, so there would have been leftovers no matter what. Do you want me to come by later?"

The momentary silence was unexpected. "No, I don't think it's a good idea. I've got some computer research on tap and I don't know how long I'll be at it. We'll catch lunch this week and, you know, do dinner later. Apologize to your parents for me, will you?"

"Yeah, sure," Bev said and had the feeling Kyle wanted to end the conversation. She said good-bye and depressed the button. She stared at the receiver in her hand and returned it to the cradle in slow motion. How strange. Kyle had been fine when she left that morning and hadn't mentioned weekend work. Well, whatever. Maybe he needed some quiet time; maybe he wasn't in the mood for a family dinner. God knows it could be moderately zoo-like at the Henderson house.

Les leaned against the doorframe of their office. "Unless you've come up with a brilliant flash, I think we should get out of here. Tomorrow will be busy."

Bev nodded. "I agree. I'm going to swing by the gym and do a workout. I've got dinner with my parents tonight and it's easier to burn off calories first than to argue with my mother about small portions."

"Working out on a Sunday? What dedication," Les said and chuckled. "If you got married, you could just say the hell with it and gain thirty or forty pounds."

Bev rolled her eyes to the ceiling. "Les, don't get on the bandwagon. My mother, my pal Helen, the Osborns and God knows who else have taken all the spaces."

He laughed and took his sunglasses from his shirt pocket. "I'm not surprised. Tell your folks hello and I'll see you in the morning."

Bev touched two fingers to her forehead in a salute and surveyed her desk to locate the pen she'd dropped while talking to Kyle. She picked the pen up, slid it into the tab holder of her notebook and pulled her purse from the bottom drawer. Her gym bag was in the trunk of the Spitfire. She said good-bye to the desk sergeant and the few officers on duty and encountered little traffic on the way to the gym. The tourists were concentrated along canals, beaches and marinas; the service-oriented populace of the town was working to keep the tourists happy and everyone else would be just trying to enjoy a day off before the regular week began again.

The gym was mid-way between the station and her apartment. The tennis courts were filled, the locker room nearly empty. Bev heard one shower running while she changed and the water hadn't shut off when she exited. A softball game was in progress on the far side of the adjoining park. It had to be one of the adult games. They didn't allow the kids to schedule on Sundays.

She stretched properly, in sequence, as she'd been trained beginning in junior high. No longer running competitively was no excuse to skip the basics and she probably needed to protect her muscles now more than she did in her teens. Bev started with an easy lope and would lengthen her stride during the first quarter mile. She had time for her five-mile route, the chance to let her body move unconsciously and her mind sort through facts and unknowns.

Her mind, however, would only partially cooperate. The facts and unknowns were about Kyle, not Cindy, not Chris. Shit, she had to call her mother to tell her he wasn't coming to dinner. Dinner was not, as she'd told him, a big deal.

Had he cancelled a date with her in the months they'd been together? A few times for unscheduled trips, although no more often than she'd cancelled for unanticipated work. He'd sounded so different – almost solemn, hesitant. And computer research? That didn't fit. Bev nodded to other joggers and cycling kids, the sweat soaking into her purple terrycloth headband and trickling between her breasts.

She hit her turn-around point and let her mind slip back to the previous night. Nothing out of the ordinary had happened. Hmmm, ordinary wasn't the right word, ordinary was a word settled couples used. Settled couples, oops, was that it? Dinner with her parents – was Kyle feeling crowded? Her crack to Les about the why-don't-you-get-married bandwagon – was Kyle getting his share of it also? Jesus, had she said anything, done anything to imply she was expecting a commitment?

Bev swatted a bug hovering around her left ear. No, no way she had. Hell, neither one of them had even said the "L" word. She nearly laughed out loud at her immediate reaction to the internal question. Christ, this was silly. She knew better than to behave like this. It wasn't a big deal and if she didn't watch out, she'd make it into one.

Cheering and clapping sounded from the ball field as she ran by. Five miles in the afternoon heat might have been a touch ambitious, but she pushed into a near sprint for a hundred yards reminding herself it was good for her. She slowed to a trot at the edge of the parking lot, breathing heavily without panting.

It took two walking turns of the building for the sweat to dry into a sticky glow. She decided to throw a towel on the seat of her car and clean up in her own apartment instead of the locker room.

She drove straight into her numbered carport and called her mother. Her mother despised talking to her on the cell phone, so Bev could keep the explanation short without a twenty-question drill as to why Kyle wasn't coming with her. That task accomplished, she peeled the soaked towel from the seat and wiped the leather for good measure. She shivered when she entered her air-conditioned apartment and temporarily switched on the ceiling fan in the den. She walked across dappled beige carpet, opened the large bay window by the dining table and inhaled the scent from massed honeysuckle vines that clung to the red brick walls. A bevy of small yellow butterflies flitted among full blooms.

Bev poured a tall glass of ice water and drank it slowly as she walked into her bedroom. She set the ceiling fan on low and then lifted the telephone. There was no bleeping notice of waiting messages. She shrugged away the thought of calling Kyle, stripped off her damp clothes and treated herself to a long shower, complete with hot oil conditioning for her hair.

She was right on schedule when she parked next to Aunt Lorna's cherry red 1957 Chevy pickup. It was the other vehicle her father pampered in addition to the Spitfire he'd restored for her twenty-first birthday. There was plenty of space on the over-size concrete pad that joined his workshop with the two-car garage attached to their pale blue cinderblock home. Bev carried a six-pack of regional microbrew. Her father refused to buy anything except Budweiser and while Bev had consumed a large quantity of standard American brews in her college days, she'd converted to craft beers as soon as her budget allowed. Her father might take one before he reverted to Bud. Aunt Lorna liked the variety and her mother was a tolerant tee-totaler as long as no one got sloppy. Bev could remember a cookout or two when her dad and Jim Osborn had been banished to the far corner of the yard of their old house.

"Emma, you know good and well those beans need a pinch more salt."

"You salt your own beans and leave mine alone."

The exchange between her mother and Aunt Lorna carried from the kitchen and Bev wished for a dime for every time she'd heard the great salt debate. The lure of grilling meat, what was probably green beans, fresh cream-style corn, mashed potatoes, and hot rolls would more than make up for habitual sisterly bickering.

She stopped between the sliding glass doors and the ample pass-through that opened the kitchen into the den. Extra leaves to expand the table hadn't been added and it was already crowded with place settings, a bowl of green tomato relish, a butter container, a bottle of hot sauce and a small plate of red onion wedges.

"Nice to know everything is normal today," Bev said and held up her offering.

"Lorna's trying to make mischief," her mother sniffed. "Your daddy has the ice chest on the deck," she said as if it was a new ar-rangement.

"Give me one of those first," Lorna said and came around to embrace Bev. She lifted on her tiptoes to plant a kiss on Bev's cheek and took a bottle in the other hand. "Good, they're still cold. Your mother said you've been having a tough weekend and everybody is surprised as they can be about this business."

Bev was solemn. "Yeah, it's different for sure."

A tap sounded on the window and Bev turned her head to see her father waving his grill tongs. She smiled and Lorna shooed her to-ward the deck. "Go say hi to your daddy. I've got to make sure your mom doesn't burn the rolls."

Frank Henderson opened the sliding door to let Bev slip through before she could hear the protest. A pan of rolls didn't dare burn un-der her mother's watchful eye.

"Give me a kiss, Kiddo," her father said and opened his arms wide.

Bev's height was from her paternal side and she stretched up to kiss his brow. "Mom and Aunt Lorna were discussing the beans. I think it's safer out here," she laughed.

"Good thing it doesn't last long," he said. "I left room in the chest for you, but give me a Bud while you're in there. How's it going, Kiddo? Anything break loose yet?"

Bev nestled the beer into the ice, extracted two and twisted the caps off. "Not so far," she replied. "It's one of those nice quiet neighborhoods where people are friendly, but not overly observant. Unfortunately the resident busybody was indisposed when she could have done some good. We haven't gotten any calls we can use."

Frank flipped a thick pork chop and doused a tongue of flame with a squirt of Budweiser. "Starting the body search tomorrow?"

Bev swigged her beer and watched him turn the rest of the chops. "We want to talk to the parents before we begin. It will have been five days since anyone had contact with her. It'll be hard, but I can't imagine they don't want us to proceed."

Frank swiped a streak of foam from his upper lip. "Yeah. Jim and I had a case way back when you were just a baby. Fella named Winslow strangled his wife, took her out 'round Miller's point and buried her. Reported her run off and didn't seem too torn up, but they'd had problems. She was known as a good-time gal and it wasn't much of a reach to believe him." He moved the meat to a waiting platter. "The woman's sister was a handful, though and, Lordy, did she keep after us. Called us every week and asked what the hell we were doing to find evidence on the son-of-a-bitch. There were a couple of points didn't quite add up, but nothing we could pin down. Must have been almost a year and a half, could have been closer to two that it went on."

"A sister, huh?" Bev said. "There's a lot of that going around. What happened?"

"Good luck for us, bad for Winslow. Some folks decided to develop the area where he'd buried the body. He'd put it deep enough for most purposes, but it had been a hand job. Once they hit the site with commercial equipment they dug it up. There was enough forensics evidence to put holes in his story and he folded. Getting rid of whole bodies on land is a problem – there are a lot of pieces they can pull together."

A horn tooted below and a group of people leaning against the railing of a boat waved to anyone in sight as they motored through the canal toward the open water. Bev and her dad lifted beers in response.

Lorna opened the glass doors and stuck her head and shoulders out. "Emma wants to know – how long?"

"Tell her if she's waiting on us, she's going backwards," Frank said cheerfully and handed the loaded platter to his sister-in-law. "Bev and I will bring the beer." He moved to the cooler, fit three bottles easily in one hand and followed Bev inside.

Emma added a plate of thickly sliced red tomatoes to the table and fluttered her hands to get everyone seated. "It's too bad Kyle couldn't be here," she said. "I'll fix him a plate you can carry with you for later. Lorna brought her chocolate cream pie and I know he's bound to like that. I've never met a man who didn't and there's a reason for the saying that the way to a man's heart is through his stomach. Oh, and we have orange pound cake left from the church dinner. He might prefer that. Oh, just take both, to be on the safe side."

Bev smiled sweetly. She'd take the plate and have it herself. It was less complicated than saying no.

"Emma, sit down and stop fussing," her father said with a grin. "I'm hungry if nobody else in this family is."

He lowered his head to say grace and Bev added a quick prayer for the Green family. It couldn't hurt to ask.

CHAPTER TEN

"I'm sorry I called so early," Chris said and took the mug of coffee. "I guess it wouldn't surprise you that I've been thinking a lot about Cindy and Jonah."

"It would surprise me if you haven't been and don't worry about the time," Bev said.

She had led Chris into the interrogation room for some privacy. The room was bleakly institutional green with gray, straight-back vinyl-seat chairs and a single rectangular table pockmarked with gouges of various origins. The lack of design for friendly chats was offset by the isolation it afforded when the wall-mounted intercom wasn't activated. Chris's expression had been one of barely maintaining control and Bev thought it might be easier if she wasn't subjected to ringing telephones and people wandering in and out of the office. She'd discreetly shoved a wad of tissues into her pocket when she offered to get coffee.

Chris took a sip, set the mug on the table and touched the silver bracelet of tiny seahorses linked by starfish. Her lips curved toward a smile.

"Funny," she reflected. "Cindy was with me the day I closed the deal on the dive shop. We went to lunch and she saw this bracelet in a store window. We went in and bought two – silver for me and gold for her. She said we should have something special to celebrate. It was cool, you know, having a sister you could do that kind of thing with."

Chris's voice thickened and her brown eyes filled with tears. She caught the first one with her finger and Bev deposited the tissues between them. Chris plucked one, sniffed and blotted her eyes.

"Some tough girl, huh?" She drew in a deep breath. "You think Cindy's dead, don't you?"

Bev kept eye contact. "It's the fifth day since anyone has seen her."

"I know." Chris wrapped both hands around the mug. "I'd give anything in the world for it not to be true, even though I know it's likely." She didn't lower her gaze. "My mom keeps talking like Cindy will call or show up and everything will be fine, but I think my dad knows, too. Grown women don't just disappear. Even if she ran scared, she would have heard about Jonah by now and if he had taken her somewhere alive, someone would have found her."

Bev nodded and spoke as gently as she could without being misinterpreted. Euphemisms could be left to others. "We were going to contact you and your parents to explain we would begin searching areas where a body might be concealed."

Chris sighed and ran spread fingers into her coppery curls. She dropped her hand and circled one finger around the rim of the mug. "I'll call my folks later and tell them. I'd like to ask you a couple of questions if you have time, though."

"Sure," Bev said and stood. "I'll tell Les you know what we're doing." She pushed the pile of tissues closer to the other woman and touched Chris's shoulder. "I'll be back in a few minutes."

She closed the door noiselessly and walked quickly into the office, told Les what was going on and topped off her coffee. When she entered the room again, Chris was sitting with her shoulders back and a calmer look. "I think I'm through with the waterworks," she said in an almost normal tone. "Can I ask you something that may sound strange?"

Bev slid onto the chair, lifted her mug and tilted her head slightly. "Something you remembered?"

"Not exactly. I know it would be a hell of a coincidence, but do you think there could be someone other than Jonah involved? Like an accomplice, maybe someone who thought Cindy was a threat?"

Bev gestured toward the door with her mug. "It's possible and we're checking for extra prints at both places. We haven't found anything yet to indicate a second person."

Chris swallowed a gulp of the cooled liquid. "Here's the deal. I'm not saying people are all they're cracked up to be. I mean, hell, priests can turn out to be perverts and sweet-looking little old ladies can be involved in cons. I'm not naïve, but part of what I do in my business is size people up, look for non-verbal clues. A good dive instructor never takes anybody's word about diving experience. It's important to watch how someone handles the equipment, how he or she interacts with other divers. What people say they know how to do and how well they actually do it aren't always one and the same."

"I'm not following you," Bev said.

Chris set her mug down again and began gesturing with her hands. "I mean, it's second nature to instructors. Look, diving is great and not dangerous if you follow the rules, but a really good instructor is always paying attention to what's going on. It's common to have people act like they know more than they do or try and hide their anxiety or get careless with technique. You have to keep an eye out for hotdogs and divers who are rusty. You learn how to read people and you don't turn that off when you leave the shop. It's like I told you, Jonah was moody a lot, but it was melancholy moody, not violent. He and Cindy never argued. I can go as far as saying, okay, the deal with Randall was a shocker, but I can't see him killing Cindy."

She blinked rapidly again as she stumbled over the last words. "What I mean is, Cindy told me his father died not long before she met him. His mother had died years before and I guess he was the only one left in the direct family so he had to take care of the estate and sold the old house. The business with his sister, suicide if I didn't tell you before, had been really hard for him and I gathered a lot of those memories came back to him while he was trying to take care of everything. I can sort of understand that if he did blame Randall, it must have just built up beyond what he could stand, but Cindy wasn't a part of his past. There would have been no reason for him to turn on her. If he had drawn someone else into the plot, that person could have been the one to think Cindy needed to be, well, you know."

Bev fanned her hands in question. "I'm not saying you're wrong about Jonah – it could have been almost an accident. Maybe Cindy found out at the last minute, tried to stop him and it just happened," she said. "He panicked and then had to react to what he'd done. It's plausible and would track with your perception."

Chris sighed again and drank the last of the coffee. "I suppose you're right," she replied. "I keep thinking about the trip we took to Turks and Caicos in the spring. Jonah was really relaxed, more so than I'd ever seen. Cindy was telling me how much he was loosening up and they did the moonlit walks on the beach, the touristy drinks in the hot tub. They were almost honeymoon like."

"Jonah was a diver?" Bev wondered if she'd met him and not realized it.

"No," Chris said. "I taught Cindy, but she had to be careful with her asthma plus she never caught the bug like I did. Jonah talked about it with me and said he didn't think he would be comfortable sixty feet underwater. In fact, I was surprised about the trip, but I had two last minute cancellations and Jonah said he'd been wanting to go to Turks and Caicos. He went out with us the first day and snorkeled and then told Cindy he wanted to wander around the island. She was going to go with him, but the visibility was absolutely terrific, conditions were calm and it was like diving in an aquarium. Jonah insisted she enjoy the water and he met us every afternoon when we got back."

A happy couple strolling along white sand beaches and frolicking in sparkling water. Bev didn't doubt it was too much of a clash for Chris to picture a follow-on scene of premeditated murder or even panicked manslaughter. A man who sipped rum punch with your sister wasn't supposed to then callously dispose of her body somewhere. Too bad there were thousands of domestic violence deaths to prove otherwise.

"Yeah, I see your point," Bev said quietly. "And something else may turn up."

Chris scraped her chair against the dingy, green-splotched linoleum and managed an imitation of a smile. "I know, you won't tell me how to calculate a decompression dive and I won't tell you how to investigate."

"I wasn't taking it that way," Bev said. "This is hard on you. More coffee?"

Chris handed the mug to Bev and tucked her purse under her arm. "No thanks. I've got a business to run and you've got a lot to do. Thanks, the talk helped. I'll call my dad and he can decide whether or not to tell my mother."

Bev hooked both mugs into one hand and walked Chris out through the bay area. She told her to call whenever she liked and silently hoped they would find the body soon. Not knowing was an additional undeserved cruelty.

Bev headed straight for the corner when she entered the office and saw the empty pot.

"It's brewing," Les said and looked at the wall clock. "They're starting a search at Graley's bridge. It'll be a couple of hours at least. Chris have anything new?"

Bev shook her head. "She's having trouble seeing Jonah as the bad guy and hopes there's somebody else." She wiped the extra mug, inverted it and put it on the table next to the coffeepot. A hot brown stream flowed into the carafe. She leaned her butt against the refrigerator and sighed. "I don't think it will be worthwhile, but I'm going to check out Jonah's office at the accounting firm. Wasn't there one woman who was on vacation?"

Les opened the folder on his desk, leafed through and pointed his finger at an entry. "Lady by the name of Marianne. The head guy I talked to is Eric Wilson. Small office, only a dozen full time employees and some temps they bring in like at tax time."

He reached for the telephone. "I'll call and let them know you're coming, if you'd like."

Bev hesitated. Face it, she was restless and doing anything was better than more waiting. Besides, the company Jonah worked for was less than a mile from the DA's office. She'd see if Kyle was free for lunch.

"Go on," Les said and grinned. "You'll start roaming around messing in all kinds of shit if you don't have something to keep you busy. If we get a hot lead, I'll call."

Bev pushed away from the refrigerator. "You've been talking to Jim again."

Les gave her a schoolteacher look – the one you get when you claimed the dog ate your homework. "It takes about a week of working with you to figure that out," he said.

Bev let the remark pass since she wasn't sure how to take it. She waved good-bye and stopped for a few minutes at Taliah's desk to see how her morning was going.

Taliah had been hired after the first of the year when the former administrative assistant's husband had been transferred out of state. Bev had been worried about Sheila's departure. Every time there was a lapse in administrative coverage, she picked up more work than she wanted and it was difficult to predict what the municipal hiring system would come up with. Taliah, however, literally blew into the office in a whirl of energy. She was ten years older than Bev, attractive enough to tease the men, smart enough to keep it professional, sassy enough to ignore the chief's indiscriminate temper and better on a computer than almost anyone in the station.

Taliah was in sharper form than usual for a Monday and Bev

was trying to hold back laughter as she finished her rendition of the latest uproar in her extended family.

"My Sweet Lord, girl, you should be glad not to have five brothers and sisters all living in the same town," she said and tapped a group photo on her desk. Her manicured nails were painted a pink bordering on florescent.

"Somebody's always stirring up silly nonsense." Taliah stabbed a pencil over her ear into the black curls that framed her heart-shaped face. "Now get yourself moving and I'll wrap up the personnel report."

Bev departed the station in a more cheerful mood than when she'd walked Chris out. She drove into town and parked in front of a square, single story concrete and glass building that housed an insurance company, a travel agency, a nail salon and Wilson Accounting, Inc. According to the directory of business names and suite numbers, Wilson Accounting was the second office on the left. The front room was standard décor; a multi-shade blue carpet, coordinated upholstered armchairs, and prints featuring coastal birds and lighthouses. The end tables next to the chairs were of the same clean line and wood as the receptionist's desk area. Maple, Bev thought. *Joyce Dunn* was inscribed in black letters on the bronze nameplate.

Joyce was in her early to mid-fifties, short hair done in the soft waves that a weekly visit to a beauty parlor produces. The light brown color was probably the same shade she'd had before lines across her wide forehead and around her green eyes appeared. The round, gold-rimmed glasses she wore seemed almost too large for her face.

"You're Detective Henderson, I assume," the woman said and stood. She smiled in welcome with the decorum one would expect in an accounting firm – no giggly sprites permitted. "Mr. Wilson is expecting you. His office is at the end of the hall and his name is on the door, or I can take you back if you'd prefer. Would you care for coffee or a Coke?"

"No, thanks, and I think I can find it with no problem," Bev said and walked in the direction Joyce pointed.

The first door to the right was open to a large office with three desks Bev could see. The door across the short hallway was partially open, the second door on the right opened on a conference room, the room next to it was evidently the break room. The individual offices were identified with bronze nameplates. The last office before Mr. Wilson's was closed and the nameplate had been removed. *Jonah Shepard*, no doubt.

Mr. Wilson's office had double doors, one half ajar with his name posted in three dimension bronze block letters.

Joyce had obviously notified Mr. Wilson, who came out of his office as Bev approached. "Detective Henderson, I'm Eric Wilson and it's a pleasure to meet you," he said, extending his hand. A firm, reassuring grip. Pudgy hands, plain gold band. A lightweight charcoal-gray suit, blue shirt with white collar and cuffs, a sapphire-blue tie and oval, disk-shaped silver cufflinks. Round, wire-rimmed gold glasses, perfectly proportioned to his face. Eyes more gray than blue, hair evenly salt and pepper, receding, yet still full on top and cut short rather than styled.

"It's Bev, and thank you for seeing me on short notice," she said. "I know Detective Martin interviewed everyone except one of your employees who was on vacation."

He swept his arm into his office. "Yes, please come in and let's get comfortable. That was Marianne Dunn, Joyce's niece, and she's here today. She's only been with us since she graduated in early May, so she really didn't spend time with Jonah and I'm afraid none of us knew the young lady, Miss Green."

He paused and gestured to the armchairs covered in jade-green chintz. The office had been done in four different shades of green with gold and cream accents. The cherry furniture was more detailed than in the other offices; architecturally interesting, not ornately designed. Framed certificates and scenic prints overprinted with clichéd management slogans substituted for artwork.

Eric settled into a chair, crossed his legs and folded his hands loosely across his stomach. His posture, tone and expression were suitably grave. "This has come as quite a shock. Jonah is simply the last person in the world that I would have thought capable of such a thing."

"I do understand," Bev said. "What I'd like to do is speak with Miss Dunn and look through Mr. Shepard's office again. We also would like access to his computer and if you don't have someone who can get into his hard drive, we have county personnel who can. We're sensitive to the nature of your clients and will allow an individual of your choice to be with us during the review of the files.

69

We're only interested in items that might give us some clue as to Cynthia Green's whereabouts. We'd like to know if perhaps there could have been another person involved, someone Jonah might have corresponded with who wouldn't match with your client list."

Eric silently ran the fingers of one hand across the knuckles of the other. "Bev, as I explained to your partner and the gentleman from Senator Randall's office, we'll cooperate in any way we can. We don't have in-house computer expertise, although the contractor that handles our systems is in town. Our attorney has outlined the disclosure issues we need to be careful of and I've told Doug, our senior accountant, to be available to answer any questions. I would prefer the work be done on-site rather than having the machine taken elsewhere."

Bev leaned forward. "Thank you, but you said someone from Senator Randall's office was here?"

Eric held his fingers still and looked puzzled. "Yes, a Mr. Noonan, head of security. He and his assistant were here earlier. The same issue about another party being involved." He cleared his throat and shifted in the chair. "Your partner hadn't indicated Jonah's office was off-limits. Mr. Noonan had proper identification and Joyce remembered seeing his photograph in the newspaper. Naturally we wanted to help a representative from the senator's office."

Bev didn't let her surprise show. What in the hell was going on? Did someone in West Palm know something? And why in the hell would someone from Randall's office be checking instead of asking them to?

"That's quite all right," she assured him. "Did Mr. Noonan spend much time in the office? And did he leave a card by any chance?"

Faint color rose in Eric's cheeks and he cleared his throat again. "Uh, I don't believe he gave me a card, now that you mention it. Joyce was with him most of the time. He spoke with her about Jonah's appointments and so forth and I don't believe he was in the office very long. He also had a chat with the two accountants who worked most often with Jonah. Would you care to talk with them about it?"

He could bet his sweet number-crunching ass she did. "Yes, thank you, I'll do that," she replied and moved to the very edge of the chair. "In fact, if I could get started, I'll look in Jonah's office and then speak with the others."

Eric stood with her, walked her to Joyce's desk and reiterated how much they wanted to assist everyone. The unexpected additional interviews delayed Bev until lunchtime and she wasn't surprised to find nothing of value in Jonah's office. The earliest she could get a county computer technician was Tuesday afternoon without getting the chief involved and considering the missing hard drives from the duplex, she assumed Jonah had deleted any useful files from his office. It was a block to be checked off though and she cajoled the technician into mid-morning.

She called Kyle's office as soon as she was out of Wilson Accounting, Inc. The secretary said he was in court and Bev told her there was no special message. She called Les and gave him a quick rundown. He said he'd call Detective Rodriguez if she'd stop for sandwiches. Yes, she remembered he preferred mustard instead of mayonnaise and he didn't like dill pickles or olives.

She tumbled thoughts around in her head about why civilians would be intruding on her turf as she made the necessary stop. She hadn't reached a satisfactory conclusion by the time she deposited their lunches on the desk.

"The bread is what's really important," Les said when he unwrapped his sandwich and looked for prohibited condiments. "Fresh out of the oven."

"Glad to oblige," Bev said and speared a radish with the plastic fork. Fruit, muffins or yogurt for breakfast, salad for lunch unless it was a social event. That left more calories for beer and chocolate.

"Did you get Rodriguez?"

Les nodded and bit into the roll. Mustard, tomato juice and shreds of lettuce dribbled from the bottom onto white paper. He swallowed and brushed across his bottom lip with his thumb. "Yeah. He knew nothing about Noonan coming down here. Also said that so far, there's no reason to believe Shepard didn't act alone. He gave me the senator's office number and said if we had anything useful, he'd like to hear it."

Les held up a finger, took another bite and then looked questioningly at Bev. "You get anything except what a nice fellow Shepard was? All business, polite, but not very sociable, never mentioned his girlfriend?"

"The same story," Bev said. "Not unfriendly, but not one for chit-chat. No new clients, noticeable absences or cryptic telephone calls. Everyone is still having a hard time believing it. The-guess-you-never-know-about-the-quiet-ones line."

Les lowered his sandwich. "Rodriguez did tell me something odd. The gun Shepard had wasn't loaded. Said they couldn't really fault Noonan for reacting the way he did, but apparently Shepard was trying to scare the senator, not hurt him."

Bev stopped the fork, put it down and stared. "What? If he wasn't planning to kill Randall, why in the hell would he have killed Cindy to keep her quiet?"

"That's a good question," Les said and resumed his lunch.

"And what function would a second person serve if Jonah didn't intend any real harm? An accomplice to help him escape, I could see, but if this was a dumb shit way of getting Randall's attention, he wouldn't have needed help with that." Bev reached for the packet of pepper, ripped it open and sprinkled it over the salad. "It's more reasonable to think Cindy found out, or Jonah let it slip, she tried to stop him, there was some kind of struggle and he killed her accidentally. He stashed the body, continued with his plan and who knows, intended to confess to everything afterwards?"

Weird, yet not unbelievable. The kind of screw-up that would be funny if it wasn't tragic.

"That would match with what we're being told about him," Les agreed and put the last bite of sandwich in his mouth. "Cindy's still dead, but involuntary manslaughter instead of cold-blooded."

"Which brings us back to the unexplained visit by members of Randall's staff," Bev said and lifted her fork again. "If they don't find Cindy today or tomorrow, maybe we should run up to West Palm. I'd like this Mr. Noonan to tell us what the hell he thinks he's doing. A lingering threat to the senator is their business, but if anybody else in this town is involved, I want a name or a suspicion. As unlikely as it seems, if there was a second person, he or she probably knows what happened to Cindy."

CHAPTER ELEVEN

Kyle propped on one elbow, captured a long curl of hair from Bev's glistening neck and laid it on the pillow. She couldn't take a full breath just yet and smiled at the gesture. Kyle had called her, suggested dinner at The Fish Hut, their favorite hole-in-the-wall place. By the time they'd gotten to the last hushpuppy, it was obvious what dessert would be.

"I think I can move," he said playfully. "How about a cold beer?"

"I know you can move certain parts very well indeed," Bev said and rolled on her side. She leaned into him and kissed his salty shoulder. "A beer would be lovely."

Kyle swung off the bed, groped for his shorts and pulled them on. Bev watched wistfully as his tanned, muscled body was made respectable for the walk downstairs. She didn't have a multitude of former lovers to compare him to, but Kyle definitely won the who-looks-best-naked award.

The telephone startled them. Kyle lifted the instrument out of its base.

"Oh, hi," he said quietly. "No, no, you're not catching me at a bad time."

He put his hand over the mouthpiece. "I'll take it downstairs," he mouthed to Bev and walked from the room, telephone pressed tightly to his ear.

Bev sat up, retrieved the tangled sheet from the foot of the bed and pulled it to her chin. The air conditioner against her bare flesh and the absence of Kyle's warmth caused a shiver to ice up her spine. Not a bad time? Well, better than if it had been five minutes earlier. All she'd caught was what sounded like a woman and Kyle didn't usually get business calls at home at nine o'clock at night.

Bev bit her bottom lip. Not her business. She reached across to the nightstand for the remote and turned on the television, trying not to calculate how long it normally took him to fetch two beers and return. Three minutes passed; five, seven, ten. The screen was filled with a dense school of hammerhead sharks, then segued to marine iguanas dashing into the ocean. The narrator was describing research expeditions to the Galapagos Islands.

"Strange looking lizards," Kyle said and walked into the bedroom with a dark green ceramic mug in each hand. The telephone was jammed part way into his pocket. "I'm not sure I'm ready to meet up with one of them yet."

He passed the mug to Bev and replaced the telephone. He plumped the pillow, leaned back and held his mug to his chest. "I'm going to have to go Illinois for a few days. I'll probably fly up tomorrow afternoon," he said in a tone Bev couldn't identify.

Bev turned to look into his blue eyes. The ardor that had shortened their dinner plans had been replaced by a guarded flatness. "Some kind of problem?"

"Uh, you know, some family business I have to take care of. I'm not sure what my schedule will be," he said vaguely and took a long drink.

Is there anything I can help with? Do you want to talk about something?

"Oh," Bev said. "Do you want me to take you to the airport?"

He shook his head. "That's too much trouble and you've got a lot going on. Plus I'm not sure when I'll be back. It'll be easier if I drive up and leave the car."

Another swig and a semi-smile, his eyes clear again. "By the way, the guy Noonan you were talking about at dinner?"

Bev mentally swerved at the change of subjects. Okay, guess they were off the personal track. "Yeah, the security man from Senator Randall's office. Les and I want to have a talk with him in the next day or two. I don't know why they didn't check in with us."

Kyle nodded. "The name sounded familiar and I couldn't place it at first. There was a cop in Chicago named Noonan while I was in the DA's office. May not be the same person and I don't remember the details, but it seems like he did some personal security work on the side. There was an investigation about money or clients or something and the name came up a few times before he dropped out of sight. If I have time to call one of the guys tomorrow before I leave, I'll check and see if it's him."

"Hmmm," Bev said. "Wouldn't that be interesting?"

Kyle drained his beer, set his mug on the carpet and killed the television. He slid his hand beneath the sheet and Bev almost choked on the swallow she'd taken. "If I'm going to be gone a few days, I should probably get ready," he said and slipped his fingers to the inside of her thigh.

Bev coughed, managed to keep from dropping the mug, threw one leg over him and pressed close. "Most people get ready for a trip by packing," she murmured.

His other hand found the curve of her waist. "I'll take care of that part later," he whispered and covered her mouth with his.

She moaned as thoughts of cases and telephone calls disappeared.

It was after eleven o'clock when Bev left to Kyle's promise to call her after he booked his flight. The streets were nearly empty. Tourists who didn't have to worry about rolling out of bed for work would be clustered in the hotel area or meandering among waterside restaurants. She rolled down the windows, although she left the top on the car. Her hair was still damp from exertion and a quick shower.

The temperature had ebbed from the humid eighties and the mellow Jimmy Buffet ballad, *He Went to Paris*, followed the lively *Coconut Telegraph* on the car radio.

Looking for answers. Christ, who wasn't? Bev idled at a light and permitted herself the luxury of wondering about the telephone call. Cancel dinner with her one night and dash off to Illinois. Family business? Sure, why not? Any old girlfriends still in the home territory, too? Why wouldn't there be? Oops, hadn't meant that to nudge its ugly little head into her consciousness.

Get a grip, she thought, when the light turned green. Everything was okay. They'd had a pleasant time at dinner and the passion that sparked as they'd sat outside was not the sign of a relationship with problems. Kyle would eventually tell her what was going on.

Would he? Bev slowed to make the turn into her apartment complex. If she couldn't ask him, why would he volunteer information? Because she didn't want to pry and if he felt close enough to her, he'd want to share his problems and feelings. Wasn't that how it was supposed to be? With someone special, someone you really cared about?

Bev parked her car, cut the ignition and sat for a moment, sounds settling around her: distant traffic, chorusing night creatures and strains of music from apartments where night people and insomniacs raised windows to take in fresh air.

Despite constantly fending off her mother's subtle but increasingly direct questions about a possible future, Bev occasionally found herself in embarrassing agreement. What exactly did she and Kyle have together? And what did they want? Shouldn't they talk about it sooner or later? Had Kyle sent signals she hadn't picked up on? Had she? Wasn't there an element of absurdity if a man and a woman could enjoy each other's company and bed for nearly a year and still categorize themselves as *taking it slow*?

Was there a relationship calendar out there she ought to know about? She'd always been skeptical of her friend, Helen, who swore she could tell whether or not a new man had potential by the end of the first date. Helen had also been target-fixated on the concept of marriage and children even though she affectionately accepted Bev's wariness of distracting emotional entanglements. Bev had been the jock pal to Helen's coquettish side. Their childhood-formed friendship remained intact since neither of them roamed too close to the ends of the spectrum. Helen was a full participant in courtship revelry without losing her personality to the boys-don't-like-smart-girls premise. Bev didn't dislike boys; she simply ignored the ego damage she wreaked when she outstripped most of them academically and physically.

Her virginity had not been something she protected, nor did she consider it aberrant to have waited until college to cross the sex threshold. The subsequent affair had been of short duration and it required an effort to recall the details. Kyle was the first of the few men she'd found time or inclination for to cause her to peek beyond the immediate validation of compatibility.

Enough already. It was late, she was deliciously yet undeniably tired and this was not the time to ponder the mystery of men, women, and feelings. Those thoughts were best saved for a leisurely, alcohol-lubed meal with Aunt Lorna or Helen.

CHAPTER TWELVE

Bev closed out a thoroughly nonproductive Tuesday with a six-mile run in the early evening. Adding the extra mile gave the day at least something of measurable value. Jonah's office computer had contained business files and an empty folder marked *Personal*. Kyle flew to Illinois with an open return date. The first search area was a bust and the second day of search was pre-empted to find two hikers who were eventually located. They were thirsty, bug-bit and clearly off the recommended trail. The honey-voiced lady in Senator Randall's office was terribly sorry, but the senator and Mr. Noonan were out of town until Friday. Yes, she would be very happy to pass along a message that Detective Henderson of the Verde Key Police Department would like to speak with Mr. Noonan at the earliest possible opportunity.

An uninspiring dinner of leftover chicken casserole was inter-rupted by her mother calling to tell her that her cousin Melissa was engaged. A nice respectable young man, manager at one of those quick-change oil places and the wedding was set for the middle of September and if she remembered correctly, wasn't Melissa two years younger than Bev? Bev tuned out the conversation, *uh-huhed* her way through the rest of it, tossed the partially eaten casserole in the trash and dished out a large bowl of chocolate fudge ribbon ice cream.

She rolled out of bed Wednesday morning feeling a muscle twinge in her right calf. She treated herself to an extra five minutes in a hot shower and indulged in an apple cinnamon muffin and Tan-zanian Peaberry instead of a regular brand. Two cups of the robust, remarkably smooth coffee and she was content enough to wish her cousin heartfelt congratulations. She'd wait a few days and ask her mother where she was registered. Bev's goodwill did not extend to making the effort of shopping for a wedding gift.

Taliah waved for her attention when she was barely in the station door.

"Good morning, Miss Sunshine," Taliah said and held an envelope between two fingers. Today's polish was somewhere between peach and tangerine. It matched her enamel hoop earrings and one of the colors in the floral print dress she was wearing. "Got the approval for those mobile data terminals you worked so hard on."

"You're kidding. I thought we didn't have a chance until next year," Bev said and smiled. "When are we getting them?"

"Probably not as soon as you'd like," Taliah grinned. "Some red tape crap in here with a projected date of late August, first part of September. That means more like October and there's a point of contact who's handling the buy. You want to go with it or you want me to call?"

The mobile data terminals were another of Bev's goals to upgrade the department's lagging technology. She'd scored big with a complete computer replacement and despite Chief Taylor's fondness for notepads and number two pencils, he'd been forced to admit it had been a good idea. The mobile terminals were essentially laptop computers for the patrol cars that, among other features, would allow the shift data to be entered during the shift and then downloaded into the desktop machines. It would be a great time saver.

"Why don't you give it a shot?" Bev replied. "You're getting good at finessing paperwork through and you can let me know if you need me to lend a hand."

She'd worked the proposal before Taliah came on board, but it would give the other woman a chance to show off a little. Taliah had grown up in a part of town where people who worked hard were lucky to keep their heads above water and college was not discussed. Pregnant at sixteen, she'd been on the well-worn path of other poor, single teenage girls – her parents wearily resigned to an event that was anything other than blessed. A high school teacher stepped in and refused to let Taliah hide behind statistics. It had meant juggling school, part-time work and the exhausting reality of an infant's demands. A community college associate degree didn't mean much in the world of academia, but for Taliah, it was proof she hadn't quit when she'd been tempted to. She'd peeled off the social label that had been slapped on her and spoke of those years with a humor Bev didn't think she could have managed.

Les had left a note on her desk about taking his wife to a doctor's appointment. Chris Green had left a message asking for her to call as soon as she could. Bev dialed the shop and heard several voices in the background. Chris sounded unsettled, but said she had a room full of students and Bev agreed to meet for a fast lunch at the Scarlet Macaw.

The search team was supposed to work the Millers' Point area and remembering her father's story, Bev thought how ironic it would be if they found Cindy there. Nothing else of interest broke the morning's tasks and she waved to Les as she passed him turning into the station.

Chris was waiting at a back corner table that provided them relative quiet.

"Thanks for coming," she said in a tone most people would have taken for normal. "They've got a grouper sandwich special, spicy black bean soup and something else I've forgotten." The circles under her eyes weren't as dark as before, although the tightness hadn't disappeared.

"I hardly ever change," Bev replied and took the chair next to her. "I'll go with the grilled shrimp Caesar and ice tea," she said to the waiter who stepped across from the nearest table.

Chris ordered the chicken quesadilla appetizer. "Want to small talk?"

"Not unless it will make you feel better."

Chris slowly rotated the napkin-wrapped silverware and sighed. "Bev, what I'm going to tell you may sound paranoid and I don't want to come across like I'm getting spooked."

Bev paused to let the waiter deliver their ice tea and smiled. "You're not the paranoid type," she said as encouragement. "What's happened?"

"I think my apartment was broken into last night," Chris said cautiously and waited for Bev's reaction.

"A robbery?" Bev hadn't seen anything on the report and no one had mentioned it.

"No," Chris said and turned the silverware bundle counter-clockwise. "Nothing's missing and I didn't even realize it at first. I had a night dive and was pretty whipped when I got in and didn't see any sign at the door like scratches or anything. There was a light on in the closet, but, hell, I could have forgotten to turn it off. This morning though I noticed things not quite right. The door to the guest room was closed and I usually leave it open. Some stuff on the desk was out of place as if someone had been looking around."

"Did you call it in?"

Chris held her hands still. "No, I wasn't sure if I should or not. I wanted to check with you and tell you…" She stopped and smiled bleakly when the waiter set their food down.

"Tell me what?" Bev prompted. She sipped her tea and watched Chris inhale deeply and exhale through her mouth.

"My ex-husband," she said, as she unwound the napkin and rolled the knife and fork out with her fingertips. "An old friend of mine from high school called to see how I was doing. She was trying to sound positive and then she said someone had told her Jarrett had been around town asking about me. She said it was maybe three or four weeks ago."

Chris picked up the knife and fork and stabbed into the quesadilla. She cut across it and divided the two halves into quarters before she raised her eyes again. "Shit," she said, "I hate talking about this part of my past. I was young and stupid and wouldn't listen to a damn thing anybody tried to tell me. Jarrett was this exciting, hunky guy that everyone said was no good for me. We eloped the weekend I graduated from high school and, for a while, it was hot, you know, a thrill a minute."

Bev nodded and chewed. She didn't need to talk.

Chris shrugged one shoulder. "I'm sure you've heard this story more times than you can count. I guess the only difference in me and some others is when the fighting started, I told him if he ever raised a hand to me, I'd call the cops."

There was no reason to make Chris give her the details. "And you did?"

"Yeah. The thing is he and a couple of his hell-raising buddies had robbed a convenience store a few days before. I didn't know that and when the cops picked him up on the domestic call, they put everything together. This was the first big trouble he'd been in, but one of them shot the attendant so it went hard. They didn't kill him or it would have been worse. The arrest, jail time because I refused to ask my parents for bail money, finding out how many bills Jarrett had racked up that I knew nothing about – what a disaster it was. As you can imagine, I was looking to make a clean start and a friend of my mother's suggested I join the Army. I went to the recruiting station the day after the trial and it was one of the best things I ever did. I got my head straight and learned I could do things I'd never thought possible. After I got to my first assignment, I sent Jarrett divorce papers through the mail and never heard from him again." She exhaled again, cut a small bite and nibbled it from the fork.

"You think he's here?"

Chris shook her head. "I don't know. But if he's been out for a while, he could have found out about the shop or about Cindy. She's been here a lot longer than I have."

Ah, now Bev was tracking. "If he's here, you think he might have gone to see Cindy?"

"That would make more sense to me than Jonah even though it would be a coincidence of timing," she said and looked at the plate as if trying to remember why the food was there. "Cindy never liked him to start with and she would have threatened to call the cops if he got ugly. I don't expect he became one of those born-again religious ones, so sure, I could see him losing control."

"Chris, you need to eat," Bev said mildly and tapped her fingers against the table. "You did the right thing by calling me. I'll send someone around to dust for prints this afternoon and I'll go into the system to see what they have on him. All I need is a full name and where he was in prison."

Chris bit her lower lip and stared unflinchingly at Bev. "If it was Jarrett, then in a way it was my fault."

Bev had seen that one coming. "No, it wasn't," she said immediately. "Don't do this to yourself. It won't change anything and if it was him, we'll find him. We'll get on it within the hour."

"Thanks," Chris said and checked her watch. "I called one of the freelance instructors to take the afternoon class. I'll come down to the station or meet your guys at my place."

Bev reached into her purse for her notebook. "Give me the name now and I'll send a car out later. It won't hurt to have a black and white seen at your apartment and I'll ask them to do extra patrols in the area until we get a line on Jarrett. And all of this can wait fifteen minutes while we get some food down you."

Chris swallowed hard and picked up her fork. "Yes, ma'am," she said. "I guess you're right."

They finished lunch and Bev swatted Chris's hand when she reached for the check. She walked her out to the parking lot, sent her toward the dive shop and called Les to make the arrangements.

"Wouldn't that be a goddamn pisser," was his only comment.

Bev beat her projected time and had the wheels in motion in forty-two minutes. What would come of it remained to be seen and, as Les said, it would be a goddamn pisser indeed if Jarrett Lloyd Langford was anywhere near Verde Key.

The afternoon passed in a series of telephone calls, emails and faxes. Lorna called to see if she was available for dinner the next night. They were discussing menu options when Les picked up the other telephone when it rang.

He lifted a finger and said, "Well, I'll be damned."

"Either one sounds great, Lorna – fix what you're in the mood for," Bev said. "Got to go – see you tomorrow."

Les was scribbling rapidly on a pad. "Got it," he said. "We're on the way." Les looked almost excited.

"On the way where, for what?"

"You know a Palmetto Paradise? Some kind of fishing camp that's closed?"

"Yeah. It's south out of town, five or six miles. It's like fourth on the list to search."

Les patted his front pocket for his sunglasses. "I'd say it's headed to the top. Some kids were messing around out there and found a hand. A woman's hand."

CHAPTER THIRTEEN

"**P**almetto Paradise has been closed for about two years, tied up in a nasty divorce settlement. It was one of those juicy scandals," Bev explained as they hit traffic on the street adjacent to the station.

Les flipped on the blue lights. "Had to be sex or money."

"Both, sort of. Bernie Madison is a big real estate agent in Miami and they used to come here on vacation. Six or seven years ago he opened Palmetto Paradise as an exclusive fishing camp. Property is on a cove, but in a spot where the water cuts back in. Land-side you have to get off the main road, turn down a two-laner and take a one-lane gravel road for another mile."

"Not a main route area," Les said.

"No, and that was part of the deal. There was no advertising, strictly word of mouth, clients who were referred. Had a dozen cabins, nice dock with marina store, boat ramp and a club house. An on-site manager who took care of things. Exclusive usually means expensive and I suppose it was pricey, but it really meant men only and I'm sure some of them might have gone fishing. Most of the action was at the clubhouse. High stakes poker, plenty of girls, dancing and otherwise, sophisticated porn collection from what I heard."

"And Mrs. Madison discovered this?"

Bev grinned. "In the worst possible way. Bernie was out of town and Mrs. Madison had driven to Key West with a few of her church ladies. They left later than they'd planned, the weather was getting shitty and, since her husband did own this 'rustic little camp,' she decided to stop to see if they had any empty cabins. The girls were willing to 'rough it' for one night."

"The religious ladies got a bit of a shock?"

"The story had several versions, but the one mostly likely to be true was that Mrs. Madison finally got directions from the nearest gas station, rolled in and went straight to the clubhouse because it was all lit up. The female bartender was topless, one girl was giving a blow job to some guy, a girl was naked on the pool table and the fifty-two inch television was not featuring a Walt Disney film, although I do believe the main character was named Bambi."

"Was Mr. Madison there?"

"No, and that's all that gave him any wiggle room. After the immediate ruckus, the divorce lawyers got into the act. Palmetto Paradise and some other assets have been tied up ever since. The buildings are still there and I think someone comes out and runs a bush hog once a year, but everything of value was stripped. Kids go out there to smoke dope, make out, and God knows what else."

The radio squawked for attention and Bev told the county cop they were on the way. Les hit the siren and the dent-pocked, rust-dotted red pickup truck that hadn't noticed the lights, or pretended not to, moved to the shoulder of the road. Les drove by and the old man who was hunched over the wheel released a gnarled hand and put it on the head of the black and tan, droopy-eared hound riding in the passenger's seat.

A county car was coming from the opposite direction, turn signal on. Bev motioned for them to go ahead. She couldn't recall the landmark for the turn-off. They followed the patrol car along the pot-holed county road, passed two narrow lanes with *Private Property* signs posted and turned when the driver ahead made a left at a boarded up wooden building with one side nearly engulfed in honeysuckle. The porch wasn't completely collapsed, although it looked as if it would break loose with one more torrential rain. Weeds flourished between broken steps.

Les bounced down rutted gravel lanes, a column of gray-brown dust churning from the lead car. Bev's insides felt wobbled as they rounded a curve and fanned into a large turn-around with a cyclone fence blocking the entry. A hinged gate, wide enough to fit an eighteen-wheeler, was thrown open; a padlock and short chain dangled from one side. Bev could see the rear end of another black and white through the stand of palmettos and other broad-leafed, densely planted tropicals. The two cars cleared the foliage screen and the property opened onto a paved lot. They pulled up next to the waiting vehicle. The driver's side was ajar, blue lights rotating silently and Bev saw one uniformed cop next to the office, talking on a cell phone. The other cop had three boys clustered on the dock where one boy was talking and pointing while his buddies bobbed their heads. Cane fishing poles, a blue backpack and a small bucket had been dropped near their feet. An opaque plastic bag was next to the cop's feet.

Bev and Les exited the car, stepped up to the county deputies they had followed and introduced themselves. Bev rolled her shoulders and did a slow turn to take in the scene.

Despite its defunct state, Palmetto Paradise hadn't suffered neglect like the building at the turn-off. The concrete block with stucco exterior had been built to withstand turbulent weather, although the original buff paint had succumbed to peeling and organic-based stains. The office and marina store were to the left, the single story, hexagon-shaped clubhouse to the right. A concrete launch ramp and wooden dock with six slips was between the structures. None of the marine support equipment was left and the discolored rectangle beneath the marina storefront window was probably where an ice machine had sat.

The dozen square cabins, identifiable by faded, different paint schemes and what had been colorful signs attached to a post in front of each, were arrayed in a winding pattern to the right of the clubhouse. There was surprisingly little debris and trash scattered around. It looked to Bev as if it could be restored without extensive repair and would bring a hefty price if the property could be released from legal wrangling.

The newcomers walked to the edge of the launch ramp and the cop who had been on the telephone strode to meet them. He pulled his sunglasses off and Bev wondered if they'd met before.

"Joel, Bill," he said to the men in uniform and thrust a hand to Bev. "I'm Marshall Reese and Mac's over there."

"Bev Henderson and Les Martin," she replied. "You the same Marshall Reese played for Florida State?"

His ebony eyes crinkled and he flexed linebacker-sized shoulders. "Yes, ma'am. Great time, but not good enough for the pro cut. Y'all the detectives from Verde Key that's got a young lady missing?"

Bev nodded. "What's it look like here?"

Marshall gestured to the dock. "Hand is in the bag. Woman's hand, Caucasian, not an old lady's, no jewelry, ragged severing at the wrist. A shark maybe or big barracuda, or if the body is on land, something might have dug it up and a piece wound up in the water," he said matter-of-factly. "The boys were fishing from behind one of the cabins when the short one in the Dolphins cap snagged it." He grinned again and replaced his sunglasses. "Scared the shit out of 'em, but I'll give them credit, the oldest one called and they stayed right here waiting for us. Didn't mess around with the hand or anything. Want to take a look?"

"I'm really more interested in what else is here," Bev said. She knew what detached human parts looked like. The rest of the body, if there was one, was her primary target.

Marshall shook his head. "Nothing to see in the immediate vicinity. It rained pretty hard a few days ago, so no tire tracks. We're about finished with the boys and one of the moms is on her way. We'll get started on a better search with Joel and Bill. The ME's office says they're kind of backed up so unless we've got more than a piece, they'd like us to bring it to them."

"This a deep water marina?" Les gazed at the greenish water.

"Yes, sir," Joel chimed in. Bill had stepped toward the dock. "No slope to speak of. It's shallow for a bit, then drops off."

"Even if you didn't have a boat, be easy to drop a body off the dock," Marshall agreed. "It's clear in the water, no trees to catch on. It would drift."

"The car is missing, too," Les said. "Roll the windows all the way down, put it in neutral and a good shove off the ramp ought to do the trick."

"You'd get better distance if you rammed it in with another car," Joel mused.

Another marked car rolled into view with a burgundy colored minivan close on its bumper.

"The sheriff and the mom, I bet," Marshall said. "I don't think the boys can tell you much else unless you just want to talk to them."

Bev looked at Les and he gave his head a quick shake. "If you know how to reach them later, it's probably better to get the area cleared," she said.

"Be right back," Marshall said, and motioned to Joel to come with him and headed to intercept the stocky man with his hat shoved to the back of his head. He'd laid a hand on the arm of the woman who was facing the dock, probably asking her to wait a moment before she went out to speak to the boys.

"Wish they'd found this earlier," Les said. "I don't think the search team can get relocated, set up and have much light left."

"The team can at least scope it out, assess logistics and be ready for first light," Bev replied. "I told them I'd call as soon as we found out what the deal was. Plus if we can bring a few more folks out, we can help do a ground sweep, see if the car is shoved in a stand of trees or if it looks like somebody dug a grave. Let's run it by the sheriff, then rustle up some more people unless he's got a better idea."

The cop on the dock was speaking with the woman who had a firm grasp of one of the boys by his ear. The other two stood, heads bowed, the excitement abated by what appeared to be an all-encompassing bubble of maternal righteous indignation. *Excuse me, ma'am, this is fill-in-the-blank from the sheriff's office. We have your son and a couple of his friends and...* No doubt the moment she was assured they weren't calling about a serious accident, the appropriate lecture was embellished for special circumstances.

Bev almost felt sorry for them even though the little shits *had* been trespassing. Besides, they couldn't keep this quiet for long and the boys would get their dose of fame. She turned away from the mini-drama and punched in the number to the search team chief. Les ambled over to make their introductions to the sheriff. The woman was herding the boys into the minivan when Bev finished her conversation. The men gathered around the sheriff who had his thumbs hitched into his belt and was listening to Marshall. Bev walked briskly to the group and hoped everyone was in agreement – she wasn't in the mood for a turf battle.

"Harry Tuttle," the sheriff said and stuck out his hand. "You're Frank Henderson's daughter?"

"Yes," she said and returned his grip with the kind of strength that nearly always startled men who didn't know her. It was a remarkably effective nonverbal tool.

"Good man, tell him hello for me," he said and made a circle motion with his hand. "We don't have another car to bring out, but Les here says y'all can get one and you were talking to Al just now?"

Bev nodded. "It will take them about forty-five minutes to get here and they'll bring a fresh pair of dogs."

"Good to hear. Marshall figures be best to start on both sides of the trees, look for any big signs and work back this way. It thickens into pretty much a mess 'bout a hundred feet past the cabins and less than that behind the office. Be hard to haul a body in and impossible to hide a car unless you hacked out an area and piled branches back in. That would be easy to spot on foot."

The collective nods of the county cops made Bev wonder how many of them visited when Palmetto Paradise was in full swing. Complimentary access to local law enforcement would have been a smart tactic.

"Sure," she said without asking the direct question about their familiarity with the property. "But I'd like to take a look at the spot where the boys were."

"I'll show you," the cop who had been on the dock said.

Sheriff Tuttle opened his car door and nodded to Marshall. "Call me if y'all find anything and let me know what the plan is for tomorrow."

The group waited until he drove away and then split to begin the initial survey. "Don McGee and everybody calls me Mac," the rangy cop said as he led Bev on the path to the third cabin. It was at the top of the first S curve and wasn't readily visible from the parking lot. There looked to be about forty feet of flat grassy area from the back door of the cabins to the water's edge. Wide-limbed mimosa trees dotted the bank, perfect for climbing and sitting against waiting for a fish to bite. It was easy to see why the boys would have picked this spot, sheltered from view and shaded from the sun. Bev stepped on an empty Cheetos bag.

She and Mac started at the edge of the bank looking for anything that didn't belong. The overgrown grass was a hindrance, the bugs a pain and the afternoon sun combined with Florida humidity added to the discomfort. It didn't take long for Bev to wish she was wearing shorts, sneakers, a floppy brimmed hat and a coat of bug repellant. Mac was silently sweat-drenched, his khaki uniform shirt rumpled in damp folds. They walked empty-handed toward the main area and both looked up when they heard cars crunching across the gravel lot.

A Verde Key patrol car was followed by a county search and rescue van. Earl climbed out of the car and waved to Bev. One of the rookie patrolmen popped the trunk of the vehicle to reveal a white ice chest. God love their pea-pickin' little hearts, as her Aunt Lorna would say!

Three men from search and rescue clambered down and one slid the side door open to let a pair of beagles hop to the ground. The rest of the men drifted in, all showing effects of being outdoors without proper equipment.

"We figured a little Gatorade and water might go good," Earl said. The rookie pulled a box from the back seat with bottles of insect repellent-laced sunscreen and some VKPD ball caps.

"You must be Al Thornton," Bev said to the oldest-looking of the search team members. He wasn't much taller than her and had the leathery skin of men who spent their time outdoors. The sides of his head beneath his cap were smooth – bald rather than shaved. His deep-set brown eyes were friendly and the slight slope of his shoulders belied the strength of his hands and forearms. Backpacker, maybe cyclist, sail-boater, not power, was Bev's guess.

"Yes, ma'am," he said and nodded to the group. "You in charge?"

Bev glanced quickly at Les and Marshall, both of whom nodded. "It's kind of joint between us and the county," she said, "but I can tell you what we've done so far."

The four of them stepped to one side to discuss the situation as the other men sorted through the layout of the property. Everyone generally agreed on how to proceed and half an hour later, the roles had been assigned. The divers had been notified and would roll in at six a.m. if the body hadn't been found by dark.

The team chief walked Bev and Les to the middle of the dock and swept his arm across the water. "The cove is protected, but you've got a regular current and we had hard rain twice this week," Al said. "Added to the runoff, we've got algae bloom, so visibility is down. If we're looking for a car, that will be easier to spot than a body and it would have been pushed from the ramp. We'll calculate potential drift, although if the body is loose, or in parts, that will make a difference. You still think it was last Thursday night or early Friday morning?"

"Mostly likely," Bev said and thought of Chris's ex-husband. "The latest would have been early Saturday morning."

Al shrugged. "We'll do the math based on the longest time, start at that point and work back."

Les frowned. "Doesn't where they found the hand matter?"

Al shook his head. "Not really. Could be the body is on land in too shallow a grave that's been opened up by the rain and a bird or wild dog got the piece and dropped it in the water. The dogs we have are good and if that's the case, they'll probably find it. Or, could be a big-ass barracuda got hold of the hand somewhere else and swam a ways before dropping it. Could be a shark got the whole body and parts came off. It's hard to tell until the ME makes the call. Even if the body is in a car, it's been five days or more and you'll get drift in spite of the weight of the car."

He spoke with pragmatic flatness devoid of sentiment, but Bev couldn't fault him for that. He'd been around long enough to have recovered bodies as well as rescued people. Emotional involvement was inadvisable over the long run.

"Well, we've got another three hours of good light before the trees and shit interfere," Les said. His short-sleeved shirt was stained and dirt smeared his pants up to his knees. Bev assumed she looked as bedraggled as he did.

"Right," Al said and answered the shrill of the cell phone attached to his belt.

"Hey, Detective," the rookie called out and held up something that glinted in the sun. "Found a gold bracelet over here."

"Seahorses and starfish?" Bev asked as they came within speaking distance.

"Yeah," he replied. "How'd you know?"

"Just one of those things," she said and watched the piece swing from his finger. A perfect match to the silver one Chris wore.

CHAPTER FOURTEEN

FIve-thirty the next morning came too soon as the alarm pierced what had been a night of ragged sleep. Bev had wakened constantly seeking a comfortable position trying to override thoughts of dead bodies and the emptiness of the bed. Kyle called late to give her a telephone number where he could be reached. He sounded distanced by more than geography and wasn't sure of his return date. Monday at the latest; no discussion of his reason for the trip or of what he was actually doing. God knows everyone had family issues and if he had some kind of problem he didn't want to talk about, that was his business. He also hadn't mentioned a dinner date when he returned. Maybe he took it for granted and didn't feel the need to ask. She shouldn't have wondered about either of those things and it bothered her that she did.

She resisted the urge to hit the snooze button, kicked the sheet off and decided the hell with making the bed. A hot shower and instant coffee would get her out the door. She'd told Les she would meet him at Palmetto Paradise rather than ride together. There was no telling how the day was going to shake out.

She made time to stop for a real cup of coffee, but when she cleared town and approached the first turn-off she saw a county black and white patrol car on the shoulder in front of a blue news van. Shit, how did they find out? Bev drove past and ignored the urgent hand of Sylvia Ruthven, one of the reporters who had been on Cindy Green's street the day they discovered she was missing.

Bev's Spitfire jarred noisily along gravel, the larger rocks pinging against the low-clearance undercarriage. She rounded the curve into the clearing and didn't see Les. Four vehicles were parked at the edge of the lot and two county boats floated, tied into slips. Marshall and another cop she didn't recognize were entering one of the cabins, although most of the activity was centered on the dock. A couple of men from the day before were at two long tables in front of the office with radios, walkie-talkies and assorted paraphernalia set up as a mini-command post. A third, smaller table held orange and white thermal containers, cups and bakery-size white pastry boxes. What was a search and recovery mission without donuts?

"Morning." Al Thornton grinned and opened the car door for her. "The divers are getting their gear ready, but we thought we'd go ahead with the shoreline search."

Bev pulled herself out of the seat. Two men in swim trunks, T-shirts and caps were surrounded by dive gear – large reels of line, buoys and several items Bev wasn't familiar with. Dry suits hung from the vehicle's open back doors.

"Dry suits?" Bev asked. "In Florida in June?"

Al nodded. "Doesn't matter. Aside from the fact they'll be moving slow and can stay down for over an hour in this depth, we don't always get clean water to work in. There's not a lot of run-off or dumping here, but go poking around in swamp or some of the other bays and there's all kinds of shit, figuratively and literally, that you don't want to penetrate a wet suit."

"Yeah, I can see that," Bev said. "What did you decide about the sequence?"

"That looks like your other guy," Al said as the unmarked car drove in. "Let's grab a coffee and donut and go over this together."

They waited until Les emerged, more casually dressed today, as was Bev. She waved her arm toward the office. They took care of the immediate caffeine and sugar need and followed Al onto the dock.

"Okay, all we got yesterday was the bracelet," he said. "The dogs were fresh and without any signs of digging in the area, we can assume she's in the water. We looked again for tire tracks around the launch ramp, but with the rain there's nothing to see. If he had a boat, he'd have gone to deep water, but if he dumped her here, it would have been off the end of the dock. We did the calculations last night using Thursday as the earliest possible time of disappearance."

He ripped a chunk out of a cinnamon roll, chewed and swallowed. "No big storms in the last month and not a hell of a lot of drift in this area. If the body isn't weighted properly, she'll have floated by now and there's a good chance she'll be snagged on the deep end of the dock or somewhere on the shore line. There's plenty of mangroves to catch on. No way to know at this point if the hand was the only part exposed. It could be that we just find pieces."

Bev was glad she'd left the pastries in the box. Les had finished his in four quick bites.

"My money is he left her in the car and shoved it in," he said. "It hasn't shown up anywhere."

"A car is easier to find," Al replied. He looked up at the overcast sky. Rain wasn't predicted until late afternoon, but the nearly solid covering of clouds was layered in white to gun-metal gray. "We've got algae, no sun and particle suspension so visibility is down to five feet, seven or eight, max. The two divers are old hands at this and I can have another pair around ten o'clock if we need them. We'll start the shore search in a few minutes and eliminate that possibility. No sense in putting divers down until we do that."

Marshall came onto the dock, cup of coffee and donut in hand. "Good morning," he said and pointed to the cabins with the donut. "We were looking for signs of a grave yesterday and forgot to check the doors. Noticed a couple of the far ones had been jimmied and looked pretty fresh. Just empty cans, cigarette butts and used rubbers." He sipped his coffee. "I'll go in the boat with you, Al and Joel can go in the other one. I sent a car out to the turn-off to keep the reporters out. Word must have gotten around and we're liable to have a lot of gawkers if we're not careful." He smiled at Bev. "You and Les okay with the plan?"

"Works for us," she said and turned at the sound of another car. The nose of the Adventures Below Dive Shop van edged into sight. What the hell? She had talked to Chris briefly last night and told her about the bracelet, but not the hand. Chris had thanked her and hadn't said anything about coming out. The cop at the entrance must have thought she was an extra diver.

"Who's that?" Al asked and frowned.

"A volunteer that I don't think you want," Bev said.

"Marshall, show me where those chocolate covered donuts are," Les said and stepped toward the office.

Bev and Al moved to intercept Chris at the end of the dock. Her face was set and she extended her hand. "Chris Green, Mr. Thornton, owner of Adventures Below. I've got better than two dozen recoveries to my name and plenty of gear in the van. Thought you could use some extra help."

"Ah, nice to meet you," Al said and hesitated. He looked to Bev for explanation.

"Chris, I wasn't expecting this," she said carefully. "I was planning to keep you posted."

Chris tightened her jaw. "Bev, I'm as good a diver as anybody and I'm tired of sitting on my ass. I'm here to help."

"Chris is Cindy Green's sister," Bev said quietly to Al. "Cindy, the lady we're looking for."

"Oh," he said and slowly shook his head. "Chris, I understand, but if you've done these, you know what five days in the water in this heat does and we're not even sure if she's still intact."

"I've bagged disintegrating parts before," Chris said stubbornly. "I'm not going to fall apart and get in the way."

"Yeah, but there's a hell of a difference," Al said, not unkindly. "You know the drill. You're feeling along and all of a sudden you've got a chunk of flesh in your hand or you're staring at a face that's partially eaten away. If your sister is in here, you don't want to see that without warning."

Her shoulders slumped enough to acknowledge his point.

"Look," Bev said quickly. "You're the one who pounded into us about knowing when to abort a dive because it wasn't right. And I bet there are things you can do on surface support." She darted a look at Al.

He cleared his throat. "Uh, yeah, the guys are going to put a line from the dock to the far shore and lay out the lanes. You can help keep track of the grid search. I'll take you over and introduce you. I knew Tom Farmer, the owner before you. Used to help us out and it kind of startled me to see the van," he said as they walked in the direction of the two men.

"She want in on the action?" Les asked as he and Marshall joined Bev.

"Les explained," Marshall said. "Not the thing you want happening in your family. Anyway, time to take the boats out."

They were Boston Whaler Guardians, nice rigs for this kind of work. Easy to maneuver in tight spaces and they'd be able to get right up against the tangle of mangrove roots and sea grass. He waved for Joel and another man that Bev didn't know and they bounded onto the pier. Joel had two pairs of binoculars hanging from his shoulders.

Al left Chris with the divers and paused on his way to the boat. "I think she'll be fine," was all he said.

The men stepped gingerly into their respective boats and kept the engines at a low pulse as they backed out. Once clear of the pilings, they split and headed directly to the top of the curve of the cove. They would start at the same spot, one boat trolling to the right, the other to the left, and work their way around to the dock. Maybe it would be over with during the first sweep.

Les snapped his fingers. "Oh, damn, I knew I forgot to tell you something. The ex-husband, Jarrett? He's in a county jail in Tennessee. Assault, I think they said, but he's been in custody since a week ago Monday. Got to scratch him from the list."

Bev stared into her empty cup, debated about a refill and shrugged. "Well, at least we checked. I'll tell Chris so she can quit worrying about him and feeling guilty that she might have gotten Cindy into this."

"I'll call the chief," Les said. "Might as well get comfortable, nothing to do except wait." He strolled to the office.

Bev approached the overlapping tarps the divers had laid down. Chris, more relaxed than when she arrived, made introductions. Ned was the tall one, with a high forehead that enhanced the narrowness of his face. His thin black hair was pulled into a short ponytail. The grizzled-faced, wiry man went by Smitty. Short, frizzed gray hair with a few dark patches clung to his scalp like a scrubbing pad. Bev looked at the equipment.

"How exactly does this work?" she asked. "I've investigated a couple of drownings, but never been in on a water search."

"Soon as the boats come back, we'll set the main line from the center of the dock and tie off on the far side," Smitty said. "We'll run lines to create four-foot lanes between the dock and wherever they couldn't see from the boats. Then it's a grid search where we move slowly up and down each lane, checking them off as we finish. If we haven't found anything on that side, we'll lay out another grid from the other side."

"The mouth of the cove is pretty wide," Ned interjected. "We'll work up until that point, but not beyond. If somebody had a boat, they would have gone to deep water." He was echoing what Al had said earlier.

"The second team will be out later," Smitty said and smiled at Chris who was holding a clipboard with a matrix drawn on a sheet of paper. "We'll find her if she's here."

"By the way, Chris," Bev said. "Looks like Jarrett has been in jail in Tennessee for several days."

Chris inhaled deeply and exhaled slowly. "I guess I'm relieved, but I still don't understand about the break-in."

Bev shrugged. "There's been a fair amount of publicity. Somebody might have thought you'd be away and were scouting the place first or got interrupted by the sound of a neighbor. We'll keep the patrols going for another few days to be on the safe side." She saw Smitty pick up a full-face diver's mask. She'd seen one like it in the display case at Chris's shop.

"Are those better?" she asked. "How do you clear your ears without being able to pinch your nose?"

"Bev's one of my new divers," Chris said proudly. "Their class finished last week."

"Congratulations," Smitty said and tapped the wide lens space. "Yes, these are better for dirty water. When you've been diving as long as we have, you get to where you can clear just by wiggling your jaw back and forth or swallowing real hard." He turned the mask over and pointed to the mouthpiece. "We don't have the communications package yet and hope to get enough in next year's budget."

"It's a two-way system for the mask," Chris said. "You get some static, but can usually hear real well up to a hundred and fifty feet with high end ones. A lot of research and salvage divers use them as well as the commercial guys. Some of the big aquariums have installed them so people wandering around can talk to the divers. Kids love it."

"I've got to decide whether or not to buy my own gear before I add those kinds of toys," Bev said.

Chris smiled. "You're hooked and so is Kyle. I can tell and I'll get you back in the water soon."

"Hey, Chris, you do any diving with a rebreather yet?" Ned asked and the three of them began tossing out jargon Bev followed in part.

They neatly aligned the equipment while talking and glanced up occasionally to watch the silent, slow motion of the two boats as they hugged the banks en route to the dock.

Marshall had already broken loose from the shoreline and accelerated slightly when the second boat swung away with no signal of discovery.

"Guess we're up next," Smitty said matter-of-factly. "Chris, you want to come with me and run the line?"

She grabbed a large, heavy looking reel, hoisted it to her shoulder in an easy motion and walked beside the older man.

Bev followed a step behind. Interesting the way Smitty and Ned had immediately accepted Chris. It was a camaraderie Bev had seen before among the divers that gathered at the Scarlet Macaw. She and Kyle had discussed it while going through the classes. It seemed to be some sort of rapid bond among people who shared a special sense of community. Now that she thought about it, she *was* ready to get into the water again as soon as the circumstances allowed.

"Don't tie up, we'll take it back out," Smitty said and caught the line that Al tossed. Marshall nosed the boat into the slip.

They swapped over, sped across the short distance of the cove and quickly rigged the line. Al, Marshall, Joel and Bev helped lug gear from the tarp to the end of the dock. She understood that Ned and Smitty would wait until the last moment to suit up. They would overheat rapidly if they stood around in the impermeable fabric with tight neoprene seals around the neck, wrist and ankles.

Al and Chris moved together to help the divers swing tanks onto their backs and get buckled in. It was teamwork born of experience and Bev wondered fleetingly if she would ever reach the stage where she could be as comfortable with the equipment.

Smitty and Ned braced themselves against Chris and Al, slipped fins onto their booted feet, straightened up, clasped one hand to the full face masks, positioned the other hand to hold the regulators to their chests and took a giant stride off each side of the dock. They popped back to the surface and Al and Chris lowered large lights to them.

"A square pattern five feet around the dock first, then the lanes," Al said as the men disappeared from sight, a trail of bubbles identifying their position.

Chris breathed an audible sigh, spoke quietly to Al and then walked to Bev. "I think I'm ready for a cup of water and it'll take them half an hour to do the dock," she said. "Thanks for backing me up before. I think I'm ready for the worst with Cindy and I'd rather be here than waiting for your call."

Bev touched Chris's arm. "I imagine I'd feel the same way. I'll come with you for that cup of water. I'm coffeed out."

The overcast sky blocked direct sunlight, although the humidity was beginning to overcome the breeze from the cove and the bugs would stir soon. Oh, well, she'd spent every year between middle school through college in track and field events and was no stranger to sweat.

The morning settled into a pattern with everyone except the divers meandering from group to group for small talk, sports talk, business talk, occasionally making radio or telephone calls and hoping for news each time the divers emerged.

Chris stayed with Al and they were busy handling the equipment, making notes and doing other things that may have been completely unproductive, but kept them moving.

The second pair of divers rolled in at ten-thirty, complete with bags of sandwiches and coolers of Gatorade. Al and Chris had them in the water in what seemed like no time at all.

Bev watched carefully as they established the lanes and swapped off. She saw lines of bubbles, ripples from unseen creatures and an occasional fish leap from the water, startled by unfamiliar invaders.

It was after one o'clock when the teams shifted to the boat launch side of the dock.

"Shit, there it is," Al called out when an orange marker was inflated thirty or so feet to the left of the boat ramp. He and Chris moved to the edge of the dock. Bev, Les and Marshall went as far as they could without getting their feet wet.

Smitty surfaced before Ned and swam directly to the ladder. He pulled off his face mask. "Got the car," he said quietly. "Woman's body in the driver's seat, still strapped in."

"Blonde hair, silver Taurus?" Chris asked in the momentary silence that followed.

Smitty nodded and passed his fins up to them as Ned broke from beneath.

"Damn!" Bev said softly as Chris wiped her hand across her eyes. Smitty clamored up the ladder and said something to her that Bev couldn't hear.

"Better than not knowing," Les said. "Let's see how they want to handle the rest."

Al stuck a handheld claxon toward the water and blared two short blasts that echoed across the area.

"Okay, we've got contact," Al said briskly. "The guys will go back down and figure out the best way to rig for extraction. We've got a pretty decent winch on the truck and we may be able to pull it with that."

"You're not going to bring the body out first?" Joel asked. "Wouldn't that be easier?"

Al shook his head. "Aside from the fact it's a crime scene that I assume these folks want to check, a body that's been submerged for this long doesn't just slip out a window and it's a hell of a lot harder to get a door open underwater than you'd think."

"What are we looking at, Al?" Bev asked. "Time-wise, I mean? Should I call the ME?"

"Call to alert him, but let the guys go down again to make a drawing. If it went straight in, I think we've got enough cable to try and winch it back up the ramp. If it's turned sideways, we may have to use the lift bags and get a crane out here."

Chris was out of hearing with Smitty and Ned, talking to the other pair of divers as they stayed partially submerged near the ladder.

"Okay, let me get with the team and we'll have this worked out quick as we can," Al said and the group scattered.

Bev took the ME and let Les contact the chief; he would take care of the media for them and Marshall would call the sheriff and arrange for a crane to be on stand-by. The pace increased with cell phones ringing and voices calling out questions and answers. People were glad to have something to do.

The pair of divers who were still in the water pushed off again and floated three more orange buoys to the surface to form a rectangular shape. The team returned with a rough sketch drawn on a large underwater slate. Al took one look, frowned and motioned for Marshall.

"No good, she's sideways and the bottom's mucky. We'll rig it for lift and then maneuver it toward the ramp. Our winch ought to handle it after that though." He spread his hands. "Probably take an hour and half or two," he said to Bev.

"Got it," she said and punched in the ME's office number. The rescue team members and Chris hauled equipment, dumped it into one of the boats and motored slowly as the divers swam to the markers. They disappeared once more while Chris and Al fed lines overboard.

An hour passed in a swarm of activity and the ME's sedan arrived.

"The chief said there must not be gory news anywhere else in the state 'cause he's been on the phone since this morning," Les reported when he wandered over, two icy bottles of Gatorade in hand. "He said you haven't had a real live murder in a while."

Could you have a real *live* murder? – Bev wondered irreverently. Probably made as much sense as the term *cold as hell*.

"Damn, look at that," she said, forgetting linguistic niceties.

The top of a car, silver underneath streaks of muddy water, appeared between four tan colored, balloon-like bags that resembled two fifty-five gallon drums strapped side-by-side. Al distanced the boat from the object and waved to the two men waiting by the rescue vehicle. The driver jumped into the cab, cranked the engine and inched close to the boat ramp, keeping the wheels on dry concrete.

The car was floating in the water and the bloated form could be seen squeezed between the steering wheel and the seat. The handless left arm, flesh ripped from several places, hung through the open window. Bev noticed that Al had shifted his body to block Chris's view. Good, she would need a minute or two to be ready, no matter what she thought.

The second man in the vehicle got out, unhooked the winch and carried the cable to the water's edge. He secured a smaller float bag above the hook and heaved it as far as he could. The divers pushed the car forward until Smitty held his hand up. One of them swam to the winch, tugged it behind him as he returned to the car and descended long enough to make the connection. He re-surfaced, flashed the thumb and forefinger *okay* signal and the divers moved to a safe distance where they bobbed until certain the procedure was successful. The winch whined, the cable pulled taut and Cindy Green, grotesquely distorted, was delivered from the water. Bev hoped she'd been dead before the car was sunk. Not that it altered the outcome, but maybe she hadn't struggled futilely, knowing she was about to die.

Water, sea grass and other debris fell in sheets, splattering the area as the car was pulled in to allow access for the other teams that would take over. There were clues to be looked for, and the body would be extricated, initially examined and bagged.

Al and Chris were on the dock, Chris's head averted from the car. She shook hands with the team and hurried toward Bev. Her face was pale under the deep tan and was as composed as one could expect under the circumstances.

"I appreciate you letting me stay," she said in a controlled tone. "I've got arrangements to take care of and I'd rather call my parents from home."

"No problem," Bev replied. Home was where she needed to be. She could let the tears fall, scream her anger, and wish that Jonah Shepard was alive so he could die a lingering, painful death.

"I called Kevin and he or somebody will be at the road with the county guy. You'll need an escort home. The press has been trying to get in here for the last few hours."

"Thanks, I'd forgotten about them," Chris said and turned abruptly to her van.

Bev waited until she was out of sight and then walked to the dripping car, the stench blossoming in the afternoon heat.

It was better to know, she repeated to herself, pushing flickering nausea out of her consciousness. It was better than clinging to unreasonable hope that somehow the obvious answer had been wrong.

CHAPTER FIFTEEN

By the time Bev finally returned to the apartment, all she wanted was a cold beer, a scalding shower and enough food in her stomach to stop the rumbles. She automatically checked her voice mail and felt only mild disappointment at no messages. She executed her plans with no interruptions, ignored the fact it was barely nine p.m. and slipped between the sheets, her eyes already heavy. Sleep came with no struggle.

An early morning rain had spent itself as she met Les at the station. Cloud formations were flattening against the baby blue sky that would soon harden to cerulean.

Dr. Cooke was waiting for them at the morgue. He saw them through the glass pane and waved them inside. His round face and stubby nose always made Bev think of a Santa Claus elf and she thought he would have been a natural as a pediatrician. It's not that pathologists should all be pasty-faced and gaunt, but the jolly image seemed incongruous.

He was drinking from a black thermal cup with a red skull and crossbones – a little ME humor perhaps. A single steel table was occupied with a sheet-covered figure, a toe tag hanging from what looked to be an old man's foot. The assistant ME was standing by the body looking at a file.

"I released the body earlier," Dr. Cooke said and pointed to some x-rays backlit on the board. "The lab rushed through the initial toxicology and there was no need for anything further."

"I know they couldn't make a call on site because of the condition of the body. Was it strangulation or head trauma?" Bev asked.

Dr. Cooke raised his eyebrows. "Neither," he said bluntly. "Cause of death was suffocation, a severe asthmatic attack."

"Asthma attack?" What the hell? "Not a homicide?"

"I didn't say that," the ME corrected. "The victim was dead before entering the water and we were able to recover a number of fibers from her lungs such as you find in carpet used in car trunks. Despite the deterioration of the body we also found signs of rope fibers around the ankles and the intact wrist."

Les held up one hand. "You're saying she was bound, put into a car trunk, had a severe asthma attack and died?"

Dr. Cooke nodded. "That would be consistent. I spoke with the victim's physician last night and she was on routine medication. Once a massive attack sets in, death can occur in minutes. The initial attack could have been due to stress, the enclosed space, or the act of binding that would have interfered with her chest muscles and her ability to breathe. Whatever the trigger, one can deduce she didn't have access to medical assistance. Whoever was responsible might not have been aware of the attack, might not have understood how severe it was or might not have given a damn. Assuming the young lady was transported from town to where the body was recovered, she would have been in the trunk at least half an hour."

"Were you able to pinpoint a time of death?"

The ME hesitated and gestured with his mug. "Not as precisely as you'll want. The stomach contents were completely decomposed; warm water and heat doesn't help with preservation. I can safely say it was at least three days, but could have been longer.

"We know it's been at least since last Saturday and we're hoping to find out if it was Thursday night or Friday morning," Bev said as if her statement would remind him of something he'd overlooked.

"Sorry," the ME said. "I'll have the report finished sometime tomorrow."

They thanked him and wandered through the basement hall to the elevator.

"Not quite what I was expecting, although it doesn't change the results," Les said when they were in the car. "Wonder why he tied her up and put her in the trunk?"

"I guess Chris could be right," Bev said pensively. "Maybe he *was* going to stash her somewhere until afterward and try to convince her to run away with him. It's not completely far-fetched and maybe he didn't understand the chance of an asthma attack."

Les shook his head. "If they'd been together very long I can't imagine he wouldn't know that. And why put her in the driver's seat later? Why not leave her in the trunk?"

Bev sucked her lower lip in thought. "It could be something crazy like he decided to let her become one with the ocean. Hell, maybe he thought it could look like an accident or voices told him to. Or, shit, maybe he was really a son-of-a-bitch like the guy my dad told me about and he was going to try and claim she ran off. If the body was in the driver's seat, there was a better chance it would get torn up. There's a whole lot of scavenging creatures swimming around and if no body was found, it would shoot the hell out of forensics evidence."

Bev's cell phone vibrated as Les cranked the car. "Henderson."

"This is Taliah. Will y'all be back soon?"

"On our way now. What's up?"

"I got a call from a woman by the name of Lusine, Sally Lusine. She sounded upset and said you left a note for them. They're neighbors of Cindy Green and got back from vacation last night. They hadn't heard the news."

"Was she calling about coming in? We'd like to check them off the list," Bev said.

"Well, she sounded like she'd been crying," Taliah said. "If you're out already, maybe y'all could go by her place instead. She said it wasn't too early for her if you didn't mind."

"Give me the number and I'll see if that will work with Les," Bev replied and copied while Taliah dictated. It was still early, but the woman was obviously up and that would take care of one more loose end.

Bev called Mrs. Lusine, nodded through the, "Oh, my God, we were so shocked," part and called Taliah to tell her they were en route to the interview. Les pulled up in front of the neighboring duplex almost as soon as Bev finished the second telephone call. She noticed that Mrs. Ridge, the across-the-street neighbor, had recovered from her indisposition and raised her shades to see who they were.

Sally Lusine opened the front door to the left side of the duplex, the one closest to Cindy's building. She stepped onto the porch and called out, "Please come in, I made some fresh coffee."

She was mid-to-late twenties, five foot four or five with a medium frame and an even tan, freckles arced across her nose and cheeks. Straight, sandy hair that hovered between blonde and brown was cut in a no-fuss style. Her jeans were the practical looser fit rather than tight and she wore a black T-shirt with the head of a white Siberian tiger emblazoned on it and the phrase *Extinction is Forever* printed underneath.

"We're sorry we weren't here," she said and led them toward the kitchen. "Hannah and Dave, the couple next door, and we had this eco-vacation to Costa Rica planned for months. We were up in the rain forest without radio, television or newspapers," she explained. "It's so awful and we didn't even know."

"Yes, ma'am," Les said comfortingly. They accepted coffee, sat at Sally's glass-topped, round dining room table and patiently got through the preliminary information.

Sally stirred some raw sugar into her cup and shook her head slowly. "Cindy and Jonah were nice people, you know? We didn't do a lot of social things together, but they were pleasant, especially Cindy. Jonah was the real quiet type. I had no idea the day we left that we'd never see them again."

Bev referred to the note she'd made. "The day you left? The Friday?"

"Yes," Sally said. "We were finishing packing and saw Jonah drive off. I guess that must have been around eight o'clock, no later than nine. We were supposed to leave at ten and I remembered I hadn't mailed the cable bill and I was out of stamps. We were running a little late and I dashed over to Cindy's."

"She was home?" Bev asked carefully.

"Uh, huh. She took care of me and told me to have a great trip. I was in a rush because they were honking the horn."

"Did she look all right?" Les asked and Bev wondered if he had done the same calculations as she had.

"Yeah. I mean, I was in a big hurry, but she was smiling and all. God, I still can't believe it."

Bev wrapped up the last few questions, anxious to get Les alone. They didn't speak until they were in the car. Les drove to the end of the block, pulled to the curb and looked at Bev.

"Shepard's appointment with the senator was one o'clock if I remember correctly," Les said quietly.

"Yep," Bev said. "Leaving at nine is more than enough time, but he wants to allow for traffic problems and being early is better than the risk of running late. I can see that."

"If Cindy was alive and well at ten o'clock that makes it tricky to back track, go into the house, tie her up, bundle her in the trunk, dispose of the body and drive to West Palm for a one o'clock. With no witnesses, I might add."

Bev tugged her earlobe. "Closer to impossible."

Les rolled the car forward. "Yeah, it does. Shit, I hope the forensics team has something."

Bev had her cell phone in hand. "I'd say it's time to go to West Palm. We know it couldn't have been Jarrett and I'd say we just lost Jonah. If this Noonan guy has suspicions about another person involved, I goddamn well want him to tell us what he's got."

CHAPTER SIXTEEN

Bev stopped to let two patrol cars ease by the front of police headquarters and saw a Hispanic man in a sage suit, white shirt, no tie, talking to a uniform cop. The man swung his gaze across the street to her. He was Kyle's height, give or take an inch, and broader through the shoulders. Black curly hair and no doubt the eyes behind the sunglasses were brown.

He slapped the cop on the back and laughed as the other man turned and sauntered toward an idling police car. He cupped his hands around his mouth. "Bev Henderson?" he called above the vehicle noises.

Bev nodded and the driver of the car motioned her to proceed.

The man took off his sunglasses and extended his free hand. "Hank Rodriguez. It's good to put a face to a name." His smile was quick and open; he had straight white teeth with a mouth that looked as if a cigarette should be dangling from the corner. A tiny scar branched off his bottom lip, a pale line against caramel skin.

"Same here." Bev returned the grip firmly. "Thanks for getting everything arranged so quickly."

Hank gestured toward the building. "No problem. We thought this one was locked down fast, and I guess from our end it was. Quite a twist on your side though. Let's go in and we can talk for a few minutes before we leave for Senator Randall's office."

"We're meeting with the senator?"

Hank grinned. "The top dog himself. Wanted to assure us he and his office would do whatever they could to help bring this terrible tragedy to a close."

His voice deepened in a fair mimicry of how the senator sounded at the last news conference.

He led her through the public area into an office with three desks. The proportional space was similar to what she and Les shared although the furniture was nicer, the floors were carpeted and the refrigerator was newer. Someone in the department must have a clean desk policy since there were almost no files in sight. Personal objects seemed to be limited to desk photographs.

"We've got water and sodas and I can get coffee if you'd rather," Hank said and waved to an empty chair next to his desk. It was the only one with no photographs on it. "It's just us right now."

"A soda is fine," Bev said, hung her purse on the chair and laid her notebook on the corner of the desk.

"I bet you're a diet type," Hank said and opened the refrigerator.

"I save my liquid calories for booze," Bev replied to his back.

Hank took two diet Cokes out. "A better use for them." He handed over the cold can and sat down, chair swiveled to face her.

"You're prettier than the newspaper photos," he said with another smile. "We read about the deal last year. Three against one was a hell of a thing and gutsy. Some folks would have frozen."

Bev felt a tinge of involuntary blush. "Oh. Well, there wasn't a lot of time to think. I pretty much reacted to what was going on." She took a long swallow.

"Gutsy, good-looking and modest," he laughed. "A great combination."

Bev cleared her throat and opened her notebook. Time to get professional. Their telephone conversations had been genial and hadn't prepared her for flirtation. Of course, she hadn't pictured him as quite so good-looking.

"Thanks. Like I told you, we had one other possible lead in the Green case that turned out to be a dead end. Kidnapping-murder isn't something we get a lot of – well, none actually – and it's a little hard to believe it was a random act. Since Noonan did come down to check around, we'd like to know why he thought someone else might have been involved. We're fresh out of suspects. "

Hank set down the can and patted a thin folder on top of the small stack of papers in his in-box. "Ready for business, huh? Okay. You're welcome to look at what we've got, but there's nothing I haven't shared with you or Les. Shepard called the senator's office and made an appointment two weeks in advance. He used the false name of Stanley Jones and referenced a Michael Adrini from Chicago. The senator had dealings with Mr. Adrini in the past, some kind of financial whiz. Shepard arrived five minutes before the appointment, had a briefcase, was dressed appropriately, was polite – serious without being nervous. The senator kept him waiting an extra ten minutes, they went behind closed doors and, within about fifteen minutes, the shit hit the fan."

Bev was impressed that he recounted the information without opening the file.

"We went over his personal effects and the car. No receipts for gas, food or overnight lodging. A blank notepad, maps, shit like that. Car was spotless, probably the kind of guy who got his oil changed every three thousand miles. Three sets of fingerprints – his and two that came up negative. One of them matched with the sister you sent earlier and I'm assuming the third set will be the dead girl you sent yesterday. Those will be run by this afternoon."

Bev drummed her pen silently on top of her notebook. "The only oddball piece was no bullets?"

"Yeah, but I saw the tape myself. Shepard and the senator were talking normally, then there's the space of a few minutes where the body language and facial expressions show a definite change of mood, then Shepard pulls the gun. Noonan was at his desk in the adjoining office, switched the monitor on, saw what was happening, buzzed for security and rushed in. Shepard didn't drop the gun, Noonan drilled him."

"No audio?"

Hank shook his head. "No, it went out a while back and hasn't been repaired. But to answer your main question, we've got nothing on another person unless those prints don't match. Noonan hasn't said shit to us about any further potential threat." He checked the wall clock and took a black and green print tie from a desk drawer. "Speaking of which, it's time for us to go. You need to detour by the ladies' room?"

"I'm fine," Bev said and gathered her things.

Hank ushered her from the building, saying hello to people as he guided her to the car. Not the strong, silent type, he bounced conversations between personal and professional. Big family, Catholic, University of North Carolina, three years in Atlanta before returning to West Palm Beach. No wife or children and no mention of a girlfriend. He drew the same kind of information from Bev except they hadn't gotten to the relationship part when they reached their destination.

"Please come in, Detectives," the young woman said when they entered the office. She rose and moved forward with more balance than Bev could have managed in three-inch heels. Not that Bev owned a pair of three-inch heels. But then neither did she wear snugly fitted short skirts to work. Or expertly applied make-up and pouffy hair.

"I'm Lila and the senator will be delayed for another minute. He's on the phone with the lieutenant governor." She cranked up her welcoming smile when she shook Hank's hand. "So nice to see you again, Detective Rodriguez. Could I get you a cup of coffee or something cold to drink?"

"No, thank you, ma'am," Hank said politely. "We're also supposed to meet with Mr. Noonan and we could start with him if the senator is busy."

"Oh, no, the senator thought it would be best if everyone met together in his office," Lila said with a shake of her head as she pursed her lips into the barest of pouts. A deep shade of pink lipstick that looked freshly applied emphasized the fullness of her lips. *The senator*, she said with particular emphasis, showing never a shadow of hesitation that his protocol would be followed.

"Well, Lila," Bev started. The double doors were pushed apart and the senator emerged with an aura of confidence that was surprisingly palpable.

"My apologies if I kept you waiting. Good to see you again, Hank," he said in a warm baritone. The handshake was a manly pump and he smoothly shifted and clasped Bev's hand in both of his. "You must be Detective Henderson. Beverly, although I think they told me you go by Bev. Suits you better, less formal."

"Uh, yes," Bev said, momentarily off-balance by the blue of his eyes and knowing that he'd gone to the trouble to find out about her name. Electric. *Whoa, this was what they meant by charismatic.* Amazing impact in the space of seconds.

"Lila, honey, did you offer these fine folks something to drink? And please tell Mike to join us right away."

Senator Randall's hand slipped to Bev's elbow and he was guiding her to his office, having inserted himself between them. Hank looked as if he was holding back a laugh.

"I hope you had a good trip from Verde Key. I don't get to the Keys as often as I'd like," Senator Randall continued and turned his head when a door on the far wall opened. "Mike," he said to the newcomer, "Come meet Bev Henderson."

Unlike the senator's projection of hail-fellow-well-met, the slender man moved quietly and the line of his mouth couldn't be called a smile. His grip was strong, a steeled warning not to mistake height for strength, the mental sizing-up reflected in his eyes. She'd seen it too many times over the years: the immediate question of whether she was a *real* cop or someone who was there because of affirmative action.

"Mr. Noonan, sorry we missed you when you were visiting," she said pleasantly. "We would have been glad to answer any questions you had." *There Ace, let's don't waste each other's time.*

"Well, now, I guess we'll skip the chit-chat," Senator Randall intervened and waved his hand across the couch and chairs. "I just want to say that this has been a tragic affair and I've been most appreciative of the support from your office, Hank," he said. He put Bev in the chair to his right and Hank on the couch to his left. "It's still hard to believe about Jonah and that poor girl. I know how heartbreaking it must be for her family."

"Senator Randall, the young lady, Miss Green, is why we're here," Hank said firmly. "Detective Henderson, Bev, I mean, has recently come into information to indicate Mr. Shepard was not the one who killed her."

Senator Randall's eyes widened. "No? Why I thought it was pretty straightforward. I understood the car was found in a bay or something. Was it suicide?"

Noonan's face didn't change expression.

"Suicide?" Bev repeated, startled at the quickness of the remark. Why would he think that? "No, sir, it couldn't have been. That's why we're trying to pin down the question of a possible accomplice in the attack on you."

Senator Randall shook his head slowly and spoke solemnly. "We do live in a time of unfortunate violence and I can see how Mike's trip may have caused some confusion, but it turns out to have been a bit premature, shall we say."

Was Mike not speaking today?

"I'm afraid I'm not following you," Bev said and turned toward Noonan. "I assume you had a reason for visiting Mr. Shepard's office and speaking with the employees."

"Well, you see," Senator Randall answered, the solemn tone replaced by earnestness. "As I'm sure you know, Jonah's animosity toward me began many years ago and obviously became some kind

111

of obsession. Once I realized who he actually was and that he still blamed me for the terrible tragedy that had befallen his family, I tried to calm him down. You know, find out if I could help him, make him see he was misguided. He used the term *we* several times and, in retrospect, he must have meant *we* as in his family. Things were chaotic at the time and I probably jumped to conclusions and indicated my misgivings to Mike."

Senator Randall flashed a smile to his silently watching security chief. "Mike, here, being the topnotch man that he is, wanted to re-assure me about the possibility of a conspiracy. He knew the West Palm police were admirably handling the investigation here and of course we had all heard about the disappearance of the girl. He assumed you were tied up with that and didn't want to disrupt your efforts with what was admittedly an overreaction to the situation. Naturally, if he had discovered anything of value, he would have contacted your department immediately. And yours also, Hank," he added.

"Of course," Noonan said in a clipped voice. "Sorry if I stepped on anybody's toes."

Sure he was.

Bev looked slowly from Senator Randall to Noonan and smiled. "When I spoke with Joyce Dunn at Wilson Accounting, she mentioned another gentleman had been with you. A Mr. Smallwood, I believe she said. Is he going to join us?"

Senator Randall shifted, his knee pressing against Bev's for a millisecond before he spoke heartily. "Rusty? Well now, Rusty's not in the office today I don't think. And to tell you the truth, Rusty's a good kid and he's an assistant to Mike here, but he's really more like a glorified apprentice – learning the ropes you might say. It didn't occur to us to have him sit in. There's nothing he could tell you that Mike can't. Am I wrong in that Mike? We sure don't want to overlook anything that might help."

If Noonan was trying to smile, it wasn't working. "Rusty was with me the whole time and didn't speak to anyone different than I did," Noonan said firmly. "As the senator said, he doesn't have any information of value."

Bev started to say that she'd like to determine that for herself when Hank cleared his throat. "Then I'm assuming you now believe Mr. Shepard acted alone?"

"Oh, yes," Senator Randall said without a pause. "Terrible thing to be so unbalanced. And I must say I was particularly shocked when Mike told me about no bullets. It's hard to imagine what he thought he was going to accomplish. He kept ranting about how I should pay for what I'd done to his family and he took that pistol out of his briefcase while I was trying to reason with him." He sighed softly. "If we'd known he couldn't actually harm me, then we could have gotten him some help, but you understand Mike simply reacted to what he saw. I'm not embarrassed to admit I was un-nerved staring into the barrel of a pistol. We all would have preferred a less violent outcome, although there was no way to realize the gun was empty."

There was a soft knock on the outer door and Lila opened it far enough to stick her head through.

"Senator, I'm sorry to interrupt, but Senator Tynsdale's office from Washington is on line one and I know you don't want to miss the call."

Senator Randall smiled at her. "That's quite all right, Lila. Ask them to give me two minutes." He shrugged in an almost deprecating manner. Powerful men calling for him. What *was* he to do?

"I sincerely apologize, but I'm going to have to take this," he said, rose and took Bev's hand again. "And since I think we've cleared up this question, Mike can show you out. It was a pleasure and please don't hesitate if there's anything else we can do to help. I wish you the best in finding out what happened to that unfortunate young lady."

Help? This was help? Senator Randall was no less charming than when he first said hello, but the pinging of Bev's internal bullshit alarm clashed with his polished dismissal. She wanted to bite her lower lip and forced a polite smile instead.

"Thank you for your time, sir," Hank said before Bev could make a comment. "We'll be in touch if we have any follow-up."

Noonan already had the outer door open and Bev carried on an internal dialog less civil than the actual parting phrases they exchanged with Noonan and the big-haired Lila.

She couldn't read anything on Hank's face and he waited until they were walking to the car before he broke into a grin. "Welcome to the world of politics," he said.

Bev matched his long-legged pace. "Care to explain why we got

113

the bullshit treatment up there?"

He shook his head, pulled car keys from his pocket and pressed the remote entry unlock button. "It's a reasonable explanation."

Bev pursed her lips and held her hand against the top of the passenger door. "It is, but something about Noonan doesn't sit right and the senator seemed awfully anxious to do all the talking. What do you know about Noonan anyway? A friend of mine thinks he might have been a cop in Chicago." A *friend*? Why didn't she say *my boyfriend*?

Hank opened his door and looked across the top of the car. "Your friend is correct. He was on the force for about eight years and went into private security. He's been with Senator Randall for four years. What I know about Noonan is that he works for a powerful man who is the son-in-law of a truly powerful man. These are kid-glove treatment kind of people."

Bev shook her head sharply. "Whoever killed Cindy Green didn't use goddamn kid gloves. If it wasn't Shepard and there's no second person, that doesn't leave me much to go on."

Hank shrugged. "Look, you have my sympathy, but if the other set of fingerprints in Shepard's car matches those of your victim, that closes it for us. We've sat down with the senator, who, bullshitting us or not, was the picture of cooperation. Unless you're holding something out on me, we've got no reason to think he's in any further danger and the dead girl is not in our jurisdiction."

He held his wrist up and tapped the face of his watch. "Tell you what. My father has this great restaurant in Palm Beach. Let me take you for a late lunch and by that time we should have word on the prints. If meeting the senator wasn't enough of a treat for you, at least you'll have gotten a terrific meal."

Bev hesitated. This wasn't what she'd been expecting.

"Come on," he said with an engaging grin. "You do eat, don't you? And if you like seafood, you're not going to find any fresher than at the Blue Garden. Oh, and there are vegetarian choices if you're one of those."

Bev laughed in spite of her disappointment. "No, I'm carnivorous. Blue Garden is the name?"

"My father is the chef, although one of my sisters is ready to take over, but my mother was the one who helped him build it from a much more modest place than it is today. She has this thing for blue and purple flowers and according to people who know plants, the garden setting is as much a draw as the food. You really shouldn't miss the chance and I guarantee we can get a table."

"Okay," Bev said and opened her door. "You convinced me." She climbed into the sedan and felt her stomach rumble. Maybe her suspicions of Mike Noonan were no more than hunger pangs.

CHAPTER SEVENTEEN

" **Y**ou keep telling me everything is under control and I've got fucking detectives in my office telling me someone other than Jonah killed the girl," Warren snapped when he and Mike were alone. "What I don't have are the papers."

"You worry too much," Mike said coolly. "We weren't seen and we didn't leave any forensics evidence. They've probably just worked out that the timing couldn't have been Shepard and that doesn't get them an answer as to who did it. They wouldn't have been so polite if the tall bitch had anything. She's got a squeaky clean, nobody-gets-a-break attitude. You can spot it a mile away."

Warren stirred the weak Scotch. "Except now they know who you are."

Mike shrugged. "So what? They're not going to plaster a photo on the news. You're too connected and they don't have a legitimate reason. The places we're going to aren't in the middle of town. We got back into the duplex with no problem and breaking into the office was a piece of cake. All the computers came up clean and it looks like Shepard was a loner except for the girlfriend, but I'm still wondering about the sister – the one they had in the papers and on the news. It sounds like the women might have been pretty tight and she's the only other one who seems to have been around Shepard much. We got into her place, but didn't have enough time for a good look. I'll give it a couple of days to settle down and maybe have another go at the sister's apartment. She's probably handling the estate and if she's taking shit from the duplex, she might have information she doesn't recognize – files or something. You can figure he didn't leave anything with a lawyer or reporter because it would have broken loose by now."

Damn it, why was there another player in the mix? Why couldn't Jonah have stashed everything in a fucking desk drawer?

Warren drained his glass. He had some minor level appointments with no one of significant influence and shit, one more drink wouldn't hurt.

"What's the deal with Rusty?" Warren thought about another round. "I haven't seen him around much. Is he okay?"

A frown started on Mike's face, but his expression quickly smoothed blank. "He's not as tough as he thought he was, but I'm keeping an eye on him," he said. "We might send him to the islands on a run. Give him a little vacation and send along a tasty piece of ass. That'll relax him."

Warren looked up sharply. "I thought you said he would keep his mouth shut."

Another flat stare and shrug. "You worry too much," he repeated. "You need me for anything else? I've got some business out of the building."

Warren flipped his hand in the air. "Go on and don't let me down on this, Mike."

"Yours aren't the only interests I'm concerned with," Mike said evenly and left the office soundlessly.

Fucking cold-hearted son-of-a-bitch with his fucking other interests. Warren swaggered to the bar to mix the second drink a little stronger than the first. Like he needed to be fucking reminded by Bassi's watchdog. Sometimes he got a laugh out of it – Freddy in DeLong's ear and Mike in Bassi's – and both the big men needing him. Him! The one with political juice.

DeLong's business ties bought influence, but made him a target whenever the liberal side played the-poor-and-struggling-middle-class tune, nor did he have patience for the subtle aspects of political give and take. Besides, his baby Cecilia liked being a senator's wife.

In some ways, Bassi was the more dangerous of the two and not merely because he had people like Noonan to take care of the dirty-hands work. Politicians willing to ensure favoritism toward one developer over another or provide passage of useful legislation were not a rare commodity. Too many greedy men though, men who carelessly allowed themselves to become the focus of investigation. That was the sort of spotlight Bassi couldn't afford to be caught in. He operated profitably beneath the radar of authorities on the prowl for big game and avoided drawing attention to his intermingled legitimate and other enterprises. No, an appropriate degree of corruption combined with finesse was a better arrangement. Warren was satisfied with the payoffs he'd negotiated and took a long-term view of the supplemental income. Oh, sure, his price would escalate as he achieved greater political status, but Bassi would anticipate that as a cost of doing business.

Warren looked at his glass, surprised to see it was empty. Could he risk one more? Before noon? No, better not. Goddamn it, why did they find the body so quickly! The West Palm end wouldn't cause any problems since the girl was out of their jurisdiction. This Bev, though, what was the story on her? How hard over was she going to be about this? Was she the kind who would let a case get cold if she couldn't find fast answers?

Mike was right about her air of moral rigidity that had nothing to do with sex. In fact, those legs went on forever and he wished she'd worn a skirt instead of pants. Pants on a woman were a waste of material unless molded to a full ass. He hadn't had a chance to get a good look at her ass and her tits weren't as big as he liked, but with that athlete's body, he'd bet she was hell between the sheets.

That was an idea. If Mike was wrong and she kept probing, maybe an invitation to the yacht with a moonlit dinner for two would interest her. A limo ride, expensive booze and a sumptuous meal. Not an open bribe. It would have to be something she could accept with a clear conscience. She would require an oblique approach, nothing overt initially, maybe a follow-up coincidental visit to the Keys. The yacht would be best though. He'd found that a sixty-five foot Horizon Skylounge usually had an aphrodisiac effect. He hadn't had to work to get a woman into bed for a while. It's not that he didn't enjoy an easy lay, yet a little challenge added spice to the mix.

Warren felt a throb as he contemplated the scene and walked to his desk to check his calendar. The last meeting should be over by three o'clock. He'd call Amber and tell her to take part of the afternoon off. Lovely little Amber might be a sure bet, but she was also energetic and inventive. It would be a perfect distraction for the day.

CHAPTER EIGHTEEN

Bev managed to zip her Spitfire through traffic and cleared Miami with minor delays.

Hank had not exaggerated about the Blue Garden. The main dining space and bar were in breathtakingly lush garden settings with multiple water features that compensated for no beach view. It was not a spot T-shirt clad tourist families would stumble across and the menu prices would dissuade rowdy college students. Hank's father and sister had been in the restaurant and when Bev said she needed something light, they brought out a crustacean salad on a bed of mixed greens that caused her to gasp with the first bite. The tastes were incredibly complex and she broke her usual rule about booze on duty. The meal deserved a glass of crisp white wine. Hank had been correct about the food almost making up for no useful revelations from Senator Randall or Noonan.

The memorable meal had been followed by confirmation of the third set of prints from Shepard's car belonging to Cindy. When Bev called Les to tell him what she found out – or hadn't found out was more like it – he suggested they go back through Cindy's background. Perhaps there had been a jilted boyfriend people had forgotten or someone who *wanted* to be a boyfriend that everyone overlooked. Either possibility was easier to imagine than a random act even though Verde Key wasn't immune. Other small, quiet towns had been shocked by kidnappings and murders, but it was just too weird to think that a complete stranger had come into town and somehow targeted Cindy Green.

She'd thanked Hank for his time and the fantastic lunch and he'd smiled in a way much too reminiscent of Kyle. It was unsettling that she'd gone through the entire meal and not thought about him. Definitely time to head south. Hank walked her out of the building and told her she didn't need business as an excuse for a visit. *Oh, yes she did!* She managed a professional sounding good-bye and spent the next thirty minutes mentally listing Kyle's good qualities.

Then she shoved brown and cornflower blue eyes to the back of her mind, cranked up the radio and lip-synced to Jimmy Buffet's *Tin Cup Chalice*. The evening shift was on when she reached the station and Les had already left. Only two messages of interest. Chris was on her way to Kentucky and would return Monday. She could be reached at her parents' house. Too bad Bev didn't have anything to tell her. Kyle was due in on a late flight and did she want to have dinner Saturday? God, yes! She dialed his cell phone, got the automated voice mail and set up the date, with time and place to be determined.

Bev booted up the computer, opened the Cindy Green file and transcribed her notes of the day's activities, less lunch. She wrote without perceptions she'd developed during the conversation: the way Senator Randall made it clear they would follow his agenda, the coldness that emanated from Noonan. Well, Randall was accustomed to people kissing his ass and Noonan wasn't being paid to be friendly. Innocuous, unemotional facts when she read them on paper. The interview held nothing of substance, a dead end when read objectively.

So why couldn't she shake the feeling that Noonan had been screwing with them? Because she took a dislike to him the moment they met? Because she was making something of nothing? Because she was despairing of finding answers? Because she couldn't figure out why an accountant who'd never even had a speeding ticket would confront a state senator with an unloaded gun? If revenge for the death of his sister was the motive, why had he waited twenty years? And who had stuffed Cindy into the trunk of her own car?

Bev sighed and printed the pages for the paper file. It was Friday and happy hour was underway at the Scarlet Macaw. She might as well soak her perceptions and questions in a beer or two.

Two beers became three and the blackened wahoo special sounded appealing. She'd had an early start the past three mornings and by nine o'clock she decided to leave while she could still drive with some semblance of sobriety.

She didn't set the alarm clock and when she roused from a heavy sleep the next morning, she realized it was almost ten. *Damn, she had been tired!* She rolled out of bed and swayed into the kitchen, ready for the blissful lift of that first cup of coffee. She inhaled the hearty aroma of the beans as she measured them into the machine with the built-in grinder. It might not have been the most romantic gift Kyle could have come up with for her birthday, but he'd delivered it with a red rose in a bud vase and a bottle of champagne.

She was well on her way to coherence when the telephone rang and she hoped it was Kyle and not her mother. She didn't have enough caffeine in her to handle either gossip or a barrage of questions.

"Hi, there," Kyle said. "Got your message."

She took the telephone from the base and wandered to the table by the bay window overlooking the park.

"Good, how was your trip?"

"Okay," he said and didn't sound as if he wanted to elaborate. "I'm going into the office for a while. Is seven tonight okay and do you want to go out or come here?"

"Make it here instead," Bev said. "You want anything special?"

Kyle laughed. "Do you mean for dinner or otherwise?"

A promising response. "I meant from a dining point of view."

"Surprise me," he said. "I'll bring a white and a red. See you tonight."

Bev smiled into her coffee mug and watched out the window as a brown lizard ran along the sill. She'd have one more cup and go for a short run to work out the kinks of sleeping late. If she was going to cook anything other than frozen lasagna, a trip to the grocery store was required. Neither her mother nor Aunt Lorna had been successful in turning her into a cook of their caliber, although she had a respectable repertoire of no-fail dishes. Kyle had been in the land of beef and pork so maybe she'd do crab-stuffed flounder. He might be in the mood for something that didn't have hooves. The lizard reversed its path and darted in pursuit of a prey Bev couldn't see – hunting and gathering time in the animal kingdom, too.

Grocery shopping was only a part of the duties to be accomplished and the rest of the day dissolved with associated chores of cleaning, putting fresh sheets on the bed and finalizing the menu. Bev had never mastered the art of multi-course meals. She made salads and homemade guacamole ahead of time and then turned to preparing the fish. She set the flounder on a lightly buttered foil-covered cookie sheet and gently mounded seasoned lump crab down the center of each fillet. She covered the sheet with plastic wrap and shoved it into the refrigerator. The bakery section had yielded cheese bread so fresh it almost got squashed on the trip back to the apartment and they'd had a rack of half-size fudge pecan pies. Twenty seconds in the microwave, a scoop of vanilla ice cream and dessert would be ready. If they made it through dessert before adjourning to the bedroom. Actually Bev was in the mood to have Kyle as the appetizer, but she didn't want to seem too eager.

She called for a mother-daughter catch-up to ensure the telephone wouldn't interrupt at an inappropriate time and then changed into a soft, cotton paisley-print caftan with jade-colored buttons down the front. *Two buttons undone or one?* One from the top and two from the bottom and a spot of perfume in the cleft of her breasts. *Hair up or down?* Down and held back from her face loosely with a malachite clasp. Wouldn't do to have strands of hair falling into the flounder.

The table was set and Bev had filled the CD holder with a stack of Windam Hill when the doorbell rang. She pushed the play button and wondered briefly why she'd never given Kyle a key. On the other hand, she didn't have one to his place either.

"Don't you look delicious?" Kyle said as she opened the door and struck a look-at-me pose. He held a paper bag under one arm and reached for her with his free hand. He stepped inside, pulled her close for a kiss and pushed the door shut with his foot.

A lingering kiss, not the perfunctory kind of a relationship taken for granted. A kiss that said *I missed you* even if neither of them had uttered the words yet.

"You're looking pretty tasty yourself," she said when they broke the embrace. "Did you get caught up at the office?"

"What I didn't get done can wait," he said and walked to the pass-through of the galley kitchen. He set the paper bag on the wide counter and lifted out a bottle of cabernet sauvignon and a pinot grigio. "The pinot is chilled so we can have it now or with dinner."

Bev took the bottle of white and pointed to one of the stools. "With dinner. You want a beer, a margarita or the red? I made guacamole." She swapped wine for the terra cotta dip bowl and took out the cookie sheet.

"Your flounder? One of my favorites," Kyle said. "A beer is good."

Bev took two pint glasses from the freezer, red ale from the refrigerator and handed the glasses, beer and opener to Kyle. She put the bowl into the space in the terra cotta chip holder and set the oven to pre-heat.

"How goes your investigation?" Kyle slowly poured the beer. "It didn't get much play in Illinois." He handed Bev the first filled glass. "They had an update and re-hash when you found the body and not much else. The boyfriend, I gathered."

"An unexpected piece of information from a reliable witness," she said with a tiny shake of her head. "Timing means it couldn't have been the boyfriend. Puts us almost at square one."

"Bummer," Kyle said sympathetically and scooped a chip into the dip. "What now?"

"Start looking for someone else with motive. I ran up to West Palm yesterday to chase down a possible lead and came away with not much useful, although I did get a dose of Senator Randall's renowned charm."

Kyle grinned. "You don't sound like you were impressed."

Bev shrugged. "The first few minutes were okay and then he started playing to the audience. Very politician-like with smooth talk and not saying much. I think Hank and I got two sentences from Noonan."

"Hank? Who's Hank?" Kyle asked and stopped a dip-laden chip part way to his mouth.

"Hank Rodriguez, one of the West Palm detectives," Bev said nonchalantly. "He's handling things from that end. Nice guy." *With a terrific body and great eyes*, she didn't add. "And speaking of Noonan, he *was* in Chicago before joining the senator."

Kyle nodded. "Yeah, my pal checked around and found someone who remembered him."

"Was he dirty, by any chance?" Bev asked. She turned for a moment to spread softened butter across the crab, squirt lemon juice on top and push the fish into the oven.

"Not officially," Kyle said and had her full attention. "He was on the force for about eight years. Active arrest record, several questionable cases to prosecute with tainted evidence, some rumblings of charges of excessive force. There was a shooting that was investigated and ruled clean, but not by unanimous vote."

Bev leaned her forearms against the counter. "Nothing from the other charges?"

Kyle lifted his mug. "Not after one of the people making allegations was found floating in the lake."

Bev raised her eyebrows. "Case never solved?"

"Drug dealer and assorted other crimes. He had dangerous business associates, no witnesses, nothing solid to go on," Kyle said and finished his beer. "Anyway, Noonan was under the wing of a senior guy who was eventually burned, but Noonan wasn't caught in the net. He did, however, quit the force not long after the heat died down and went into private security work."

"Saw the light and became a model citizen?" Bev asked and pointed to Kyle's empty glass.

Kyle shook his head and put his hand over the top of the glass. "Fell off the scope is more like it. The DA's office had nothing else on him. One of his major clients is periodically poked into by the organized crime guys, but Noonan was never a target. No specific interest in his leaving Chicago. Sorry."

Bev kept her head turned toward Kyle as she moved to the refrigerator. "I imagine we could check up on him if I needed to and I've got nothing real to go on. I also have no problem believing he's dirty. He's got the look and the attitude if you know what I mean." She handed the salads to Kyle.

"You ready for me to open the wine?" he asked and took the plates. The wine holder, designed like a galvanized tin bucket with a cooling liner filled with cracked ice, was on the table.

"Sure," Bev said, peeking into the oven window. She switched the dial to broil setting. Enough about work. She hadn't seen Kyle for days and she had to watch the fish carefully. The delicate crabmeat atop the fillets would go from perfectly cooked to charred and rubbery within a minute if left unattended.

She wasn't going to solve Cindy's murder tonight and ruining their dinner wouldn't change that.

CHAPTER NINETEEN

"I'm telling you it comes in threes. You can laugh if you want to, but it's the God's honest truth," Taliah said crisply to Les as Bev came into the station on Monday.

"What comes in threes?" Bev asked, not really caring.

"Death," Taliah answered and shook her finger to emphasize. "It all started with that Jonah boy. Him, the poor girl next and now this other fellow. Hardly a week between them. I don't know what the senator did to bring bad luck on himself, but he should be thanking his guardian angel it was no closer to home than it was."

Bev gave herself a mental shake. What on earth was she talking about? From the look on Les's face, he was ready to retreat. If Taliah was winding up, they could be in for a litany of examples from both sides of her family to illustrate folksy philosophy.

"You have a good weekend?" Bev asked to divert the subject from whatever had gotten her started.

Taliah grinned. "I did and I bet I'm not the only one. I understand there was a certain Explorer seen at your apartment building until late yesterday morning. You've got a fine man and I agree with your mamma that y'all should be making plans instead of dillydallying around. If you keep it up, some other woman is going to think he's there for the taking."

This was hardly the track Bev intended her to jump to.

"Uh, Bev, we really ought to go discuss the case," Les said in exchange for her earlier rescue. "Talk to you later, Taliah."

Two lines rang simultaneously and not even Taliah could carry on three conversations at a time. She waggled her fingers in acknowledgement and chirped a hello to the first caller.

"Nothing like a small town," Les said and followed Bev into their office.

She snatched the mug from the top of her desk. "As long as you don't expect any goddamn privacy in your personal life," she said with more exasperation than rancor. Another cup of coffee would make it tolerable. She held the pot up to Les. "Who died that got

Taliah going?"

"It was a guy in West Palm," Les said and walked over for a warm-up. "Someone on Senator Randall's staff nose-dived his car into the water and it's the three people connected to him that got her started. Taliah doesn't know about Cindy not being exactly a connection anymore." He took a sip and grinned. "According to her calculations, the senator has one more coming."

Bev didn't know how large Senator Randall's staff was. "Who was it?"

Les shrugged. "Started with an *S* – not Smith – Small or Smell something. I think he was a young guy – booze and speed – it was on the news."

Bev hadn't turned the television on when she'd come back from her morning run. "Smallwood?" Noonan's assistant, the second man who'd come down with him.

"Sounds right. He was in his mid-twenties. You meet him when you were up?"

"No," Bev said and sat down thoughtfully. "I was expecting to, but he wasn't in the office and the senator assured me he didn't have anything of value to add."

"Well, he's not the only one," Les said and flipped open the disturbingly thin file. "I got to thinking that since Cindy was a teacher, maybe some kid had a bizarre crush on her. It's a reach, but who used to think teenagers would go on shooting rampages at school? The school's sending a list of students who've been in trouble for any kind of violence in the past year and another list of her students, to include any extra-curricular activities she sponsored. Figured we'd see if there was a cross-match. Then, hell, I guess check the paperboy and if she had regular pizza delivery from anyone."

"Okay," Bev said, logged on to her computer and clicked the regional news tab. The entry in the paper was brief and the headline followed Taliah's theme. *Senator Expresses Dismay at Traffic Fatality.*

The death of Dwayne L. (Rusty) Smallwood, a junior member of Senator Warren Randall's staff, came as another shock to the senator who only recently suffered an assault at his office. Mr. Smallwood apparently lost control of his car sometime in the early morning hours...

Bev read the article as she sipped her coffee. Single car accident, not on a major road, discovered by a county patrol around sunrise. No seatbelt, alcohol was suspected. Two photos – one of the red sports car being prepped for extraction and one of Smallwood that looked like a yearbook entry.

Kevin came into the office with a handful of papers.

"Morning. This fax came in from the high school," he said and glanced at Bev's computer screen. "That the wreck on Smallwood? At least he didn't take anybody else out with him."

Les took the papers and Bev raised her eyebrows. "Did you know him?"

Kevin shrugged. "Not *know* exactly. We booked him and two other kids a couple, three years ago. We got to talking about it after we saw the news this morning."

Be was startled. "What? He used to live here?"

Kevin scratched his head. "Naw. He and his buddies were down and had a run-in with 'Gator Rogers. Busted up Gill's and must have had eight or nine guys going at it by the time we got there." He grinned. "Come to think of it, it started because of Palmetto's."

"Palmetto Paradise?" Bev pointed to one of the straight back chairs. "Why don't I remember anything about this?" Brawls at Gill's were commonplace, but large scale ones usually meant extra hands for paperwork and it wasn't like Bev to forget the big ones.

Kevin turned the chair backwards, straddled it and crunched his face. "Seems like you were gone for some training course. Jim helped us out on it." He turned to Les. "You met 'Gator yet?"

"Don't think so," Les said.

"You'd know if you had," Kevin laughed. "He stands damn near six foot seven, fucking shoulders barely fit through most doors and got hands can palm a basketball like you and me hold a baseball. Used to wrestle 'gators for side money."

"Got it," Les said.

"About Smallwood," Bev prompted.

Kevin propped his forearms on the back of the chair. "Oh, yeah. There was this girl – don't remember her name right off-hand – worked at Gill's and subbed out at Palmetto's when she got the chance. Hell of a lot better wages from what I heard." He winked at Les and Bev made a rolling get-with-it motion with her hand.

"Okay. Smallwood and these other guys had been out at Pal-

127

metto when Crystal – that was it – when Crystal was working and I guess Smallwood took a liking to her. She didn't come back though and he found out she worked at Gill's and went looking for her. Thing is, he didn't know 'Gator was sweet on her. Smallwood thought he was a macho man and he had two sidekicks, although anybody from around here could of told him three against one didn't mean much to 'Gator. Folks told us 'Gator even gave the guy a chance and he made the mistake of trying some karate shit." Kevin grinned and shook his head.

"The buddies jumped in and then, hell, you know Gill's. Things got out of hand and we wouldn't have bothered with it, but the mayor was on one of his clean-up-the-town kicks. We rounded everybody up, booked the batch of them and let the DA sort it out. Wasn't anybody hurt too bad and I think Judge Pickett just fined everybody. The out-of-town boys went home with their tails tucked and Crystal married 'Gator because she said nobody had ever cared enough to fight over her and she wasn't interested in some city kid."

"Nothing like a good love story," Les chuckled.

"Do we still have the file with the statements?" Bev asked.

Kevin shrugged and stood. "Probably, but that was when Mae Jean was here, so there's no telling where they are. Back in the storeroom, I guess."

Bev groaned. Mae Jean, possibly the most incompetent administrative assistant ever foisted on the department and cousin to the mayor's wife. How badly did she want to look at the file? Maybe she could get Taliah to start searching.

"Small world with Smallwood, if you'll pardon the pun," Les said and picked up the lists from the school.

Bev sat still for a moment and sucked her lower lip between her teeth.

Les tilted his head. "Something bothering you?"

"Yeah, but it's hard to put my finger on," she said reluctantly. "I'm not sure of the last time I paid attention to Randall's name and now it's like a daily thing." She shook her head. "Plus I haven't told Chris yet about the timing letting Jonah off the hook. On the one hand, I think she'll be relieved to know it wasn't him, but we don't have a damn thing to give her and we have to start digging again. As hard as it would have been on her, I almost wish it *had* been her ex-husband."

"Too convenient," Les said and passed stapled sheets to Bev. "Why don't you start with the longer list since you grew up here. Maybe a name will jump out."

Bev took the papers and checked her watch. She'd wait an hour and call Adventures Below to see when Chris was coming in. Maybe she'd had some new ideas while she was with her parents. They were due a break.

Bev and Les worked the lists and the telephones for most of the day with no significant progress. Chris called and Bev volunteered to meet her at the dive shop to save her a trip. Chris told her there was a class in session. That meant the shop would be too crowded for a private talk and she suggested the Scarlet Macaw instead.

Bev arrived before Chris. Only one table in the front was occupied and two mid-afternoon bar flies were engrossed in a Braves game. Steve was behind the bar, held up a beer glass and filled it with club soda and a slice of lime when she shook her head.

"Thanks, Chris is coming over and using this as her spare office again," Bev said and took the glass. "She's got a class going and I didn't want her to have to come to the station."

"No problem," Steve said and smiled. "Take the back table. There's better than an hour before the afternoon boats come in. I saw Chris before she flew home and told her that if there was anything I could do to let me know."

Bev nodded and they both looked toward the door when Chris came in. Steve leaned across the bar to receive a peck on the cheek. "Thanks for the beautiful flowers," she said. "It meant a lot to mom and dad. Everyone has been really thoughtful."

"Sure," Steve said. "You hungry?"

Chris brushed aside the offer. "No, and I'm making a point to take it easy on the booze, but I could use an ice tea."

"Brewed a fresh canister toward the tail end of lunch," Steve said and filled her glass. You ladies go take care of your business and I'll make sure you're not disturbed."

"I'm doing okay," Chris said to Bev's unasked question as they wove between wooden tables. "I'm behind at the shop with as much time as I've been out. Danny's been a big help and one of the dive masters who's between jobs is filling in at the counter. There are enough instructors around to call on for classes, but there's business paperwork I have to handle and, of course, there's Cindy's house to get settled and well, you know, stuff."

They sat and Chris looked at Bev. "And there's Jonah's stuff, too. I don't have a clue as to what to do about it. I don't think he has any family at all. I mean, I don't even know what happened to his..., well, him."

Bev pushed the straw to the side of her glass. "Uh, there's a procedure when there's no next-of-kin," she said. "And it's Jonah I wanted to talk to you about. Something came up right before you left."

She gently explained what they'd been told and discreetly looked away when she saw tears glisten in Chris' eyes.

Chris inhaled a deep, wet breath. "Then it wasn't Jonah," she said after a moment.

Bev regained eye contact. "No, but unfortunately that doesn't put us any closer to finding out who it was."

Chris shook her head. "I understand, but you can't imagine how glad I am to hear this. For days now, I've been going over every-thing I knew about him between what Cindy told me, I mean, and the times I was with them. I tried to think about how it might have hap-pened and kept coming up blank. Jonah was a real introvert and could go for days without much interaction, but he had this sad sweetness about him, a real gentleness. I still have trouble believing what he did at that senator's office, but him hurting Cindy was too hard to picture."

Bev picked up her notebook. "Since we also know it couldn't have been Jarrett, we're going to have to dig more. We have to look for anyone who might have had a real or imagined grudge against Cindy."

Chris frowned in concentration and then took a long drink of tea. "I'll try, but I can't remember her ever saying anything about prob-lems like that." She paused and gave Bev a tentative smile. "Uh, now that I know it wasn't Jonah, there's something that may sound strange, but I feel like I should ask because, well, Cindy really was in love with him and I'm sure he was with her. All the tragedy with his family left him what I guess you'd call emotionally stunted and Cindy was convinced she could pull him out of his shell. I have to admit, there were times when he seemed to be happy, like the trip last spring."

Bev was puzzled. "Something you want to do about Jonah?"

"I don't have a lawyer. I mean I haven't needed one and Cindy didn't have one either. Can Kyle recommend somebody? I'll need help taking care of things for Cindy and, well, there's nobody to do for Jonah," she said softly. "If we can work out the legal piece, I'd be able to now. I mean I just couldn't have before, not when... well, you know."

Bev nodded. "Yeah, sure. I'll give Kyle a call this afternoon."

Chris rose and put her hand on Bev's shoulder. "Thanks. I'll get back to the shop if we're done."

Bev stood, picked up the empty glasses and walked with Chris to the bar. A trio of older men had escaped the afternoon sun for the coolness of the bar. They were gesturing toward a ball game in progress on the screen.

Chris said good-bye and Bev tried to pay Steve for the drinks.

"Don't insult me," he said with a smile. "I get enough of your money. Speaking of which, how about a beer?"

Bev laughed. "It's early yet and I'm not done with work today." She glanced at the television to check the score of the game and it flashed to an advertisement before she caught the numbers. "What's with the game?

"Braves up by three, top of the eighth," the nearest man said. "They're number one in the league if it matters this early in the season. Give us another round, Steve."

Bev nodded. A distinguished looking, fifty-something man was speaking sincerely into the camera as text scrolled underneath his image.

"What a jerk," one of the other men said, the sound of Virginia Tidewater in his voice. "The man flip-flops more than I do on a bad mattress. He wouldn't know the truth if it came up and bit him in the ass."

The man who'd ordered the round grinned. "Well, you know what they say. The only way you can tell when a politician is lying is if his lips are moving."

"Ain't that the truth," the third man agreed and exchanged mugs with Steve.

Bev stared at the television screen as the man's face faded. *Son-of-a-bitch! Joke or not, what if the guy had a point?*

Bev waved in parting and drove directly to the office, her mind working from a new angle. Damn, Les was already gone. She'd forgotten he told her he was leaving early. She deposited her purse in the bottom drawer, looked up Hank's number and called.

"Hey, there," he said. "I was hoping you'd be in touch and wasn't expecting it to be this soon. Shall we make a date for dinner?"

Bev laughed, not sure if he was serious. Better to leave it alone. "Actually, we saw the thing on Smallwood down here. Hell of a thing, huh?"

"Yeah, but what can you say? Fast car, booze, and late at night."

"So there's nothing about it that seemed unusual?"

There was a brief silence from the other end. "Bev, what's this about?"

She kept her voice steady. She didn't want to alienate him with what could be interpreted as wild speculation. That was sure as hell what the chief would say at this point.

"It may not *be* about anything, but I was wondering if you could see if this is as straight up as it looks. I would really appreciate it and if there's nothing out of sync, no sweat. The timing strikes me as odd."

Hank laughed. "Any chance this is just an excuse to talk to me again?"

How far should she play that card? No, not a good idea.

"Not my style," Bev said lightly. "Look, I know it's kind of an out-there question, but I really would appreciate it," she repeated.

"Tell you what," Hank said quickly. "I'll do this on the condition you'll come up here if I find something of interest. Fair enough?"

"I can probably manage that," Bev said without a full commitment. *What the hell was she doing?*

"Deal," he laughed. "It'll probably be late tomorrow. Remember, we do have more than one crime at a time in the big city."

"Cute," Bev said. "Very cute."

"That's what my mother says about me," he said and Bev imagined a grin on his face.

"Uh huh. Anyway, thanks and here's my cell number in case I'm not in when you call," Bev said and rattled it off before the conversation could get more personal. "Talk to you later."

She disconnected and mentally shooed away the tickle of chagrin. She was not falling back to feminine wiles to get what she

wanted. Hank was simply one of those flirtatious men and he probably acted the exact same way with every woman.

She punched the speed dial for Kyle's office and for some reason felt a flash of relief when she heard his voice. First she explained Chris's dilemma and he promised to give her a call.

"Uh, the other thing is I was wondering if you would get in
touch with your buddy in Chicago and see if he can find out, or put
me on to someone who can, what went on with Mike Noonan between the time he left the force until he joined Senator Randall's
staff."

Kyle didn't sound surprised. "Yeah, I can try and catch him tomorrow. Are you looking for something specific?"

"I don't know," Bev admitted. "It's one of those feelings and
I'm not going to be rid of it until I check it out."

"Hunch time, huh? The case is pretty much a dead end?"

Bev would have resented that comment from anyone else. Well,
she would have resented it more from anyone else. "I'd rather not
put it like that," she said. "Hey, how about dinner tonight?"

His hesitated for longer than seemed necessary. "Uh, I'd love to,
but I've got some business I have to take care of tonight, well, the
next couple of nights. Let's plan something for the weekend, okay?
I should be free by then."

"Sure, that's fine," Bev said quickly. "Can you let me know tomorrow about the Chicago thing?"

"Yeah, and we'll talk about the weekend later. I may have to go
out of town again. I should know in a day or two."

"Okay, talk to you later," Bev said and slowly replaced the
handset when she heard the dial tone in her ear.

What the hell was going on? Whatever business Kyle had
wasn't likely to be work. The DA himself had been complaining
about the monotony of their caseload with nothing big or exciting to
handle. And another possible trip? What was this problem he was
dealing with? And why the hell didn't he want to share it with her?

She jumped when the telephone rang. Maybe Kyle changed his
mind.

"Honey, we haven't seen you in days," her mother said. No
sense in starting with a cheery hello.

"Why don't you come for supper tonight? Your father had another full charter today and he has to do some thing to the boat so we

133

won't be eating until later. Seven-thirty, I figure. You could come on whenever you're ready."

Oh, why not? Maybe she could get her father alone and they could talk about her fledgling suspicions. He'd been a damn fine cop in his day and could keep conversations to himself when she asked him to.

"Sure, Mom," she said. "I'm about done here and I'll run by the apartment and change. "You want me to pick anything up?"

"No, I've got a mess of purple hull peas on the stove, I'm doing rice and tomatoes right now and I'll fry the chicken in a bit. Myrtle brought me a bunch of nice fresh cucumbers from their garden and I did an icebox lemon pie earlier. And hot rolls, of course. You think we need more?"

Bev couldn't help laughing. "For three of us? It sounds like more than enough. See you in a while."

She wondered briefly if her talent for track and field throughout school hadn't been a defense mechanism against her mother's firm belief in hearty meals and the ever- present freshly baked snacks and desserts. Why Bev hadn't developed the Mitchell women's knack for cooking might be puzzling to Bev's mother, but it seemed pretty simple. Why should she go to the trouble when weekly dinner at her parents and Aunt Lorna's was guaranteed?

Bev shrugged off her disgruntled feeling about Kyle and left the office. She'd set some wheels to turning and it would be interesting to see what kind of answers she'd get. She decided against talking to her father. It would be better to wait until she had a few dots connected. If she were truly flailing about, it would be less embarrassing if no one heard her budding accusations.

CHAPTER TWENTY

W arren wasn't interested in the sound from the talk show. He knew the words had been on target. Terrible tragedy, completely unexpected, a fine young man, our deepest sympathy extended to his family, blah, blah. He was watching his screen presence as he always did. The words were secondary. Any decent speechwriter, and he had a damn good one, could get the words. Delivery. Delivery was the important piece. He'd had too many restless nights lately, sleep long in coming and punctuated with bits of dreams he couldn't recall when he woke. It was all right though. His color was good, eyes clear, jaw firm. There was no sign of extra Scotches to ease his tension from the Shepard fuck-up.

He heard the knob from the adjoining door turn. He clicked off the television, tested the Scotch and water for the right mixture and looked up when Mike came in.

"Lila said you wanted to see me."

"Nearly two hours ago," he said testily. "DeLong is on his way here. Where the fuck have you been?"

"Had business to take care of," Mike said with the lack of deference he'd been displaying since the Shepard killing. At least he was keeping up appearances when other people were around. "DeLong is coming here instead of you to him?"

Warren swallowed half his drink and didn't offer one to Mike. "He likes to pretend he's a regular guy sometimes. Listen, he's going to bust my balls about Rusty. He doesn't believe in no-such-thing-as-bad-publicity. I agree it would have been better if Rusty hadn't been drunk, but it's not like he took out a busload of school kids. Is there anything I should worry about? He wasn't wearing women's clothes or anything, was he?"

Mike made some kind of unidentifiable sound, a cross between a snort and a low chuckle. "No," he said slowly. "Everything looks exactly like it's supposed to. Young guy, too much to drink, out late, fell asleep at the wheel and tanked into the water. Happens three, four times a year in this area."

It took a moment for Warren to fully process what Mike said – or maybe it was his delivery instead of the words. He walked to the closest chair and gripped the back with one hand while clutching his drink in the other.

"Supposed to look? What the hell do you mean?"

Mike brushed past him, took a glass, splashed in a small amount of bourbon and downed it, neat.

"It means Rusty is dead," he said calmly.

Warren lifted one hand and focused on keeping it from shaking. "What the fuck did you do?"

Mike set the glass down carefully. "Rusty wasn't as hard-assed as he thought he was. He got spooked about the detectives coming around. I took care of it."

A flash of light-headedness blinked behind his eyeballs. "Fucking hell! Was that necessary?"

Mike shrugged. "I've got to check out the other sister in Verde Key and thanks to the broad who was here, I have to be extra cautious. Rusty had become a liability. Mr. Bassi is as anxious as you are to get things resolved. He wants to send help, but I told him to hold off and let me handle it. So if that answers your questions, I've got a day or two of stakeout ahead of me."

Warren opened his mouth and realized he didn't know what to say. The intercom buzzed. He walked to the desk and put the receiver to his ear, not sure if he could talk yet.

"Mr. DeLong is on his way into the building," Lila announced without him having to speak. And Mr. Hartwell is with him."

"Thank you, Lila and make sure no one disturbs us," he said in a trained, steady voice. Mike had disappeared.

Goddamn, motherfucking, son-of-a-bitch! He drained the Scotch and wished he had time for another one. Goddamn it to hell! Who the fuck did Mike think he was? Christ, he thought they were going to send Rusty to the islands on a cash run and to get laid!

The door was flung open and DeLong forged in, Freddy Hartwell at his heels. Shit, he didn't need them together, but wasn't it like DeLong to want an audience? He'd just as soon avoid Freddy, but it was virtually impossible considering the flap with Rusty and another round of media curiosity.

Warren swallowed hard, willing his face to relax. "Bill, good to see you," he said jovially and came out from the protection of the desk. "I was surprised at your call."

"Freddy, get me a club soda," he boomed and gestured Warren to the chairs. "Sit down, Warren, while I tell both of you about my lunch with Buddy Skyler."

"Buddy Skyler?" Warren repeated politely and moved into his customary chair before his father-in-law laid claim to it. Freddy would be relegated to the couch.

"Yeah," DeLong said with the sort of smile he usually reserved for lucrative deal closings. "No sense beating around the bush. Buddy won't be running for re-election next fall."

"He told you that?" Freddy sounded surprised. "Who else knows?"

"No one other than his wife and doctor," DeLong said and accepted the glass. "Buddy's got a couple of health problems he's been hiding and they're getting the better of him. Doesn't matter what, he won't be making the announcement for another few months," he said to cut off further discussion. He lifted his glass to Warren.

"You did a hell of a job impressing Tynsdale and his crowd when they were down. Buddy agrees the time is right to put you in Washington."

"The U.S. Senate," Warren said immediately. He'd play it cool with DeLong, rein in the excitement until he heard the rest.

"I'd rather have you as governor, to be honest. It would be more immediately useful," DeLong mused as if it was something he could order from a menu. "But, shit, the incumbent's still strong and with Buddy's backing, you should be on solid footing for his seat. A couple of terms and we'll see which way the wind blows. Well, what the hell you got to say for yourself?"

Warren adjusted his tie. "I'm flattered, naturally," he said smoothly. "I had no idea it would be this soon."

"Keeping your eyes open and taking opportunity before the other guy sees it is what makes for success. I've had an understanding with Buddy about this from the day you won your first re-election." DeLong turned to Freddy. "We'll have a shit load of work to do though revving up the machinery. You'll have to work out a timetable, let me know what you need for resources and all that horse shit. Get things lined up, but keep it quiet until Buddy makes his announcement. We want it coming from him, then a little delay while you graciously acknowledge his endorsement," he lectured. "Okay, Freddy, I need to talk to Warren for a minute, so go start planning your end."

"Yes, sir, Mr. DeLong." Freddy couldn't have scrambled up any faster if there'd been a scorpion stinging his ass. "I'll be in my office when you need me." He had the decency to direct the last comment to Warren.

Fucking toady! But too good at keeping political gears turning for Warren to get rid of him even if he could.

"Okay, goddamn it," DeLong said flatly. "You got anybody else on your staff who's going to do something stupid in the near future?"

How little he fucking knew! "It was too bad about Rusty, but unforeseeable and we got nothing except good play from the thing with Shepard," Warren countered.

"Guess you're right about that," DeLong conceded and stared directly at Warren. "I want you to listen to me, son. This is a big step and once you've made it to Washington, a hell of a lot of other doors will open. Cecilia has got the style for this and she'll do well for you. Way back when you caught her eye, I figured it was a hell of a lot easier to take you under my wing than try and talk sense into a nineteen-year-old."

Cocksucker. He always made sure everyone knew his place.

"I realize I wasn't in the league Cecilia could have had, but I like to think I've made her happy and I've always worked hard for the support you've given me," Warren said levelly. What a balancing act between challenging this asshole and backing off too far! He'd go straight for the throat in either case.

"Hmmm," DeLong said without dropping his gaze. "If she's not happy, she hasn't told Margaret and you've held your end up so far. My point is I'm ready to take you up a few more rungs. Junior senators don't get a lot of immediate attention unless it's bad. I'm not saying become a born-again Bible thumper, but once the campaign gets rolling, you don't need Freddy scrambling around trying to explain why the goddamn cops are in your office."

"Not to worry, Bill," Warren said. "How many off-the-wall things can happen? This weird shit has run its course."

DeLong set his glass on the round table. "I sure as hell hope so." He stood and re-buttoned his jacket. "It's going to be a hell of a thing having a U.S. Senator in the family," he said, good humor evidently restored. "Margaret and Cecilia will probably have to buy whole new wardrobes. That might be the most expensive part of the deal."

Warren stood and laughed. "I'll have Cecilia add the Skylers to the invitation list for next week."

"Not a bad idea," DeLong said and began to walk toward the door. "Make some informal appearances with him, let folks start wondering." He stopped at the door, his hand on the knob. "Don't forget how well Freddy knows the Washington crowd. It's a different ball game and you'll need to pay attention to what he says."

"Wouldn't think otherwise, Bill," Warren said. "My love to Margaret."

He closed the door behind his father-in-law and pressed the cool glass to his forehead. Motherfucking son-of-a-bitch! What a hell of a goddamn time to bring this shit up! The fucking U.S. Senate! Skyler had rolled over his opponent the last two elections and with his support, Warren's success was as guaranteed as anything ever is in politics. This fucking mess with Shepard had to get resolved.

He moved to the bar and debated about one more light Scotch. He didn't debate long – hell, he was celebrating. He filled the glass with ice and trickled the amber liquid over the cubes. It was too bad about Rusty, but what was done was done. Mike had to get to the bottom of the business with whatever Jonah had stashed away and he sure as hell didn't want any interference from Chicago. Too high a probability of clumsy muscle instead of low-key efficiency. If two dead bodies could be considered low-key. Well, three counting Jonah.

Maybe the sister of the dead girl did have access to something she didn't know about or maybe Jonah had been bluffing all along, thinking the threat of exposure would be enough. That would have been pretty stupid, but, hell, the whole damn family had screws loose. If nothing came to light soon, he'd have the financial end under control.

He stepped into the bathroom, switched the light on, took a good look in the mirror and toasted the next junior senator from the great state of Florida.

CHAPTER TWENTY-ONE

Bev strolled into the station, unsure about when to discuss her idea with Les. She'd worked through the revised scenario again during her morning run and flipped it this way and that as she showered. If both Kyle and Hank came up empty on their ends, it would blow her theory to hell and it would be prudent to hold off until she heard from them. Prudence, however, was not her strongest characteristic.

Taliah was waving her forward. "Good, saved me a call," she said. "The chief threw his back out early this morning and has gone to the doc's. Les is on a follow-up about the Stop 'n Go robbery. The chief is the guest speaker at the Lions Club luncheon today and he said to get you to cover it. It's eleven-thirty at the Marlin Inn."

Bev dropped her head and looked up suspiciously. "What? Come on, Taliah, tell me this is your idea of a bad joke."

Taliah shook her head hard enough to set the orange hoop earrings swinging. "Sorry, Miss Sunshine, it's just the way the morning is shaping up. The chief couldn't even drive himself and you know the doctor is going to give him those pills that make him dopey. Les might get here in time, but it's hard to say, so you're up."

"When the hell are we going to get the deputy chief position filled?" Bev asked in exasperation. "The deputy is the one who makes public appearances when the chief craps out."

"Well, it certainly won't be before eleven-thirty this morning," Taliah said with less sympathy than she should have. "It's the same talk he gave to the Kiwanians in February, but with the updated statistics. You know, the one about plans for the new, consolidated, emergency services facility, and the ratio of population growth with the crime rate. It's sitting on top of his in-box. I cleaned it up yesterday before I went home. Go over it a few times and you'll be fine. Oh, there's a copy of the agenda and a list of the attendees. No one but the usual group."

Bev sighed and walked into the chief's office. Yes, she was familiar with the talk and aside from the fact it was boring, she truly despised public speaking. She never knew what to do with her hands and forget trying to tell a joke. The Lions Club regulars were as harmless a crowd as one could hope for and, Christ, better than eighty percent of them had known her since before she was born. Still, what a pain – roaming around the banquet room, shaking hands, swapping small talk, sitting at the head table, for God's sake, with more polite exchanges, then standing behind the podium to tell them not one single thing they didn't already know, saying pro-longed good-byes as someone suddenly remembered another story about her dad. Ugh! Or worse, someone could want a blow-by-blow description and update on the Green case. No, this was not what she had envisioned as she'd driven to work.

Bev picked up the papers, trudged to her office and made a face at Les's empty chair. Shit, if she'd come in to work instead of run-ning, she'd have gotten the follow-up on the robbery and he could spend a chunk of his day spreading goodwill among stalwart com-munity members. At least he'd made fresh coffee. She dropped the packet Taliah had prepared on the desk, retrieved her mug and stared longingly at the telephone. Maybe Hank or Kyle would call early with something urgent and she could dump the task onto Kevin. He was senior enough in a pinch.

The instrument was stubbornly silent, her voice mail had no messages and when she logged onto the computer, her email was in-significant. She sighed heavily for the sake of anyone who might be listening and took comfort from the idea of the Marlin Inn's blue-ribbon winning pie baker. A wedge of her silk chocolate, pecan or strawberry would almost make up for the aggravation.

Bev spent the morning tweaking the chief's stale presentation, memorizing numbers and transferring key words to note cards. De-spite her reluctance, the gathering was pleasantly banal and the Lions Club president gave a thorough and complimentary introduction considering the short notice in swapping speakers. She rarely lin-gered on the fact that she had made police department history as not only the youngest detective, but also the only female one. Damn, she was a role model for young people and she did bring a fresh per-spective to local law enforcement.

She was in a better mood when she finally slipped away and brought Taliah a slice of peach pie. She'd relented and brought one for Les, too. She wasn't surprised to see that the chief's office was dark.

"Oh, your fellow is in with Les," Taliah said as she peeked into the container. "He's looking might fine, too, I might add. Such a nice build and, oh, those blue eyes of his."

"Thanks," Bev said and felt a smile start. Did he have something of interest or was he trying to make up for his recent lack of attention? Either would do and both would be better.

Kyle had rolled an extra chair from the corner rather than taking the one at her desk. He uncoiled his tall body when she came in.

"Hi," he said with a grin. "Taliah told me what happened. Les said he was really disappointed in missing his chance."

Les held his hands wide as though protesting the statement being attributed to him.

Bev laid the wedge-shaped container on Les's desk and wrinkled her nose at Kyle. "Just for that, I'm not going to feel badly about bringing only one piece of pie."

"I'm not sure I need to eat for the rest of the day. I got roped into a breakfast meeting my boss didn't want to make," Kyle said and patted his stomach. "If I tell you my buddy in Chicago got back to me quicker than I expected, will I be returned to favor?"

Bev slipped past him with a squeeze to his shoulder and slid onto her chair. "Only if it's the kind of information I want to hear."

Les observed them in a paternal sort of way, an automatic expression he probably didn't think about. "Is this one of those conversations where I should excuse myself or do you want to let me in on it?"

Bev touched a finger to her forehead. "This is business," she said. "I haven't had a chance to tell you that I asked Kyle and Hank Rodriguez to do some checking for me. Did he call, by the way?"

"Not since I've been back," Les said. "Oh, and before you start, I was explaining to Kyle that the Stop 'n Go turned out to be what we expected. It was the kid they fired and a pal of his. They got tanked up the other night and mouthed off about their daring crime. The search warrant should be ready shortly. They're both in town and as far as I can tell, they think we're not on to them so they should be around later."

"Cool," Bev said and turned to Kyle. "Your turn."

He extracted a faxed sheet from his briefcase and passed it to Bev. "Noonan is not a target for anyone, although he does have some interesting connections. After he quit the force, he opened a private security agency and a Mr. Michael Adrini, who works for Victorio Bassi, were clients of his."

Bev cocked her head. "I don't know the players in Chicago."

Kyle nodded. "Bassi is the big fish, relatively speaking. He can't compare to some of the more notorious names and his global reach is definitely limited. He warrants periodic federal and local interest, to include my checking when I was there, however, he doesn't always make the cut for the application of law enforcement resources."

Les scratched his head. "Not big enough to go after?"

Kyle shook his head. "That's part of it, although he's smart and Adrini is a whiz-bang. Bassi is into a lot of shit, but he's got a labyrinth of legitimate businesses set up, plus banking in places like the Caribbean, all courtesy of his financial guru, Adrini. It would take a lot of digging to crack through the barriers."

Bev sucked her bottom lip in. "Where does Noonan fit in?" The name Bassi didn't mean anything, but where had she heard of Adrini?

"Noonan had an exclusive contract for many of Mr. Adrini's, to wit, Bassi's, enterprises in Chicago and he also worked personal security. Not the muscle stuff, but the higher level, electronics and so forth. He did this for three years, then sold his security agency and went directly to work for Senator Randall." Kyle pointed to the paper. "Now for the part that was verbal, not written."

Bev smiled. "Bassi has business dealings in Florida and contributes to Senator Randall's campaigns?"

"Damn, and you've got a dynamite body, too," Kyle said, either forgetting about, or unmindful of, Les. "Okay," he continued when Bev gave him a reproving look. "A lot of the Chicago guys favor Florida and while contact between Bassi and Randall has been infrequent, they have been seen together. It was not long after one such meeting, very above board on the surface, that Mr. Noonan joined the senator's staff."

Les rubbed the back of his hand. "What's the speculation?"

Kyle shrugged. "Like I said, Adrini has set up a number of companies, many legitimate, tax-paying enterprises, not sure how many are in Florida, but I wouldn't be surprised to find out there are several in the Palm Beach area and that Noonan makes routine visits to them."

Bev chewed her lower lip for a moment. "I hate to say this is out of my league, but it is," she said quietly. "Is there any way to check on this or could maybe Hank Rodriguez give us a hand?"

An expression Bev couldn't quite read passed across Kyle's face. "These are the questions you normally have to call favors in for, or give a good reason why you're asking," he said carefully. "I'm not sure I can give a good reason and I'm not sure I want to call in a favor until I have a better idea of where you're going."

Les leaned forward, elbows out. "Have you picked up on something?"

Bev hesitated. Shit, she could handle telling Kyle or Les separately, but she didn't really want to get into this with both of them together. At least not until she heard from Hank. "Not exactly," she said. "The whole business with Noonan has an odd feel to it."

Kyle cleared his throat. "Bev, I sympathize with your problems on this case and don't get pissed, but from a professional perspective, you don't want to go barreling down this path on just a feeling."

Les stood and grinned. "I need to hit the men's room," he said. "Good seeing you, Kyle." He closed the door behind him with a soft click.

"I'm not barreling down anywhere," Bev said with an effort not to snap. "I've asked Hank Rodriguez for some information and if it comes back the way I think it will, I'll want to check more into Noonan. If Hank doesn't have what I think he will, I'll drop it. Okay?"

Kyle glanced at the door. "Two things. First, I know better than to try and tell you to ignore your gut, so I'll only say you need to be super careful with whatever you're up to. Second, what's this Hank like?"

"Like as in how?"

"Is he like Les or Jim or some hotdog?"

Bev narrowed her eyes slightly. "Do you mean is he young or old? Fat and bald or good-looking? Is that what you mean?"

Kyle shrugged. "If you're going to climb out on some limb, maybe you should make sure you're getting reliable information."

Was Kyle jealous?

"I was impressed with him," Bev said. "I think I can trust what he tells me." No reason to mention his bargain about her coming up. He probably didn't mean it.

Kyle picked his briefcase up from the floor. "Uh huh. Look, I'm due back at the office. Sorry about being tied up lately and time is kind of tight the rest of this week. Dinner Friday?"

"You're not going out of town?"

The corners of his mouth turned down quickly and then the semi-frown disappeared. "I don't think so. Let's make plans anyway." He pushed away from the chair.

Bev rose, stepped close and put her hand on his arm. "Kyle, is there something I can help with?"

He tightened his jaw, but his voice was steady. "Look, there's sort of a family thing at home. Nothing that involves us. Think about what you want to do Friday."

Shit, what was the deal? Why wouldn't he tell her?

"Sure, okay," she said. "Thanks for the word on Noonan."

Kyle stepped to the door, opened it and paused. "Yeah. I'll call you later."

Les must have been watching for the coast to clear because he came into the room almost the moment Kyle left.

He took the container of pie, put it in the refrigerator and looked at Bev when the telephone rang.

"Henderson," she said crisply.

"Hi, gorgeous," Hank said silkily. "How's my favorite Verde Key detective?"

"Les will feel slighted," she said. "What timing though. I was just talking about you."

"All good, I hope. You're in luck by the way. One of the cops at the site of Rusty's wreck used to be here and he was in a group I play poker with. He and his wife moved out of town last year and he got on with the county. He didn't mind talking to me."

Bev motioned to Les with one hand. "Hank, Les is here. Okay if I put you on speaker?"

He laughed. "You think I won't dirty to you if he's listening?"

She really ought to tell him to quit that nonsense. "Very funny," she said as Les pushed the door closed and sat down. Bev punched the speaker button. "What have you got?"

"Hey, I thought we had an agreement about you coming up here," Hank said in mock protest. "This telephone stuff only goes so far with me."

"If it's good, I may seriously need to make another trip," Bev said.

Hank's bantering tone switched to pensive. "I'm not sure how good it is. There are a couple of details that may be nothing at all. The investigation wasn't intensive. There's a bar and grill a few miles away and the waitress remembered Rusty with two other guys. Said they were there until late, but left before last call. Said Rusty had been putting away tequila shots and the others were drinking beer. The bottle found in Rusty's car was bourbon. The car went headfirst into the water, but there were some scratches on the rear bumper that looked fairly new, although as loaded as the blood alcohol level showed, he may have bounced off a tree before he plowed in."

"Who were the guys with him?" Bev asked quickly.

"Nobody in sight when the cops found the car, no evidence of anyone else having been on the scene," Hank said. "No one called in a report. Whoever it was must have gone their separate ways beforehand. Either they didn't realize Rusty was wasted or didn't care."

"One other question," Bev said and gave Les a hang-on-I'll-explain signal.

"Yes, I'm open for dinner tomorrow and I think you should plan on staying overnight. It's too long a drive to start back late at night."

"I mean about the accident," Bev replied. "You said the county cops found him. Where was this place?"

"It's between here and Fort Pierce. The bar is at an intersection of two county roads. Why?"

"Seems like a long way to go for a drink," Bev said and realized she was doodling on her notepad. "Rusty didn't live out there, did he?"

She could hear the sound of papers being moved. "If this home address is correct, the answer is no, he didn't. Want to tell me why you're asking?"

"Because it bothers me that Rusty Smallwood got killed in an accident right after we're in the senator's office."

Les opened his eyes wide and Hank made a noise that might have been a muffled yelp. "Are you and Les the only ones listening?"

"Yes," Bev said cautiously.

"Les, I thought this woman was highly intelligent in addition to being hot, but I'm beginning to wonder. Is she prone to fits of insanity?"

"That's not funny," Bev said abruptly. "Look, I admit we don't know much about each other and I don't want to get you in trouble, but I have a feeling that won't go away. If I ask nicely, can you please talk to the ME and see if he or she noticed anything unusual? I swear I won't ask another question if they say everything was normal."

The silence on the other end was punctuated by a small sigh. "I have no idea why I'm going to agree to this, but it will cost you a dinner, either way."

"Thanks, I truly appreciate it," Bev said before he could change his mind. "You still have my cell phone number?"

"Yes, but I get your home phone as part of the bargain," Hank replied. "It's only fair and it might be late when I get to the ME."

Bev recited her number and ended the conversation when she saw Les drumming the fingers of one hand impatiently.

"I need to look up one more thing and then I'll explain," she said in a rush and flipped back through the report that Hank had given her the day she was in his office. Adrini. There it was.

"Time's up," Les said bluntly. "What kind of wild goose chase are you on?"

Bev shook her head vigorously. "I heard a comment yesterday and got to thinking that maybe we've been looking at this backwards."

Les raised his eyebrows. "What do you mean by backwards?"

Bev swung her chair from side to side. "Let's forget about Cindy for a minute and start from the real square one of Jonah and the senator. We agree it makes no sense for Jonah to have confronted the senator with an unloaded gun."

"Hell, maybe he thought it was loaded. We are talking about an accountant. What does he know about guns?"

Bev spread her hands in the air. "Bear with me. No one has an audio of the conversation between the two men. When the report came out about Jonah's sister, the senator's explanation of why Jonah confronted him made sense. You have to ask yourself though why Jonah waited so long. And if he was there for revenge, why the unloaded gun?"

"Delayed stress shit. Built up over the years. The man was crazy or thought the gun was loaded," Les repeated. "And he hadn't thought about someone like Noonan who would be so quick on the trigger."

147

Bev poked the report on her desk. "That's possible, as would be the death of Cindy at his hands. As we have discovered, however, Jonah couldn't have killed Cindy. Nor could Chris's ex-husband. So let's look at what we know as facts. The name Adrini? Jonah used it as a reference when he made his appointment to see the senator. According to Hank's report, he finished getting Noonan's statement around two-thirty in the afternoon. It was well after six o'clock the same evening when Chris tried to call Cindy. It's two hours and change to drive from West Palm if you miss traffic. Rusty made at least one trip to Palmetto Paradise, an out-of-the-way place. Cindy's body was recovered from Palmetto Paradise. Noonan and Rusty were at Jonah's workplace. Hank and I went to see the senator and Noonan. Rusty was nowhere to be found and we were assured he had nothing of value to tell us. A few days later, Rusty is dead, killed in a single car accident, late at night or early in the morning, in an area where he did not live, no witnesses. Add in the fact that Noonan is an ex-cop, considered to be dirty and has connections with alleged criminal types."

Les stared at her thoughtfully. "Coincidences?"

"Do you honestly believe that? Change it around and say Jonah wasn't there to seek revenge about his sister, or at least not to shoot Senator Randall. If he just wanted to get his attention and scare him without taking the chance on actually hurting anyone, an unloaded gun would be the way to go. Not smart, mind you, but the way someone like Jonah might think."

Les rubbed one hand across his cropped hair. "You figure Jonah had something on the senator? Financial because of the accountant tie-in? Noonan shot him without realizing what was going down and then what? Noonan and Rusty came here, broke into Jonah's place to look for it and Cindy interrupted them?" He worked his jaw and continued in a stronger voice. "They hustle her out of the house for some reason, she dies and they dispose of the body. They still couldn't find what they needed and eventually got into Jonah's office." He slapped his forehead lightly. "The missing hard drives from the computers and the clean one in his office. Okay, for some reason, Noonan decides Rusty can't be trusted and he's eliminated too."

Bev watched as Les blinked rapidly. "Holy shit. No fucking way."

"Except it fits," Bev said in a low voice.

"Oh, man, Jim warned me you could get like this," Les said and blinked again. "Damned if it doesn't fall into place better than what we have." He shook his head again. "No, no, no fucking way."

"Why not?"

"Because it's a hell of a lot easier and smarter to pin this on Jonah," he said with a lop-sided grin.

"Sure," Bev said. "It is, isn't it?"

Les sighed. "Who else have you told?"

"Lucky you, you're the first," Bev said and passed her hand over the telephone. "Notwithstanding Hank's joking around, I'm willing to bet you he finds something not right about Rusty's body and, if he does, I'll have to go up there. I don't want to get too much into this on the telephone."

"When are you going to tell the chief? This ought to send him right up the wall."

Bev sucked in a deep breath of air. "I thought I would wait for Hank to call and if I'm right about Rusty, we'll go in to the chief. We'll have to get West Palm and maybe the county involved."

"I love the way you went from I to we without missing a beat," Les said sardonically. "I don't want the Green case to go unsolved, but I sure as hell hope you're wrong. If you're not, life is going to get way more exciting than I need at my age."

Bev smiled grimly. "And you came to Verde Key looking for small town calm."

Les picked up the telephone and paused. "It was a good plan," he said. "Speaking of small town, let's go wrap up the Stop 'n Go business while you're still available. If the chief doesn't fire your ass, you'll probably be in West Palm a day or two."

Bev smiled coyly. "The chief can't fire me. I'm a role model for young people and bring a fresh perspective to local law enforcement. The president of the Lions Club said it, so it must be true."

CHAPTER TWENTY-TWO

The fledgling robbers of the Stop 'n Go were together in a battered trailer, stoned to the point of being placid about the warrant and talkative about their crime. They'd considerately kept cash in the store's marked bank deposit bag hidden in the inventive spot of underneath a mattress. A pistol, which had been brandished instead of fired, was found in a shoebox along with the cashier's watch. The search, arrest and booking process were time-consuming rather than arduous.

Hank had not called by five o'clock. Bev rearranged some files, tried to think of the best way to approach the chief, gave up at six o'clock and went home. She was contemplating limited choices in her freezer compartment when Hank called.

"I hope I didn't catch you at dinner. I'd like to think you eat at a civilized hour," he said by way of greeting.

"Depends on your definition," Bev said and shut the freezer door.

"I'm more of a nine o'clock person, but I can manage at eight," Hank said, playfully. "Even though we had an agreement, my mother would be distraught if she thought I made a lady pick up the tab. So we'll eat at their place where I don't get charged and call it square."

"You talked to the ME?" Bev could feel the excitement low in her stomach.

"Don't get too carried away," Hank said, his voice less playful. "The ME said there was a contusion to the right temple not consistent with the position of the body. Death, by the way, was from drowning, although the victim was unconscious at the time. What is it you think you know? Why did you want me to check?"

"It's probably better not to get into details over the telephone and I have to talk to Chief Taylor here before I can come up," Bev said carefully. "Is your schedule clear tomorrow? I can get in with the chief first thing and be on the road right afterward."

"You obviously don't believe this was an accident, but it would be nice if you could give me an idea of what the fuck you're up to, if the word doesn't offend you."

"No offense taken," Bev said. "How much would it upset your day if I suggested someone take a very hard look at where Mike Noonan was that night?"

He hesitated long enough to make his point. "Didn't I mention Mr. Noonan works for a powerful man, who is the son-in-law of a much more powerful man? And if I don't end this conversation immediately, how much trouble are you planning to stir up?"

"No more than I have to in order to find out who crammed a really nice lady into the trunk of a car and then dumped her where fish tore off pieces of her body," Bev said calmly.

"I'll drop the attitude if you're not just grasping because you've run out of ideas," he said in a low tone.

"I wouldn't waste my time or yours on that. Chief Taylor will probably rake me over the coals and when he's finished screaming, he'll tell me to get to your place. We can go through lots of formal bureaucracy or you, and whomever you choose, can hear me out and decide whether or not to cooperate."

"I can't promise how it will shake out on this end, but I'll try," Hank said, no trace of flirtation. "If it's going to get nasty, I'll call and alert you. Let me know when you hit the road."

"No problem. What I'd like to do is go to the site where they found Rusty and walk the ground," Bev said. "Look, Hank, I know this will piss some people off and I do appreciate it."

"Hey, I always have the restaurant business to fall back on," he laughed. "I'll see you tomorrow."

Bev replaced the receiver slowly and exhaled. She'd better turn in early. Tomorrow would be a long day and Hank was right about spending the night if she was going to make good on having dinner with him. Gods knows if she found what she was looking for she would owe it to him.

She selected a packet of chicken divan from the freezer, popped it in the microwave, rummaged in the cabinet for a rice and vegetable side dish and pulled a package of salad from the refrigerator. One serving left and no slimy smears of spoiled lettuce. Opening bags and punching buttons was as much culinary challenge as she was up for this evening. She thought about calling Kyle to tell him she might not be home the next night.

Why? They didn't have plans and it wasn't like they'd been spending a hell of a lot of time together lately. Like most couples, they'd started with only weekend dates. Their pattern of dinner once or twice a week had evolved without either of them making it a formal arrangement. Kyle had said whatever he was dealing with had nothing to do with them, but maybe he felt like they were spending too much time together. Thanks to her mother's nagging, she *had* been inviting him to more family gatherings and maybe he thought she was trying to send him a message. She'd put an extra toothbrush, a can of shaving cream and a packet of disposable razors that never touched her legs in the bathroom to make it convenient for him when he slept over. He might have misconstrued her intentions, although it wasn't as if she'd offered him closet or drawer space.

The microwave beeped. Oh, the hell with it. If she spent the night, she'd check her voice mail for a message. If he weren't trying to reach her, it wouldn't matter if she were in town or not. She looked at the meal she was preparing and thought about the Blue Garden. Staying over would have some good points.

Bev was on the road by ten o'clock the next morning nonplussed by the chief's profanity-laced warnings. It was Les's first experience with Chief Taylor's temper cranked up, although as Bev explained on her way out, full scale was reserved for genuine, preventable screw-ups.

His, *"Are you out of your fucking, goddamn mind with this bullshit?"* actually meant, *"I wish to hell you hadn't come up with this, but it sounds like you might be on to something and I'd rather know the truth than worry about political fallout."* Chief Taylor was a good cop with a depth of integrity that in no way included gentleness with his staff. As he once remarked to Bev, "Mentoring means you get your ass chewed and not fired – now get the hell out of my office."

Les wished her luck and said he'd keep working the so-far dead end idea of another individual in town who had grievances against Cindy.

Bev called Hank from a gas station and told him she was on the way and please not plan on a leisurely lunch. He told her he'd left word at the front desk and she could come straight to the office when she arrived. She took that as a good sign.

She paid more attention to her route and how long the drive took than she had on her previous trip. She felt total satisfaction at confirming the time frame would have worked for Noonan getting to Verde Key after his interview with Hank.

The woman on the desk buzzed Bev immediately after she flashed her badge and Hank walked her down the hall to the office of the deputy police chief.

Owen Barrett shook her hand with a respectable grip and waved them both to sit. He was an inch shorter than Bev, had a desk-bound softness to his body that might have once been sturdy and a square face with pale eyebrows. His green eyes were not unfriendly and he spoke with little inflection.

"Your Chief Taylor telephoned this morning and Chief Holland has delegated to me until we have a better idea of what our real situation is. Detective Rodriguez and I had a discussion earlier and I think it would be easiest if you explain exactly what your theory is."

Bev took advantage of having laid it out for Chief Taylor and quickly covered the salient points.

Hank was silent and Deputy Chief Barrett nodded. "For the sake of argument, let's assume for a moment that Mr. Smallwood's death was not an accident and your homicide is linked to it. From your perspective, are you saying Senator Randall should be a target of investigation?"

Bev spread her hands. "I could go either way. Noonan has markings of a loose cannon. I'm convinced Mr. Shepard had something on the senator, something Noonan didn't know about at the time he killed Mr. Shepard. If the senator dispatched Noonan, as I believe he did, in order to try and recover some sort of incriminating evidence, everything that happened after that may have been independent actions," she said and saw relief flash through Barrett's gaze.

"Again, for the sake of argument only, you have no actual idea of what Mr. Shepard's evidence is, if it exists? You assume financial, but could it be something else, like some sort of marital indiscretion? Additionally, if Mr. Noonan felt Senator Randall's career was being threatened, he might have taken independent action without prompting."

"Uh, yes, I suppose so," Bev said.

Deputy Chief Barrett did not blink. "In other words, we have no solid reason to believe Senator Randall is personally involved in any criminal activity? After all, when you told him about the girl, he would not necessarily have leaped to the conclusion Mr. Noonan was at fault and there is certainly no reason for him to think Mr. Smallwood's death is other than as reported. Are those fair statements?"

Bev understood then. Was the man part lawyer? If forced to investigate Noonan, they were already providing Randall with cover.

"I can't really say," Bev replied flatly. "We don't know enough about Mr. Noonan."

"My point precisely," Barrett said. "I've authorized Detective Rodriguez to work with the county solely on the question of Mr. Smallwood's death. If, and I emphasize, if, the death appears to be homicide, it will be treated as such. If Mr. Noonan becomes a suspect in the course of normal investigation, Detective Rodriguez will act accordingly. We see no grounds for bringing Senator Randall's name into this and we assume you will cooperate in this position."

Nothing like weasel-wording. Bev bit back her initial response. It wouldn't be smart to poison the well just yet. "I understand your concern and I'm only asking that we look carefully at all the evidence." Chief Taylor would have been proud of her restraint.

Barrett stood. The discussion was obviously over. He smiled politely. "Good. As I explained to your Chief Taylor, we're always glad to help fellow law enforcement officers as long as we proceed with due caution. Detective Rodriguez is clear on what he should be pursuing. We'll meet again if anything of merit comes to light."

"Yes, sir," Hank said quickly and opened the door to the office. "We're clear on this." He put a hand to the small of Bev's back and exerted pressure she took as a "don't say anything else" sign.

He hurried her back to his shared office that was thankfully empty again and began to laugh when they were alone.

"I hope you don't play poker, because I bet you don't bluff worth a damn," he said.

Bev was more irritated than angry and she didn't think she could blame Hank. "Are you going to tell what that bullshit was about?"

He drew a diet Coke out of the refrigerator and held it like a peace offering. "Some good old-fashioned cover-your-ass talk is all. Nobody is trying to do a cover-up, but ain't nobody going to stir this around if you're wrong. Politicians aren't popular, but the guys at the top aren't messing with William DeLong's son-in-law unless it looks iron-clad."

Bev swigged the diet Coke and narrowed one eye. "You don't think Randall is totally in the dark, do you?"

He shrugged. "Active denial can be a wonderful tool and if Noonan can't be directly linked, you're sure as hell not going to make anything stick on the senator."

Bev pursed her lips and waited a moment. "Okay, I'll leave it for now. I want to talk with the attending ME and go out to the site. What sequence suits you?"

Hank shook his head in mock reproach. "I caught the ME this morning before I went in to see the deputy chief. She's gone until tomorrow. I'll tell you about it while we drive."

Traffic was moderate and soon after leaving the station, Hank pointed out a heavily trafficked boulevard.

"Remember when we went to Senator Randall's office? It's down that street, a left, then two streets over. Anyway, there are several apartment complexes on the major street, a bunch of bars and restaurants. The residents are mostly singles or younger couples without kids. It's a cut below waterfront, but a swinging kind of area."

"You live there?"

He grinned and tapped the window with a knuckle. "No, I'm closer to my parents' restaurant. Rusty had an apartment there and a couple of favorite bars."

Bev raised an eyebrow. "You checked up on him?"

"It wasn't much out of my way last night and you piqued my curiosity. I had his home address and it didn't take a lot of legwork."

She shifted to face him. "What did you find out?"

"No current girlfriend and in both places where he regularly hung out, they said he'd been boozing more than usual. He'd come in late, drank until closing time and stagger out. Seemed kind of down, but wasn't talking. He wasn't causing trouble for anyone so they figured it wasn't their business. Care to guess what his drink of choice was?"

"Tequila?"

Hank grinned. "Nope. He was a bourbon man, usually Black Jack. One of the bartenders said he only drank tequila when he was really looking to get wasted."

Bev sucked her lower lip between her teeth for a minute before she spoke. "So, if you wanted to make sure someone thought Rusty had been drinking and driving, what would you put in his car?"

"A bottle of Jack Daniels, Black," he said and accelerated when they cleared the city limits. "Like the nearly empty one they found."

"Well, what do you know," Bev said. "The ME had something good, too?"

Hank passed a truck with a load of watermelons and cut behind a red Explorer with two kayaks mounted on top. "She said it was suspicious. He didn't have his seat belt fastened and the impact to his face was consistent with what you would expect. There was, however, a contusion to the right temple. Given no seat belt, he could have flopped around, but, in that case, the damage should have been to the left temple and signs of impact from the door frame would be to the left cheek and jaw."

Bev made a fist and moved it gently into contact with Hank's right temple.

Hank whipped past the Explorer. "Rusty was decent size. It would take a big man to knock him out with a punch."

Bev curled her hand around the neck of an imaginary bottle. "Well, how about a full bottle of bourbon?"

"I think that would do it," he said quietly.

CHAPTER TWENTY-THREE

Hank turned at an intersection, went another mile or two, made a second turn and jerked his thumb behind them. "The Orange Blossom is back up the road three or four miles. That's where they were."

He came around a curve and slowed, a county patrol car pulled off the narrow shoulder, partially onto the grass, blue lights flashing. "Jerry Hooper, the pal I told you about."

Bev clamored out of the car as soon as Hank tucked in behind the other one. A man unfolded from the vehicle. His tall, lanky frame was that of a high school or college basketball player, but not the size pros ran. Big hands and a wide mouth with a slower smile than Hank's quick grins. "Hey, Henrico," he said and punched his arm in lieu of a handshake. "How's life uptown? Your mama and daddy doing okay?"

"They're good," Hank said and waved his hand to Bev. "Bev Henderson, meet Jerry Hooper, who goes by Hoop. He's a piss-poor poker player, but got a sweet jump shot."

Hoop's large hand engulfed Bev's. "Nice to meet you," he said and ignored the other comments. "Hank likes his little mysteries and I'm not sure why we're gathered at the river, so to speak."

Bev studied the layout. The water banked into dense shrubs and trees. The shoulder and a short strip of grass were all that separated it from the two-lane road. It was logical to accept a car making a deadly mistake. The sod was still torn from where Smallwood's car plowed in. There was no traffic even though it was mid-afternoon and the road was straight. At night car lights would be visible from a long distance.

Bev lifted her chin in the direction the cars were pointing. "What's further that way?"

"Nothing except a boarded up fruit stand for about five miles," Hoop replied. The road T's into one of the big orchards; got small towns both ways a few miles after the T and you can connect back to the main route you were on. That's why you don't get much traffic."

Bev covered the few paces to the water's edge. "When did they find the car?"

"After daylight and morning shift change," Hoop said. "My partner and I were second car on the scene around seven o'clock. The car was nearly submerged and if anyone had been along, they wouldn't have seen it in the dark." He swept his hand to the road. "No skid marks, so probably fell asleep at the wheel and swerved in. Body was in the driver's seat, no seat belt, air bag collapsed down, no sign of struggle to get out."

He and Hank walked down to stand beside Bev. "Anytime y'all want to tell me what this shit is about, I'll listen," he said.

"There was no sign of another car or any footprints or anything?" Bev asked instead. "And were the windows down?"

"Hoop, we've got some loose ends from another case we're trying to work through," Hank explained. "Smallwood wasn't from this area and the ME found a couple of things that raise questions."

"No shit," Hoop said and tromped across the grass. "It was a single-car entry, no other tire prints, no footprints. Windows were down and the bottle was underneath the body's feet, but if you look where our cars are, you can see a degree of slope. It basically launched from the road, which is why it didn't drag much on the ground before entry. Speed will do that."

Bev and Hank turned and looked up. It wasn't steep, but was a slope, nonetheless. Hoop strolled to them and followed their gaze. "It looked like a garden-variety accident. Only reason we checked the Orange Blossom is because he wasn't local and that seemed like a good place to start. The Blossom closes at midnight and no one remembers seeing him drive away. Sally said he and the two men he was with left maybe an hour before closing, might have been closer to ten-thirty. A crowd came in around ten and they were short one waitress so it got busy."

He stared at Hank. "I showed her the photo like you asked and she couldn't say for sure. Said the other men were white, both wore caps, nothing special. The reason she remembered the kid was he had one bourbon and switched to tequila."

It was Bev's turn to stare. "What photograph?"

Hank motioned them up the shallow slope. "Tell you later. We've got two cars. Let's try something Bev and I are thinking about."

"We have to reverse direction," Hoop said. "He was in the right lane, crossed the road and went down."

"The opposite way from if he'd left the Blossom and gone back to West Palm," Bev said reflectively.

"Unless he missed the intersection," Hank pointed out. They got into their respective cars and re-positioned. Hank stopped several feet in front and got out to speak with Hoop. He returned in a few minutes and looked at his watch. "Okay, Rusty is behind the wheel, now what?"

Bev held her hand as if around the neck of the bottle. "Maybe we've taken a swig or two. I look, see that the road is empty, but too dangerous to hit him while moving. How do I get him to stop? I tell him I've got to take a leak?"

"Sure," Hank said and nearly jerked his head when Bev swung her arm toward his temple. He slumped to the side. She took a tissue from her purse, wiped the imaginary bottle clean, pressed his hand around the neck twice and thrust her hand holding his toward his feet. She unsnapped his seat belt, jumped out of the car, ran to the driver's side, reached across through the open window, worked the stick as if to put it into drive and signaled to Hoop.

He rolled forward, front bumper to rear and cut his wheels sharply to the left.

Hank straightened up and checked his watch. "Shit, right at five minutes and you'll notice not a car has come by. Rolling the windows down wouldn't have taken long either." He pulled onto the shoulder and waited for Hoop.

They walked across the road and stared into the water.

"Smallwood's car was a Firebird. Something heavy like a truck or an SUV could do it," Hank said after a moment.

"If the first blow didn't knock him out, it would have at least dazed him and he was drunk," Bev said. "Even with the air bag activating, he doesn't have his seatbelt on, he slams forward, probably rendered unconscious."

"You stand here and watch. Car fills up, he drowns within ten, fifteen minutes. If someone comes by, you jump down the bank and act like you're trying to help," Hoop said, getting into the scenario. "If he manages to get out of the car, you can risk active intervention. If it all falls apart, chances are he won't remember what the hell happened and you take another shot at it later."

"Son-of-a-bitch," Hank said softly.

A car appeared in the distance and the old black man driving a dented Dodge slowed to a crawl as he saw the lights flashing, but Hoop waved him past. "There was one truck came by right before y'all got here," he said. "and that's been damn near twenty minutes. The deal is, you got nothing to show it wasn't an accident," he said with a grunt. "Remember, I was here and if you put me on the stand, I'd have to tell what I saw. I wouldn't mind speculating, but a smart lawyer would pick me apart."

Bev took off her sunglasses and rubbed her eyes. "You're right, but we had to see if the logistics held up," she said. "We know it's physically possible and that's a big step as far as I'm concerned."

"That's because you're not Deputy Chief Owen Barrett," Hank said with a grin.

Hoop spat on the ground. "Who was the photo of? It looked like a newspaper clipping, but if it ain't the sports section or the funnies, I don't pay attention."

"You don't want to know," Hank said. "Lots of politics."

Hoop made a cross of two fingers in a warding-off sign. "You can keep that shit, for damn sure. You need me for anything else? The radio has already been quiet longer than I was expecting."

"No," Hank said. "I've got a copy of the report you sent."

Hoop nodded. "As far as I know, the case is closed until someone higher than you and me says it ain't," he said simply. He touched his hand to the brim of his hat. "Nice to meet you, Bev. Hank, tell your folks we'll be up for our anniversary dinner next month. My mamma said they'd take the kids and we can go have ourselves a night in the city."

Hank shook his hand and they waited as he flipped off the blue lights and sped away. "I sent him a clipping of Noonan from the paper. It was a nice color shot, text cut off. Too bad nobody recognized him, but Randall makes appearances in this area for ceremonies, shit like that," he said. "And, as you may have guessed, Noonan drives one of those big-ass luxury SUVs, the kind that would eat your Spitfire as a snack."

He grinned when she tried to smother a laugh. "By the way, I went ahead and booked you into a place that's decently priced, near the restaurant and has all the basic amenities. I'll call and cancel if you made other plans."

Bev bit back a retort about being goddamn presumptuous. He'd probably just say he was trying to be helpful and he had done everything she'd asked him to, plus some. Damn, an ID from the waitress would have been useful!

"That was nice of you," she said. "I'm sure it'll be fine." The chief said she was getting soft when she mentioned she might spend the night.

Hank was holding the door open for her and she slid in with a sudden thought that the dress she'd packed might be too revealing. She assumed the Blue Garden was not a blue jeans kind of place and she'd grabbed an emerald green outfit that wouldn't wrinkle in the confines of an overnight bag. It was sort of clinging though and had a slit up one side. Maybe she should have gone with something more conservative. Well, too late to worry about it.

"Any idea of the second man?" Hank asked and cranked the car.

Bev shook her head. "Not a clue. I guess Noonan would have access to extra muscle if he needed it. I'm fuzzy on how the guy in Chicago ties in, to be honest."

Hank pulled onto the road. "I can answer that in a general way. The really big boys have places like Miami carved up and I doubt Bassi is in their league. On the other hand, we've got a high tourist/transient population like the rest of the coast. Hotels, restaurants and other service businesses are mainstays, not to mention land development deals going on every second. Those are great means for washing cash."

Bev twisted in her seat. "How?"

"I could use the restaurant as an example, but I wouldn't want you to get the wrong idea," he said and smiled. "Didn't you say your dad had his own fishing charter business?"

Bev nodded.

"Okay, he has maintenance like marina fees, supplies and what have you and gets paid from customers. He probably does some cash transactions, but check and credit cards mostly from his customers. Suppose he never had to write a check to a supplier and could use all cash? And suppose the cash came in from a non-taxable, external source so he could declare as profit practically every dime he took in from clients? Perfectly legal profit he pays taxes on, but a high percentage of the overhead is covered? That would be a good deal, wouldn't it?"

161

Hank was using his hands as he spoke and Bev almost wished she hadn't asked the question.

"Guys pick up several cash heavy businesses, have couriers run money down and pump the profit through a series of legitimate corporations. Spread it out, keep it at a low, yet steady level, make it hard to figure who owns what and the money-trackers will spend their time going after the billions instead of smaller amounts. If Bassi has someone smart enough to set it all up, he doesn't need but one or two guys in each business who actually know the deal and he has someone else who serves as a watch dog."

"Like Noonan?"

Hank slowed for the red light at the intersection of the main road. "Having a state senator in your pocket is helpful, too," Hank said and shot forward faster than Bev would have. "Men like Bassi are big on family, but he might not have enough relatives to cover here and Chicago, so he could bring in a guy like Noonan. If that turns out to be the case, though, it could get real sticky, real fast."

Bev didn't want another reminder of Deputy Chief Barrett. "Let's do this one thing at a time. I probably ought to care about potential political corruption and money laundering, but right now I'd rather deal with homicide. It seems cleaner than money laundering."

Hank's grin was just too damn cute for his own good.

"Alleged homicide for us," he said. "Oh, come on, it wasn't a home run, but I'd say we got a double," Hank said when Bev frowned. "We've scoped out the scene and we know Senator Randall has been here which means Noonan has been, too. We know Smallwood was with two men."

"A positive identification would have been nice. Your deputy chief was rather explicit about circumstantial evidence."

"Yeah, and he also said if we can show it was a homicide, we could proceed. The car is still impounded and I can put the forensics team on it. Maybe they can find something."

Bev frowned. "No good. I'm willing to bet that Noonan was the one in the car and since they work together, he could have ridden with Smallwood a hundred times."

Hank grinned. "You're impatient," he said. "Listen, what you've come up with makes people uncomfortable. You've convinced me it was Noonan and he'll have overlooked a piece of evidence or someone we didn't expect will come forward. It's tough to cover all the details in two homicides without making a mistake somewhere."

"And Senator Randall? What's your feeling about his involvement?"

He made a face like sucking on a lemon and then relaxed. "I'm invoking your comment about one step at a time. Let's go back to my office, lay out what we have and decide what the next step should be. On a more pleasant note, is eight o'clock okay for tonight?"

"Sure, but I want to get an early start in the morning," she replied. "I thought I'd take off around seven."

"How business-like. I was planning to show you the town. Have dinner, maybe do a little dancing. You know, enjoy the nightlife and keep going through breakfast."

She didn't want to ask precisely what he meant by *nightlife*. "Not on a school night," she said lightly. "I'll have a full day tomorrow and I can't afford no sleep and a hangover. It's harder than in my college days."

"Ain't that the truth," Hank agreed. "We'll keep it to a leisurely dinner and save dancing for another time."

Maybe she should mention that she and her boyfriend, Kyle, didn't usually go dancing. No, too awkward. An opportunity would come up to work him into the conversation during the evening. Right this moment, boyfriends and disconcertingly attractive, single detectives were second priority to a murderous ex-cop, a slippery politician and whatever other snakes might be hiding under more rocks she was planning to kick over.

CHAPTER TWENTY-FOUR

Hank set her at a desk with an empty in-box, a round plastic container with pens protruding, an open calendar with *Vacation* scrawled across the week's entry and no papers in sight. A pewter frame held a photograph of a pretty woman standing on a lawn holding an infant on her hip. A small boy clung to her leg with one hand and held a toy space ship in the other.

Bev had yet to meet Hank's office mates, their presence made known from scribbled notes stuck to computer screens. She had no desire for an update session with Deputy Chief Barrett and she deftly by-passed Chief Taylor by waiting to call Les when she thought the chief would be out of the building. Les had been methodically pursuing the Verde Key end and was philosophical about no progress.

"It's like elimination prints," he said neutrally. "You take them so you can cross them off the list. If the West Palm end breaks loose, the shit is going to hit the fan and we'd better be able to show we exhausted every other possibility."

Bev remotely checked her voice mail before she contacted Les. Their conversation trailed to a stopping point. "Uh, Kyle didn't happen to stop by, did he?"

"Haven't seen him," Les said. "You need me to get hold of him?"

"No," Bev said quickly. "I'll give him a call later."

She and Hank ran out of productive tasks and he offered to lead her to the Tropic Breeze hotel. "It's not on one of the major streets and it's close to my route home," he said when she told him she didn't want to put him to any trouble.

Bev waited in the visitor parking lot and Hank pulled his black Porsche along side her. The pay scale for detectives was apparently high in the city. He used side streets instead of main ones and Bev wondered if it was due to traffic or because he liked the way the car cornered on the zig-zag course. The Tropic Breeze was a place that could be easily missed if you weren't familiar with the area. Upscale retail shops and restaurant signs filled the short street with an art gallery directly across from the hotel.

It was a three-story, coral stucco building with arched windows, flowerboxes and terra cotta roof tiles. The U-shaped drive was only four car lengths and Bev didn't see a parking lot or garage. She followed Hank and a valet stepped from behind a desk in the arched, deeply recessed entrance. He approached Hank, opened his door, and proceeded to Bev's car.

"You're with us for one night, Miss? Will you need help with your luggage?"

Bev gathered her purse and briefcase from the seat and swung out of the car. "No, I'll get my bag from the trunk." Hank had said the prices were not bad here, although the term *boutique hotel* came to mind.

Hank took Bev's bag as she swapped keys for a tag from the valet. He flashed her a smile and said, "I'll go in with you and make sure you get the special discount."

"Ah, there is a catch," she said and admired the mosaic of tropical birds in the center of the lobby floor. Four pairs of French doors opened onto a covered portico with empty tables and chairs. Large bouquets of fresh flowers and leafy green plants in clay pots decorated the room. Seating arrangements were quartets of red and gold striped chairs with low wrought iron and glass tables.

Bev didn't see a bar or restaurant sign, although one arrow did point to telephones and restrooms while another indicated elevators.

"Ms. Henderson for one night," Hank said to the woman behind the desk. "She's a guest of Mr. Rodriguez."

"Yes, of course, we have you right here," the woman said brightly as she quoted an absurdly low rate, parking included and Bev gave her a credit card. She'd press Hank for details later. Which Mr. Rodriguez was she a guest of?

"Okay," he said, satisfied that everything was in order. "I'll pick you up at eight."

Bev nodded and turned to the professionally pleasant woman giving the spiel about the location of her room, complimentary breakfast on the patio and an extensive room service menu.

Bev thanked her and found her way to the top floor. She didn't know if all the accommodations were the same, but her room was spacious and airy, tastefully decorated in pastels with better-than-average prints on the walls. The desk was equipped with a telephone and an extra line for a computer. It was obviously a hotel designed for business travelers who wanted a break from franchise giants.

Bev was surprised to see the ice bucket had been filled and the mini bar contained the usual assortment of snacks and beverages. The milkshake she'd had as an on-the-road-lunch had long since disappeared from her system, but she suspected dinner would be a drawn-out, three or four-course affair. She didn't want to spoil it with an over-priced candy bar. She settled for an over-priced diet Coke, kicked her shoes underneath the desk and checked to see that she had a clear signal on her cell phone. She argued with herself and decided against calling Kyle. He could reach her if he wanted to. The voice mails at home were from her mother, Aunt Lorna and Helen. She took care of them, indulged in an episode of the old television show, *The Avengers,* and took a long shower. She was approaching stomach-rumbling hunger as she wiggled into the sleeveless dress. The simple scoop neck stopped just shy of showing cleavage and the fluid fabric fell to above her ankles with a slit up the side almost knee high. She'd remembered to throw in a gold sunburst pendant and matching earrings. She twisted her hair into a knot at the nape of her neck and secured it with a fake tortoise shell clamp. Not fancy, but passable. Okay, more than passable. She was a few minutes early and went downstairs to wait in the entrance so Hank wouldn't have to bother with coming in. After all, it's not like it was a date.

The same valet was on duty and she assured him she didn't need assistance. The art gallery across the street was filled with people and music floated out when a man opened the door.

"There's a special show tonight to benefit one of the community arts programs," the valet said when two black limousines arrived. A tall man emerged from the first vehicle and reached to take the hand of someone inside."That's Senator Randall and his wife," the valet volunteered. "She's big into the art and music programs."

Senator Randall glanced across the street and his eyes stopped for a moment when Bev nodded. He smiled expansively, a politician taking note of a citizen, helped his wife get her balance and turned to speak to a man who had stepped out of the gallery to greet them. Bev couldn't imagine that he recognized her after only one meeting. Hank swung into the driveway and Bev waved him to stay in the car. The valet opened the passenger door almost before Hank had the car stopped.

"Wow, you look terrific," he said and eased out on the street. "What's the occasion and is that Senator Randall?"

A photographer appeared and was taking a group shot of the Randalls, the man who'd come out of the gallery and the couple from the second limousine.

"Thanks, some kind of benefit and, yes, it is," Bev answered in sequence. "I wasn't sure what the evening wear was." Hank was wearing a pair of cream linen slacks and a blue print silk shirt.

"You look perfect and I hope you're hungry. My sister is on tonight and she'll want to show off," Hank said.

"I'm practically starving," Bev admitted and refrained from seizing the dashboard when Hank took a corner considerably faster than she liked. "By the way, what's the deal with the hotel?"

He laughed and patted the steering wheel. "I told you I had a big family and they cover a lot of territory among them. One of my uncles manages the hotel, another one has a Porsche dealership and a cousin runs a men's clothing shop not far from here. Family discounts are why I can look like I'm on the take and yet be an honest and hard working public servant."

Bev grinned. "Oh, good, now I don't have to feel like I'm getting over, but I'm still paying for the evening. We had a bargain."

"You can discuss that with my sister."

The Blue Garden was even lovelier than during the day, the patio setting beautifully lit to highlight the flowers and fountains. Bits of conversations, a jazz group Bev couldn't see, and the clatter of the hustling wait staff blended in a surprisingly harmonious way. The hostess, a cousin, kissed Hank hello, smiled warmly at Bev and sent them to one of the few open tables.

"Mariella has your dinner planned so I hope you're in the mood for seafood," the waitress said when she glided to them. "She said you could select your drinks and everything else is out of your hands."

Hank grinned at Bev. "I would advise you not to argue," he said. "Would you like a cocktail or start with wine?"

Bev could tell it would be a losing battle. "I have to pace myself," she said. "A glass of white for me, but you go ahead with your usual."

"Bring us a bottle of Cumbrero, please, Angela," he said. "I imagine that will go with whatever Mariella is cooking up, if you'll pardon the pun."

"I won't tell her about it," the girl giggled.

"And speaking of telling things," Hank said with a smile. "I know why I don't have a wedding ring on my finger, but we haven't talked about why you don't."

Shit, nothing like being direct.

"You first, you brought it up," she lobbed back with a tiny shake of her head.

"I have enough nephews and nieces to keep my mother busy for now, so I get to slide for a while longer and be the one who parties," he said boyishly. "It goes with the car and the clothes."

"Ah," Bev said and looked up when Angela brought the wine in a bucket atop a stand. She went through the tasting ritual with Hank who nodded in approval. Angela whisked away again and Hank let Bev get one sip in. A Spanish white, not one she was familiar with. Crisp, dry, excellent.

"Quit stalling," he said. "My guess is you're focused on your career."

"Wow, what a leap," Bev laughed. He raised his eyebrows and waited. "Okay, I do get nagged by my mother, but the job does take up a lot of time and Verde Key isn't exactly a large town." Shit, why was she hesitating? She should tell him to keep things on the level.

She lifted her glass and paused. "I am, however, in a relationship."

Hank shrugged. "I'd be surprised if you weren't, but evidently it hasn't reached the ring stage yet."

Bev hesitated. "No, it hasn't," she said and drank some wine. *Did she want it to? Should she even be here with Hank? Was this a date? No. Yes. Maybe. She hadn't meant it that way. Absolutely not. Had she?*

Hank's smile was relaxed, no pressure. "Look," he said and reached for the wine bottle. "I kid around, I'm enjoying working with you and I definitely like the way you fit into that dress, but I don't want to make you uncomfortable. I'm okay with just having a great dinner with a hottie and you can decide how you want the evening to end. Fair enough?"

Bev fought back a flush and stared into his eyes to make her point. "I appreciate the compliments and I'm not a tease, so I'll tell you right now the evening will end in the lobby. If you change your mind about dinner, I'll understand."

"Not a problem," he said and filled their glasses. "I don't intend to take it personally. I only hope Mariella isn't sending out oysters as the first course."

Bev laughed and the budding sexual tension faded.

Angela approached with a tray holding a basket of bread and two silver-domed dishes. She set the bread on the table. "You're starting with lobster in a light curry cream sauce stuffed in avocado," she said and lifted the covers from the plates. "The next three courses are every bit as good, if not better."

Bev looked at chunks of sauced lobster meat spilling from an avocado shell and was glad she'd waited to eat. It wasn't every day she sat in a lovely restaurant and dined on a chef's special selections. Thank God Hank had broached the subject of the evening in the way he had. Kyle's existence was acknowledged and she could relax without guilt interfering with her taste buds.

CHAPTER TWENTY-FIVE

Warren Randall sat on the darkened portico, ice bucket and bottle of Scotch at his elbow. What did it matter that the residents of the neighborhood, less the security patrol and heavy party people, were in their respective beds? Why should he bother? It was more restful to watch the liquid glistening of reflections in the manmade lagoon than to lie in bed waiting for sleep eventually to come only to be shredded with overlapping images and faint whispers that if he listened, would be words of damnation. After a while, the Scotch would fold him into a protective cocoon. It took minor adjustments to begin his schedule later in the mornings. Lila had begun to deftly decline requests for breakfast meetings and wisely asked for no explanation.

Night creatures chorused croaks and chirps as Warren replayed the scene outside the gallery where he'd spotted the female detective at the hotel and seen the Porsche arrive. What the fuck was she doing back? He'd been startled, her presence and attire out of context. An edge he possessed, however, was the ability to register a face with a name, a tidbit of personal information and retrieve it with immediate effect. *Why, Senator, I can't believe you remember me. We only met once and there was such a crowd of us. Well, yes, the restoration project is coming along wonderfully, thank you, and we were so thrilled to have you as a speaker...*

Rodriguez and Betty, no, one syllable, B..., Bev, that was it, hadn't appeared as if they were on business. Perhaps it was a purely social matter. She was a tasty looking piece of ass and he wouldn't blame Rodriguez for making a run at her. A drive from Verde Key on a weeknight for a date? Bev hadn't struck him as spontaneous. Maybe Rodriguez had concocted a plausible excuse or, hell, maybe she was taking a couple of days off. In the middle of an investigation? Not very damn likely. They hadn't called him though, hadn't been around the office. Lila surely would have mentioned if there had been further police inquires.

He shifted in the chair. Goddamn Noonan and this heavy-handed business with Rusty! Hell, he could have sent the boy away someplace where no one would have cared if he'd blabbed his mouth. If an accident had been necessary, there would have been more time and distance with less press coverage for damn sure. And how long was Noonan planning to stalk this other woman, this sister? He said another couple of days and, if nothing turned up, they could figure they were clear.

He was probably right about Jonah not having left whatever he had with a lawyer or reporter. He would have been contacted by now. He couldn't shake it though – he'd seen the look in Jonah's eyes – he'd been too confident to have been empty handed. It had to be financial. He never would have waited this long if he'd known the truth about Lottie and anyway, how could he?

Even if he had gotten the autopsy report and an independent review, the result would have shown death by suicide. There was no way he'd found proof about the baby. She'd only found out a few weeks before and no paternity tests had been run. Warren was certain she hadn't told anyone other than him and Andy was the only one he'd confessed to.

Christ, he'd used a goddamn rubber. How in the hell had she gotten pregnant anyway? What had it been – three times? The bet only called for once, but shit, he and Andy were seventeen and, God, had she been a sweet fuck. Then she'd started in about being in love, getting married and the rest of that horseshit. The tears came, followed by the urge to unburden her sins, cleanse them within the sanctification of the church, she'd said. He had to keep her quiet until he could work out a plan. Then the goddamn baby. What the hell was he supposed to have done? Get saddled with a wife, a brat and her idiotic family?

He tried to talk her into an abortion, he really had. If she'd agreed, it could have worked. He had it all arranged and could have faked his way through the procedure, holding her hand, being sympathetic, promising her they'd be together and have a baby later when the time was right. Kept stringing her along, headed off to college, let her down easy. She would have been too humiliated and afraid of her father to admit what happened. Her father would have beaten her in retribution before he would have demanded Warren do right by her and without the baby she couldn't prove paternity. He could have coolly denied everything and depended on Andy to back him up. Painted her to be delusional or falsely accusing him for reasons unknown.

But, no, she'd been so damn stubborn and he didn't know what else to do. It wasn't really his fault when you thought about it. If he wasn't destined for money and power, why would his life have turned out the way it did? He couldn't be sidetracked by a shotgun wedding. Once he'd come up with the solution, Lottie had been so easy to play. How could he be blamed for her naiveté?

The discordant screech of a bird yanked him from his mental wandering. Let the dead rest. That's what Jonah should have done. If anyone was to blame, he was. Why couldn't he have left everything alone? His own death, the Green girl, Rusty. None of it would have happened if it hadn't been for Jonah.

Warren's glass was empty, but the tension in his neck and shoulders hadn't dissipated. He needed a distraction. Sensual care by Amber would be his first choice, but Cecilia's denial would not encompass him leaving the house at this hour. She had her own limits as to what she would tolerate and he couldn't afford to risk pushing those right now. He'd settle for another Scotch and maybe sit in the hot tub to loosen up until the booze kicked in. He scooped ice into the whiskey glass, poured liquor half way up the sides and added another splash. He wandered to the hot tub, laid his silk dressing gown and shorts across the back of a chair, lowered himself into warm water and hit the button for the bubbles. The hum of the motor wouldn't penetrate up to the master suite.

Water frothed chest high and he leaned his head back to see the few stars not obscured by clouds. He let his thoughts drift away from the distant past, away from unsettling recent events. He focused on the memory of another hot tub in Dallas with an incredibly skilled stripper from a discreet club that catered to men who preferred not to be seen in well-advertised establishments. The statuesque blonde had been impressed with his over tipping, was as limber off-stage as on and was not the slightest bit interested in exchanging real names. He'd introduced himself as Samson to her Delilah. He'd thought that was amusing and had a bit more class than John Smith.

CHAPTER TWENTY-SIX

" You didn't tell me you were going to West Palm and certainly not to spend the night," Kyle said as he looked up from Bev's desk. "Les filled me in before he left for an errand. I was going to write you a note." He was holding a pen, a blank notepad underneath.

"Well, hello to you, too. Yes, I'm fine thank you," Bev said and swung her purse off her shoulder.

Kyle stood and pushed her chair toward her. "Sorry," he said more perfunctorily than apologetic. "How was the trip?"

"I thought Les told you everything," she replied with a bite to her voice she couldn't quite explain. Was she angry at him? Why? Because if he'd bothered to call her, he would have known where the hell she was.

Kyle rubbed a knuckle in his right eye. Darkened circles showed a lack of sleep. "What have I done to piss you off?"

Bev dropped her briefcase and purse and angled her body toward the coffeemaker. "What makes you think I'm pissed? Do you want a cup of coffee?"

He shook his head. "No, I've to go in a minute, but you always hold your shoulders like that when you're upset and since I'm the only one in the room, I expect I'm the target."

Bev turned her mug right side up, poured steaming coffee she didn't want – she'd had two cups on the road. She wasn't in the mood to discuss their personal life. Or lack thereof would be more accurate.

"This case bothers me," she said, which was true. "What did Les tell you?"

Kyle sighed and Bev couldn't tell if it was because she changed the subject or he didn't approve of what she'd done. "He said you and that detective were poking around the kid who got killed and you thought you could connect some dots."

That detective? The inflection was unmistakable.

"You mean Hank?" Bev asked mildly. "Yeah, he's being a big

173

help. We're still in the circumstantial phase, but there are way too many coincidences piling up for my taste. I think Noonan is up to his cold gray eyes in this."

Kyle hesitated and consulted his watch. "That's a hell of a limb you're climbing out on," he said. "Look, are you free for dinner to-night? We haven't had much time lately."

"Except for last night, I'm not the one who's been busy," she said edgily. Jesus, why was she being so bitchy?

Kyle closed the distance between them and stared into her eyes. "Bev, I know I've been tied up lately and I thought I explained it had nothing to do with us. Is that what's got your feathers ruffled? Is that part of the deal with this Hank?"

Bev set her mug down with a soft thump. "This Hank is helping me with a case that, whether you agree or not, is probably a hell of a lot more complicated than it looked like when we started," she said. "He's got nothing to do with us, to use your phrase."

Kyle sighed again. "I don't have time for this," he said. "Din-ner, okay? Seven? You pick where."

"Yeah," Bev said, suddenly embarrassed with the way she was behaving. "Seven is fine and I'll think about a place. Maybe the Fish Hut." God knows she didn't need to eat for a day or two after the meal she'd had, but probably not a topic she should bring up.

Kyle nodded and pecked her cheek. "Hey, I know this case has gotten under your skin and I haven't been around as much as usual."

"No big deal," Bev lied. "I'll call you later."

She waited until he was out of sight, then sat at her desk and turned the computer on. What was the matter with her? Hank was attractive, but her real interest was in the case, so why was she play-ing the jealousy card? It was juvenile and she needed to get her head straight instead of toying with silly games. She clicked onto the internet connection and almost stopped the absurd voice that said, *"He started it first. If he would tell you what was going on, you wouldn't have to keep guessing. He says it's not you, but he won't share what it is."*

"Oh, shut up," she said out loud and logged onto her electronic mail.

"What?" Les asked from the doorway.

Bev hoped she wasn't blushing. "Nothing," she said quickly. "Just fussing at the computer."

Les tossed a small pharmacy bag into a drawer. "If it's that little helper, I hate him myself. It's as bad a back seat driver. You made good time getting down."

She smiled. "Yeah, reinforcing the fact of how long it takes to buzz between West Palm and here if you're not bogged in traffic. Anyway, how are you coming on our lists?"

"Bone dry and I've checked every name," he said with a shrug. "Chris called and said she was coming by this afternoon. She found a key to a safe deposit box she didn't know Cindy had. Apparently there was a book in it she thinks must have belonged to Jonah and she wasn't sure if it was something we ought to look at. She's got a class and will be here between four and five."

Bev perked up. "A book she thinks was Jonah's?" She reached for the telephone. "I'll go get it from her."

Les held up his hand. "Not so fast. She was on her way out to the boat when she called and won't be back until later."

"Oh, an open water session," Bev said, disappointed. If it were a full class, they'd be gone until lunchtime, have equipment clean up, a discussion about how they had done on their skills and maybe another lesson or an end-of-module quiz. Inevitably there would be at least one student who wanted to talk afterward and Chris would need time to shower and change – late afternoon would be about right.

Les shoved a folder to one side and set his elbow on the desk, chin in the palm of his hand. "Run through this car wreck business with me again so I understand what you're thinking."

Bev rummaged in her briefcase for her notebook and the file that was more robust than when she'd penned the label. She gave Les a detailed description of the business parts of her visit and they spent the morning arranging facts, unknowns, questions and pure speculation. They broke for lunch and Bev went to her apartment instead of the gym since she didn't have her gear in the Spitfire. She normally avoided a workout at noon in the summer, but she was sluggish after two days on the road and the incredible meal from the night before. If she were going to meet with Chris late and have dinner with Kyle, there wouldn't be time for all three activities. She'd make it a long, slow run to stretch her muscles and eat up the afternoon. Besides the physical boost, she could pound out some of her bitchiness about Kyle. There was nothing like losing herself in sweat for mental cleansing.

The old trick was as effective as it had always been and Bev's mood was significantly improved when she returned to the office. Taliah told her that Les was in the interrogation room with the Thompson boys, who had been caught shoplifting again, and their father, whom they'd managed to find in a sober state. She said Les was trying to put the fear of prosecution into the entire family, although in her personal opinion it was a waste of breath since they were no-account trash with no respect for the law. Bev didn't need to get involved and it wasn't going to take long to knock out the little bit of paperwork sitting in her inbox.

She finished a few minutes before Les came in muttering and waving away questions.

"What an asshole," he said as if that was a revelation. "I swear to God, there ought to be a way to require a license to have kids. Screw it, let the judge or social services deal with them."

Bev wiped a quick smile from her face. Taliah was right – most everyone in town knew the Thompsons, particularly the judges.

Les snatched his telephone when it rang and slapped his hand to his forehead. "No, no, of course I didn't forget. I just got tied up and I'll leave here in ten minutes." He hung up and grinned at Bev. "Damn, I forgot. The roofing guy is at the house and I'm afraid we're talking replacement. You need me for anything?"

"No," Bev said. "I'll call if Chris has something worthwhile."

Les was still muttering when he hurried out the door, although Bev wasn't sure if it was about dysfunctional families or leaky roofs. She heard a muffled, "Oomph, sorry" and saw her Aunt Lorna nearly collide with him. The older woman peeked into the office, smiling. "I know I usually call, but I had some business close by and thought I would personally deliver this."

She held out a topaz-colored bud vase with three pale yellow roses, one in full bloom and the others on the verge of opening. Sprigs of baby's breath, greenery and a white and gold striped ribbon completed the arrangement.

She laughed at Bev's surprise and put the flowers on the corner of the desk. "He dashed by right before lunch, scribbled the card and said he would be everlastingly grateful if we could get it to you this afternoon. How was I going to turn down a request like that?"

"How nice to have a florist who's so accommodating," Bev said, trying not to be flustered. "You have time for a cup of coffee?"

Lorna eyed the pot across the room. "If that's been on all day, I'll take a Coke instead if you have something other than diet."

"We have both," Bev said and started to get up.

"You read the card, I'll get the drinks," Lorna said.

Bev dutifully opened it. "If I did something wrong, I really didn't mean to and I apologize. See you tonight. Kyle."

"Three roses couldn't have been much of a fight," Lorna said, passed a diet Coke to Bev and perched in Les's chair. "He did seem a little distracted though, not as outgoing as usual."

Bev slipped the card into the middle desk drawer and shrugged. "I know. I mean, I don't know. Something's been bothering him lately and he doesn't want to talk about it. There's some kind of family issue."

"Ah," Lorna said. "and you're wondering why he won't confide in you. After all, it's not like you aren't practically living together."

Bev squirmed and took a swallow.

Lorna laughed. "Honey, I'm not prying. You've been awfully tense lately and I know the Green girl has you upset, but when Kyle came by and seemed anxious to get these to you, it wasn't difficult to put two and two together."

Bev sighed. "I'm probably being silly," she said. "It's just..., shit, I thought we were closer than that, you know? I don't know if I can help with whatever it is, but maybe I could. And if we can't talk about whatever this is, how are we going to talk about anything serious? Not that we have anything serious to talk about," she added quickly. Oh, hell, what did she mean? Christ, she didn't know what she meant and she hated being off-balance.

Lorna smiled in the way older people do when they're trying to be supportive instead of amused. "I hear you and even though I try not to sound like your mother, you and Kyle have been keeping company for longer than anyone else you've dated. I would think you have certain expectations and this is making you wonder if you've read the relationship wrong."

Bev felt the color in her cheeks. Jesus, this was like some stupid advice column letter.

"Don't get peeved," Lorna said quietly. "The two of you will work things out in your own time, but after more than twenty years in the florist business, I guarantee you men don't go to the trouble of sending non-birthday or holiday bouquets unless they care. Oh, or unless they're trying to get laid and I know you're past that stage."

Bev felt her mouth curve involuntarily. "I suppose you're right," she said. "He didn't have to do this and it was sweet of you to bring it by."

Lorna smiled again and stood. "Glad to oblige. I'll take my Coke and run along. Are we on for our regular Thursday night?"

Bev nodded and rose. "As far as I know, but I'm not too busy to walk you out."

They chatted about innocuous subjects on the way to the parking lot and when Bev stepped away from Lorna's classic Chevy truck, Chris pulled her PT Cruiser into the adjacent slot. She let Lorna back out, then opened her door and waved to Bev.

"Hey, did Les give you my message?" Her hair was a mass of damp curls and she was in her work clothes of shorts, sandals and an Adventures Below T-shirt. Today's ensemble was orange. She held up a large manila envelope with the bottom portion bulged out.

"Yeah, he said you had something for us," Bev replied.

"It may not be important, but I don't feel right about looking through it," she said and followed Bev into the station. "It's a diary or journal and I know it wasn't Cindy's."

Bev took her into the office instead of the interrogation room and shut the door. Chris took the chair Lorna had vacated, declined a drink and unfastened the envelope's metal prongs. She extracted a light blue leather-clad book, more journal size than the square of a diary, devoid of lettering on the front or spine. The leather was cracked and a dark blob stained the bottom left corner. A thick rubber band held it closed.

"Les may have told you I didn't know Cindy had a safe deposit box," Chris said with a shake of her head. "I found a key when I was going through the navy blue purse of hers I borrowed. The people at the bank have been really nice. They said they didn't realize I didn't know about it or they would have mentioned it before."

"You think this belonged to Jonah?" Bev hadn't reached for the item yet. It looked too old to be anything Jonah would have been working on recently.

Chris tapped it with her finger, her voice slightly shaky. "Cindy had mostly papers in the box, an antique locket from our grandmother and this. Cindy never kept a diary as a kid and I only opened it to make sure it wasn't her handwriting. If it's Jonah's, I don't want to be reading something obviously meant to be secret. If he'd asked her to put it in the box for safekeeping, Cindy probably never opened it – that's the kind of person she was."

Bev reached across, lifted it gingerly and tugged the rubber band loose. It was too pliant to have been the same age as the journal appeared to be. There was a faint musty smell and the cover pulled away with the stickiness of old paper. Saturday, 6 November was centered on the lined page written in a delicate cursive, the faded ink still easy to read. She unstuck the blank second page and read the single line on the third page. *Junior English, Honors Class – Lottie Shepard.*

"This must have belonged to Jonah's sister, the girl who committed suicide," she said quietly and set the book down with a shiver that she felt rather than showed.

"Eew," Chris said softly and backed her chair up slightly. "Then for sure I don't want to touch it. I know it isn't your problem either, but could you stick it in a file or whatever until I've at least had a chance to figure out what to do with all his other belongings? I keep hoping a long-lost cousin will materialize."

"Yeah, we can hold it," Bev said. Too bad Chris hadn't uncovered an accountant's ledger of shady dealings or a stack of computer disks.

Chris drew a breath and searched Bev's face. "Les didn't sound as if you had much new," she said, the question hanging in the air.

It would be irresponsible to tell her about West Palm. "Chris, we're looking at some ideas I can't talk about, but we're doing everything we can and we'll keep you up to date."

The woman closed her eyes briefly. "It's not that I don't trust you – it's just hard," she said. "You hear shit like this on the news and it never occurs to you it can happen to your family. Anyway, thanks for taking that off my hands. Business is starting to pick up for the summer, so call me when you and Kyle want to go diving and I'll make sure to have spots on the boat open for you."

"We will," Bev said and escorted her to the front door. There were several cars waiting to exit the parking lot. Shit, it was shift changeover and she hadn't called Kyle about dinner. What was she in the mood for? Italian? Crispy conch fritters and a batch of spiced steamed shrimp?

She wandered into her office, punched the speed dial for Kyle, got his voice mail, thanked him for the flowers and said she'd be at the office for another hour. The short sleeved pants suit she had on would be fine for anywhere they went and she might as well leaf through the journal.

The can of diet Coke had gotten warm. She dumped it, retrieved a fresh one, sat down with the old volume and began to scan the feminine script of a girl who had taken her own life when Bev was a toddler.

The first third of the book was a chronicle of nonstop religious activities, school and domestic chores. There was no gossip of giggling friends, no invitations to parties, no dates. It was a depressing recitation of a teenager who must have been practically invisible if she was lucky and the object of cruel jokes if she'd caught the attention of students always willing to mock kids who didn't fit in.

Bev slowed her reading when she came to the first entry about Warren Randall.

I can't believe Warren asked me to help him with English and civics. He's so handsome and popular, any girl would say yes. He said he thought I was really smart and he'd pay me well for the tutoring. I'll be glad to help him, but I couldn't take his money. I hope my parents say it's all right.

It was the passage dated a month later that caused Bev to widen her eyes and sit up straight. She skipped ahead a few pages, nearly gasped and started over again from the original introduction of Warren Randall into Lottie's writing. Holy shit, no wonder he'd sent Noonan on a search!

Her disgust deepened to righteous anger as she read the astoundingly naïve words describing seduction and betrayal, the utter miscomprehension of Randall's malevolent manipulation. She sat, nearly numb with outrage, and jumped when the telephone rang.

"Hi," Kyle said. "Sorry, it's later than I thought. Do you want me to come pick you up or meet somewhere?"

"Kyle," Bev said, her voice sounding vaguely hollow to her ears. "Can you come right away? I need to get a legal opinion, fast."

"Sure," he said. "What's wrong? You sound odd."

Bev cleared her throat. "It's too damn unbelievable to tell you on the phone, but get here fast and be prepared for a hell of a shock."

"I'm on the way," he said and a dial tone replaced his voice. Bev felt her nose sting and she breathed a wet shudder for the girl that Warren Randall murdered.

CHAPTER TWENTY-SEVEN

"What?" Warren screamed into the telephone. "What the fuck do you mean, she found something in a safe deposit box and turned it over to the cops? That's what you're supposed to be preventing! What the fuck were you doing?"

"Take a drink and listen to me," Noonan's disembodied voice instructed sharply. "I followed her to the bank this morning. She went in, had a conversation, then went into the vault. When she came out, she had a bundle of papers and some kind of notebook."

Warren groaned and clutched the receiver until his knuckles turned white. A notebook! Son-of-a-bitch, the notebook Jonah threatened him with.

"But, and I think this is important, she didn't rush right to the cops. She drove to her office, then went out on the boat with a group of people, didn't come back until lunch and didn't go to the police station until late. She wasn't in there very long and didn't act upset when she came out. She went home and hasn't budged."

"I don't give a goddamn about where she is now! You said she's already been to the police!"

"If you'll calm down for two seconds, what I am saying is that if she had something where Jonah laid everything out, she probably would have been in a big hurry and a lot more excited. I think she must have found something else, something she wasn't sure about, but nothing obvious."

Noonan's words penetrated the panic that had swept across Warren. "Look," he continued, "the tall bitch, the detective, met her outside, they walked in and the sister couldn't have been with her for more than ten minutes. If it had been the goods on you, I can promise they'd have been going over shit for a lot longer. Cops don't get a smoking gun and let a person walk off without a shitload of questions."

Warren wiped a line of beaded sweat from his brow. "She was here last night."

"Who?"

"The detective, the female one. Bev – with the detective – Rodriguez."

"They came to the office?" Noonan asked slowly.

Warren loosened his grip, his fingers beginning to stiffen. "No, nothing like that. I happened to see them downtown, at a hotel near a gallery where we had a reception. It looked like a date, but I can't believe it was just that – she doesn't seem to be the type. If she doesn't think something is going on, why was she here?"

Noonan didn't answer immediately and Warren imagined him processing information with no expression on his face. His voice didn't waver. "I don't know why, but if no one has contacted you, it can't be too serious. A town like this doesn't get big crimes. If they have a tie-in to you, they're not going to sit on it."

A tie-in to me, you prick – I'm not the one fucking killing people. "What are you suggesting?" Warren asked in a more normal voice. "What's your next brilliant idea?"

"Keep as low a profile as possible and continue with business as usual," he said calmly. "I'm going to stick with the sister for another day or two. She's starting to go through things. I saw her hauling extra loads out to the trash and she's been by a lawyer's office a couple of times. If Jonah had access to a safe deposit box and the shit wasn't there, it may be buried so deep no one will find it. If he had anything in the first place."

"You're sure nobody has seen you?"

"I know my job," Noonan replied curtly. "You just stay calm."

"I'll be a hell of a lot calmer if you knew what the cops have."

"If it's bad, you'll know soon enough," Noonan said and disconnected without giving Warren time to respond.

He stared at the receiver, replaced it with a trembling hand and pressed the heel of his hand against his temple. Shit, was this it? Was it about to all come down? He'd give Noonan up no problem. They couldn't pin him with the deaths, but the Feds would be all over him on the deals with Bassi. Christ knows if they would even leave anything for the state's people. How much time did he have? Should he alert his lawyer with a hypothetical situation just to get him thinking about the possibility?

He gathered as much strength as he could and buzzed his assistant. "Lila, honey, is Freddy around?"

"No, Senator, he wasn't coming back to the office this evening.

Do you need me to reach him for you?"

Thank God for small favors. He couldn't face anyone right now. "No, thank you, and, Lila, you go ahead and take off. You've been working awfully hard lately and I do appreciate it."

She hesitated. "I hate to leave you alone," she said. Granted it didn't happen often.

"I'm not staying much longer," he said quickly. "Really, you go ahead. You don't have me scheduled for anything early tomorrow, do you?"

"No, your schedule for the next two days is on top of your calendar,"she replied. "There's nothing before one o'clock."

"Good, good and, Lila, I may sleep in a bit in the morning. Don't be surprised if I'm a little late," he said, not sure how much longer he could sound nonchalant.

"Well, all right. I'll see you tomorrow," she said.

He hung up and walked to the bar. A little ice and a lot of Scotch. A robust drink to steady his thumping heart. Shit, what had Noonan said? The part about being in the police station for only a few minutes.

He clicked on the television, tuned to a sports channel for noise and sat heavily on the sofa. Noonan had a point. Jonah could have encoded everything of course, but wouldn't the girl have noticed? Wouldn't she have wanted to alert the police immediately if she'd found an item like that? And if what he had were as detailed as he had indicated and in plain language, the girl would surely have recognized Warren's name if no others. But if it wasn't Jonah's documents, what was it?

He let the Scotch slip down his throat. Think, think, think. If they knew Jonah hadn't killed the Green girl, but they didn't have anything solid to go on, they would be still looking for suspects, right? Logically they would have asked the sister to keep an eye out for anything that might help them. Perhaps something in the papers in the safe deposit box was out of the ordinary enough to cause her to consult with the police. Something she didn't understand, so she turned it over just in case. Whatever it was, however, hadn't required much of the girl's time. Then it couldn't have been Jonah's documents. Even if she hadn't looked at them before, which would seem unlikely, once the detective saw them, she would have questioned the girl at length. Noonan had said she hadn't seemed upset or excited when she left. If she had thought there was any substance to what she'd taken from the box, she wouldn't have been business as usual.

Warren drained his glass, the few cubes mere slivers of ice. Noonan was an officious cocksucker who'd fucked this situation up six ways to Sunday, but he could be correct about what the girl had given the detective. Shit, he was tired of waiting! He couldn't risk asking Noonan to go faster though – they were suspicious enough.

He felt a stab of pain above his left temple and pressed the cold crystal to it. He'd have one more drink and go home. The direct telephone cut through the calm he had talked himself into. Shit, who was it? Should he answer? No, let the voice mail get it. The telephone stopped after four rings. He waited, breathing shallowly as he heard his wife's voice.

"Warren, I don't know why I'm getting this machine instead of Lila. Mother called. She simply must settle on the menu for next month's luncheon and she's asked me to come over for the meeting with the caterer. I'll probably stay for dinner. Come join us if you feel up to it. I've got to dash, call me when you decide."

Warren shook his head at how relieved he was – he had to get a grip. Soon, soon, it would be over with soon. He straightened his shoulders and picked up his cell phone. Cecilia and Margaret would have no need of his company and he could use the excitement of Amber's uninhibited tongue. If she didn't give the best head of any woman he'd ever been with, she was certainly in the top three. Thank God he'd had the foresight to put her in a luxury apartment and find her a cushy job. She made few other demands and was as discreet as she was nubile – a disenchanted mistress was the last thing he needed at this stage.

CHAPTER TWENTY-EIGHT

Bev went to the ladies room after alerting the desk sergeant to expect Kyle. She splashed water on her face after she washed her hands and stared into the mirror. That was better. Okay, she'd been on the wrong track, but her original theory *had* made sense. Financial or long buried secret, the essence and subsequent consequences were the same. It so happened that Senator Randall was simply more of a reprehensible bastard than your ordinary on-the-take politician. Hell, he was probably guilty of both. She recalled the charm she'd felt during the initial part of her visit with him, the immediate draw to his handsome face and persuasive voice. It was easy to imagine how overwhelming his raw presence would have been to a lonely, sheltered teenager.

Bev stepped into the hallway and heard Kyle in the central bay as he spoke to some of the men. He saw Bev, ended the conversation and hurried into the office.

"What in the hell is going on?" he asked quickly when she closed the door. "Are you all right?"

Bev nodded. "Yes, but I've got evidence against Senator Randall that's sure as shit not what I was expecting. I haven't told anyone else yet because I just got it and I want to know the legal implications."

Kyle took her elbow and led her to her chair. "Whoa. Sit," he said noncommittally. "What do you mean by evidence?"

Bev reached for the journal instead of her chair and opened to the third page. "I mean a journal from Lottie Shepard, Jonah Shepard's sister, the girl who committed suicide. Except it wasn't suicide – Warren Randall killed her. It wasn't financial stuff he sent Noonan after, it was this."

Kyle squinted one eye and held a hand up. "Stop."

Bev drew a breath in sharply, but he put his hand on her forearm and pushed her down into the chair.

"Bev, you're right – I'm glad you didn't tell me this on the telephone. Before we go any further though, I'm going to get a pad and sit at Les's desk. Then I want you to tell me how you got the journal and then tell me what in the hell you're talking about."

"You might as well get yourself a Coke while you're at it," she said with the tiniest touch of sarcasm. She needed a legal opinion, not lawyerly mannerisms. The damn journal was not obtained through improper search.

"Good idea," he said, went to the refrigerator and took out two diet Cokes. He popped the tabs, exchanged one of them with her for a clean notepad, took a pen from his pocket and sat down.

Finally! "Okay," Bev said and gave him a fast but complete version of Chris bringing the journal and why she was alone when she read it. "Satisfied?"

He nodded tentatively.

"The first reference to Warren Randall isn't until later," she said. "So even if Chris had looked at the first pages, she wouldn't have seen what I found. You can tell from what Lottie wrote that she didn't fit in with the other kids at school. Her family was some kind of hardcore, fundamental religious type who didn't believe in dancing, music, make-up, all the things girls Lottie's age would have been doing. There's a bunch of references to church meetings and activities, the only form of social interaction she had. Anyway, she starts tutoring Warren Randall in a couple of classes they have together. It's obvious the girl has a crush and at first, they work at her house, then shift to his house, although his mother is usually around. It all sounds very proper for a while."

Bev couldn't sit still any longer – Kyle should know that about her by now. She jumped up and began to pace the length of the desk. "You can see it plain as day, the compliments he begins to give her, the physical contact. Lottie was so swept away with emotions she didn't know she could have, she wrote it all down. The kissing that turned into more, her drawing away, him convincing her there was nothing wrong with it."

"I thought his mother was around," Kyle said, making few notes.

"At first, yes, and then Warren asked to change the time they worked together and Lottie didn't know his mother would be gone. This is when it picks up fast and I don't know, maybe a girl more experienced than Lottie could have figured it out, maybe not." She stabbed a finger at the journal. "The son-of-a-bitch makes it with her and gets her pregnant."

Kyle raised his eyebrows. "Bev, maybe she wasn't as innocent as you think. Maybe she wanted to be seduced and you're still a long way from him killing her."

Bev shook her head vehemently. "Trust me, when you read the way she wrote it, you'll agree with me. Anyway, she tells him she's pregnant and he wants her to get an abortion. Not surprisingly, she doesn't want to and since he's been telling her he's in love with her, she assumes they'll get married, have the baby and make a lovely little family."

"He dumps her instead, she becomes depressed and kills herself?" Kyle asks. "He might be considered responsible in a moral sense, but that's not the same as killing her."

Bev gave him a time-out signal. "He goes way past that. He makes a suicide pact with her."

"What?" Kyle jerked his head to the book.

There, I knew that would get your attention. "Yeah," Bev said. "He spins a story about how his parents would never approve of a marriage because they're so young, they'd cut them off without a dime, her parents would never allow her to keep a baby born out of wedlock, and they would send her away in shame. Apparently he convinces her that if they commit suicide together it will be this great romantic ending and they'll be joined in death for eternity."

"That's what she wrote?"

"Almost verbatim," Bev said. "We know for a fact Warren Randall is alive and he's the one who called the police about Lottie. Obviously he was there with her when she took the pills instead of responding to her telephone call the way he claimed. She lays it all out – how she'll go first as he holds her in his arms to make sure she passes without pain."

Kyle's usual objective demeanor slipped. "She actually described the plan?"

Bev slowed her breathing; it had become more rapid as she remembered the searing passage. "Bigger than hell," she said grimly. "If you think about it, if no one knew when he arrived, it wouldn't be hard to pull off. He carries out the first part, waits until she's dead and then calls for help."

Kyle stretched out to take the journal and kept his eyes on Bev. "Wonder why no one found this back then?"

Bev sank into her chair and nudged the book in his direction.

"With what she was writing, I'm sure she had it well hidden. I bet she did leave a note explaining everything, but Warren would have had plenty of time to destroy it. They may have done a cursory search for a diary, but she mentions early on that she'd never kept one. She only started the journal as an English assignment. She probably never mentioned it to anyone."

"So this is what you think Jonah had and why he confronted Senator Randall? After all these years? Why wait this long?"

Bev passed a hand across her forehead. "I've gone through the old reports a couple of times and he was quite vocal about believing Randall was the father. He wouldn't have hesitated to use this if he'd had it early on. No, Chris told me that one of his parents died a few months before she met him and the other one had died several years ago. I don't remember the exact order. The point is, he was the only one left in the family so he would have been taking care of their belongings. I bet it was too painful for her parents after Lottie's death and they boxed everything up without looking through her things. That's not unusual and it means Jonah wouldn't have found it until recently, when he was clearing out the house."

"Now you're speculating," Kyle said in his courtroom voice.

"Yes, and it passes the common sense test," Bev said impatiently. "He's hated the guy for years and maybe he's been trying to get something on him with no luck until he finds this. I'm not completely sure why he goes to see Senator Randall before he releases it. He wanted to make him sweat, I suppose, and it turned out to be a huge miscalculation. Maybe he didn't tell Randall exactly what he had, so Randall sends Noonan and Smallwood to look for something. Since the ME said Cindy died as a result of a severe asthma attack, maybe she really did surprise them and everything spun out of control. You know the rest."

She blew out a stream of air. "At least we have proof of motive. Now it's figuring out what to charge whom with, but that will be up to your boss. I bet Noonan will roll on the senator to try and save his hide."

She stopped when she saw Kyle's expression. It was not the look she was hoping for. "What? Do you want to read the journal for yourself?"

"Bev, don't go off the deep end on me," he said in much too quiet a voice. "What you have is explosive on the surface. What you have, in fact of law, is an unauthenticated book which, if it can be proved to be genuine, contains unsubstantiated allegations."

"Jesus Christ," Bev snapped. "It's all there! Deathbed confessions are legal. It's practically the same thing."

"No, it isn't," Kyle replied. "Bev, please, I can see why you feel the way you do and I'm not saying you're wrong. Take a drink and let me give it to you from a legal point. That's part of why I'm here – remember?"

Bev slumped involuntarily and caught herself. Pouting could come later. "I'll be good," she promised.

"I'll set aside questions about chain of custody before Chris delivered it to you and give you one of the biggest holes first. Jonah could have had this written himself."

"You've got to be kidding," Bev shot back.

Kyle shrugged. "He blamed the man for his sister's death. The family is dead and, for all we know, there isn't a sample of her handwriting left. Jonah could never get anything on Senator Randall so he buys an old, blank journal in a second hand shop or whatever and had this made up so it looks authentic. He knew enough of the details of his sister's life that he could have. He might not have planned to go after him legally, but deliver it to a reporter. There are those who wouldn't be meticulous about verification."

Bev snorted. "How likely is that?"

"It's plausible – likely doesn't matter, but for the sake of argument, let's say it is genuine and can be validated as Lottie's journal. As you say, she was an outsider, lonely. She develops a crush on a popular boy and creates this fantasy world. He rejects her, she delves deeper into the fantasy she's written, reaches a point of complete desperation and commits suicide."

Bev held up a finger. "But we know she was pregnant."

"And paternity never established. Maybe she gave in to some other boy and didn't want to admit it. She transferred all her hopes and feelings to Randall."

Bev massaged her temples. "We know she tutored Randall."

"I agree," Kyle said, "and that gets us no closer to verification of what she wrote. And the final, incontrovertible point is that there is no way to cross-examine a document like this. Unless you can somehow find an individual who observed her making the entries and knew the contents, these are only words on paper."

"Probable cause, though," Bev retorted. "You just admitted it could be politically damaging. That's probable cause to want it found. We can prove Noonan was here. We home in on him. We get him, he gives us Randall."

Kyle was shaking his head as she spoke. "His explanation for being in town was reasonable and the level of potential political damage is only if it's handled badly. Remember, even if everything Lottie wrote is accurate, it could somehow be shown to be so, and Randall admitted it, he was only seventeen. He could claim he intended to go through with the suicide pact, lost his nerve and panicked when he realized he couldn't save Lottie. Senator Randall and the DeLong family have plenty of money to hire the kind of people who could find a way to turn this to Randall's advantage. I can't think of a judge who would rule for probable cause based on this book."

Shit, shit, shit! Bev clenched her jaw to keep from shrieking the words. How could this be right? She was looking at goddamn evidence!

"Bev," Kyle said softly and leaned far across the desk. "Thank God I called before you launched off with this. I wish I could tell you what you want to hear and I can't. There are legal issues you can't ignore."

"Stupid goddamn issues," she said petulantly. Cops, lawyers and judges – weren't they all supposed to be on the same side? Hell, anyone with half a brain would realize the journal was authentic.

Kyle reached for her hand. "I know this is one of those cop-lawyer moments when you think we don't care. If you can look me in the eye and say a cop has never been sloppy with gathering evidence, or there have never been incidents of illegal search and seizure, and there's never been a case of someone manufacturing evidence to frame someone, I'll agree with you."

Shit, shit, shit! Bev slid one hand to him and bumped the topaz vase. "You think it's real, don't you?"

He clasped her fingertips between both his hands. "I think Lottie wrote it and I can see how she might be telling the truth, but I don't know enough about her or her state of mind to say yes. I see why you believe it though and how it lines up neatly to account for Cindy and Smallwood. If Smallwood was with Noonan, he could have lost his nerve after disposing of Cindy and become a liability."

Bev exhaled more breath than she'd taken. "Randall is a lying son-of-a-bitch and is directly or indirectly responsible for the deaths of four people. I will, by God, find a way to prove it and bring the bastard down. I don't care how long it takes me."

Kyle's smile was slow – showing understanding, not amusement at her statement. "I wouldn't want to be in either Senator Randall's or Noonan's shoes," he said. "The only thing I'll ask is that you cross the *t*'s and dot the *i*'s. If Chief Taylor agrees, and particularly if you need the cooperation of the West Palm end, everything you do from this point on is subject to being under a microscope. Please tell me you also recognize they will probably never let you run with this."

"That's two things," she said and swallowed hard. "I promise I'll be excruciatingly detailed and I know this will not be met with joyful enthusiasm." She couldn't blame Kyle for his assessment – her belief in justice and his belief in the law weren't always the two sides of the coin they should be.

She doused her smoldering frustration and pointed to the vase. "By the way, those are lovely and you didn't need to send them."

"Yes, I did," he said and hesitated. "Tonight's been pretty charged, but maybe we can have some time to talk this weekend."

Guilt tickled Bev's brain. She'd been pissed at him for days and ready to bust his balls until she started in on the journal. A solid lead in her case and concern about her relationship with Kyle had fallen totally off her mental scope. Not much question as to her real priorities, was there?

"I'd still like to have dinner if you're up for it," he was saying.

"Now that you mention it, I am kind of hungry," she said. "The Fish Hut, or would you rather go somewhere else?"

He tugged his tie. "I'm not sure they allow suits. Let's swing by Paradisio's or we could grab take-out and go to my place."

Shit, she could put the journal out of her mind for the duration of a short dinner, but despite Kyle's warning, she wasn't going to be able to leave the issue untended for the entire night. She smiled at him. "As tempting as your place would be…"

"I understand," he said. "You need to be alone to game plan how to handle this with Les and Chief Taylor. No sweat. We'll save catch up for the weekend."

"Thanks," Bev said. "Let me secure the book in the evidence

room and leave Les a note in case he gets in before I do. If you want to go ahead and order me a red wine and find out what the specials are, I won't be far behind you."

"Sure," Kyle said, stood, lobbed his empty can into the waste-basket and left the office.

Bev whipped out a cryptic note for Les, taped it to his computer screen and picked up the journal. She stared at the roses as she shut the lights off and fleetingly wondered what Lottie Shepard's favorite flower had been.

CHAPTER TWENTY-NINE

Bev hurried into the office, exchanging rapid morning pleasantries. She and Kyle had enjoyed dinner, although they mutually avoided a conversation about why he sent the roses. The promise to deal with personal matters over the weekend sufficed. They parted in the restaurant parking lot and she stayed up later than she intended creating dialog for potential scenes with Chief Taylor. She envisioned derision, denial, a flat refusal for her to pursue Senator Randall and the longed for response of, "brilliant work, go get the bastard."

She wasn't surprised to see Les at his desk, the journal open. He followed her movements quizzically as she dumped her purse in the bottom drawer.

"Why didn't you call me last night? I would have come in."

She picked her mug up and took his when he pushed it within reach. "I was blown away, to be honest, and Kyle called so I asked him to come over for a sanity check." She walked to the coffeepot and paused when she lifted the carafe. "You finish it?" She refilled Les's mug, one sugar, no creamer.

"Yeah," he said calmly. "Was Kyle looking at this as a person or as an assistant DA?"

Bev tried not to smile and walked carefully back to her desk, mugs topped to the brim. "The lawyer part took over."

"Does the chief know yet?"

Bev blew a stream of air across the surface of the liquid. "Just the three of us so far."

"This is goddamn dynamite," Les said finally. "You think they'll buy it or make us bury it?"

"I hope the hell we get to move on it," she said bluntly. "Kyle wasn't what you'd call encouraging, although he agrees that if you take it at face value, everything falls into place. I was off-base about the financial piece, but if Jonah told Randall about the journal, it makes sense he would have launched Noonan. They must be going bat shit."

Les wagged his head thoughtfully. "I bet they don't know about it. If you remember, hard drives or files were missing from the computers Jonah had access to. There's no way Noonan could have thought this would be on a computer. It's more likely Jonah told him he had something and didn't get into specifics. Randall's crooked, he thought like you did and Noonan fucked it up by killing Jonah prematurely. He didn't have time to find out about the whole ball of wax."

Bev blew a puff of air. "Shit, you're right. Randall must be involved with this Bassi guy, otherwise why would Noonan be in the picture at all? The financial items would have been computerized with paper back up. Noonan would have found that and thought he had everything. If everyone buys Smallwood as an accident and they destroyed whatever Jonah had, they think they're good to go."

Her forefinger worked a silent, rapid rhythm against the handle of her mug. "The truth of the matter is we don't have anything solid against Noonan, and Kyle made it clear we can't go directly for Randall. What we need to do is track Noonan's movements from when he shot Jonah. Get access to his telephone records and vehicle, interview people around him. We need a complete and intensive investigation with our West Palm pals, but Randall knows he has enough pull to shield Noonan."

She stilled her finger, took a sip of coffee and scrunched her face in thought. "On the other hand, if we hit Randall with the journal, it might really throw him for a loop. Even if it wouldn't stand up in court, just the idea of it would have to come as a shock to him. If we shake him up enough, maybe he'll throw us Noonan with the loose cannon angle. And Noonan might roll on Randall."

Les swiped a dribble of coffee from the side of his mug and licked it from his finger. "Thin, Bev, it's thin. Randall's been lying about this for more than twenty years. If you believe what the girl wrote, he didn't have any conscience back then and he sure as shit won't have improved."

Bev lifted her hands slightly and let them drop to the desk. "Les, this is what we have. It's our first real break and we've got to find a way to make it work."

"I guess you're right," he said slowly. "You going to call Hank or talk to the chief first? Taliah said he won't be in until almost noon."

Shit! Why this morning of all mornings? "I probably owe it to the chief to talk to him before we tell anyone else," she said reluctantly. "Even though we have every right to pursue Cindy's death, the deputy chief I talked to in West Palm didn't want Smallwood to be linked to it. Hank will be cool, but he's in the same situation we are – his bosses won't be happy. "

"How do you plan to approach the chief?"

"No beating around the bush," Bev said immediately. "He already knows why we suspect Noonan. We add this to it and tell him Kyle's objections. He'll holler and carry on, but he'll make the right decision."

Bev's direct line rang. "Henderson," she said, assuming it was Kyle.

"Bev, I hate to bother you at work, but I'm in a jam," the voice of her father boomed through.

Bev did a quick mental adjustment. "No problem, Daddy. What's up?"

"I'm on my way to Miller's Point. I've got a split pick-up on a charter and one of the engine belts seems to be slipping. It's not too bad, but I don't want to risk the son-of-a-bitch going on me while we're out and not have a spare. I called ahead to Bill Miller and he doesn't have this one on the shelf. I know Bedford's has them and I was going to ask your mother to run by, pick one up and meet me. Then I remembered she's teaching ceramics class at the church today."

"Got it," she said. "Give me the part number and I should be at Miller's Point by the time you get there."

She wrote down the information and grinned ruefully at Les. "I need to run an errand for my dad. I'll be back before the chief."

"No problem," he said. "I'm not going to try and explain this to him by myself, but if he comes in, I'll make sure he stays put."

Taliah was at her station and Bev knew better than to try and slip past again without talking. She stopped to tell her where she was going and that she and Les needed to see Chief Taylor as soon as they could.

"He doesn't have anything for this afternoon. Now tell me about those pretty roses Lorna brought yesterday," she said with no hint of remorse for prying.

"Later, got to go now," Bev promised. Right, as if she hadn't weaseled the story from Lorna. She respected Taliah, but goddamn was she nosy! On the other hand, she was cheerful, not malicious, and in general, did not pad personal information she dispensed about dozens of families around town.

Bev spun the Spitfire out of her spot, glad in a way her dad called. She hated sitting around waiting to make a move and she really shouldn't be discussing the case with anyone else until they told the chief. He'd understand about her talking to Kyle even though he'd bust her ass about it just for good measure.

Bedford's wasn't overly busy; Bev located the correct belt and was on her way within minutes. Unless there was a sudden surge of traffic, it wouldn't take long to get to Miller's Point. She tucked the bag with the belt underneath the weight of her purse and lowered the top on the car. She might as well take advantage of the breeze and thin veil of clouds that would burn off by noon.

She zipped through town and slowed near Miller's Point when she was caught behind a full-size, late model blue van hauling a pop-up camper. Ohio plates – that must have been a fun trip with the three children she could see through the windows.

The van continued beyond the turnoff and Bev whipped into a slot at the edge of the large parking lot. Miller's Point had been de-veloped as a waterfront mixed-use community with a combination of single-family homes, condominiums, marina facilities and a popular bar and restaurant on the second floor above a convenience store.

Bev strolled to the charter boat area and scanned for Dawn's De-light, a name derived from her dad's partner's wife rather than sun-rise. Their thirty-six-foot Luhrs was at the far slip. A quartet of men garbed for a day on the water clustered on the dock, handing canvas bags to her dad's partner. Her dad waved to her and leaped off the boat.

"Thanks, Bev, I hated to interrupt you," he said and gave her a quick hug. "If I hadn't though, sure as the world, the damn thing would have broken on us."

"No problem, and you're right – always be prepared," she said with a laugh and gave him the sack. "Looks like a good day for fish-ing."

"Better than being behind a desk," he said and grinned. "Now skedaddle before Claude accuses me of diverting police resources for personal use."

She laughed again, stood and watched until he had the final passenger aboard and retraced her steps toward the restaurant. She rounded the corner when her cell phone rang. Faint static distorted the voice.

"Hey, Bev, it's Chris. Can you hear me okay?"

"A little static, not too bad," she said.

"Look, this is kind of screwy, but Les said you might be at Miller's Point. You know where Callahan Cottages are?"

"Yeah, I'm at Millers and it's four, five miles from Callahan's. Why?"

"I'll explain more later. A friend of Jonah's called this morning from Washington D.C. He's been out of the country and just got word about what happened. Asked me about his place at Callahan's. It's a place he and Jonah sort of had together. He told me where the spare key was and asked if I could check on it. I don't have...afternoon...meet...what..."

Chris's words were breaking up badly and Bev couldn't catch the rest.

"Chris! Chris! I'm losing you," she shouted. "Try again!" Shit, what the hell was that about?

Bev climbed into her car, hit the call back feature and was greeted by a mechanical message that said the number dialed was out of range. Damn, Chris must have hit a dead zone.

Had she understood correctly? Jonah had a cabin at Callahan's? That didn't make sense, but it wasn't a far drive. She could swing by and still make it to the station without keeping Chief Taylor waiting.

Bev took a dogleg and cut through the far side of town to avoid the traffic lights. She hadn't gotten which cottage at Callahan's although Chris' PT Cruiser or the Adventures Below van would be easy to spot.

Callahan's was laid out in typical U-shape of waterfront establishments. The calmer and relatively shallow water of the cove was darker than sparkling open water; mangroves and other vegetation lining the shores instead of sandy beach. Unlike Miller's Point, it was an older area being slowly renovated by individual owners, not land developers. Two bedroom, one bath wood shingled structures were being replaced by two and three story painted concrete houses. Within a few years, a handful of stilt houses would be the only remaining original properties. Rumor had it the younger Callahan was planning to tear down the admittedly ramshackle main building and try his hand with an upscale look.

The asphalt entrance to Callahan's was deeply rutted, probably from construction equipment. Bev saw three cabins in throes of renovation; two water-side and one on the water view side of the single paved street. Clanks of heavy machinery and shouted instructions echoed from building crews. She downshifted into first and rolled past the dock and store as she looked for one of Chris' vehicles. Two older men were loading gear into a Sea Ray as what looked like an Edgewater skirted around one of the gray stilt houses built on sturdy concrete pilings. Two sets of round pillars, more durable than the old-fashioned frame buildings, had become perches for gulls and brown pelicans. A small flat bottom, motor-less boat hugged the shore, one of three boys poking a paddle into mangrove tree roots.

Bev spotted the silver PT Cruiser three quarters of the way down the street, pulled to the side instead of into a driveway. Bev realized it was difficult to read the faded house numbers. Was Chris in 101, 102 or 103? A dark green Taurus with a rental sticker was parked at a nearby cottage with a For Sale By Owner sign posted in the yard. Bev stopped behind Chris's vehicle, got out and looked around for movement. White shades obscured all the windows and Bev couldn't hear music, television or muffled voices.

She sighed, stepped to the house directly in front of her, called out and knocked on the doorframe. No answer and the screen door was latched. Bev proceeded to the second house and cocked her head at an odd noise when she reached her hand to the door. There was no response to her knock and then she heard what could have been a back door slam.

"Chris, it's Bev," she said loudly, opened the unlocked screen door and turned the knob. It twisted freely and Bev blinked when she found herself in the dusky interior. She registered the sight of a cell phone on the floor first, then saw the sofa pushed to an angle.

Shit! She snatched her gun from her shoulder holster, swung into a two-handed stance toward the open door to her right and pushed it with her foot. An empty bedroom.

The second bedroom had the desk. Drawers were yanked open and papers strewn. Bev covered the distance to the back door in seconds. Steps led to a wooden walkway that was a straight line to the dock. Chris was being pushed forward, something black tucked under her lower left arm, the man at her side gripping her elbow.

"Police, Noonan!" she shouted. "Give it up!"

Bev dove as he turned and fired twice. She scrambled up into a crouch, no way to get a flat out run at him or stop for a steady shot. He maneuvered Chris to where she was a partial shield and by now he was only paces away from people on the dock. The two men were immobile and stared at the man barreling toward them, the girl in tow. The man in the approaching boat swerved in a wide arc, his body bent forward, head down.

"Police!" Bev screamed again, advancing as quickly as she could in the awkward position.

A back door opened and a woman stuck her torso out.

"Stay inside!" Bev yelled and rose to a stand when Noonan turned his back to her.

He sent one man sprawling on his ass and was screaming at the other, his pistol in the man's face. Bev raced down the walk, but Noonan effortlessly twisted and released two more rounds in her direction.

Without cover she was forced to drop again, nearly losing her balance. She looked up to see Noonan push Chris face down into the boat, the second man floundering in waist-deep water. Noonan fired one more shot up the walk, jumped into the boat, reversed it and sped away, spraying sheets of water. Bev pounded onto the pier, took aim at Noonan and fired ineffectively as he zigzagged. The other boat bounced through the water on the side away from Noonan and the man called to her.

"You need to get him?"

She snapped her head to see him idling the Edgewater. "I'm retired Navy – get in!" he yelled above the engine's noise. Bev jumped with no hesitation and banged one knee hard as she landed ungracefully.

"Call Verde Key police," she shouted to the man on the dock when she righted herself. "Tell them what happened!"

She clung to the side of the boat with one hand as her unknown assistant shoved the throttle forward.

"Floyd Armstrong. I used to run boats for Navy SEALs," he said over the roar. "This baby will catch him." His creased black face was split with a wide grin and he lowered his profile so he could see where to steer yet provide virtually no target for Noonan.

Bev braced one foot against the side to try to stabilize herself as the hull slammed into the water. Floyd raced left of Noonan to cut him off from the mouth of the cove.

"I'll get him into the shallows," Floyd called over his shoulder.

Bev saw Chris pull up on her knees. Noonan was having a hard time steering with one hand and clutching the pistol with the other. He kicked his foot at Chris to force her down again. She swayed to her right and edged closer to the side, giving Bev a better sight on Noonan. She squeezed the trigger twice. Noonan jerked his arm and slumped slightly, then swung the wheel hard to the left.

Bev saw Chris vault herself over the right side and land in the water before Noonan could snag her. She disappeared below the surface.

"Don't worry," Bev yelled to Floyd, "keep on him, she'll be okay!" Water was Chris's element and there wasn't much chance she'd been hurt in the fall – a little winded maybe. She'd understand Bev not stopping to check.

"He's circling to get behind us!" Floyd warned and turned so suddenly it knocked Bev off balance again. Shit, she was never going to get a shot lined up.

Noonan buzzed past and she and Floyd both automatically ducked when he raised his gun arm. This time Bev could see the blood smeared on Noonan's other arm. Good, she'd hit him, although she needed him alive – him and whatever he had in the boat.

Chris bobbed her head up and went under again, but it was a pike dive, not a struggle.

"Got him," Floyd crowed as he swooshed by Noonan, hitting him broadside with the wake, rocking the smaller Sea Ray violently.

Damn! He accelerated instead of slowing to regain control. He plowed through the turbulence, fighting the wheel. Floyd moved just outside the wake and was gaining on him when Noonan let go, twisted clumsily, took a two-handed stance and fired. Half the windscreen crackled and Bev threw her arm up instinctively as she dropped her head.

"Motherfucker!" Floyd bellowed. Noonan had miscalculated the timing and Bev looked to see him wrenching the wheel too late as the boat slammed into a protruding concrete piling. The prow exploded, shot-gunning debris through the air while Noonan's body was hurled among chunks of fiberglass, wood and metal.

Floyd killed his engine to avoid sucking fragments into the propellers and Bev watched in dismay as blood bubbled around the man floating face down.

CHAPTER THIRTY

The wail of sirens behind Bev split the sudden silence as Floyd drifted into the wreckage. A marine patrol sturdy Grady-White powered into view and Bev hailed them, her badge held aloft. Floyd had a boat hook ready, but Bev shook her head.

"Let them take over. There's going to be a hell of a report on this one," she said and peered anxiously into the splintered stern of the boat. A life vest, the lid of an ice chest – no black object. God-damn it, how far could it have gone? Was it still intact? What was it?

The guy on the patrol cut his engines to a throb and eased to a halt. Bev leaned across the broken windscreen, glad to see Boone Reynolds.

"Bev, looks like a hell of a mess," he said without preamble. "Let us get in and see what we can do."

"The son-of-a-bitch is dead and probably murdered two people," she said flatly. "He had some evidence that I'd rather recover."

Boone raked his eyes across the scene and shook his head. "We're not equipped for deliberate search. What are you after?"

"I'm not completely sure," Bev admitted. "A large book, I think, could be more than one in a plastic bag. And I need anything else that looks like personal effects."

"I've got to get the body out, Bev – that's protocol – but there's shit scattered all over and the bottom will be stirred up like crazy. I'll radio Search and Recovery for you and see if they can hustle out. Sorry, but they're your best bet," Boone said and waved his arm to the dock. "Not to mention you've got a crowd waiting."

Bev turned, saw uniforms, witnesses, Les and Chris. Damn! Chris would know exactly what they should be after and she ought to check on her anyway. What the hell happened in the cottage? She swiveled her head between Boone and the wrecked boat and exhaled deeply.

"You take care of your business and ask the search guys to get here as fast as they can," she conceded. "We'll run on in."

Boone nodded, his piece said.

"They must have called for an ambulance," Floyd said quietly and Bev looked at him closely for the first time. He grinned and stuck a callused hand out. "Floyd Armstrong, ma'am, if you didn't catch it earlier."

"Bev Henderson," she said and smiled. "You always jump into trouble like that? Not that I'm complaining," she added immediately, "I'm damn glad you were around."

"Just lucky," he said. "This is the most fun I've had since I retired last year. The wife and I are renting a small place while ours is being remodeled," he said and pointed to the group of people. "I imagine the wife is up there, cussing me a blue streak. She'll think it was dangerous."

"I'll see if I can get her to go easy on you," Bev said. "And if you'll hang around, I'll make sure someone gets the information they'll need for a claim on your boat."

"Appreciate that, but I think the gent who owns the Sea Ray will be a whole lot more concerned about his paperwork," he drawled and backed gently from the site.

The small crowd seemed to be under control. Uniforms had separated witnesses to one end, although a thin, middle-aged woman who might be Mrs. Reynolds was gesturing animatedly in their direction. The ambulance was centered at the head of the dock. A male and female emergency medical technician stood next to a gurney, their posture indicating they knew they were waiting for a corpse rather than an injured party.

Chris was chatting with them and didn't appear overwrought for having been kidnapped at gunpoint. She had a black beach towel wrapped around her sarong-like, a pool of water at her sandaled feet. Bev groaned when she saw the reporter, Sylvia Ruthven, working the curious crowd that another patrolman was keeping in the parking lot.

Les was waiting to take the line when they nosed into the slip. "Goddamn, Bev, you're full of surprises this morning and you look like shit. Want the medics to give you a once over?"

She tossed him the rope and grimaced. "I'll live. You talk to Chris?"

"Damn near as tough as you," he said, and leaned down and secured the line. "A hell of a story you'll be interested in." He pointed his chin to the shattered Sea Ray. "A laptop computer, notebook and a couple of disks are what he got."

Bev shook her head rapidly. "Shit. It's down there somewhere. The search crew should be on the way, but I don't know."

She climbed out and introduced Floyd Reynolds who comically ducked his head when the thin woman dashed across to throw her arms around his neck. He lifted her aboard as if she was weightless and winked at Bev.

"Hey, Chris, sorry about not stopping for you," Bev said and felt a sharp pain knot her calves. Her knee was beginning to ache and she saw her reflection in the wide store window. Christ, she looked awful! Her braid was loose, sweaty hair matted on her face, and the front of her clothes was streaked with dirty water.

Chris moved forward, her wet sandals squelching against the planks. "If that motherfucker is dead, it was worth it," she said, her voice low. "Les and I talked."

Bev glanced around. Les was waiting quietly and everyone else seemed occupied. "Broken neck, I think, but the stuff he had went in. The search team should be on the way and if you're feeling up to it, I'd like you to go over everything again with me."

Chris gazed past Bev to the mass of floating remnants. "Sure, but I want to be in on the search this time. It was a laptop, notebook and two disks and if we don't find them soon, they'll be worthless to you."

Les casually shepherded them to the far end where they couldn't be overheard. The patrol boat skipper revved his engines and swung his craft toward the pier.

"Chris got blind-sided," Les said and handed Bev a comb from his pocket. That seemed a silly thing for him to carry considering his chosen hair style, but Bev took it and began to gently repair her hair as she listened intently.

"It started earlier," Chris said. "I've got the guy's name and number in my purse. It's Neil or Niles and he's in Washington, D.C. with the IRS. He and Jonah have known each other for a long time. Jonah worked for the IRS office in Tallahassee for a few years. I'm not clear on the details, but they kept track of each other and a while back, Neil or Niles, bought this cottage as an investment property and Jonah was connected to it somehow with keeping an eye on it or something. Anyway, the guy just found out about Jonah being dead and it took him a while to find someone in town to help him – people at the bank must have thought I would be a good contact. When he called me this morning, he said it would be really hard for him to get down here right now and asked if I could possibly come out and check on the place. He thought Jonah used it sometimes and that seemed strange since Cindy never mentioned it."

The patrol boat came into Bev's peripheral view. An ME had joined the emergency medical technicians and they cleared an area to lay the body for initial assessment.

Chris paused until she had Bev's attention again. "The guy sounded okay and I didn't mind running out to take a look, but I called you because things have been so bizarre lately. When Les told me you were at Miller's Point I thought you could meet me, but I wasn't sure you'd heard me. I was going to call again after I got into the place." She shook her head.

"Like I told Les, it was all fast after I went inside. It couldn't have been more than five minutes, I don't think. I got some light on, did a quick spin through and had the phone out when that bastard" – she pointed to the boat – "came through the door, knocked the phone out of my hand and told me to keep quiet if I wanted to live."

She tightened her jaw. "I did a six-month rotation in the Balkans and saw some stone cold killers while I was there. This cocksucker would have fit right in. He went for the desk as soon as he saw it. I tell you, if we hadn't heard you drive up, there's no doubt in my mind he'd have killed me and shoved me in a closet."

Her nostrils flared. "Is Les right? Did that son-of-a-bitch kill Cindy to protect some asshole politician?"

Bev swallowed hard. There was only so much they could tell Chris. "We don't know for certain, but it seems likely."

"Shit, shit, I should have tried to get the case when I broke away," Chris said morosely. "I just reacted and I should have known you would need it."

"Chris, you did the right thing," Les said immediately. "More than most people would have been able to do."

The arrival of the search and rescue truck saved Bev from agreeing with Chris even though she knew Les was right. Damn it, if she'd been able to snatch the bag, it would have been perfect.

Al Thornton loped onto the pier. "Boone Reynolds gave me a thumbnail sketch and I was able to bring four divers," he said and pumped everyone's hand vigorously.

"Five divers," Chris said promptly. "I'll send for my gear."

Al raised his eyebrows.

"You'll get the whole story later, but Chris knows exactly what to look for," Bev said evenly. Shit, her shoulder hurt, too.

"We've got extra equipment," Al replied. "Fill me in on the situation while we walk back and tell the rest of the crew what we're doing. We brought the inflatables for this one. I'll put Smitty and Ned in, then Chris and the other pair."

They trooped to the end of the dock where the driver was backing the trailer with a four-passenger Zodiac down the launch ramp. A second vehicle with another trailer-mounted boat was being waved past the policeman.

"We're about done," one of the EMTs said. "Smashed his face – crushed the bones and probably drowned in his own blood. Be out of here in a few minutes."

Well, hell, if he had to die, Bev hoped it had been painful.

Al delivered Chris to the team, returned and motioned Bev and Les to the side.

"We're going to do what we can, but you need to understand the first rule of recovery is that knowing where an object went in does not mean you know where it will wind up. It's shallow and we've got a point of entry, although you can see a fairly wide radius of wreckage. And laptops aren't designed for submersion," he said quietly.

Bev tried not to snarl. Al wasn't at fault. "The notebook should be recoverable and Chris said there were two disks."

Al's expression was not optimistic. "Much lighter weight than a laptop and there's a mild current today. If we don't luck out in the first couple of hours, I doubt we'll locate them."

Goddamn it, not when they were this close!

Bev sighed and suddenly felt every throb, ache and an intense thirst. "Just do what you can, Al. Do what you can."

He nodded once and turned when Smitty called his name.

Les touched Bev's elbow. "Hey, let's get you a drink and a wet paper towel. In fact, you want to run home, clean up and come back? It's liable to be a long damn day."

Bev did a slow neck roll clockwise and then counterclockwise. "I'll start with some water in me and on my face and see if I can make myself a little more presentable." She looked at her empty hands and patted the waistband of her slacks. "I must have dropped my purse in the cottage. I'm lucky the cell phone didn't fall off."

Les pointed toward the walk. "Why don't you go up and I'll bring water and Cokes? We'll call the Washington fellow and find out his story."

Bev surveyed the scene. Everyone except the group lingering beyond the police barriers was involved in activity. Neither she nor Les would be missed for a short absence. "Okay," she said and gave him a half-smile. "I'll see how long it takes at a regular pace."

Les clapped her on her back. She stifled a yelp and had a sudden desire for the days when cops kept medicinal bourbon close by. She straightened her shoulders instead and retraced the path to the cottage. The store manager would no doubt question Les as to when business could resume. There was nothing like a good killing to get the cash register cranked up.

Bev went through the back door and stopped at the kitchen sink. She let the brackish accumulation run out and then slurped water from her cupped hand. God, was she thirsty! A partial roll of paper towels was on a plastic under-the-cabinet holder. She ripped three off, dampened them, made a cooling swipe across her face and the back of her neck and dropped the grimy wad on the short counter. That was good enough for now.

She stepped around the peninsula and found Chris's purse, most of the contents strewn between the couch and floor. A pale blue sheet with an Adventures Below imprint was stuck outside of Chris's checkbook. *Nile Vandevere, IRS, DC, 202-555-3456 x 110 and Callahans, 102,* were scrawled on the sheet.

Bev took the note to the square, wooden table and pulled open the vertical blinds. The picture window provided an impressive cove view. She unhooked her cell phone and punched in the numbers. She wondered what Mr. Nile Vandevere of the IRS had to say about Jonah Shepard.

CHAPTER THIRTY-ONE

Nile Vandevere spent half an hour on the telephone with Bev and told her to use his place as long as they needed. She was about to pass his explanation on to Les when Chief Taylor shoved the door open without knocking and commandeered the armchair. He sat heavily and Les handed him an empty Coke can for an ashtray.

"Les told me about the journal business," he rumbled without preliminaries and waved his hand around the room. "Now explain this and why we have another dead body, a woman who was kidnapped, plus a taxpayer whose boat was swiped and demolished."

Bev inhaled silently. No embellishment – the chief was a *just-the-facts* boss. "You know we suspected Jonah had something on Senator Randall which set Noonan into motion and resulted in Cindy's and Rusty Smallwood's death."

Nod.

"We didn't have any idea about the journal until yesterday. We thought Noonan found whatever Jonah had because of the missing files and hard drives from the computers at the duplex and Jonah's office."

Nod.

"Chris, and we assume Cindy, didn't know about Nile Vandevere or this cottage. Nile and Jonah have been friends for several years, although he'd never met Cindy. A little over a year ago, Nile was looking to buy a vacation place he could afford without having to rent it out. He wanted one that he might later remodel into something larger. He asked Jonah to check around and this fit the bill. Jonah handled the transaction and asked if it was okay for him to use it as a second office for some private work. Jonah gave the impression he was working on a book about money laundering. Nile also thought Jonah might be trying to develop his own accounting/tax firm to go independent and that was why he didn't want anyone at the office to know what he was doing. He didn't have a problem with Jonah setting up a base because that meant he could keep an eye on the place and Nile wouldn't have to pay a management fee."

Chief Taylor held up a glowing cigarette. "This is where Jonah was doing his digging into the senator?"

"A good set-up," Bev said. "He had a place he could work undisturbed, totally clean from his name. There's a high speed Internet connection installed. It looks like he worked on a laptop and unfortunately kept minimum paper files. We didn't realize Noonan had come up empty in his other searches. He must have decided Chris was his best shot as she started to sort through Jonah's possessions." Bev bit her bottom lip. "Damn it, I should have put it together after the break-in at Chris's apartment. I could have nabbed him before this happened."

"Water under the bridge," Chief Taylor growled. "The bottom line is, Noonan followed Chris here, got whatever Jonah had, it all went into the water when the boat crashed and that's what the team is searching for?"

"You could add in the fact that Bev showed up and saved Chris's life," Les commented.

"And managed to get the primary murder suspect killed as well as lose hard evidence that could have linked us to Senator Randall," Bev said.

"*Might* have linked us," Chief Taylor said and knocked burning ash from the tip of his cigarette. "Noonan may have been a loose cannon and the senator may only be guilty of corruption."

"You're forgetting the suicide of Lottie Shepard," Bev said tiredly.

"Sorry, can't see that one. A political hot potato at best. You're talking about assisted suicide if he supplied the pills and was present. The statute of limitations must have run out if we even still have the law – I can't remember."

"He convinced her it was a suicide pact with no intention of going through with it. That's got to be manslaughter or something," Bev argued. Goddamn it, the girl was dead because of him!

"To you and me, but I imagine your DA fellow is right about not from a legal view," Chief Taylor said and let the smoldering cigarette fall into the can. He hoisted himself to his feet and looked at the open door. "Okay, I've got enough to beat the mayor and media back with," he said. "I'm not going to give them Noonan's name until I've alerted the mayor. Give me a call if they find anything, but I can't see making this a multi-day effort. The Green girl is our only concern and I'd say you've solved that. There won't be a trial so we don't have to get into beyond-reasonable-doubt shit."

"Goddamn it, Chief, Senator Randall…"

"No." He gave her an unyielding look. "If, and only if, they recover something intact that shows real dirt on Senator Randall, the DA might be willing to go after him. Twenty-year-old, uncorroborated moaning by a teenager who might have been delusional won't cut it. You can pass on whatever you want to the West Palm folks and let them decide whether or not to pursue the deal with Smallwood."

Bev literally bit her tongue as her temper flamed. This wasn't right! She wasn't sorry Noonan was dead, but damn it, she should have taken him alive. Even if Senator Randall hadn't told him to kill Cindy and Smallwood, she'd bet her next year's paycheck he was an accessory after the fact and that sure as hell wasn't some old news or delusion!

Chief Taylor paused as she glared at him. "I know you're pissed," he said softly. "This is the kind of thing you'll make yourself crazy over and Les is right. You've got to think about the fact that if Noonan were guilty of the other two killings, he'd have taken Chris out without blinking an eye. You did good – not perfect, but good. Every once in a while, you need to let it soak into your stubborn brain there's nothing wrong with good. I learned a long time ago that a D was a passing grade."

"I never made a goddamn D in my life," Bev said before she could stop the words. She rubbed the tip of her nose with the back of her hand. "Anyway, the computer is probably a loss, but a few hours in the water won't have damaged the notebook too badly."

Chief Taylor opened the door. "Don't pin your hopes on it," he said. "We're minus one murdering son-of-a-bitch. That's not a bad day's work."

He shut the door behind him and Bev looked at Les in frustration.

Les shrugged philosophically. "I think we're done here. Want to walk down and see how it's going?"

"Sure," Bev said, the blood pulsating in her head, her muscles shrieking for an analgesic. "It's not right, Les, it's not goddamn right."

"You're a cop, Bev," he said and reached for the doorknob. "Sometimes the bad guys get away. That's why cold case files sit in desks and not every acquittal is because the defendant is innocent. Besides, maybe Noonan's actions will convince your buddy up the road to go after the senator. If nothing else, the press is going to be asking questions about a connection. They can make lots of people uncomfortable."

Bev recalled Deputy Chief Barrett's reluctance and wondered if he would consider Rusty Smallwood's death worth a run-in with the power elite. *That*, she wouldn't bet on.

"I'll try and sell them," she said reluctantly. "Les, you got aspirin or something?"

He fished into his pocket and produced a tin. "Hell, yes. At my age you do the aspirin regimen and keep some around, just in case," he laughed without humor. "Come on, I'll buy you another diet Coke to wash it down with."

They walked slowly as Bev twisted and stretched the different aching body parts. No damage the aspirin, a long hot shower and cold beer wouldn't fix, although she might avoid wearing shorts until the bruises faded. Kyle would be a good sport about it. Kyle! Shit, she hadn't talked to him! No telling what kind of story he'd gotten. Wait. Why hadn't he called or come out to check on her? Maybe he was in court and hadn't heard.

"What's wrong?" Les asked. "You look like you just thought of something."

Bev shrugged. "Sort of. I need to call Kyle."

Les snapped his fingers. "Oh, hell, I'm sorry. He called the station right before all this broke loose and left a message to tell you he had to fly home. It completely slipped my mind."

Bev stared at him. "What? He meant today?"

"Yeah, some kind of family emergency. Said he wasn't sure how long he'd be gone and would telephone late this afternoon or tonight. He's got his cell phone with him and his laptop if you want to send an email."

Well, goddamn!! The case was coming apart on her, there was a better than average chance she would be in a really rotten mood by evening and now she didn't even have a shoulder to cry on about it. Not that she would cry, but that wasn't the point. Family emergency? What family emergency? Why in the ever-loving name of hell didn't he just tell her what was going on? Damn it, how male could he be?

"The boats are still out," Les said and interrupted her seething thoughts.

Just as well – she was going to spiral into an old-fashioned hissy fit if she wasn't careful – momentarily satisfying and not very productive.

"All five divers must be in," Bev said as she looked at the deserted dock. The crowd in the parking lot had dissipated and she saw Sylvia talking with one of the uniforms. She would have quickly cornered the men who owned the stolen boat and Floyd. She'd probably gotten everyone except her and Chris and that was no doubt what she had in mind.

"Hey, it's way after lunchtime and there's probably no reason for us both to stand here watching," Les said. "Why don't you get a bite, maybe get cleaned up and start your report? Boy Scout's honor, I'll phone you within seconds if they find the shit."

Bev shook her head rapidly. "No goddamn way," she said evenly. "I may look like shit, but I'll clean up good later. A diet Coke and a pack of crackers will hold me. I'm not hungry to tell you the truth."

"They might be out there for the rest of the afternoon," Les said and scratched his cheek.

"I'm not leaving," Bev said firmly and shooed him toward the car. "Go on and see if you can deflect the fearless reporter for me. I'm not up to talking with her and if she sees me alone, she's liable to flash her boobs to get past the barrier."

"If she flashes her boobs, I'll talk to her," he said with a smile. "Besides, I did see the crash. That ought to be worth a little skin."

"I'm afraid the other witnesses beat you to it," Bev laughed.

Les glanced at the marina store door. "Speaking of people, we need to let the guy's customers start coming back in. The body is gone, photographs were made and as long as nobody interferes with the dive teams, we shouldn't keep them out."

"I know," Bev said, resigned to good citizen-police relations. "Ask one car to hang around though in case something else strange comes up or if I need an official vehicle for some reason. If they recover evidence, I want to make damn sure the chain of custody isn't broken."

Les nodded, patted her on the shoulder and ambled away. Bev went inside the almost chilly store.

She gently rebuffed the manager's complaints by assuring him business could return to normal and agreeing that yes, it had been a hell of a thing and who'd have thought something like this could go on in broad daylight. Yes, the divers were looking for evidence and no, she couldn't say much more about the case at the moment. She escaped into the ladies room with a diet Coke and a package of trail mix.

She downed the aspirin before she faced the mirror. The hasty repair in the cottage had helped some. She soaked a paper towel, wrung it out and cleaned the rest of the caked dirt from her face, neck and hands, then used another towel to minimize the streaks on her clothes. She unbraided her hair and gently untangled the rest of the snarls. By the time she finished, she had achieved a level of acceptable disarray.

"Damn, I wanted to get you truly disheveled for the camera. It would be more dramatic," Sylvia said from the doorway.

Bev leaned her head against the mirror.

"Nice touch, although not quite the look I'm going for," she said cheerfully. "Come on, we'll make you a heroine again. *Pursued gunman with no thought of personal safety*, etc., and, by the way, I really want Chris Green. Is she actually underwater?"

Bev kept her forehead to the glass, but turned her head to the right. "I'm not in the mood, Sylvia."

"Tough shit," the woman said without rancor. "I happen to know you've got nothing but time on your hands until they find these mysterious items or give up trying. You might as well give me an interview. I know damn good and well you're deliberately stalling on the identity of the man. I can feel it and that's only one of the things I want a scoop on."

Bev straightened and raised her eyebrows. "People in hell want ice water, too."

Sylvia barked her throaty laugh. "Amusing comeback. Listen, you know I play fair, but I can't believe Chris Green's involvement is coincidental. My antenna is buzzing and I want the good shit first. If this has something to do with the Cindy Green case, give me a break – it'll all come out anyway. Let's go outside, find a little shade, catch a breeze and you can unburden your soul."

Yeah, right. Shooting my mouth off to the press ought to really help this situation. "Sylvia, I plan to go outside and do my job. That does not include helping you with yours. Chief Taylor will have a statement for everyone later this afternoon and if we're done here, I'll be with him."

The reporter shook her head slowly. "Such a hard ass you like to be," she said with no trace of irritation. "I may not get you to lighten up, but bet you a cold one I'll have Chris talking. I was superb in my earlier write-up if I do say so myself."

Bev flicked her hand to move the persistent woman away from the door. "I'm sure you were and Chris is a private citizen. If she wants to give you gory details, that's her business. I don't know when they'll be coming up though."

"No sweat," Sylvia said and opened the door for her. "I've got my laptop and can while away the afternoon writing my story and fill in the blanks later."

Bev gave her a half smile and pressed past her. She liked Sylvia as a person, appreciated her writing style and enjoyed the few times she'd been able to sit down with her in a social setting. Bev's aversion to dealing with the press was more general in nature than specific. She understood enough about editorial prerogative to know what she said would not necessarily be reflected accurately in print. And there might possibly have been occasions when perhaps she'd made comments that were not entirely appropriate. Her description of a group of spoiled, thrill-seeking kids obviously devoid of parental guidance who had committed a rash of burglaries had been one of the times Chief Taylor had scathingly explained that her job as a detective did not include providing social commentary about the general public. He didn't give a good goddamn about the spoiled kids, but he didn't need fucking complaints from the parents.

People were milling about the store and the manager was talking knowingly to a knot of men at the cash register. Good, Sylvia could interview *him*. Bev looked toward the inflatable boat when she emerged from the building. Al was leaned forward speaking with two divers who grasped the side of the boat and made gestures around floating wreckage.

She wandered to the far end of the dock, snatched her cell phone when it rang and tried not to be disappointed at the sound of her father. She cleared up the exaggerated version he'd heard and assured him she would call her mother and calm her down. That process took longer than she liked, but she tucked the phone to her ear, paid virtually no attention to worried admonishments and watched the divers as they surfaced empty handed, conversed and submerged again.

The conversation with Hank was easier, although he spent a lot of it grunting and groaning. No, he didn't know if Chief Taylor had notified his chief yet and he wasn't going to run find out. He would hold off for a while and think about what the hell to do next. She promised he would be the second call after her chief if they recovered something useable. The thought of the journal did not fill him with warm fuzzies. Now that they had discussed business, when was she coming up for another overnighter? Bev side-stepped the question with a vague *we'll see.*

She paced and watched for almost an hour until one of the divers finally came up with something tucked against his side. Al leaned down and took it from him. Squarish and black. Bev rushed to the edge of the pier and waved to the boat. Al held it up and she nodded eagerly even though she was certain he couldn't see her gesture. Al turned to speak with the man in the second boat and then gave Bev a signal that he was coming in. She jiggled one foot impatiently. She caught the line he tossed as soon as he was close enough and flinched when she saw his expression.

"Don't get too excited," he said, and lifted a sodden, black canvas bag from the bottom and passed it to her. "There was no protection and the notebook and disks must have been flung out of the side pocket. What you've got is a thoroughly soaked laptop."

Bev held the dripping mass. "Maybe they're inside."

Al climbed out of the boat. "Not according to Chris. She said he stuffed them into the side pocket."

Bev set the bag onto the dock, knelt and struggled with the zipper. It was jammed in several places as she tried to keep her temper. Hell, she'd cut the damn thing open if she needed to. She worked the zipper loose and surveyed the machine. Water, mud, bits of plant matter and debris covered the computer and the bottom of the drenched canvas.

Al crouched beside her and spoke low. "Listen, I hate to give you more bad news, but I've been watching the current flow and the divers are telling me what I kind of expected."

Bev clenched her jaw and looked at him.

"I can keep them out until we max on time and I can try again tomorrow, but my professional assessment based on a lot of experience is that it's not going to happen. The disks are so lightweight, they would have floated already and from the way Chris described the notebook, there was nothing to send it to the bottom and it didn't catch around the pilings. My bet is that it's long gone, too."

Bev swallowed hard and blinked her eyes rapidly. "Seems like I heard once there are ways to recover data from damaged computers."

Al shrugged. "You can take it up with your experts, but this is a standard make with no hardening and a couple of hours in saltwater is not ordinary damage. It might help to rinse it in fresh water, though."

Bev inhaled deeply and searched his face. Sympathetic, not encouraging. "Give me another hour? In the meantime, I'll let the computer whizzes know what we've got."

Al took his cap off, wiped his brow with the back of his arm and nodded. "Sure. We're looking hard, Bev. It's tough to suspend the laws of physics – lightweight objects float and move with current."

She managed to paste a smile over her total frustration. "Physics wasn't one of my favorite subjects, but I remember the basics."

Al uncoiled and eased back into the inflatable craft as Bev lifted the sodden case. Noonan dead, Jonah's evidence gone, the only link to Randall a journal that a rookie lawyer could get tossed out. Great, just goddamn great.

Bev unclipped her cell phone. She'd have Les come get the computer while she waited the extra hour, then take his advice and run by her apartment for a quick shower and change of clothes. If the recovery effort failed, she didn't want to make the admission during the middle of the chief's press conference.

CHAPTER THIRTY-TWO

Bev slumped in her chair. She was cleaner than she'd been and aches were edging in as the aspirin wore off. The lack of support from conversations with Chief Taylor and the DA seeped through her like cold rain. With Kyle gone, they had to deal directly with the DA whose legal acuity was combined with severe risk aversion. He hadn't been receptive to leaning on a state senator, although they extracted a promise for him to call the West Palm DA, whom he knew socially as well as professionally. She'd had less luck with the issue of Lottie's death.

"I wouldn't fucking touch that with a fucking ten foot pole," had not been difficult to interpret.

Goddamn it, why was she the only one – well, two, counting Jonah, who wanted to see Warren Randall pay for that? She wasn't about to dismiss Lottie's journal as depression-fueled make-believe. She'd been close enough to Randall to recognize thinly veneered amorality. He was the kind of man who would have used women all his life. Okay, used people in general, but especially women.

She frowned when the sound from the telephone broke her concentration.

"Bev? Did Les give you my message? And what in the hell happened today? Are you okay? I'm sorry I didn't get to talk to you earlier, but I had no idea," Kyle said without letting her answer the first question.

She gripped the receiver and swung her chair to watch the door – she didn't need an audience strolling in. "I'm a little bruised up, but nothing broken and no stitches," she said calmly. "Today's been sort of complicated so why don't you start by telling me why you flew out the way you did?"

"Bev, I was going to explain everything this weekend," he said slowly. "I'll save the details for when I get back, but I'm at the hospital with my dad and practically the whole family. He has leukemia and they're going to do a bone marrow transplant. All of us who might be a match are here to get tested."

Bev stared at the wall, his words lagging behind her comprehension. Leukemia and bone marrow transplants?

"Jesus, how's he doing? I mean, how bad is it?"

His voice dropped lower. "It could be worse. He's in a great hospital with a super medical team. There are some new treatments and with the bone marrow transplant, there's a real good chance he'll go into remission. Look, Bev, this came at me out of the blue and... well... I guess I should have told you from the beginning. I couldn't believe it was true and then..."

"I understand," Bev said quickly, "and it's all right. I don't know how I would have reacted if it had been my dad. What happens next?"

My God, no wonder he'd been distracted! Kyle and his father had the kind of closeness that came from genuine affection rather than obligatory family ties. Not that he'd discussed it with her. It was in the way he talked about him, the respect and admiration woven with the stories of childhood outings, adolescent challenges, and shared passion for the law. You could tell it was more than the favored status of oldest son. There were all the signs of two men who were proud of each other.

They spoke for almost thirty minutes. Bev heard his voice gain confidence as he related the prognosis and information he'd gleaned from hours of on-line research. After he explained what they'd been told about the bone marrow match test, he pressed her for an accounting of the day. He ran through a spectrum of awe, concerned chastisement, sympathy and irascible agreement with the DA.

"As much as I hate to sound like my boss and Chief Taylor, you should pat yourself on the back for saving Chris and getting the bad guy."

"I only got one of them though," she protested. "I want Randall."

Kyle said something she couldn't hear. "Bev, I've got to go in a minute. Look, if Jonah found something on Randall, other people can too. I'm not making any promises, but I have a contact in a watchdog organization. They're not law enforcement, but if they're willing to start digging, they could pique the interest of someone who could take other action." He spoke again away from the receiver.

"At this point, that's better than what I'm getting," Bev said.

Shades of Truth

"Listen, you go ahead. Your place is with your family right now."

"Yeah," Kyle said. "I'll know what my time frame is like tomorrow. I'll call you as soon as I can. Take care of yourself for me, okay?"

"Sure and give my regards to your mom and dad," Bev said. She cradled the receiver against her shoulder after he hung up and closed her eyes to imagine him somewhere in a large hospital, one among hundreds waiting for news. There would be excitement for new parents, relief for patients whose afflictions were pronounced healed, dread of the unknown for others, grief for some who would be told nothing more could be done.

Bev shook her head sharply to dispel the morbid thoughts. Even though she'd never met his father, he was bound to be strong and a fighter. There was every reason to have confidence in his condition and she refused to feel guilty because she was glad to find out the relationship between her and Kyle wasn't at stake.

Christ, what a long day it had been! She'd bargained with her mother to have dinner at their house tomorrow instead of tonight. She wouldn't mind a father-to-daughter cop conversation at all, but she didn't think she could cope with inevitable *what-ifs* from her mother. Her view was she'd worried enough when her husband was on the force and it wasn't fair to expect her to handle it with her daughter, too. *What if you'd been really hurt? What if next time you...* Although she always came around after gentle coaxing by her father, Bev wasn't in the mood for emotional ritual.

She was trying to decide whether she had energy to handle dinner out or if pizza delivery at her apartment would be better when the telephone rang again.

"Shouldn't you be gone by now?" Chris asked in a hoarse voice.

"I was delayed by another call," she said. "Where are you?"

"Home with a stiff drink," she replied. "It got pretty crazy with the search and talking to my parents and all. It wasn't until a few minutes ago that I realized I hadn't properly thanked you."

Bev waved her hand dismissively to an unseen audience. "You took a chance, too, the way you kept your cool and bailed out of the boat."

Chris laughed without humor. "Yeah, you and I are a couple of bad-ass chicks. At any rate, don't plan on ever paying for another dive with me. You've got unlimited boat privileges from here on and I may throw in free beer as well."

"I'll let you sleep on that offer for a few days," she said and took her purse from the desk drawer.

"Listen, there was one other thing. I managed to avoid most of the reporters, although I had about a dozen voice mails waiting. The one lady, Sylvia, buttonholed me. I was impressed with how she'd done the other articles, so I spent some time with her. Anyway, I don't remember exactly how it came up, but I mentioned that journal to her. You know, the one from the safe deposit box." Chris hesitated. "She asked me some questions and I told her I hadn't read it. I didn't think about whether I should have said anything or not. I hope that was okay."

Bev squeezed her eyes shut for a moment. Shit, was it okay? It was evidence, sort of, and not something for public disclosure. Except not really, if you took the DA's view that without an active investigation, it wasn't something to be shielded. Bev hadn't given up on the point, however, which would make it something they wanted to keep closely held.

"Uh, that's no problem," she said, not sure how long Chris had waited for a response. Only a few seconds according to the clock. "We don't know how it plays in this, if at all," she said, not wanting to sound critical. Chris had enough on her mind.

"Good, I wouldn't want to dick up anything you might be doing for the rest of the case," Chris said sluggishly. "I'm going to unplug the telephone, take what may be the longest shower of my life and then crawl into bed and sleep until I wake up. I don't know when I'll go in tomorrow, but if you need me I'll either be at the shop or here."

"Sure," Bev said. "Get some rest. You deserve it."

They said good-bye and Bev logged off her computer. Not dick up the rest of the case. That was the big question, wasn't it? What was the rest of the case? Was she going to be able to get anyone in authority to let her go further, to target Randall?

Not based on the opinions of the DA, Deputy Chief Barrett and practically every other person she'd argued her position to.

Bev shook her head sharply, mired in the circle she couldn't break out of. The fatigue of the day and finding out about Kyle's father was dulling her ability to think. She rarely took baths, although she was tempted by the idea of a long soak in a tub while holding a cold beer. Trying to drink a beer in the shower could be tricky. She narrowed dinner to definitely pizza delivered to the apartment. The number was on her speed dial and they had her regular order in the computer – no decisions required. She shut out the lights and nodded goodnight to the evening shift without stopping to exchange gossip.

She stepped into the early evening, the sun softened by the lower angle, a light breeze reducing the perpetual humidity. A tan Jeep Cherokee she didn't recognize was parked near her Spitfire. The engine was running and as she stared at the vehicle, Sylvia Ruthven swung out and grinned, a lit cigarette hanging from the side of her mouth.

Bev tried not to let her shoulders droop. Sylvia wouldn't have been sitting in the parking lot just because she had no other way to spend her time.

"Oh, don't look so reluctant," she said and closed the gap between them. "I know your ass is dragging and I'll even buy you a cold beer if you'd like. More than one in fact."

Bev looked at her sideways and tried not to smile since it would only encourage her. "I don't have the energy for this," she said simply. "My plan for cold beer entails being alone."

"Okay, then I'll try to take advantage of your weakened state," she replied good-naturedly. "Tell me about the dead girl's journal."

Bev paused at her car, opened the driver's door and threw her purse inside. "The what?"

"The journal written by Lottie Shepard, found by Chris Green and delivered to you. A journal that one can assume contains fascinating revelations by the young lady who may very well be the root of all kinds of things that have been happening lately," she said briskly and waved her cigarette vaguely in the direction of West Palm.

"You know I'm not likely to comment on evidence of an ongoing investigation and certainly not without clearance from the boss," Bev said tiredly. "You can ask him."

"I did and he brushed me off with a comment about not knowing either the authenticity or the relevance and I think that's bullshit. Unless, of course, everyone wants to help cover the illustrious Senator Warren Blaine Randall."

Bev snapped her head up and looked Sylvia directly in the eyes.

"What do you mean?"

She moved the cigarette into an arc behind her so the smoke trailed away from Bev's face. "You may lump all reporters together as a pain in the ass, but that doesn't mean I'm not good at my job. I spent my waiting time productively today and accessed some old files from Lottie Shepard's suicide. To say that it was rubber-stamped isn't much of an exaggeration. I also know about the fact that when Jonah Shepard confronted the good senator, he did so with an unloaded gun."

Damn, where had she gotten that from?

"I told you I can feel this story is big," she said earnestly. "Right this minute, no one else has the pieces I do, but I'm not sure how long that will last. Did you hear Senator Randall's statement to the press?"

Bev shook her head.

"He's completely shocked and dismayed and can't comprehend what Mike Noonan was up to," she paraphrased. "He has a press conference scheduled for tomorrow. He probably delayed it to have time to polish his act. I try not to get into conspiracy shit mode, but four people die violent deaths within two weeks of each other. Three have direct links to Senator Randall and it ought to raise some questions. Questions that can get ugly for a man in his position, questions that men like his father-in-law will not want asked. I never thought of you as afraid of that kind of pressure."

Bev jerked herself upright and glared from her height advantage.

Sylvia raised her eyes and chortled. "Ah, I am right. You're pissed because they're trying to gloss over possible involvement by the senator. Better to lay it all off on a dead man." Her voice became husky. "Bev, I'm not going to deny this is a huge chance for me to break out of local coverage and I will make the most of it. That doesn't negate the fact I think Warren Randall is lying through his handsome smile. Money and power will work their magic to let him slide by with no hardball questions. If you can't do it officially, maybe I can stir shit up my way. I swear I won't quote you, I just want to know what's in that journal."

She ground the cigarette out against the sole of her shoe and crossed her arms loosely across her chest.

Bev inhaled silently, her eyes searching Sylvia's resolute face. This wasn't her style. She was tenacious and the right answer was to press forward with her arguments and let Kyle seek out his contact. Leaking information could backfire and it was unprofessional as hell. There was a system to work through.

Lottie Shepard's delicate script flowed before her, Warren Randall's betrayal obvious to anyone who wanted to see it; in the journal he showed the same charming willingness to lie that Bev sensed that day in his office. He was a man who understood the system, who bet on its protection. He belonged to a network of wealth and privilege that could buy brilliant legal maneuvers and positive public opinion spin. Some fell from grace, while most had the resources and lack of conscience that allowed them to lie with utter and believable sincerity, to smile with pained regret as accusations barely pricked their rich hides.

"He's probably more slimy that either of us know and William DeLong has the wherewithal to bury every bit of this along with Mike Noonan," Sylvia said softly.

Bev wondered fleetingly what her father would do and then remembered the sight of Cindy Green's bloated, mangled body. She drew a deep breath and began. "Hypothetically speaking, suppose there was once a fragile, seventeen year-old girl....."

CHAPTER THIRTY-THREE

Warren felt molded to the chair, barely able to lift the heavy glass to his mouth or the bottle of Scotch to pour a refill. Ice, water – superfluous elements that masked the relief the liquor brought. He needed solace without demand. Too many demands from too many directions.

DeLong, ranting and throwing instructions to him, to Freddy. He bellowed threats to his senior lawyer to keep the stink of whatever the fuck was going on from the family name. Freddy was simpering in his desire for reassurance that it was all some terrible, tragic mistake. Lila repeated a frenzied plea for statements she could give to the endless calls. Cecilia's silent rebuke had meant who the fuck knew what – she found the whole matter to be socially embarrassing?

God, he'd been on stage since Freddy had rushed in with the unimaginable announcement. Warren refused to believe him at first. How could Noonan have been so stupid, so careless? It was all over with, then. It would be merely a matter of hours before the pieces were fit together. The weight of inevitable disclosure lightened as Freddy wheedled vital information from his sources.

Nothing recovered except Noonan's body? Something he'd taken, but the girl didn't know what? Warren grasped those statements even as he'd spun his shocked dismay in the only salvageable direction. Yes, Noonan had obviously gone off the deep end. Poor man, perhaps he'd been more affected than they realized by the incident with Jonah's death and Rusty's accident. Perhaps he'd taken it all personally, beginning with his failure to prevent Jonah's confrontation with the senator. Despite early signs, he must have developed some off-the-wall theory about a conspiracy and launched on his own. Who knew why he would have involved the other Green girl or what he thought he found? Yes, it was most puzzling and mysterious. Freddy tweaked the verbiage and held his ground while DeLong screamed obscenities about damage control.

Warren delayed his appearance with the promise of a formal

press conference the following day. He had to let Freddy arrange a structured platform under controlled circumstances. It was vital to have a venue they could game plan. He fled home and shut himself in his study. A futile search, they were saying. A recovered laptop computer, but somber laments that the contents would have been destroyed and the search was to be terminated for the other items. Interviews with witnesses, a reminder of the chain of events since the day Jonah had been shot.

Freddy's words began to take shape in speculation. Even using disjointed pieces and having more questions than answers, a version of the truth could be fleshed out by a skilled practitioner. Take a thread of truth and weave it expertly among the lies. A solemn demeanor was the key. He would stay calm, project dignity with only a hint of admission that perhaps Noonan's steely competence had been a veil over harnessed violence that those around him had not recognized. A brief sigh of error in perception and heartfelt praise for heroic actions that saved the life of Chris Green. He played it to himself, barricaded in his study, modified the phrasing and was adept with the rendition by the time the cameras started rolling at the press conference.

He was poised, concerned, as mystified as anyone else would be under these circumstances. Did he have knowledge of allegations against Noonan during his days in Chicago? Why, no, Mr. Noonan had come to him with solid recommendations.

It had been toward the end of the allotted time when a woman he didn't know had stood and fired the question about a diary from Lottie Shepard.

"Pardon me?"

"A diary, Senator. A diary about her pregnancy, her decision to commit suicide."

"Preposterous, a nonsensical rumor."

"A reliable source."

"A vile hoax then by someone seeking to profit from this entire horrible chain of events. Completely irresponsible."

The impertinent bitch trying to toss out more information as Freddy mercifully regained the initiative and thanked everyone for their time, expressing regret that the senator had a pressing engagement. She'd still been trying to force her way through the throng when he'd stalwartly exited the room, ignoring her shouts to him.

The rest of the day, evening and night had been a trade-off of huddled private meetings and public appointments he couldn't cancel and an endless dinner party Cecilia refused to attend alone. Warren had allowed himself to be sucked into the wake of a boorish man who was known to talk at length with little encouragement. An occasional word and periodic nods were the only contributions required. His companion's reputation ensured few other people would seek him out. Cecilia finally relented with a brittle smile and made their farewells to the hostess. Her rigid posture had not relaxed during the drive home, nor did it when they entered the house, freed from the sight of others.

She'd kicked off her high heels, but made no move to change from evening clothes. "I have some correspondence to catch up on," she announced icily and disappeared into her study down the hall.

Warren had thrown his jacket and tie onto the bed, snatched the bottle of Scotch and a glass from the small wet bar and retreated to the terrace. It was a smaller version of the ground floor terrace with a view of the lagoon, the stone apron and part of the garden. He swallowed the first Scotch like water, the second nearly as quickly, the un-tempered bite a balm to his battered psyche. Lottie had left a diary? Could it be true? He didn't doubt she had one. He'd feared that at first, certain it would be produced by a vengeful Jonah. Nothing, though, nothing but the note she'd written, the one he'd set fire to after he was sure she was no longer breathing. God, it had taken longer than he thought. It had been nearly an hour after she'd swallowed the pills. It had been a mixed batch, some filched from several bottles of his mother's, some Andy had gotten for him, some over-the-counter ones thrown in for good measure.

After Lottie had grown still, he'd waited an extra ten minutes before taking the note and three blank pages beneath it. He'd ripped the sheets into shreds, burned them to ash in the cold fireplace, scraped the ash into a paper sack and carried it with him when he left. He'd checked for a pulse when he'd finished and slipped out the back to walk to his car, hidden in a wooded lot three blocks away. He'd opened the sack and let the ashes drift out.

He'd been certain no one would show up at the house while he was there. The real risk had been if someone saw him or the car. It had been dark and he'd been careful, watching the quiet streets for movement. He'd originally thought about leaving Lottie to be found by her parents or whomever, but decided he had more control if he was the one who called it in. After he retrieved his car he'd driven with the lights on, the radio volume up and knocked loudly at the front door – an anxious friend, no, acquaintance, no, fellow student, who was innocently responding to a confused call from a sobbing girl. As it turned out, no one had seen his staged entry, but it hadn't mattered. Thank God they hadn't checked telephone records like they did today. No, as he assumed, the Shepards weren't important enough for an intensive investigation. It was routine for the police and Lottie's parents accepted it as judgment from God. They mournfully prayed forgiveness for a child who had been weak in the flesh. Only Jonah had demanded answers, had guessed a part of the truth.

How could a diary appear now though? Where had it been? Was that what Jonah had meant all along? If so, what had Noonan found? Warren poured more Scotch to the brim of the glass. Who had the diary? Could it be the reporter? Was there any way to prove it was Lottie's or would he be able to sell that it was a fake? With Noonan and Rusty dead, there was no one to dispute his claims. He would be careful not to blame Rusty for anything – his family might take exception. If the truth came out about the wreck, Rusty would be another victim. Right, a protégé misled and betrayed by his mentor. No, no reason to jump into that one yet – maybe his death would be officially left as an accident. It was easier to remember the lies if he kept them to a minimum.

No one was likely to defend Noonan's character. He'd been a loner and the Chicago connection would write him off as a business loss. Warren's arrangement with Bassi would dissolve and while that was regrettable, it had been adequately profitable.

Don't panic was the first rule of survival. If the diary could not be verified, all he had to do was ride out the furor. He would have Freddy increase his appearances with senior and children-centered organizations. They needed a full-court press to get beyond this.

He'd take Cecilia for a romantic get-away and it was probably time to sacrifice the affair with Amber in a shower of expensive gifts. She was a practical woman and had known it would end someday. The press and public tired of stories quickly. After a few months of impeccable, community-building behavior, most would forget. Thank God the election was not on top of them!

DeLong would require more delicate handling, but he, too, would re-embrace his son-in-law. He'd already invested too much to walk away if the polls either held steady or only down-ticked for a short while.

Warren chuckled quietly and lifted himself from the chair. Enough, enough of sitting still. The reporter had caught him off guard and he needed to take charge of his fears. He leaned over the marble railing, peered at the light-dappled water of the manmade lagoon and spat in contempt of the people who underestimated him. He'd kept the secret of Lottie Shepard for more than twenty years. He could bluff his way though it again.

CHAPTER THIRTY-FOUR

Bev jerked awake as she realized she heard the telephone and not her alarm clock. The large red digits displayed 5:33. Shit, this couldn't be good.

"Henderson," she said, her mouth dry. Was it Kyle's father?

"Sorry for the time, Bev. It's Hank and I didn't want you to hear the news before I talked to you."

"What news?" The sheet fell to her waist when she moved into a sitting position.

"Warren Randall took a header off his second floor balcony about four hours ago," he said flatly. "Dead on impact or shortly thereafter."

"Holy shit! He jumped?"

"Don't know," Hank replied slowly. "We just finished at the house."

"Wait," Bev interrupted him. She was on her feet, the receiver crooked into her shoulder. "I can be on the road in fifteen minutes," she said hurriedly.

"Why? Not that I mind buying you a cup of coffee, but this is purely local," he said, his voice more puzzled than flirtatious.

"I'll explain when I get there. Your office best?"

"Yeah, I guess," he said. "Why don't you tell me what the hell you're talking about though?"

"I don't want to get into it over the telephone," Bev said sharply. "Hang up so I can jump in the shower." She depressed the button without saying good-bye, her brain calculating as fast as it could without coffee. Shit, shit! She'd seen replays of the news conference and Sylvia had called her late in the afternoon, exultant about the bedlam she'd created with her questions. Oh, God, what if Randall had crumpled because of the journal? Christ, she wanted to shake him up to make a mistake, not commit suicide. Was that possible? He didn't seem the type. Shit, what if he'd been nearer a mental edge than anyone thought?

She blasted herself with cold water for the alertness effect as well as distraction from the wave of guilt pulsating in her veins. Damn, that was cold! She relented, turned the faucet to a warmer setting and let the rational part of her brain override the initial emotional response. She would have time to think as she drove.

Soon she was in fourth gear, a large coffee wedged between her left hand and the steering wheel. She tuned the radio to a Miami station and pressed the accelerator. She'd left a message for Les at the office although he would probably catch the bulletin over breakfast.

Bev wasn't surprised that few details of the breaking story were being broadcast – DeLong would have clamped the lid on if the cops hadn't. She called Hank from the car when she was at an intersection close to the police station.

"Damn, you weren't driving the posted limit," he said more cheerfully than he should be at this hour. "Change of plans. It's crazy here between the chief foaming and reporters trying to get a scoop. Meet me at the Randall's home. I'll give you directions and then I'll be on the way."

"Hang on a sec, I'm near a Burger King," Bev said and whipped the car two lanes to the right. She parked in the first slot, wrote down the instructions and then dashed inside for a bathroom and another coffee.

Bev drove carefully to avoid a wrong turn, although the patrol car and a lingering television station van made for good landmarks. Under other circumstances, she would have enjoyed a leisurely pace to admire the ritzy neighborhood. Hank was talking to one of the patrolmen and waved her through. She tucked the Spitfire next to his Porsche, got out and whistled reflexively – it was a hell of a house. The absence of yellow police tape spoke of the family's influence – wouldn't want the place to look like some tawdry area where nasty things happened to lesser mortals.

"I may break a personal record for cups of coffee consumed before ten o'clock," Hank said as he joined her. He was holding a brushed aluminum travel cup in one hand and had his other slipped into the pocket of his beige slacks. It was the *Miami Vice* look again with a loose fit matching jacket, a cobalt blue shirt and no tie. "Want to small talk or get down to business?"

She stared for a moment at the impressive front door. Christ, it looked like something from a castle. "Any better idea of what happened?" she asked, not sure of what she wanted the answer to be.

How was she going to feel if Randall committed suicide because she leaked information about the journal to Sylvia?

Hank lowered his voice. "It's hard to tell at this point. Mrs. Randall was the only one home with him and she made the call a little after 1 a.m. – she called 911 first, then her father – or at least that's the claim. I was notified because one of the officers who responded to the scene is a cousin and he thought I would be interested. Like I said, folks are scrambling."

"Where is everyone?"

Hank grinned. "The housekeeper, her husband and a junior member of the law firm that handles William DeLong's legal concerns are in the house to keep the riff-raff out. Mrs. Randall has been whisked away from prying eyes. The preliminaries are over with, but as long as we don't look as if we're conducting a search, the lawyer bulldog won't howl too loudly if we do a walk through. Let's go around back and you can see the impact spot. Not too messy – severed his spinal column – although true cause of death has to be determined."

He led her by the outside stone path instead of through the house. Bev wished Aunt Lorna could see the layout – the landscaping was almost as luxurious as the house. Or did it qualify as an estate?

"Goddamn, did they steal the lagoon from a movie set?" she asked as they stepped onto the spacious stone border. The housekeeper was no doubt distressed that she hadn't been allowed to wash away the stains yet. At least it hadn't been a direct head wound – that would have splattered blood, bone and tissue.

"Could be," Hank said and walked her to the right of the covered area. He pointed out the gracefully designed marble balustrades and railing above their heads.

"According to Mrs. Randall, they attended a social function last night and returned home late. Despite the hour, she had some work to attend to in her study, also on the second floor of the house, down the hall from the master suite. Her husband, to the best of her knowledge, decided to have a nightcap while sitting on the balcony – or upper terrace, as she referred to it. She heard nothing, was occupied with her own matters and when she entered the bedroom almost two hours later, she didn't see her husband. She went onto the terrace, saw the bottle and glass on the table, didn't see him, assumed he was in the bathroom and went back inside. When she realized the light was off, she became puzzled and thought perhaps he'd gone downstairs. She went to look for him, saw no light except for the ones they usually leave on, called out and then became concerned. She went back upstairs onto the terrace, walked to the edge and saw him on the terrace below, face down and dialed 911 before she rushed down." He took a sip of coffee.

"No, the house staff doesn't live in," he continued, "and as you can see, all the houses are walled and set a fair distance apart – no one around, no witnesses, no note. Mrs. Randall was still in her evening clothes; he was in a dress shirt, trousers, no jacket and no tie. No signs of struggle. The ME hasn't ruled out that he might have had a mild heart attack or something and fallen. On the other hand, Mrs. Randall acknowledged he had been drinking more than usual with all the, what did she call it? Oh, yeah, all the 'recent turmoil.' It's possible he was totally wasted and tumbled over. I don't know the blood alcohol level."

Bev studied the distance and turned to stare at Hank. "What's it like upstairs?"

He shrugged. "We'll go up, but the layout is the way she described it. We've already done a discreet, unscientific test and sound doesn't carry. This place is solid and you can't hear a damn thing from the study if the door is closed."

"Money does buy nice things," Bev said mildly. "Show me the choreography, please – I'm curious about something," she said, still wondering about Randall's state of mind. Possible mild heart attack from stress and a fatal fall? Could be – it wasn't an uncommon cause of vehicle crashes. The son-of-a-bitch sure as shit should have been stressed.

Hank grinned. "No tour until you tell me why you shot up here like a bat out of hell. I'm easy though and I'll accept that you find me irresistible and want to make up for cutting our dinner date short the other evening."

She smiled automatically. Damn, he was handsome! "I really don't think I'm your type even if you do know how to show a girl a good time."

"That only answers one of the questions," he said without moving.

Bev sighed and shifted her purse strap higher on her shoulder.

"The deal is that I did something I'm not very proud of in a moment of complete aggravation and now I'm feeling guilty and totally unprofessional."

He frowned for a moment and then opened his eyes wide. "The journal and the news conference yesterday," he said.

She nodded.

"Hot damn, I wondered where that came from," he said with a laugh. "I didn't know how many people were in on it. The good senator was pretty flustered." He lifted his coffee toward the upper terrace. "You figure him for the suicide type? And with what you told me about the journal, wouldn't that be fucking ironic?"

Bev lifted her shoulders and let them drop. "You've been around him more than I have. Between a monster-size ego and everything I think he's been responsible for, I wouldn't have pegged him for it." She sucked her lower lip into her mouth and then tried to smile. "I mean, hell, I was getting a load of legal bullshit from the DA about wrapping everything up since Noonan was dead and Sylvia Ruthven, the reporter, is okay for someone in the media. The stress thing causing a heart attack or a spell might be right, but if so, that would kind of be my doing, too."

"Come on," Hank said quietly. "I'll walk you through." He took her across the terrace through one of the sets of French doors and around the kitchen. Bev could hear a man's voice, but couldn't distinguish the words. She halted in the formal foyer and sucked in a breath at the intricately carved staircase and the richness of exotic wood.

"Yeah, it's something," Hank said and slowed to let Bev have a good look.

"The master wing is to the right," Hank said as they reached the head of the stairs. "Three guest suites are on the left."

Wide double doors were open, but he walked to a single door another twenty feet down the hall. "The lady of the house has her own study; the gentleman's is downstairs," he said with a slightly mocking flourish.

They entered the immaculate room that gave the impression of the garden brought inside. Thick cream carpet and some sort of silky fabric on the walls with alternating panels of cream and multiple shades of green, except for one wall devoted to a mural that brought to mind the pictures Bev had seen of famous European gardens. A towering bouquet was on a small, round table near the doorway. Furniture was minimal, however, it was not a lounging room at all. A slightly larger round table with two chairs, a rectangular writing table with chair and a desk with closed cabinetry completed the picture. A stack of what was probably monogrammed stationary, a gold pen in a gold and silver holder and a telephone done in an old fashioned style were the only items visible.

Bev let her eyes roam, but didn't move inside and turned to Hank. "It looks like it would be quiet." She raised her eyebrows. "On the other hand, with only two people in a house this size, why would she shut the door?"

Hank drank more coffee. "Maybe she likes to play heavy metal music and didn't want to disturb her husband. Or there's a computer in the cabinet and she was surfing porn sites."

Bev scratched her chin. "Sure. Let's see – they've been out late, but she's still pissed off, doesn't want to be around him and comes in here as an escape. I can't imagine a woman like her having pressing business at practically midnight."

"Who says she was pissed at him?"

Bev raised her cup and circled her hand. "This is a woman of elegance – all the *recent turmoil* would piss her off. Doesn't play well in high society. No matter what kind of front she puts on, there is no way she wouldn't have been pissed."

"She's classy, all right," he said and pointed down the hall. "This is a bit too froo-froo for my taste, but wait until you see the master."

Unlike the first floor with polished woods and tiles, the entire second floor was more of the thick, padded carpet, their steps making no impression and no sound. Did the house have its own set of night noises? Creaks and squeaks? Maybe not.

The lights were on in the open master and the room was almost as large as her apartment. Not feminine, nor what could be categorized as masculine – West Indian plantation perhaps. Deep rain forest colors blended with pale yellow and a set of double French doors; one set open.

A tuxedo jacket lay on the elevated king-size bed. She didn't see the tie as they crossed to the balcony. Terrace. Too large and impressive to be a balcony. There was an array of stone planters filled with hibiscus, japonica and flowers Bev didn't recognize.

A round, glass-topped wrought iron table, four chairs with cushions, two matching chaise lounges with their individual tables, the frame for a retractable awning nearly flush with the house. A whiskey glass on its side on the table, liquid almost evaporated, the bottle of Laphroaig two thirds empty, a chair pushed back as if someone had risen.

"You notice there's no ice bucket, no water," Hank said quietly. "Serious drinking, although the argument could be made you wouldn't contaminate Laphroaig with either."

"Wonder what level the bottle was at when he started," Bev said. She stepped to the railing – well, ledge was a more accurate description. It was all marble, wide enough to hold a wine bucket. The upper terrace was to the right of the lower covered terrace and had a great lagoon view.

Hank fanned his hand to the exterior of the grounds. "There's no house to the back and you can see how trees have been planted to shield the view above the walls on both sides."

He stepped to her left. Bev saw that the ledge was barely hip-high to him. "This seems unusually low," she said.

"It is," he replied. "The housekeeper was happy to talk about anything other than the tragedy and she gave us a history lesson. The original owner was some big movie star from the early days and had a lot of custom work done. She wasn't very tall and she hated sitting down and having an obstructed view of her domain so she had this built to her specifications."

"You're about as tall as Randall, aren't you?"

He grinned. "Oh, I'm bound to be an inch taller."

"Naturally," Bev said and bumped her hip hard against him.

"Shit!" He swayed forward and grabbed the ledge with one hand as Bev clenched his belt and braced herself. His coffee mug bounced off the marble tile.

"What the fuck was that about?" His face flushed briefly as he regained his balance.

"Just checking," Bev said without expression and released him.

He slowly shook his head, bent to get his mug, straightened and looked her full in the face. "No."

"It wouldn't have been difficult if he was drunk. No strength required and no struggle."

"No," he repeated, a breeze carrying a mix of scents from the surrounding blossoms. "Not without an eyewitness beyond dispute – you know, like the Pope, maybe."

Bev did a neck roll left, then right. "Since when is the spouse not the favorite suspect?"

Hank twirled the empty mug around on one finger. "Still is for a homicide. This, however, looks to be an accident and when the ME completes the autopsy, we may even be told it was death by natural causes with an associated, but not causative, fall. Or, as you mentioned earlier, perhaps a very late onset of conscience and a suicide without note to avoid further embarrassment to the family."

"You don't believe that," Bev said and cocked her head. "And the other possibilities would be remarkably coincidental, don't you think? A not totally tidy, yet effective end to a very untidy situation."

"Excuse me, is there something I could help you with?" a man's voice cut in, more curt than solicitous.

They turned to the open door. A man in his early thirties regarded them with a pinched expression. He was dressed in corporate attire: light-weight dark blue suit, white shirt, silver cufflinks, blue striped tie and matching pocket kerchief. "I'm Bernard Smith, Mrs. Randall's representative from Collier and Leland. I was under the impression you had completed preliminary inquiries," he said and all but tapped his foot. He was probably the finger-wagging type given a chance.

"Right, Bernie," Hank said with a smile and moved close enough to force him back a step. "Detective Henderson and I had a little follow-up to take care of, but I think we're done now." He swung his gaze to Bev. "Wouldn't you say so, Detective Henderson?"

Bev wondered if they should screw with Bernard, who probably detested being called Bernie, and decided it wouldn't be much fun.

"Sure," she said and exaggerated the downward tilt of her head down as she spoke. "I'm satisfied with what I've seen."

"Well then, I'll show you out," Bernard almost huffed, unable to look either of them in the eye without standing on his tiptoes. He fluttered his hand toward the hall.

"Thanks, Bernie," Hank said and bowed slightly to let Bev precede him.

Bernie didn't exactly hustle them along, but he stepped quickly and didn't offer chit-chat.

He opened the front door and Hank expanded his smile. "Oh, Bernie, do me a favor and tell Adam that Hank said hello and I'll give him a call soon for a tee-time."

Bernard's thin cheeks tinged red and he blinked his pale blue eyes rapidly. "Mr. Collier, you mean?"

"Yeah, Adam. I've known him since I was a kid. He's a great guy, isn't he? Thanks for your help."

"Uh, yes," Bernard said and fingered the knot of his tie, the earlier disdain in his voice dissolved. "A great guy," he agreed with a puzzled smile before he retreated into the house.

"Adam Collier would be his boss?" Bev asked as they walked to the cars.

Hank tried not to laugh and cut his eyes to Bev. "Yeah, and I've been told he's a flaming asshole."

"Which means...."

"I've never met him, but goddamn, I hate to be condescended to by a high-priced flunky. *Mrs. Randall's representative*, my ass."

So much for not screwing with Bernard, the snobby little twerp. Bev rested her butt against the front fender of the Spitfire and looked at Hank to remind him they were there on business. "Now, as I was saying..."

Hank reached out, tucked a fly-away curl behind her ear and dropped his voice low. "It's over, Bev. Lottie, Jonah, Cindy, Rusty, Noonan and Randall. They're dead, all of them. Isn't that enough?"

Bev sucked her lower lip in, then stared at the house as Hank waited for her response.

"I wanted to get him the right way," she said finally. "Through the system, Hank – brought to trial and found guilty. I wanted everyone to know the truth."

His eyes were as serious as she'd seen them during their short acquaintance. "Bev, as much as I admire your body, your mind and your guts, you must have Calvinism somewhere in your Anglo ancestry. Truth is like a lot of other things – it comes in shades of more than black and white. People like Randall paint it the way they want and no matter what we did, the chances are that he would have come out on top."

Bev sighed. "That's it then. You drop it, close the file?"

Hank shrugged. "If the ME has a substantive finding, we won't bury it. Mrs. Randall's explanation is plausible though."

Bev smiled weakly. "If it turns out that the Pope was visiting one of the neighbors, happened to be looking through a telescope and comes forward as a witness, you'll pursue it?'

"On my word as a product of twelve years of Catholic schooling," he replied. "May I take you for a late breakfast?"

Bev touched his cheek with her fingertip and withdrew her hand. "I think it would be better for me to leave," she said. "I need to notify Chief Taylor and everyone about what happened up here, make my report and…" She shook her head at his playful eyes. "Time for the small-town cop to leave the big city," she finished and slid to the door, the handle pressing into her lower back.

Hank leaned forward, reached behind to open the door, pecked her cheek and stepped away to give her clearance.

"It's been good working with you," he said simply. "Give me a call sometime if the boyfriend falls out of the picture."

"Tell your sister hello for me," Bev said instead and got into her car with a parting smile. "Thanks for the help."

He nodded and was walking to the patrol car as she drove away. She honked a farewell and popped open the glove compartment, groping for the *Beaches, Bars, Boats and Ballads* tape set. She inserted a cassette, turned up the volume to Buffet's *Pirate Looks at Forty* and headed home.

CHAPTER THIRTY-FIVE

Cecilia Margaret DeLong Randall sat alone on the window seat of the far rear bedroom that she had claimed after her thirteenth birthday. A tray sat on the small table that had been placed within easy reach. It held an uneaten bowl of fresh strawberries, a croissant with red currant jam and a tranquilizer. She'd drunk the tall glass of freshly squeezed orange juice and the cup of café au lait.

She watched Carlos move methodically among the shrubs, a nip, a trim, a cut – each precise and born of decades of experience. She should be sleepy and knew her mother wanted her to take the pill, to rest. That would come later, she thought. Exhaustion would win out and it might be better to wait for that, to let nature work its course as they said.

It was true that she was tired. The rage and adrenaline had drained most of her reserves. Her lie had flowed with little effort, although there was a certain amount of strain. It was, however, no greater a lie than she'd been living for years.

Cecilia stared at the turquoise blue of the swimming pool – more conventional than the lagoon she'd insisted on – and wondered how Warren could have fallen in slow motion while plummeting. There had been such disbelief on his face. It was an oddity she couldn't comprehend. The frozen moment and instantaneous plunge existing side by side. How curious.

She hadn't meant to kill him – well, she hadn't killed him – not really. It was as if she'd been two parts of herself for the entire afternoon, evening and night. The composed Cecilia who dwelled in her enviable house and the enraged Cecilia, a character who was not permitted to intrude into privileged society. While her existence might be grudgingly acknowledged, she was appropriately banished into controlled recesses.

Cecilia had been too busy to see the news conference live. It was afterward, before she was ready to dress for the evening. She'd been alone, like now, and the only segment on the television was where that rather tackily dressed, brassy woman had shouted out about Lottie Shepard – about a diary or something.

Warren's expression had stirred the fury – the flash of naked fear that he covered so quickly she doubted anyone else had seen it. Warren was such a master of expressions – so practiced. *Lottie Shepard.* A name that had been repressed for so long and then, there it was in newspapers again, on the television. The first time she'd heard it had been during Warren's campaign for senator. He'd assured her of his innocent involvement and disbelief in what the poor, distraught girl had done to herself. Cecilia had embraced his story, as had the public.

It was the name, she thought, the name and the look on Warren's face that demanded Cecilia remember the day she'd glimpsed the truth about that name. The truth about the handsome young man who had seemed so much more real and exciting than the ones of her own circle. The truth about the man she'd championed to her parents, pleading with them to accept him.

When exactly had that day been? Six months after the election? Sooner? Later? Not that the actual time mattered. Warren and Andy Sims had been drinking all afternoon. They were on the ground floor terrace, unaware that she had padded barefoot into the kitchen. The door had been open; it was one of those beautiful, soft days when it would have been a crime to have the house completely closed up.

Andy had a voice that boomed, more so when he was drinking. "Lottie," he'd said. "Fucking Lottie Shepard damn near got you this time, man!"

"I made it okay," Warren had slurred, his voice nearly as indiscreet as Andy's. "and it should be buried, just like she is. Don't say that fucking bitch's name ever again. I'm done with it."

Andy had laughed. "Well, at least she was a sweet piece of ass. Let's drink to her for that."

"I'll give her credit for that, but goddamn it almost wasn't worth it," Warren had said. "Here's to the last of Lottie Shepard."

She'd withdrawn from the kitchen without them seeing her. She could still remember that she'd felt dizzy. Was that one of the last times she'd believed Warren about anything? Or had that come later, too? The many nights when he called with a stale excuse, the trips out of town. The hints of perfume he thought he'd scrubbed away, the looks he exchanged with so many women when he thought she wasn't paying attention.

Cecilia saw Carlos pick up the handles of the wheelbarrow and trundle toward the back wall of the estate. It wasn't so much Warren's unfaithfulness – wealthy, powerful men were given more opportunity than others. No, she had her life, as he had his, as did many of their friends with unspoken arrangements. It was the contempt she'd heard in his voice that she couldn't reconcile – a depth of callousness she began to see too often, derision that winked through the silken charm he was admired for – fractions of undisguised arrogance. The resources laid at his feet through her that never seemed to be enough for him.

The role of separate lives within a showcase marriage had become tiresome, although Cecilia had contemplated a series of trips with her mother rather than a divorce. Divorces could be bothersome and her father did so enjoy playing the King Maker with her husband. The shooting of that boy had been the start of the endless focus of attention and low-voiced questions and comments.

More deaths, not that she ever liked that horrid man, Noonan, and finally the reporter who didn't sound as if she was bluffing. *Lottie Shepard.* Cecilia didn't even know what the girl had looked like. Had she been pretty? Probably, but it wasn't important. The fury had emerged from her appointed, hidden chamber when she saw the truth on Warren's face. Did he honestly think she hadn't noticed the change in his behavior – the increased drinking, the inability to sleep? Had he always taken her for a fool as well as a trophy?

She acquiesced to the furious harping as she switched off the television and proceeded to dress for the evening, knowing he wanted to beg off, determined that they would go. It might be their last appearance as a couple. She wasn't sure if she would throw him out of the house or take a more subtle approach. She'd gotten through the evening by ignoring the covert glances and rehearsing how she would tell him of her decision.

He'd been oblivious, of course, taken aback by her rebuff on the way home. Why had she waited to talk to him? Funny, she couldn't remember. She'd gone into her study, as she had said, and more time passed than she thought. He'd been out on the terrace when she'd told him it was over – she was through. The anger ceded to the composure. This was a subject to be dealt with coolly, intractably.

He'd stared at her and laughed a drunken, gloating laugh.

"Oh, God, that's rich," he said and didn't bother to stand. "You're joking."

She'd been at the railing, the night breeze catching the folds of her gown, the fabric pressed to her body, whispering around her ankles. "No, I'm not. I'm tired of it all, Warren. The women, the lies, this mess you've dredged up from your past. I want no more of you."

He had risen heavily, knocking the glass over. He hadn't been quite quick enough to replace anger with contrition. "Cecilia, sweetheart, I know this has been troubling and..."

"Oh, shut up," the fury had snapped at the insulting display. "Save your breath for the cameras."

She'd turned to go – a dramatic, composed exit and then what? What exactly? He'd stepped close, reached for her and she'd snatched her arm away. He'd lost his balance. She'd snatched her arm away and shoved him on the back? He'd tripped? It had been a strange blur. The look, the falling. The suspension of time.

Had she heard the sound? A gasp, not a scream. How long had she stood there, staring down? It couldn't have been long.

She could have called for help – perhaps he wasn't dead. She stared into the darkness past the outside lights. It was still – no movement of any kind, no other human noises, no one had seen. She was sure of it. It had been so simple then, the fury dismissed, too unpredictable a creature for what needed to be done.

She'd slowly descended the stairs and made her way outside, properly composed. She heard no moans, saw no sign of breathing in the dim light. It didn't seem likely he was alive, although she couldn't bring herself to check for a pulse.

She practiced her conversation softly, the frogs and insects providing a background.

"Why no, I don't know when, it might have been earlier...."

It didn't take long. It was close enough to the truth with only a few details to be altered. She repeated them over and over as the sirens drew near and as she'd anticipated, her father arrived within a few minutes of the ambulance and the police. One of the highly compensated lawyers whose name she'd forgotten wasn't far behind.

They had taken charge. Her role of stunned silence was acceptable. Anyone could see that she was in shock. She'd been required to say very little and no one seemed skeptical of her explanation.

A knock on the bedroom door beckoned her from replaying the scene. "Come in," she called weakly.

Her mother crossed the carpeted floor and looked at her with concern. "Cici, my dear, won't you try to eat and get some rest? Your father has everything under control and you're going to need your strength. I know it's awful, but we'll try and make it as painless as possible for you."

She smiled tremulously. "Thank you, Mother, but I'm all right. I thought I might take a soak in the tub and lie down for a while. If I can't sleep, I promise I'll take the pill."

Her mother nodded, bent and kissed the top of her head. "That's a good idea. After you've napped, come down for a late lunch. Everyone is extending their sympathy with this dreadful accident, but we've told them you'd like to be alone for a while."

"How kind of them," Cecilia said and touched a delicate hand to her cheek.

A widow did draw more sympathy than a divorcee. She wasn't terribly fond of black though – perhaps a burgundy trimmed in black or a deep purple would be socially appropriate.

CHAPTER THIRTY-SIX

Bev lifted the pot lid and stirred the spaghetti sauce for no reason other than to occupy her hands. The salads were in the refrigerator and the pasta pot was filled with water, salt and a few dribbles of olive oil. She didn't want to start the water boiling until Kyle arrived and she'd already drunk more of the Chianti than she'd intended. They would have to open a second bottle. Kyle had telephoned from the airport while he was waiting to board and offered to pick up Chinese food. She'd told him no, she was taking the afternoon off so she could cook if he was in the mood for something easy.

Taking the afternoon off hadn't been totally her idea. Taliah and Les had chased her away from the station. Granted, she was still tense from the day before with the questionable demise of Warren Randall.

Chris had called and when Bev explained they might never be able to tie up all the loose ends, she'd echoed Hank's sentiment. "If all the sons-of-bitches are dead, that's okay. Fuck the details."

Verde Key was devoid of serious crimes, her paperwork was caught up and Les said the best thing for her unsettled feeling with the Randall/Shepard/Noonan/Green situation was to get drunk and laid. Taliah had taken the original message that Kyle was booked on an afternoon flight and she wanted Bev to do something romantic.

"You've been wound way too tight, honey. You and that man need some time to get reacquainted and I don't mean watching television together," she'd said with something that resembled a leer.

Bev had given in to their urging, stopped by the grocery store for provisions, then gone for a long run in the mid-afternoon. She'd blanked her mind and let the heat and humidity sweat away the lingering feeling that she'd failed in her quest. Maybe it had been a sloppy end and maybe Mrs. Randall deserved investigation, yet all things considered, she had put the pieces together for Cindy's family.

The run, a bottle of Gatorade and a hot shower restored her perspective. She contemplated two different sets of underwear, decided on none at all and slipped into a pair of blue denim shorts and a red stretchy top that left one shoulder bare. Hair loosely pulled back with a gold clamp and a thin gold chain with a turtle that fell just below the hollow of her throat. Her attire was sexy, yet kitchen-friendly with no draping sleeves to catch fire.

She added two more grinds of black pepper to the sauce and almost jumped when she heard the knock at the door.

"It's open," she called and met Kyle halfway across the den as he came in with a sack in one hand and his overnight bag in the other.

She pulled him to her and kissed him with a tenderness that intensified into tongue and tingling feelings.

"Well hi to you, too," he said when they pulled apart. He dropped the bag and circled her waist with his free hand. "I don't mean to presume about tonight. I came straight from the airport."

"You can presume all you wish," she said with a smile. "How about a glass of wine? Or something else?"

He glanced at the stove. "That smells great. Will it hurt to let it simmer for a while?"

She shook her head.

He kissed her bare shoulder and felt the spot on her back where he would have ordinarily encountered a bra strap. "In that case, if you could pour me a glass of wine, maybe we'll delay dinner for a while."

Bev caught her breath and nodded again. Damn, she was having trouble talking.

He followed her to the pass-through and as she filled the waiting glass, he withdrew a bottle from the sack. He set it on the counter, flicked the ribbon that was tied around the neck and smiled. "We'll open this later. It's kind of a special bottle."

Bev looked at the key that dangled from the ribbon, raised her eyebrows and held out the glass.

Kyle took it and held her fingers in his grasp. "I know we've both been distracted lately, but I think it's past time when I should have given you that."

Bev smiled and suppressed a giggle. She'd found an extra key to her apartment and put it on a hook next to the front door. She was going to see how the evening went before she offered it to him.

She leaned her forehead against his chin. "Let's take our wine into the bedroom," she said softly. "We've got all night to talk."

THE END

Printed in the United States
106318LV00005BA/113/A

9 781598 000931